Coming Together

at last

volume 2

PHAZE
Cincinnati, Ohio

www.Phaze.com

Coming Together

at last
volume 2

edited by

A Phaze Production

PHAZE
Cincinnati, Ohio

Phaze Books
6470A Glenway Avenue, #109
Cincinnati, OH 45211-5222
Phaze is an imprint of Mundania Press, LLC.

To order additional copies of this book, contact:
books@phaze.com
www.Phaze.com

Cover art © 2007, Debi Lewis
Edited by Alessia Brio

Trade Paperback ISBN-13: 978-1-60659-094-2

First Print Edition – January 2009
Printed in the United States of America

10 9 8 7 6 5 4 3 2 1

Coming Together: At Last

is dedicated to the memory of

Mildred Loving

1939-2008

Loving vs. Virginia

[N]ot a day goes by that I don't think of Richard and our love, our right to marry, and how much it meant to me to have that freedom to marry the person precious to me, even if others thought he was the "wrong kind of person" for me to marry. I believe all Americans, no matter their race, no matter their sex, no matter their sexual orientation, should have that same freedom to marry. Government has no business imposing some people's religious beliefs over others. Especially if it denies people's civil rights.

I am still not a political person, but I am proud that Richard's and my name is on a court case that can help reinforce the love, the commitment, the fairness, and the family that so many people, black or white, young or old, gay or straight seek in life. I support the freedom to marry for all. That's what Loving, and loving, are all about.

~ Mildred Loving
June 2007

Table of Contents

Introduction

© L.A. Banks

What is the color of the most powerful force in the universe, love? When we look at hope and freedom and change and passion, do these words conjure a race or ethnicity, or are they values and ideals that cross the boundaries of form?

These are the questions I ask myself as I watch the world news. Surely a mother down on her knees wailing at the sight of a collapsed school building in earthquake-ravaged China is no different than the aggrieved father searching desperately for his children in cyclone-stricken Myanmar, who cannot in my mind be distinguished from the traumatized grandmother clutching pictures of her grandchildren to her breast as rescue workers look for survivors in the tornado-ripped heartland of America, any more than those people's cries are different than those of a mother in Darfur lifting her child up to a UN truck begging for mercy... or Baghdad's suicide bomber-embattled children wondering where their parents are after an explosion.

Then is there any difference between the people mentioned above and their losses than that of the inner city mom standing over her shot teenager calling on the Lord for mercy, than there would be for the suburban mother who has just learned that her teen has tragically wrapped their car around a tree on prom night and didn't make it? Images, images... oh, we have all seen them, paused, and held our palms against our hearts when we have. Maybe we've said a silent prayer for those people caught in the grip of tragedy because we can identify with their pain. For that glimmer in time, we don't see differences; we see the feelings and emotions of our fellow man and woman.

If we are really thinking, feeling members of humanity, we are called upon to reach down into our souls to ask fundamental questions. Can one deny that the waters of Katrina or those of the dreadful tsunami refused to delineate between religion, ethnic heritage, age, or gender? Did helpers who scrambled to assist survivors weep less for an orphaned child because of that child's hue? That's not what we saw during and after the 9-11 disaster. We saw people of all races and origins rushing in to help, some even giving their lives for strangers. We saw love sublime, strangers helping strangers, just because it was the right thing to do.

Therefore, it seems that the only logical conclusion one can come to is that love, hope, passion, pain, suffering... all these things are a condition of being human, and are not conditional upon what type of human one happens to be according to labels. A baby crying pulls at one's core, no matter what ethnic group that child was born into by the accident of birth... laughing children have that same effect. Tears shed for a profound loss also move us and break down walls. But if tragedies are so compelling, then let's step back for a moment and peel away the layers to consider one additional level of awareness. If we can understand the cries that follow a bridge collapse in Minnesota, and/or any number of horrific events that have happened, why can't we understand the colorblind nature of love?

It is one of the greatest conundrums in the world, in my opinion—because if people are laid prostrate from a loss of a loved one, doesn't that mean that they had to love whomever the tragedy befell? Doesn't that mean they loved their child just as you would love your child... that they loved their parent or spouse or friend or partner just as you would have loved yours? If we accept that as truth, then how can we regulate love to an artificial parameter like race, when we've just gone around the globe in this small exercise of recalling current events to show that all people have been touched by loss (which means they have also all been touched by love)?

For how can you have loved deeply and not weep when you have lost? It wouldn't matter, then. You'd remain dry-eyed and stoic. But that's just it. We've seen communities and families devastated and the pain of that spread out in roiling waves that effect us, even a half a world away while watching the news. Thus we can only conclude that where the tragedy hit, people were connected to others that loved them, and once the victims were no longer in the world, that bitter reality created indelible suffering for someone who cared that they were alive.

With that as a premise, rather than wait for a disaster or an act of God to create a glaring media frenzy to show just how human we are, why not embrace love for all people when the skies are clear and calm, when the waters have receded, when the shelling has stopped, and while there is laughter in our midst? Love is joy. Love is freedom. Love is hope. It is something that we all deserve and is provided for in abundance in the universe and on our planet, like air, as an ultimate act of God.

I personally believe in love and light... and the indomitable human spirit. I believe in hope and grace and caring, and in heroes and sheroes, maybe that's why I write about them... just as I believe in a Higher Power that levels the playing field, eventually... and I believe in angels. Most of all, perhaps, I believe in the ability of people to change for the better, to open their hearts and to receive the greatest power in the universe (and to use it for good)... and that is the power of love.

Peace and Stay in the Light!

~ L.A. Banks

♥

www.vampire-huntress.com

A Little White Lie
© Steve F. Young

When she reached across the table
And laid her hand on my arm
I jumped
I was immediately paranoid
That she thought I jumped because
She was black
Her nails were long and dark red
Deep caramel fingers tipped
In fuck me red
I let my eyes follow the slim
Line of her arm
Until it disappeared
Past her shoulder
Into a thin blue blouse
Her neck was unimaginable
I was staring
She squeezed my forearm
I looked up at her face
She was happy I was staring
Parted smiling lips painted
In fuck me red

Red looks good on you
Thank you
She leaned back
And took a slow sip
Of a gin and tonic
I swear that drink was sweating

I wanted to tell her

This was a fantasy
At last coming true
I wanted her to ask
Why I thought red fingernails
And unimaginable necks
Looked so much better to me
On black girls
Than any other
I wanted to try to explain
Maybe because where I'm from
Most black girls
Won't bother with white boys
That look like Opie all grown up
Maybe racism in America
Had made what I wasn't
Supposed to have
The very thing I covet
But I didn't tell
And she didn't ask
Because none of that mattered
This was two people
Strolling along a familiar path
With an unfamiliar
And somehow very exciting twist

She did ask me
Have you ever been with a black girl?
And not long after getting inside
Her house
She knew I had lied
When I said yes.

♥

renaissancejones@yahoo.com

Love Under the Endless African Sky
© Aliyah Burke

[One]

Capitol Hill

"I don't give a damn! That's my baby girl that's over there!" the masculine voice thundered, causing the other man to back up from the venom in his tone.

"I know that, Congressman, but we don't have any authority to get into Zimbabwe for a rescue mission. Our military has no reason to go. I've contacted the embassy, and they said they'd do their best to find and protect her."

Congressman Thomas Buxton ground his back teeth and frowned at his aide. "Jason, I am not leaving her alone over there. Get me a way to get her out. I don't care what it takes, find me a way." He looked up as the other members began filing back into the room. *What a time for Congress to be in session. I'll not fail you this time, baby girl. This time I will be there for you.*

Wiping a hand down his face, Thomas looked at Jason. "She's all we have. I can't lose her."

"I'll do whatever I can. I promise."

With a heavy heart, Thomas Buxton reclaimed his seat. Shoving personal issues to the back of his mind, he focused on the session.

It was after ten at night when Thomas entered his office and shut the door behind him. He needed to call his wife, but until there was something tangible he could tell her, he didn't want to.

His gaze landed on the tri-fold picture frame on his desk. The middle one was of his whole family; there was a copy of his wedding photo on one side and the other was his only child. His daughter.

A knock on the door had him wiping away any trace of tears. "Come," he announced.

The door swung silently open and in walked Jason Holden, his aide, and his wife, Jacqueline Buxton. Forcing a smile on his face, he stood.

"Jason, I thought you'd gone for the evening." He walked around his desk and kissed his wife gently. "Hi, honey."

Jason smiled. "I was on my way out when I ran into Professor Buxton, so I escorted her up. Goodnight, Congressman, Professor."

His wife smiled at Jason. "Goodnight, Jason. Always good to see you. You'll have to come for dinner soon."

"I look forward to it." Jason nodded and kissed her on the cheek. He left them alone in the room.

His wife's expression lost all cheer as she approached one of the chairs before his desk. "Tell me you've got some news."

Shaking his head, he sat beside her, reached for one hand and squeezed it. "Not yet. Jason's been looking and I've put in a call to Colonel Nowell."

Her shuddering gasp made his heart wrench. Pulling her close, he pressed a kiss to her head. "She'll be okay, Mother. We raised a strong girl."

For a few moments, they sat there huddled together, sharing strength with one another as they prayed for their baby girl.

* * * *

Skynomish, Washington

The man rolled over and reached blindly for the phone. "What?" he barked into the receiver.

"Did I wake you, Matthews?"

"Yes," he growled.

"Lounging away in bed after noon? You drunk?"

Squinting against the sun that shone in through the windows, the man sat up and rubbed a hand over his eyes. *Am I drunk? Not really. However, I do have one hell of a hangover.*

He reached for a cigarette and lit it, taking a long drag as he pushed up out of bed. The blonde woman in the bed rolled over, exposing creamy breasts to him. He ignored them. "What do you want, Nowell?" Barefoot he padded to the sliding glass door off his bedroom and stepped out onto the porch.

"Can't I just call to see how my old friend is doing?"

"You were my superior officer. Since I've been out you haven't called me a single time." He took another puff on the smoke. "What do you want?"

"I need your help, Ryder."

Ryder Matthews leaned on the railing and snubbed out his cigarette. His gaze took in the pristine wilderness of the Cascade Mountains. "With what?"

"My goddaughter is in trouble."

Ryder ran his tongue over his teeth. He'd heard about Colonel Richard Nowell's goddaughter. Seen pictures of her. Cute. Colonel Nowell didn't have a wife but his best friend did—and a daughter. And the colonel looked at their daughter like she was his own.

If he remembered correctly, her name was Henrietta. Her father was Congressman Thomas Buxton. A democrat but one who worked hard to keep bases open and increase base pay for those who served.

The colonel had told them how proud he was of her. Ryder hadn't had the pleasure of meeting her, however.

"What kind of trouble is she in?"

Ryder sat down on a chaise and listened to his former boss tell him the situation. Before he knew what had happened, he'd hung up the phone, kicked out the still sleepy blonde, and began packing a bag to grab a flight. It was going to be a long one.

He settled into his plane seat and closed his eyes, mentally going over the information he'd gotten from Colonel Nowell. There wasn't an exact known location on Ms. Henrietta Buxton. He knew where the missionary group started, but according to Nowell, they were travelling between villages.

So his plan was to hunt her down, hopefully quickly and before the trouble reached her. There was serious tension between the army and the rebels. He was getting into the country under the guise of going to their embassy.

What the hell am I doing?

Ryder had agreed solely for the respect he had for his former commanding officer. Colonel Nowell had defended him staunchly when the United States Marine Corps tried to say he was psychologically unfit for duty.

Ryder agreed to resign his commission and leave the Corps quietly as long as they kept their opinion of his mental status off his permanent record. They had, and so he quit the only thing he'd ever loved doing.

Looking out the small window, Ryder glanced down at the ocean. From this height, everything looked so peaceful. He sighed and reached in his pocket, pulling out his iPod. Turning it on, he called up a picture of Henrietta that had been sent to him by Nowell and downloaded.

Ms. Henrietta Buxton. In the photograph, she wore a black tank top and khaki shorts. She sat on a rock, a lake and mountains behind her. Her walnut brown eyes twinkled at him from behind her rectangular eyeglasses. A beautiful grin teased the corners of her full, lush lips.

Ryder felt his cock stir. With a groan, he shut his eyes.
What I don't need is to be attracted to her.

Even as those words skated around in his head, he realized it was too late. His body was already reacting. *And that's just from her photo.*

Opening his eyes, he touched the image of her face, backed out of the photo screen, and shut it off before shoving it back into his pocket. Hopefully, it wouldn't take him long to find her, get her out of there, and then he could get back to doing what he'd been doing when Nowell called. Drinking.

The woman beside him smiled as she covered herself with a blanket and closed her eyes. He shut the shade and got as comfortable as he could.

His dreams were filled with images of Henrietta. In fact, he and Henrietta in bed together. The blonde from his bed this morning had faded into nothing. Ryder couldn't even remember her name.

As the plane continued on, Ryder slept and dreamt of a woman he'd never officially met, but was supposed to save.

[Two]

Zimbabwe

The harsh afternoon sun beat down upon the back of her neck as she leaned against the door of her old Scout. Wiping her hand across her forehead, she smiled at some of the locals.

"It's really warm today," she said, taking a drink of water.

"Yes, very," a tall muscular black man answered in accented English.

"Let's take a break for lunch, Taurean. Then we can dig and lay more pipe for the system after it cools down a bit.

Especially since we have to go around that corner up ahead."

"Sounds good. I'll pass the word along."

"Awesome."

She reached through the open window of her Scout and grabbed a pad and pencil. Then she headed for the quickly-erected tent that had people hanging out, trying to get a break from the sun.

"Hey, Quanda," she said as she took a bite of the fruit her friend handed her.

"Afternoon," Quanda responded with a smile. "Going good?" she asked.

"Yes. Just taking a break. I'm going up around the bend to see what's in store for us, so if anyone wants me, that's where I'll be."

"Be careful."

"Of course." With a wave of her notepad, she headed off.

"Eddie! Eddie!" a voice yelled.

"Over here," she hollered back, without turning around.

"There's someone here asking for you."

That got her to turn. Jevonte strode closer and behind him followed a man she didn't know. She stood slowly as her gaze moved over the unknown man.

Powerful was the first word that popped into her mind. He stood tall and straight as he moved, as if unaware of his own fluidity. He wore dark khaki cargo pants and a light gray tee shirt. A shirt that hugged his muscular torso showing off his rippled abs.

Damn! Her gaze traveled up to linger on his face. Hard angles, sunglasses kept his eyes hidden, and there looked to be two or so day's growth on his face. Nice firm lips.

"And who might you be?" she questioned, walking toward the duo.

"Henrietta Buxton." He made it sound like a statement and not a question. His voice was smoky and gravely, setting her nerves on high alert.

A burst of laughter escaped from her. "Henrietta? Wow, not many call me that. But yes, legally that's my name, although most call me, Eddie. What can I do for you, Mr. ...?"

He stepped closer and stuck out his hand. "Matthews, Ryder Matthews."

Delightful shivers ran up and down her spine as his large hand closed over her smaller one. "Okay, Mr. Matthews. What can I do for you?"

He tipped his head to the side as if watching her. "I'm here to take you home."

Pulling her hand free from his, she narrowed her eyes. "Take me home? I don't think so. I'm not done with this project. Besides, I don't know you well enough to go anywhere with you."

"Look, lady, I didn't fly around the world to have you tell me no. Get your things and we'll get going." There was a bite to his tone.

Glancing around him to where Jevonte stood, she said to him in Shona, "Send Tinashe down here, will you?" Then she turned her attention back to the imposing man before her. "Who sent you?"

"Your godfather. Apparently your father is very worried about your safety."

"You know my godfather? What's his name?" Doubt tinged her tone.

"Colonel Richard Nowell."

"Where do you know him from?"

"He used to be my CO."

"So you're military," she stated. She knew he was telling the truth; she'd heard stories about him from her godfather, but she had to ask. There could be more than one Ryder Matthews in the world.

"Ex. We're wasting daylight." He gestured behind him. "Let's go."

"I'm not going anywhere. These people need my help and I plan to do just that."

"And this conflict brewing between the rebels and the army? What are you planning on doing about that?"

Tinashe and Jevonte returned, and she headed over to them, leaving him standing there all alone.

* * * *

Ryder couldn't believe she just blew him off. Still, instead of following after her, he just watched her as she spoke to the two men who had walked up. Whatever they were talking about he couldn't understand; it wasn't English.

Henrietta "Eddie" Buxton wore tight khaki shorts that hugged her toned legs, the color of whipped mocha. She had a white tank top on covered by a dress shirt that was rolled up past her elbows.

Her voice rang husky, and it affected him in ways he wasn't ready to acknowledge. He groaned. He needed a drink. Her godfather would kick his ass six ways to Sunday if he even had a glimmer of the thoughts Ryder was having about her.

"Must be the sun," he muttered.

"What must be?" Eddie asked.

"Nothing," he mumbled. "Are you ready?"

"I already told you, I'm not going."

He sighed in exasperation. "Look, I don't want to get in the middle of this trouble, so get your things and we can leave."

"The fact that there are problems isn't anything new. There will be strife today and tomorrow as well. I'm staying. But I understand how you may not wish to get exposed to it. So go, tell my godfather thanks for his concern, but I'm fine." She turned and headed off toward a huge boulder and hollered over her shoulder, "Tell him to tell my parents: it's all okay."

Damn woman, it's like she doesn't think she's in danger. Rolling his shoulders, Ryder followed her and stood beside her as she talked to the others. He glanced down at the notepad in her hand. It looked like an engineering plan, but for what he wasn't positive.

Against his better judgment, he asked, "What are you all doing?"

"Building an irrigation system. The children and women in the village spend too much time going back and forth between the only water source and everything else. It's not always safe. So with this, we will give them the ability to pump water right in the village."

She glanced at him, and his heart caught in his chest. There was such conviction in her stare. "We're almost done digging the trench and laying pipe, but not all the way done yet. And now we have to get through all that rock ahead of us. So we're going under the boulder. Between the two huge slabs of rock."

"With what? I didn't exactly see huge machinery back there."

"Nope. And you won't. We make do with what we have."

Impressive. If it works. "What's the chance you'll leave willingly with me?"

"Slim to none." She turned her attention back to the men who were talking amongst themselves.

He sighed again. Ryder took off his sunglasses and touched her cotton-covered shoulder. "I can't protect you if you don't let me."

Her brown eyes met his gaze. "I'm not asking you to protect me. I know the danger. It's the same danger that was here when I first got here. It hasn't changed, and I'm not going to let my father's insecurities send me home."

"I can't leave you here unprotected."

The smile she flashed him made his knees melt. "I've not had a protector in a long time, Ryder Matthews. What makes you think I need one now?"

"The fact your godfather asked me to do it." He leaned in close, inhaling the evocative scent she wore. "And I'm not about to go against the colonel."

She blinked slowly and held his gaze. "Your eyes are amazing." He arched a brow at her words and enjoyed the flushed look her skin acquired. "I mean," she cleared her throat, "you are more than welcome to stay and work. Or you can leave."

"I'm not leaving without you. But, when I say I'm staying with you, I mean *with* you, same tent and everything."

Her eyes darkened before she pushed her glasses up on her nose. "Suit yourself." Then she put her attention back to the task before her.

Ryder watched in silence as she spoke with the two men and they lit the fire beneath the boulder. His eyes kept drifting back to the lone woman of the group. He knew she was a civil engineer, her mother was a college history professor, and her father was a congressman.

Her parents didn't concern him at the moment. Right now, he just longed to release her hair from its confinement. He wanted to see her standing, glistening in the shower as the water cascaded down across her body.

His erection grew. He shifted his stance to keep it concealed and to try and alleviate the pressure. It didn't work. Eddie sank down on her haunches, which gave him a direct shot of the firmness of her ass tightly outlined by her shorts. His cock grew harder, and he had to look away in order to try and control his reaction.

Her laughter trailed over his skin, and he put his attention back on her. She seemed so comfortable with them, spoke their language, and had created a wonderful rapport.

Patting the men on the shoulder, she turned and looked at him. She wiped her hand across her forehead before heading toward him. "Well, let's go get you settled in. I have to come back down here in a while, but Tinashe said he'd watch the fire for a while."

He nodded and turned to walk beside her. "Tell me about you," he ordered.

She shoved her hands in the back pockets of her shorts. "Not much to tell. Something in particular you're looking to know?"

Marital status. Boyfriend status. Will you sleep with me?

"Whatever you wish to share."

"Well, I don't share much. I'm really a very boring person."

"I highly doubt that, Henrietta."

"Oh, please call me, Eddie. Henrietta is a mouthful."

"Eddie is a man's name."

She shrugged easily. "Well, some think I do man's work, so it fits."

You don't look anything like a man. He looked down at the top of her head. She was about seven inches shorter than his six-two frame. "I'll try to call you Eddie."

"Thanks. Henrietta is something my father calls me. Well, him and Richard."

Ryder smiled. "What about your middle name? Is it more to your liking?" She laughed again and he realized how much he liked her laugh. "What's so funny?" he asked as the tents came into view.

"My name is Henrietta Ossian Buxton. I was named after Henry Ossian Flipper."

He furrowed his brows and queried, "Who was that?"

"An American soldier and the first black American cadet to graduate from West Point. Very impressive especially considering he had been born into slavery." She smiled. "My mother teaches African-American History. And up until the moment I was born, they were under the impression I was going to be a boy. My father went to West Point, and so even though I came out a girl, they wanted to honor him."

Ryder heard some hesitation in her voice. It stopped him and made him reach out to her. "I'm sure they are very proud of their daughter."

A small smile crossed her face. "Perhaps. But somehow, I feel inferior. As if no matter what I do, the daughter of West Point graduate Congressman Thomas Buxton is still just a daughter."

He couldn't help it; he had to touch her. His hand cupped the side of her face, his thumb tracing over her cheekbone before touching her lips. Ryder leaned in close and whispered, "You are selling yourself short, Eddie. No one would ever think of you as 'just' anything."

"Sweet talkin' me ain't getting me to leave and go home with you, Ryder." She touched his face with her fingertips. "But thank you for saying them." She moved away and began talking to a group of women.

The second she touched him, he was rock hard, and the moment she stopped, he longed for more. *Oh hell, I'm in trouble.* Colonel Nowell had teased him about a woman who would knock him for a loop the second he laid eyes on her. Well, damn if it wasn't his former CO's goddaughter that had done it to him.

[Three]

Eddie only half listened to what Amadika was saying. Her mind was focused totally on the feelings that single touch from Ryder had created in her.

I must just be very, very horny.

Her gaze drifted over to where he stood talking to two men. His arms were crossed, showing off his intense arm muscles. He hadn't put his glasses back on. She had been amazed by the look of his eyes. They were a swirling mix of grays, blues, and greens. Such passion lurked in their depths, such awareness to everything around him.

He was large all over. Tall, brawny, full of what seemed to be unending muscles. She gulped trying to moisten her throat. The sun shone down on his tanned skin. His hair looked brown with blondish highlights, and it was kind of shaggy, hanging unruly around his face. She liked it on him.

There was the hint of a tattoo that she could see peeking out from under the sleeve of his shirt. *I wonder what kind of tattoo you have, Ryder.*

He stood there talking to Tinotenda. Still, his eyes were waiting for her to look at him. A slow, sensual smile crossed his rugged face as he dropped his gaze to look up and down her body.

She burned in response. Her nipples tightened, and she felt her belly quiver as his stare moved over her. He made her feel like she was standing there totally naked before him. Despite the heat of the day, goose bumps erupted all over her body.

"You like him, Eddie, don't you?" Amadika asked.

"He wants me to go home with him," she replied, making sure she still spoke in Shona, just in case he was listening.

A brilliant smile crossed her friend's dark face. "You can use my home."

She blushed. "Not exactly what I meant."

"Please," Amadika admonished, "I've been with you since you got here. No man has turned your head until this one strolled in here looking all handsome."

Eddie sighed and looked away from Ryder. She couldn't even attempt to argue the point. Amadika was dead on in her observation. Her senses had kicked into overdrive the moment she'd laid eyes on Ryder Matthews.

What kind of name is Ryder Matthews, anyway?

"Here he comes," Amadika said with a teasing note to her voice.

With a fortifying breath, she turned to watch his approach. She lost her breath. Her pussy throbbed, and she *knew* she was in trouble with this man. Serious trouble.

"A word, Eddie," he purred.

It was like he knew what timbre to speak in to make her turn into a puddle of mush. She shoved her lust into the back of her mind.

"Sure. Oh, this is Amadika. Amadika meet Ryder Matthews. The man my father sent to bring me home."

"A pleasure," her friend said, shaking Ryder's hand.

"Indeed it is," Ryder returned.

"Oh, enjoy this one, Eddie," Amadika said in Shona as she walked away leaving them alone.

Eddie bit back a groan as her body seemed to agree with her friend's statement. "What'd you need to speak to me about? Did you get your bag put away?"

"Yes, Tinotenda placed it in your tent." His eyes darkened before he said, "I mean our tent."

She shivered again in the hot sun. "Something you needed to say to me?"

"I want to know why you aren't going home. This truly is admirable what you're doing, but very foolish and risky."

"Look, Ryder. I don't want to hash this out with you. Bottom line, I'm not going home. If the army or the rebels

25

come, I'll deal with them just like the rest of those who live here."

"What makes you think they won't try to use who you are against you? Hold you for ransom." He grabbed her arm and yanked her in close.

"No one knows who I am here. And furthermore, they don't give a damn. The man who put your bag in the tent, he's a prince. I'm not anything special. My worth is what I can offer them, not who my father is." Her nose flared and she was swamped by his masculine scent. He smelled so good.

"Besides, I know the U.S. doesn't negotiate. I accepted that when I came over here. My father didn't care I was coming, so if he's worried now it's to show concern to my mother."

Ryder shook his head and placed his nose to where it touched hers. His warm breath floated over her. "I don't know your father, but I would bet he loves you more than the colonel, who happens to think the world of you."

"We all have our own versions of the truth," she breathed.

"I have to know," he whispered.

"Know what?" she asked in the same low tone.

"If your lips taste as good as I think they do."

She whimpered as his mouth covered hers. He tasted divine. Warm, heady, addictive, and totally masculine. His tongue swept confidently into the depths of her mouth. She slid her tongue against his and shuddered as he thrust it deeper.

Ryder moved through her mouth like he owned it and was checking out each nook and cranny. Each swipe of his tongue, sent electrical impulses straight through to her pussy. It convulsed in time with the strokes he delivered.

Her hands moved up and latched onto his large arms. Her fingers dug into his biceps, and she used them to help hold her up for her legs wanted to give out on her. She sighed into his mouth as his arms wrapped around her and pressed her close to him. She could feel the muscles plus the ridge in his pants that told her he wanted her. Moisture drenched her panties.

His fingers splayed across her bottom, gathering her close to him. His mouth devoured hers, and she gave as much as she got. He wasn't gentle, and she didn't want him to be. She wanted him to demand from her.

He wrenched his mouth off hers. His eyes met hers, and she got lost in the dark gray-green surrounded by a blue ring. They took her breath away.

"Well?" she asked trying to control her heart beat.

"Better than I expected." He dropped his arms from around her and stepped back. His eyes still burned with a fierce fire she longed to release.

"You weren't too bad yourself," she snapped. "Of course, I've been without a man for a while." Eddie stomped off, heading out to where a group of men dug into the hard earth.

* * * *

Ryder mentally kicked himself as he followed her over to the ditch. His eyes were glued to the sway of her hips and the way her shorts clung to her stunning, smooth legs. How could he have kissed her? *How could I not? Her lips just begged me to kiss them.*

He knew the colonel would skin him alive if he found out, but he didn't give a damn. If he had his way, he'd be doing a lot more of kissing her and other things.

His eyebrows rose as she picked up a pickaxe and began to work alongside the men. For a moment, he followed the movement of her body. It was obvious she'd done this many times before. Her motion was practiced and easy.

He'd felt calluses on her hands as she squeezed his arms. Walking up to the trench, he nodded at a guy who handed him a shovel and got to work.

The time was passed with them swinging tools and the locals singing. The music was uplifting and had a wonderful beat to it. Ryder noticed that Eddie sang along with them. As they worked the line nearer to where the boulder was, he reached up and wiped the sweat off his brow. His body ached, muscles burned, but he felt better than he had in a long time.

Her laughter reached him, and he turned his head to look. She stood beside another man, one he didn't know, and they were sharing water. He bit back the growl that threatened to erupt from his throat.

She nodded at something the man said and then got back to work, swinging that pick in an effortless motion. Her body was full of lean muscles, each second in her presence his appreciation for her grew. He'd met many children of senators, congressmen, and other wealthy people, but Eddie was the only one who seemed to care about others more than herself.

A call for dinner stopped the work, and everyone gathered around fires and talked while they ate. Ryder sat beside Eddie. It was a tasty rice dish with small pieces of meat in it. Filling.

"So tell me about you, Ryder. What did you do in the military, and why aren't you in anymore?" Eddie asked, fixing her brown eyes on him.

"I was a Marine." Ryder saw no reason not to tell her. He expected her to trust him. "But the Marine Corps decided I had become a bit unstable. We came to a mutual agreement, and I left."

He glanced at her. There was only acceptance of his words in her eyes. No fear, disgust, or mistrust.

"What rank were you?" she asked, turning her attention back to her plate of food.

"Major."

"Okay. And what exactly did you do for the Marine Corps?"

Setting his fork down, he asked, "Doesn't it bother you they think I'm unstable?"

Her head was shaking before the question died from the air. "Nope. The fact Richard sent you speaks enough for your character," she paused briefly, "even if I don't need you here."

Ryder wasn't sure what to make of her. Still, it seemed the right thing to do to brush a loose strand of her hair away from her oval face. "You need me. You just haven't accepted it yet."

She wiped her mouth and sent him a devilish grin. "Ain't but one thing I ever needed a man for and since God's created batteries," she leaned in close, "I don't even need a man for that."

His eyes widened before they narrowed in amusement. He winked and said, "Baby, batteries can't *begin* to compare to what I'll do to you."

"You'll be snoring before I even get to the tent, but thanks for the offer." She wrinkled her nose at him and walked off.

Ryder took his time finishing dinner. He knew full well his erection would be blatantly obvious. Some of the remaining men watched him with huge knowing smiles on their faces.

When his body had calmed down a bit, he left the fire and headed to the tent. He pushed past the flap and froze. Eddie stood with her back to the entrance in only shorts and her bra.

He could only stare.

Her skin was all the same dark shade of rich, tempting mocha. The white of her bra sliced through the darkness.

He groaned aloud, and she turned. Her breasts appeared as tasty as he'd believed.

"Sorry," he muttered, "guess I should've knocked."

She reached for a shirt on her cot. "Don't worry about it." Eddie covered herself. "I'm sure it's nothing you haven't seen before. I'll be back in a bit."

Those words shoved his desire to the rear as the need to protect raced to the foreground. "Where are you going?"

He didn't want her going alone, but she spoke before he could voice an objection.

"Jevonte and Taruean are going with me back to the boulder. I'll be fine and back before you know it." She smiled and slipped out before he could say anything else.

Ryder told himself that she knew the area better than he did. And with some of the locals, she should be fine. So he readied himself for bed. As his tired body stretched out, he sighed in relief. It'd been a while since he'd worked that hard.

His mind drifted toward Eddie and how he felt around her. He felt good, like he actually had a purpose.

[Four]

Eddie rubbed the back of her neck as she walked toward her tent. She was exhausted. Today honestly seemed hotter than the previous few days. The addition of that hottie, Ryder Matthews hadn't done a damn thing to help either.

She was content the boulder wouldn't create too much hassle. They had a good fire burning under it. Four men were there to keep an eye on it, and each other.

Opening the flap, she stepped in, her gaze immediately drawn to Ryder. He'd left a lantern on low for her. He lay on his back, eyes closed, and there were deep, even breaths coming from him.

Eddie hesitated as she reached for the light after checking her bedding. Her eyes lingered over the way Ryder's lashes rested against his cheeks.

"Goodnight, Ryder," she whispered as her fingers turned off the light.

She stretched out and had just closed her eyes when a low voice reached her. "How're your batteries?"

Eddie grinned in the dark. She should have known he was not really asleep. "Never better."

"You should upgrade," he said in a whisper.

"Upgrade to what?"

"Me," he said right by her ear.

Eddie knew it might not be the smartest thing, but she didn't care. There were parts of her body she'd ignored *way* too long. Tossing back her blankets, she said, "I hope you aren't bluffing about how good you are."

He slipped in beside her. "I'll let you decide."

She groaned as his hands began to explore her body. Callused skin slid under her shirt, skimming her ribs, and teasing the undersides of her bare and sensitive breasts.

"Take it off," he commanded, tugging on her tank top.

She did and groaned as he covered her body with his own. Strands of his chest hair teased her taut nipples. Eddie trailed her hands down the muscled expanse of his bare back.

His lips nibbled along her jaw line, his stubble sending extra shockwaves through her. One hand moved toward a breast. She moaned as he cupped it and flicked the pebbled tip. Ryder licked and nipped his way down her neck and sternum. His tongue swiped the inside slope of each breast before he sucked one tip completely into his mouth.

Oh, shit! Her back arched off the cot, and her hand threaded into his thick hair, pressing him as close as possible. His mouth moved between her breasts, keeping her tense and so close to an orgasm. It was like he knew and backed off before she reached it, and then got her all worked up again.

Torture. It was exquisite torture.

Eddie could feel the moisture leaking down the inside of her thigh. Her hips undulated against him, his long, hard cock pressed against her, tantalizing her.

She spread her legs wider, craving the feel of him between her thighs. Desperate to have that ridge stroking her clit. She whimpered as she felt it. Eddie tried to move faster, but he wouldn't let her.

"Impatient," he murmured in her ear.

"Stop teasing me," she growled trying to push down his pants.

"I'm not teasing. If I was I'd do this."

Before she knew what happened, he'd shoved two of his large fingers deep inside her pussy. Lights flickered behind her eyes as the orgasm swarmed her. "Ah!" she screamed.

A scream he cut off with a kiss.

The kiss was anything but gentle. His fingers slammed into her over and over as his tongue plundered her mouth.

He stopped as fast as he'd started. "If I was teasing, I'd leave you like this."

"No," she begged. "Please don't leave me like this." Her body longed for so much more.

"Don't worry, Henrietta," he purred. "Your hot pussy needs to be fucked. Thoroughly."

"Yes," she sighed, her skin on fire. All that mattered was his touch and the ecstasy it brought her.

Ryder helped her out of her pants, and when his body rubbed against her, she reveled in the feel of his nakedness. His thick cock pressed against her wet slit but didn't enter.

"I can't wait to feel you milking my dick," he rumbled against her ear. "I know you're so fuckin' tight just by the way you squeezed my fingers. My cock was made to fit in this hot pussy."

She dripped even more onto her blankets. Reaching between them, Eddie wrapped a hand around his warm erection and guided it into her pussy.

"Yes," he groaned. "Bring me home, baby." His hips flexed, and he sank completely into her heat.

"Oh!" she hissed in pleasure. *Dear God, this feels so good.*

Ryder kissed her, gently this time as he slowly began moving inside her. Deep, even strokes.

She dug her nails into his shoulders as her ankles hooked behind his back. The cot squeaked with every thrust and was followed by a low moan.

Eddie sucked hard on his tongue and clenched the muscles in her pussy as an orgasm bore down upon her.

"So tight," he muttered into her mouth. "So blessed tight."

"Faster," she ordered, desperately needing the relief he could bring her.

Ryder was rapidly losing his control. Her hot, wet channel held him like a custom made suit. There was only one person designed to wear it. For him, it was Henrietta Buxton.

His balls were so close to exploding. He had known she'd be amazing, but this... this was off the charts.

Each stroke brought a mewl from the back of her throat, which enhanced his passion. He began to thrust faster, sinking balls deep in her velvet heat and drawing back groaning as her muscles clenched around him as if begging him to stay.

Ryder had no intention of leaving the bounty before him. Her body writhed beneath him, hips arching to allow him deeper penetration.

"More," she begged over and over until it became her mantra.

"Oh yeah," he promised and picked up his speed again. He placed his hands by her ears and plunged in and out.

Harder.

Faster.

Deeper.

A low rumble was born in his chest as he pounded into Eddie. His balls tingled, and he knew he couldn't last much longer.

"Please," she panted.

"Please what?"

"I need...I need..."

He knew what she needed. Supporting most of his weight on one hand, he slipped the other between them and played with her clit.

"Ah!" She bit back her scream and pressed her face into his shoulder.

Her body shuddered as she orgasmed. Her pussy contracted hard around him, the rippling muscles working him like no woman had ever done before.

Once.

Twice.

Ryder propelled himself as deep as he could and unloaded his sperm within her. The roar escaped from him as his cock ejaculated. On shaky limbs, he lowered himself on top of her.

"Are you okay?" he asked, feeling the rapid speed of her heart rate.

"Uh huh," she mumbled.

Rolling in the narrow cot, Ryder maneuvered them so he was on the bottom and her body lay on top. He pulled the blankets up to the top of her shoulders and fought to find his breath.

She sighed and burrowed her face into his chest, raining little kisses all over it. "I bet that wasn't in the colonel's plan."

Ryder wrapped his arms around her and pressed a kiss to the top of her head. One hand moved in an idyllic motion. "No, I don't suppose it was."

And I don't give a damn.

"While I'd love to further my exploration of your talents, I have to get some sleep." Her words were soft and laced with exhaustion and contentment.

He smiled in the dark. His heart melted as she reached up and kissed him once. Softly. It wasn't long, and Ryder knew she was sound asleep.

He woke alone. Voices from outside of the tent were loud, and with a groan, he sat up. He was still in Eddie's bed.

"Ryder," a man said before his dark face peeked in the tent. "Come, Ryder. Breakfast almost finished."

Who is he? His mind scrambled for the man's name, and he sat up exposing his bare chest. *Oh, I know.*

"Thanks, Jevonte. I'll be right out."

"Okay." A wide perceptive grin crossed Jevonte's face. "Bye." Then he was gone.

Ryder got dressed in moments. Rubbing the sleep from his eyes, he stepped out into the early Zimbabwean morning.

His eyes scanned the wide open plains, and he couldn't stop the smile. Africa was truly a magnificent place.

"Excuse me," a woman said.

Ryder looked down at a woman holding a bowl out to him.

"Thank you," he said.

She smiled and turned to leave. "Wait. Do you know where Eddie is?"

The woman nodded and pointed behind him. "There."

"Thank you. How do you say it in your language?"

"Thank you, *Maita basa.*"

"*Maita basa,*" he repeated.

She smiled again and walked away. Ryder ate the bowl of fresh fruit and washed it in the water that sat there. Then he headed off in the direction she had pointed, toward the boulder.

He heard them before he saw them. The fire was burning hot under the boulder. All of them were shoveling mud and digging a trench. The same ratty vehicle he saw when he arrived was down there as well.

He couldn't understand what was being said, although the gist was clear. Jogging toward the group, he allowed his eyes to travel over the woman he'd spent the night with.

Dried mud caked her arms and legs as she worked alongside the men. Her hair was gathered back in a loose ponytail, and she wore another pair of short shorts and a tank top. The only difference today was the shirt was blue and there was no longer shirt over it. His eyes traveled over the muscles in her arms and legs as she worked.

"Morning," he said.

"Ryder," she responded without stopping. "Morning. Can you go to the vehicle and bring over some of the long pipes on the top, please?"

"Sure." He strode quickly to the vehicle and grabbed two of the pipes. *Damn, these are a lot heavier than I thought they would be.* Ryder took them over to her and set them down. "Here you go."

Eddie stopped and walked over to where he was. "Thanks," she said with a smile.

"Hey." He latched onto her arm, his body reacting to her nearness. "Are we okay?"

Her gaze rose up to meet his. In an instant, Ryder was lost in them. Eddie winked at him. "Unless you've done something you regret."

"No. I most certainly don't regret it." He reached for her and wiped a smear off her face. "Not at all."

She held his gaze for a moment before she stepped in closer to him, reached up with one arm, and grabbed his shirt, yanking him closer to her. Then she kissed him. His cock was rock hard the second her tongue thrust inside his mouth.

He groaned and reached around to cup her ass with his hands, his fingers massaging the tight muscles. His hips rocked against her, allowing her to feel his rock-hard erection.

When she pulled back, her eyes were dark and swirled with building passion. Her tongue ran over her lips and she said, "Good." She ran her gaze up and down him, igniting flames along the way. "Not afraid of getting dirty, are you?"

He flashed a grin. "Not at all. I *love* getting dirty. Will you help me get clean afterward?"

She licked her lips and sucked the lower one in her mouth. It was like a jolt to his groin. "Perhaps."

"Work me hard, woman. Work me hard."

Grabbing his hand, she led him back to the narrow and deep trench. "We have to keep digging this down, so the pipes will be hidden and not scare the wildlife."

"How will they get water at the village, and what the hell is going on with the fire under that boulder?"

Wiping her forehead, she crossed her arms, drawing his eyes to her breasts. "We'll be pumping it up. And the fire is to explode the boulder, so we can move the smaller pieces and keep going."

He was very impressed. "I didn't have any clue about using fire like that."

She grinned. "Me, either. But I must tell you. They are very resourceful here. Very."

"So," he gestured toward the trench, "why is it so deep everywhere?"

"Don't want the rains to expose it. There aren't many outrageous storms here, but there's no reason to take a chance and have to do the same amount of work again."

Ryder glanced down at the woman beside him. Her eyes oversaw the work, and he could tell how proud she was just by watching her. He wasn't positive what he was feeling standing there next to her, but the need to get her out of the country was not anywhere at the top of his list. She was happy here, and he was as well.

[Five]

Eddie smiled as she sat in the modified roof seat area of her vehicle. She'd taken out the seats, except one, and had left the metal railings. A few clouds had rolled in, and she enjoyed the breeze that blew across her.

Masculine laughter drew her attention down toward the Sabi River where the men were playing football, true football. Ryder had joined the game and ran shirtless with everyone else. He had an anchor and globe tattoo.

He was working hard to keep up with the natives. Her eyes lingered over the tanned skin as he wove in and out of the other men. Her first impression of him had been wrong.

Her godfather had said he was awesome at his job, just too serious. She hadn't seen much of that. He seemed very laid back to her.

Shaking her head at their childish antics, she turned her attention back to what she was doing: designing a windmill so it would do the work of irrigating their crops. At the moment, her problem was trying to figure out what material to use for the blades. Pursing her lips, she began jotting down ideas.

"Look at you sittin' up there looking all sexy." Ryder's voice reached her.

Glancing over the side, Eddie smiled. "And look at you, all hot and sweaty. Come on up."

In moments, he was settling beside her on the blanket she had laid out. "What are you doing?"

"Trying to figure out what's the best material to use for the windmill."

"Anything I can do to help?" he asked in a smooth tone.

Eddie ran her gaze over him, lingering on his crotch. Ryder had awakened within her an insatiable hunger. His hand guided her face to meet his. Right now, his eyes were bluish-green tinged by mercurial gray.

"Right now?" he questioned.

Dropping her pad, she nodded. "Yes."

Ryder covered her mouth with his. She was pressed gently back against the thick blanket. Shudders engulfed her as his tongue traced her lips before sweeping into her mouth. Her breasts tightened, and she rubbed against his bare chest.

Ryder pulled back and stared down at her. Eddie reached up and touched the hard angles of his face, still covered with that sexy stubble. He turned his head and kissed her palm.

"I want to make love to you," he murmured.

His hand moved down, and he unsnapped her shorts. Eddie lifted her hips so they could be removed. Her panties followed suit, the warm breeze blowing against her mostly bare pussy.

"Ryder," she moaned as his fingers teased the swollen lips.

"One second, baby." That was about how long it took for him to begin sliding inside her.

"Ah!" she purred with contentment as he stretched her again.

"I second that," he uttered as he moved within her.

Eddie closed her eyes and undulated beneath him. Their bodies moved in perfect tandem with one another. His mouth had slanted over hers, and he made slow love to it as his hips thrust into her. With one large hand, he pinned both of her wrists over her head, her feet were braced on the metal railing surrounding them.

In and out.

In and out.

In and out.

Ryder created a fiery yearning deep inside her. She opened her eyes and whimpered trying to get him to move faster. Sweat dotted their skin, making it slick.

He sat up on his knees, his strong fingers digging into the flesh of her hips and drove into her wet core even faster. When she moved her hands, he shook his head until she placed them back over her head.

The fire within her began to spread. Inside her boots, her toes curled with ecstasy. "Ryder," she mewled.

"Are you close? I can feel you tighten around me."

"Please," she panted.

"Are you burning for me?"

Faster his pelvis moved.

"Oh, God, yes!" she shouted.

Deeper his strokes rubbed her. She watched his face. Beads of sweat ran down his tanned face. His mouth set in a line of fierce concentration, and his eyes burned with a passion she'd never seen before.

She licked her lips and begged, "Please. I need to come."

Ryder almost blew his load at those words. Gritting his teeth, he fought back the urge to come, ignored his body's demand for release.

Half open, he observed Eddie. She was beautiful in the throes of passion. Flushed skin, full lips parted, eyes dilated. The sight of her alone was enough to make him relinquish control.

He watched his pale cock slip between her dark nether lips. Eddie had a small triangle of hair on her pussy with a point guiding the way to her own entrance to heaven. Otherwise, it was bald.

He was shiny with her juices. He groaned at the sight, and his erection felt like it grew harder. Glancing back up her dark mocha body, Ryder held her gaze, loving how full of passion and desire it was.

Lifting her hips to a greater angle, he moved even faster. Her eyes began to flutter, her pussy muscles tightened.

"Come on my cock, baby."

She did. Her entire body tensed before she arched against him. Her mouth screamed his name to the sky.

Ryder lost it. He echoed her cry with one of his own and collapsed on her. In the distance, the roar of a lion filled the air. He stiffened but relaxed when she didn't move.

Rolling off her sweaty body, Ryder brushed a damp tendril of hair from her face. "Thank you," he murmured against the top of her head.

"Oh no, thank *you*."

He frowned as she pulled on her panties and shorts before lying back down. "Is that your way of telling me we have to get back to work?" he asked.

"Yes," she hesitated, "kinda."

Wrapping his arms around her, he grinned. "I like kinda better."

* * * *

He'd been there going on two weeks now. Working alongside Eddie and the men during the day and sharing a bed with Eddie each and every night. It was the best time of his life, helping out these amazing people.

He couldn't believe it. He wouldn't have if not for the fact he had helped with the work. He stood with Jevonte and watched as Eddie ran the pump for the first time.

The windmill was up and functioning, allowing their new irrigation soaker system to work on the crops. The pump had been more temperamental, so she'd been working on it all day. And now it worked.

Ryder stared as smiles filled everyone's faces. His heart skipped a beat when she glanced at him. And yet, he knew she needed to get stateside. Now that the project was over, he would insist, getting her out of here. The instincts he had were screaming at him that there was trouble on the horizon. He didn't want her caught in the crossfire.

Her husky laughter skated across the air and reached him, making his heart swell with a feeling he was experiencing more and more around her. He scoffed and shook his head. Ryder knew exactly what it was he was feeling for her. He was teetering very close to love.

That night in the village there was a huge celebration. Ryder sat along the edge, more watching than participating. His eyes drifted over to where Eddie stood with a group of women.

His breath caught in his throat. She'd changed into a dress. Well, he thought it was a dress. Her breasts were barely covered by dark purple material, stomach was left completely bare and then she had on a tight sarong the same color. Her feet were bare, and he saw beads around her ankles.

She was beautiful.

As one, the women began to dance. His groin lurched as her body began to move to the music.

"Your Eddie certainly is beautiful," a deep voice spoke from behind him. Tinashe settled beside him, his ebony skin shining in the firelight.

"What makes you think she is mine?" he asked even though the words made him smile.

A deep chuckle emerged from his friend. "The feelings between you two have been growing since the moment you walked into this camp. What you share is something many look for their whole lives."

"You think she feels the same way?"

"Yes. She positively glows when you are near her, or watching her."

Ryder smiled wider.

"She is something special, but she needs to be protected. You have to keep her safe."

Those words made the smile vanish like a puff of smoke. "You feel it, too?"

Tinashe nodded. "Yes. But she is stubborn and won't want to leave."

"If I have to carry her off over my shoulder, I'll get her to go. We'll leave in the morning."

"I will miss you, my friend."

"Thank you for everything, Tinashe. You've taught me so much."

"It is good to see that cloud that was over you gone. She will be very good for you."

Ryder couldn't respond for Eddie had stopped right in front of him, hips swaying and one hand beckoning him toward her. When he just sat there staring, she reached down and took hold of his hand, pulling him to his feet.

"Dance with me," she said looking at him with her big brown eyes.

"I'm not a good dancer," he whispered as her hips moved against him.

"Stop thinking so hard. Feel the music; let the beat move through you." Her hands put his on her full hips and the result was his body hardening instantly. "Close your eyes," she ordered.

He did and lost himself over to the privilege of holding her in his arms and the hypnotic beat of the music. It wasn't until two songs later, that he laughingly guided her to the side and said, "I need a breather."

"You're not that bad of a dancer, Ryder Matthews."

His thumb skimmed her cheek. "You make it look that way."

Her face lost some of its joviality. "Is this where you tell me it's time to go?"

Ryder sighed. "We can't avoid it. I have a job to do, and that's get you home safely."

"A job," she snapped, stepping away from his touch. "So that's what I boil down to... a job?"

He frowned. "That's not how I meant it to sound."

A mask settled over her face. "Whatever. I don't want you to think that because you've fucked me, I'm just going with you because I am in love with you. I know there is a group of rebels on their way. And while I despise running to safety when these amazing people have to deal with the danger, I don't want to put them in more danger by my being here."

Reaching for her, Ryder scowled when she stepped further back. "You aren't just a job, Eddie."

She held his gaze for a moment then walked off, leaving him alone in a village full of merriment. *Go after her,* his mind screamed. His feet were planted firmly upon the packed earth. He saw her climb up onto the top of her vehicle.

Five minutes was all he gave her before following her to the outskirts of the village. The sun was setting and the ground had been cast in a golden glow. Without hesitation, he climbed up and sat beside her on the sole remaining seat.

[Six]

Eddie fumed in silence for a while. She didn't know why hearing him say he had a job to do made her so furious. It wasn't like he hadn't said that from the very beginning. For a moment, though, she imagined that there was something more, given the intense sparks that had flown between them and, subsequently, what they'd shared since that first kiss.

She shuddered as the vehicle leaned to the side and Ryder appeared. Eddie closed her eyes against the emotions that swamped her being in his presence. She would have to be an idiot to know there wasn't something more than just physical with the man who sat beside her, stretched out his powerful legs before him, and took up more than his share of her air.

A low roar vibrated through the air, bringing a smile to her face. There was just something majestic about hearing the raw power of a lion. Another roar was followed by another and another, until the impending night was filled with them.

"What are they doing?" Ryder's voice was hushed.

"Talking. Finding out where everyone is. Isn't it beautiful?"

"Haunting."

"That, too."

"I don't want you to be mad at me, Eddie," he said.

"I'm just frustrated all the way around. It's not really at you, per se. I'm worried for my friends, and it makes me sick I can get out of harm's way but they can't. They are faced with this all the time."

"You can't help them if something happens to you. You can always come back."

He draped his arm around her, tugging her close to his warm body. She sighed and allowed the masculine scent that surrounded him to fill her senses. Contentment filled her as the dark sky began to fill with stars.

"I love it here. I don't want to go back to the States." Eddie watched as the sky looked liked diamonds spread out on black velvet. She pulled the thick blanket they'd made love on earlier over them and sighed.

"I have to get you home, baby," his words were hushed.

"But you can't make me stay." She knew where she belonged. It was here. She had abilities that could give many people freedom from their hard life, and that was what she wanted to do.

"No, I can't."

Turning her face toward him, she looked over his profile. The light from the fire in the village casting a very soft, flickering glow around him. "Make love to me once more," she whispered. "I want to feel you under this endless African sky."

In moments, she moaned in ecstasy as his rigid erection slipped inside her. Sitting on his lap, she hissed as he filled her full. She didn't argue as he removed her shirt and dropped it beside them.

His hands moved up her sides, reaching her breasts and skimming over them. Eddie whimpered as he began pulling on them with his fingers. They were so sensitive, and each tug sent another wave of desire through her.

She continued to ride his cock, not slamming down on him, just a nice easy motion that kept her hanging on the edge of her orgasm. Eddie wanted this to last.

Ryder moved his hands down to settle around her waist, and his mouth latched onto her breast. He suckled one and then moved to the other, his teeth nipping gently upon her pebbled tips.

She dug her fingers into his shoulders as she began to move faster upon his lap. Her head dropped back as a satisfied groan left her. Up and down her skin, his hands moved, the calluses heightening her pleasure.

Biting back a scream as he grazed her taut nipple with his teeth, she looked down at him. He pulled back and met her gaze. Their mouths met in a blaze of passion.

His hands rested on her hips, and he helped her increase the speed as he rose up to meet each stroke. She mewled into his mouth as she felt the orgasm bearing down upon her. Eddie drew back, her mouth bringing his lip with her for a moment, and then she let go and tipped her head back and really began to ride him in earnest. Desperate to find the star-blinding feeling she knew he would bring her.

Ryder's deep grunts were audible around her groans. Her breasts jiggled with each powerful thrust he delivered into her.

"Tell me when, baby," he commanded.

"Now," she begged. "Please, now!"

His fingers tightened into her hips before he surged into her one more time and came with a low roar. His release triggered hers, and she clamped her muscles as she slammed onto him one more time and came around his pulsing cock.

Shuddering and exhausted, she slumped forward. His heart pounded hard against her, and she pressed a kiss to his neck, enjoying the salty taste of his sweat.

"We should get going now, that way we can catch an earlier bus."

He tilted her head up toward his. "Is that what you want to do?"

"No, but hanging around isn't going to make leaving any easier." She moved out of his embrace and shoved quickly into her clothes. "I'll go say my goodbyes and grab my gear." Eddie climbed down and hustled back to the village.

She ignored the tears that ran down her face as she drove them into the night, the fires from the village swallowed up by the blackness. Her eyes worked hard to keep them on the faint road and then the tire blew. Carefully coming to a stop, she turned off the engine and climbed out.

"Damn it all, I thought I checked the tires better than that." She kicked the useless tire with her shoe.

"I'll help," Ryder said materializing beside her.

"Here," she opened the tailgate and grabbed a gun and handed it to him, "get up on top of the truck and keep an eye out."

Ryder frowned as his hands closed over a gun. He had no idea she'd even had something like this in her possession. Walking to the front, he held it in front of the very dim headlights. It was a Vektor R4 assault rifle. On top, there was a scope.

Turing away from the light, he put it up to his eyes and smiled. It had a night vision capability. With a bound, he jumped up on the hood and made his way to the top of the vehicle.

Every now and then, he scanned down around where Eddie worked quickly at changing the tire. The gun was ready to fire just in case as he checked their perimeter. He frowned as his heart leapt to his throat. A lone man was making his way toward them.

"Eddie," he barked low, "we're about to have company."

He jumped down to the ground, his body filling with the familiar adrenaline of battle.

"What? Man or beast?" she asked him, and he noted there was no fear in her voice.

"One man."

"Army or rebel?"

"I don't know. How the hell do you tell the difference?"

"Let me see. It's most likely a rebel. The army doesn't normally travel solo." She never stopped working on changing the tire.

"He's getting closer, and he's picked up speed. I want you to hide," he ordered as his body tensed. The man had drawn a knife. "I don't think he's looking to make friends."

"I'm almost done," she argued.

"Now, Eddie! Move!" he snapped.

"If I hide, and he gets here, we lose our ride. Our only chance is for me to get this finished, and we haul ass out of here."

Not our only one. "Hurry," he said, maneuvering so he was hidden but could still cover Eddie.

"I'm not putzing here, damn it." She lowered the jack and went back to work on tightening the lug nuts.

Ryder tensed the closer the man grew. He yelled something out to Eddie, but Ryder couldn't understand it. His lip lifted as she lifted her head and answered him. Why was she doing that?

I'm here, Eddie. I won't let him hurt you.

The man moved into view better and was gesturing with the knife. Eddie shook her head and answered him.

Two more steps, and I'm shooting him.

The man gestured toward the vehicle and again, Eddie gave a negative shake of her head. She stepped to her left and hefted the tire iron in her hand and said in English, "There is no way I'm giving you sex or my vehicle."

A low growl erupted from Ryder. *Hell no! Ain't no man touchin' my woman.* He raised the muzzle and moved out of the dark. "Back the fuck off, man."

The shock was obvious, but when he reached for his gun, Ryder shook his head at him. "I wouldn't do that if I were you. Eddie, tell him to drop his weapons."

She did and the man did as he was told, very reluctantly.

"Gather them and put them in the vehicle, Eddie," he ordered. "I've got you covered." A grin crossed his face as she did what he said immediately. *That's my girl.* "Now, get in the driver's seat and get ready to leave."

When she did, he walked backward to the door, jumped up on the foot rail, kept the gun trained on the man spitting daggers at him and said, "Drive now. Let's get going."

With a flurry of spinning wheels, Eddie got them out of there and in seconds they couldn't even see the man. She stopped when he told her to, and he climbed in on the passenger side. Silence reigned as she drove again.

"You may as well get some sleep, Ryder. I'll drive for a few hours then we can switch off."

It sounded like a good plan to him. He rested his head against the window and settled the assault rifle between his legs, where it was within immediate reach, and closed his eyes.

* * * *

Ryder looked at the woman sleeping beside him. She had been very quiet since they boarded the plane. The captain had just announced they would be landing in a few minutes, and she had still not awakened.

"Eddie," he said softly. "Come on, baby, wake up."

When they had changed planes, he'd placed a call to Colonel Nowell, telling them when they'd be arriving. Now that they were circling the Dulles International Airport, he wanted to stop time.

She stirred and looked up at him, her amazing walnut brown eyes still cloudy with sleep. "Are we landing?" Her question was hushed.

"In a few minutes."

"Thank you for saving me. I know I didn't want you there, but when it came down to it, you saved my ass. Thank you."

He leaned over to her and kissed her. "You don't ever have to thank me."

They held hands as the plane landed and taxied to the gate. There was no rush to get off the airplane, so they waited for the others to disembark.

A heavy silence fell over them as they walked toward baggage claim. Ryder continually rubbed his thumb over the back of her hand. Her face was stoic, and she refused to look over at him. They maneuvered slowly through the crowd that seemed frantic to get back to their loved ones.

A few steps away from when baggage claim would come into view, he stopped. "Look at me, Eddie." His heart wept from the amount of sorrow he saw in her amazing eyes.

Cupping her face, he used one thumb to trace her lips. She kissed the pad before she pivoted on her heel and disappeared into the crowd.

Ryder walked disheartened into the baggage claim area and saw her in the arms of her parents. Colonel Nowell was there as well and headed toward him, reaching out and pulling him in for a giant hug.

"Thank you for bringing her back safe."

"Right," he mumbled, trying not to stare at her.

"She's fine, Ryder. Although I am curious as to why you are watching her like she's yours."

"I have to get back through security. I have a plane to catch. Goodbye, Colonel." Ryder turned and began walking off.

"It's better this way," Colonel Nowell hollered after him.

Better for whom? Because I'm pretty damn sure my heart is being ripped out. Ryder kept walking without looking back.

[Epilogue]

Eddie kept playing it over and over in her mind. Ryder Matthews walking away without a single look back. She'd longed to run after him and hold him to her. She wanted to beg him to keep her, because she loved him.

Her parents were smothering her. She just wanted to get away, and today when she told them she was going back, they just about blew a gasket. Eddie didn't care.

"I'm happiest when I can use my ability to help people in need," she'd told them. Her mother had understood, but then she'd never had a problem with her little girl's need to help those less fortunate.

So after talking to them, she'd made two more calls, and she was soon in an airplane heading to the stop midway to her destination. She smiled as the plane banked to the left and headed toward the runway.

She got in her rented vehicle, stowed her gear, and began driving. It took a few hours, and it was dark when she shut off the engine. Taking a deep breath, she climbed out and headed for the door, knocking gently.

Her heart caught in her throat as she was faced by the man on the other side of the door. Ryder Matthews still looked so wonderful. His hair was a bit shorter, and his scruff was lighter but nevertheless there.

"Hi," she said by way of a greeting.

"Eddie," he breathed, pushing past the door and pulling her into his embrace. "What are you doing here?"

She stared up at him, her heart pounding erratically. "I couldn't stop thinking about you."

His mouth lowered until his lips teased hers. "I wanted to come to you so many times, but wasn't sure you'd want me."

"There's no one I'd rather have beside me. I love you, Ryder Matthews."

"Jesus, Eddie. Do you have any idea how much I've longed to hear those words from you. I love you, too, baby. I love you, too."

He kissed her. Their tongues met in a flare of passion. Ryder picked her up and carried her to his bed where he made long, sweet love to her.

When she woke later, totally satisfied, she opened her eyes to see him watching her.

"What's next?" he asked.

Eddie smiled. "I'm going back to Africa. Be my bodyguard?"

"Forever, baby. Forever."

♥

aliyah-burke.com

Slice
© Ralph Greco

[One]

Germane's three-inch heels lightly spanked the wet patio. Sliding the glass door slowly open, she stepped up and into the dark kitchen, walked across the tan linoleum floor, past the small butcher-block table to the far right corner of the room, and stood at the silent basement stairs. She descended painfully slowly. This was the important part; mustn't rush the sound of her heels clicking on the thin wooden stairs.

So much fucking ritual, she mused as she artfully fell into darkness.

"Took your time," the low voice greeted her from the silence of the basement.

"It took me a while to get ready," Germane explained when reaching the bottom step. She paused to straighten her wrinkled raincoat then stepped off the last stair, around the wooden banister, and walked forward onto the cold tile.

"I called you an hour ago," Lila admonished from her ratty high-backed chair. A splash of blue haze peed from the television in front of her. In the light, Germane could just see the tops of Lila's bare knees.

Germane continued her creep, past the closed laundry-room door, past the high video shelf, finally stopping at the high back of Lila's chair. She reached her long arms over its cloth back, resting her bright red nails on her lover's pale shoulders.

"I'm sorry," Germane said, kneading Lila's pale skin through her strong thumbs. She lowered her arms over the thin silk of Lila's bra and began tickling the smaller woman's pointy breasts.

"You're just delaying your punishment," Lila spat, not moving her eyes from the television.

Germane slowly removed her hands, straightened, and opened the belt around her raincoat. Lifting one sharp three-inch heel at a time, she deftly walked from the rayon splash and around to the front of the Lila's chair.

"Keep your back to me," Lila ordered as the black woman stood in front of her.

Germane watched a silent David Letterman make faces at a guest she knew she should recognize but didn't.

"You know..." Lila started, lifting her foot to rest on Germane's bare ass. "I can't tell if I like you with or without the G-string."

I like it with, Germane thought, but Lila had ordered her bare tonight, so she was.

"Spread your legs and bend," Lila sighed, and Germane did so, grabbing her ankles and spreading her ass wide as she had been instructed to always do.

"Sorry?" Lila mocked, removing her foot and moving forward on the squeaking chair. "If only you were."

Germane yelped as Lila thrust her stubby middle finger up into her dry anus. She grabbed her ankles tighter as Lila thrust her finger up to its first knuckle.

"Sorry," Lila repeated, sliding forward off the rocker, kneeling down to meet Germane's wet sex with her hungry mouth.

[Two]

"Ge, move down just a bit," Doctor Birch coaxed.

New baby keeping you up, huh? Germane thought; she could hear the raspiness in his usually liquid voice.

Doctor Birch's voice had been one of the reasons Germane had first started coming to the gynecologist. He seemed a nice enough man with his wide face and little blue eyes, but when he started talking—the wet patter of his speech, the delicious way words just splashed off his tongue—Germane had been convinced to trust the guy.

"Any pain?" he asked from somewhere between her legs.

"No more than usual," Germane answered, the pressure building a bit in her pelvis. She looked up at the ceiling and tried to find the Quintan triplets, attempting to forget her endometriosis.

"Any time you want to go for that..." Doctor Birch started but stopped as Germane felt a pinpoint of pressure poke her lower left side.

"Little inflammation here," he continued. "I'll give you something for it."

Two minutes later, Doctor Birch was taking off his gloves as his nurse left the room. The curly-haired man continued speaking to the chart in his big hands.

"You know, I forgot to thank you for a referral."

Germane sat on the examination table coaxing the flimsy robe to close over her heavy breasts. She shifted her bottom to allow the robe to close even more and then stopped herself, nearly chuckling at her modesty.

Referral? she thought as the doctor's words rang in her head.

"Who?" she asked.

"A.J. Janson," Doctor Birch continued, making a few markings in Germane's file. "Real nice young lady."

"Oh yeah, I remember," Germane said and suddenly did.

She had met A.J. and her mother two weeks ago in the mall, and the younger woman had taken her aside and asked if Germane could recommend someone for her "little problem." More than a decade ago, Germane and A.J.'s cousin had been roommates in college, and Germane guessed that her rather liberal reputation went a long way in establishing a quick confidence. Germane hadn't asked what exactly was the young girl's problem... and wouldn't dream of prying now. Still, she would like to know if everything was all right.

"You and her hit it off?" Germane asked as innocently as she could.

"Yes, real well. She's a real nice young lady," the doctor reiterated, looking up from his notes to add, "with not a problem in the world."

Thanks, Germane thought, smiled at the chubby man, and jumped off the table.

"Um..." the doctor started, reaching for the door, "she should be here any minute."

"Alone?" Germane asked, too late to have caught herself. Doctor Birch only smiled. She knew he knew.

"Alone," he agreed, smiled widely and left the room.

Good, Germane thought.

A.J.'s mother was okay but could be a bit of a bitch when she wanted to. She was one of those neighbors who never started a rumor but could be counted on to keep the flood going. There would be all the usual prying questions, and Germane just wasn't up for that.

A.J. she could handle, though.

Actually, Germane smiled, putting on her sweater, *I'd love to see her.*

There was something about the almost tomboy type of girl that was very attractive to Germane; the young girl had a quality about her that could best be described as 'bouncy.' She was a stunning package of long blonde hair, soft features, and big brown eyes, all tempered by a mind that seemed to flitter quickly from one thing to a next. And although Germane had not caught the girl at her best, as A.J. had been worried about her 'little problem,' she had been sufficiently smitten by the early twenty-something year old that she imagined she could affect some harmless flirting now.

At the very least, she could ogle the girl for a few minutes before Doctor Birch called her in.

[Three]

Good deep curves, sharp contours, and long lines; the body in the mirror was a delight to Germane. In her younger years, she had never enjoyed looking at herself; hastily drying herself after showers; masturbating with eyes shut and room dark; never checking slowly toning muscles after a workout. Love was made with lights low and music loud. But now, thirty-three and holding, Germane was digging her shape, her dark wispy turns and rises, her full open spots. She liked the woman she had grown into and delighted in taking any and every opportunity to stare long and hard at her long and lean body.

"The Peak Early Theory," Germane whispered as she opened her legs and grabbed her right breast even harder.

Germane had seen clear evidence of the PET at her ten-year reunion. With vindictive aplomb, she had sashayed through that hotel ballroom, cutting sharp corners with her tight brown hair shining and her even tighter dress clinging. Every girl considered a babe back in 1979—or every guy called a fox—now looked old. Very old. Hell, Germane's father had those guys beat, and he was double their ages!

The girls fared worse. What marriage hadn't done to them, post-childbirth letting-go had. And all of them, from petite Lori Simons to busty Mary Ellen Reynolds, who'd all been incredible looking in high school, had "peaked early." Germane, who at seventeen had been battling baby fat, a too long body, and hair that was always natty, looked sleek and fine in her black taffeta and lace. Hence, the proof she needed and the salvation she secretly burned for came when guy after guy—who never paid her any mind in high school—flirted with her that cool November evening. She, of course, had no interest—since her homosexuality was one of the few things about her that had peaked early—but it was a victory all the same.

And now she sat naked, her old red rocker gently moving back and forth, sneaking peeks at her long, taut, brown legs in the mirror. It was almost as if she wasn't even looking at herself, but rather that she was gazing at an attractive nude, a woman she would like to see a photograph of. A woman that Germane was delighted was herself, but at times like these could trick herself to believe possibly wasn't.

"Damn good," Germane said aloud, and her mind drifted to the long legs of A.J. Janson. *Man, how great they would look in a tight miniskirt!*

"God, that little ass," Germane whispered to herself as she spread her legs a bit more. The young girl's little rump had never once stopped moving in the waiting-room chair today—boundless, intoxicating energy.

Probably tastes as sweet as honey, Germane thought, slowly curling the dark hair on her pubis.

"Let me teach you," she whispered, licked her lips and draped her legs one over each arm of the rocker. She repositioned her ass so her wet chocolate sex was well in view of the closet door mirror, licked her middle finger and began to tickle her waiting, hard clitoris.

"Just once," Germane said and pushed her finger further down, stopping at her silky full lips.

"Wait 'til I get you at lunch," she threatened her empty bedroom. With a deep sigh, Germane thrust her index finger into herself, lifting her other hand off her plump breast and splaying it across her wide belly.

It was all Germane could do to not fall off the rocker as she watched herself in the mirror, cupping her whole hand in her crotch, lurching forward in the chair as she imagined A.J. there, kneeling between her spread legs. The swell had begun inside her as it had when she was speaking to A.J. but of course, now German could do something about it.

"Oh, let me just kiss your ass, just once. Please!" Germane growled to the still June night as she imagined watching the young girl's little bottom bounce as she kissed its bare rise.

God. Germane needed to come. She thrust her finger in as deep as it would go and grabbed her shaking right breast. Ten seconds more, and she'd explode.

"Oh, God, A.J.," she growled and shook as the first wave rose to full height within her steamy long body. Reluctantly, with steel resolve and eyes wide, Germane peeled her hands away, her wet sex aching for the finish of her finger fucking, her breast quivering.

Not yet. Got to save it, she thought, breathing heavily and laying back in the rocker.

Germane's ass was slightly sticky on the hard wood seat. Her sex flooded strong juices as she tried hard not to think of how hot she really was. She slumped further back into the rocker, afraid now to stare at her heaving reflection, afraid of the deep hunger she knew would be evident in her pulsing brown eyes.

She had to have A.J. That was all there was to it! Germane's need was growing into an obsession she knew could be dangerous. Her current situation with Lila was testament to that. Germane had never wanted that 'relationship' to be anything more than an occasional meeting when both she and her neighbor were horny. But it had grown into much more than that. Much, much more, and Germane shuttered as her hand poised over the portable phone. It was at quiet, desperate times like these that she remembered...

* * * *

Both women had slowly displayed their sexuality in front of one another. It was a small town, and since Lila had been living in her house for close to twenty years, Germane quickly heard the gossip about her new neighbor. But separate lives, friends and careers, proximity of family kept the women from any real contact. It wasn't until the languid pose of summer—as greetings across front lawns grew into iced tea breaks and cookouts—that the women learned of their shared homosexuality and slightly unusual predilections.

At first Germane had considered herself lucky; a willing partner living right across the street! Germane had harbored a desire to be dominated from as early an age as she could remember sexual feelings. But it wasn't until she met Lila that she really had the luck to explore these feelings. Sure, there had been those few encounters with girlfriends early on... very early on. Rolling around at a slumber party when one girl manages to fall across another's lap and a quick swat is greeted with giggles and light protest. Germane had thought the heat she felt was simply the close proximity of another girl. At the time, Germane had no idea what S&M was.

But as her sexual need for women grew and Germane realized that there was not only a word but an entire subculture built for her homosexuality. She also learned that she really did enjoy the feel of a quick playful swat to her behind, or delighted in the resound a open palm made across soft panties... or at the very least, thinking about such things! And as she grew into her teens and early twenties, the tall black woman fantasized more and more about being taken across someone's lap—even a guy, if need be—and spanked hard and long.

The few times that Germane did convince a lover into this type of play had been more of a tit-for-tat arrangement, with Germane reluctantly giving as much as she received. But she knew, even during those few tentative encounters, that she really wanted just to receive and receive much more than a brief bottom warming. She began to realize that she wanted to be degraded, humiliated, and beaten within the context of a very kinky night of domination.

As Germane often remarked to herself, she had been dealt a double whammy of socially unacceptable needs: lesbianism and masochism.

Lila Little had spent plenty of time with non-sociability. She had been in the trenches—as she called it—ever since coming out to her parents at thirteen. A thin girl with deep blue eyes, a strong chin, a button nose, and an almost regal air about her, Lila had been the dominant in over a half dozen relationships—even one with a guy she had enjoyed whipping on occasion—and didn't want her sex life any other way. Not exactly her type, with her wide hips and soft-spoken retorts, Lila still became Germane's top. Need often bests knock-down, drag-out attraction.

But as much as Germane had enjoyed being subjugated, beaten, tortured, and taken by Lila, she knew the 'relationship'—and Germane always considered that word with little quotation marks in regard to Lila—would eventually run out of steam. The simple act of undressing for her neighbor, which used to flood Germane's sex only months before, now left her cold and wanting. It wasn't that Germane didn't want to be dominated; it was just she didn't really want to be dominated by Lila anymore...

* * * *

Lila barked for Germane to be over in ten minutes. There had been a time when that alone would have brought wetness between Germane's legs. Now she only felt sickened as she hung up the phone and slowly rose from her rocking chair.

[Four]

"He's a real nice man," Germane agreed.

"I was worried," A.J. said, whispering a bit over her frosty glass. "I mean, I was so happy I ran into you that day. I was really desperate."

"Why didn't you just ask your cousin to—"

"I... I just couldn't. I mean, we're close but..." A.J. tried but took another gulp of her iced tea instead.

Germane watched as A.J.'s long fingers held the glass, how the young girl's palm arched easily around its wet side. She imagined her black breasts—big, plump and sweaty—in the girl's hand, caressed just as tight.

"What are you getting?" A.J. asked, changing the subject and looking up too quickly.

Germane was caught, she knew it, and A.J. knew she knew it. The two women exchanged a silent moment, during which Germane was convinced the younger girl would just get up and leave. Germane's stare had simply been too predatorily.

"Just order two of whatever you get," A.J. said, shrugging off the moment.

"Yeah, sure," Germane said, more than a bit startled.

"I'm so glad we're doing this," the young girl said after another drink. "Outside of school, I don't have too many friends."

What the fuck? Germane screamed to herself. *I know her mother has chewed her ear off about me! I'm sitting here*

63

smiling now, but there is no way she didn't see me looking at her...like that. The girl can put two and two together.

"Well, you have one now," Germane said, her mind back to the conversation.

"Great," A.J. beamed.

"So, tell me about you," Germane continued. "I'm sure you know a lot about me from your cousin."

Germane shuttered at the thought of Bonnie repeating anything of their dorm years. There had been a lot of girls, even a few guys. And beer, lots of beer. Bonnie's recollections would not be tempered by prejudice. She knew about Germane from the moment they had met and held a healthy curiosity that never manifested beyond questions. But it was still always better to get any real information right from the horse's mouth, Germane knew.

"Not much to tell," A.J. said and then fixed her gaze straight at Germane. In their short acquaintance, Germane had never seen the young girl with such a serious face. Where was the broad smile, the dimple in her right cheek?

"What's wrong, honey?" Germane asked and reached across the table to take A.J.'s hand in hers.

"I don't want to spoil this," A.J. said. Her big brown eyes filled with tears. "I really want this to work out."

Shit, here it comes, Germane thought. *Is there a back door out of this place?*

"Ask if you think it'll make a difference," Germane said, leveling A.J. with a cool stare.

She wants to know now, I'll fucking well tell her, Germane thought, sliding her hand back across the table. Just then, the lanky waiter in red suspenders reappeared, as if on cue.

"Two lunch special salads," Germane barked, without looking up. Despite his youth, the waiter must have been able to read a strained conversation and left the two women without a word.

"You know Lila Little and I are friends." Germane tried to hide the terseness in her voice. "I'm sure your mom has told you about Lila," she continued, not expecting a reply.

Shit, this is not going the way I wanted! she shouted to herself and shifted her butt just enough to relieve the pressure the wood chair was exerting on her right cheek; Lila had been especially brutal on that side last night.

Goddamned Lila, Germane thought. *It's all your fucking fault. I'm going to blow it with this girl because of the shit her mother has heard about you!*

"It's none of my business," A.J. said, trying to change the subject with her usual thin-lipped smile and another long gulp of her iced tea. "I just, I don't know. I..."

"Yes, is the answer to your question," Germane said and then screamed in her head: *You okay with that? Cause if you're not, fuck you very much!*

"It's a small town, people talk," Germane continued, softening a bit. This girl was not her mother, wasn't accusing, just curious.

"You also want to know if I asked you here because I'd like to sleep with you," Germane continued. *What the hell, it's all out in the open now.*

"Yeah, I..." A.J. said, her smile widening to reveal perfect porcelain teeth.

"Yes to that question, too," Germane managed.

A moment of silence passed, and Germane reached her hand across the table again. A.J. didn't recoil.

"Whatever you want this to be, it can be," Germane continued, whispering. "Friends, lovers, whatever. I do find you attractive, but I'm not one to force myself on anyone. I just thought we hit it off nice at Doctor Birch's, so why not lunch?"

"No, I wanted to come," A.J. softly defended.

"Well, I'm glad you did," Germane agreed and lightly smiled.

"I'm not sure what I want this to be," A.J. said. "I mean I've had thoughts all along, but I never..."

Never knew one of us before, Germane thought, but said: "Let's just have lunch, okay?"

"Yeah, I'm hungry as hell," the young girl exclaimed and sat back in the high-backed wicker chair with a sigh.

If you only knew how hungry. Germane thought, smiling back.

[Five]

"I was wondering when you'd call," Lila said, relighting the candle.

"It's only been three days," Germane protested.

What the fuck am I doing? she thought as she pushed her face deeper into Lila's fluffy pillow. She heard the clap-clap of the double swatter and braced for another swat.

"For three days, you get the full treatment," Lila said, checking the tight scarves at Germane's wrists.

"Lila, hit the left side. The right is still sore," Germane pleaded.

If I keep to the pain, I'll get through this, she thought.

"Fuck you," Lila said and landed another two swats. The second landed just below Germane's cheek on her upper thigh, the sting lifting her from the bed.

"You're not going anywhere," Lila snickered. "I tied those tight this time."

"Bitch," Germane growled. *God my ass is stinging*, she thought as she tried to move her ankles.

"You never tire of trying my patience," Lila teased and pinched Germane's welted backside. "I think it has to be the dildo tonight."

"No, Lila. No," Germane pleaded. *Yes, do it. Anything to keep me from having to touch you*, she thought, but a bit of fear was creeping into her mind. It had been a long time since Lila had dildoed her.

"This will teach you not to take so long calling me," Lila said and left the bed. She checked the bonds at Germane's hands again and at her ankles.

"Nice and warm..." Lila commented as she ran her fingers up her spread legs. "And wet," she added, pushing a bony index finger into Germane's soft sex.

"Please let me come, Lila," Germane pleaded as her lover strummed her engorged clitoris. *Let me come so I can get dressed and out of here!*

"It's going to take a lot more than your pleading," Lila said and removed her hand.

The smaller woman left the bed, walked across her bedroom, and fumbled through a drawer. A minute later, she returned, kneeling between Germane's spread legs.

"Just a touch of this," Lila teased. "Don't want to make this too easy."

Germane could hear Lila breathing heavier and then felt a cool, wet sensation shoot up her anus as Lila applied the cold lubricant. Lila's fingers were shaking as they plied Germane's anus.

Fucking nervous after all this time? Germane thought as the wetness between her legs cooled slightly.

"It's been a bit. It's gonna hurt," Lila said, continuing to apply the greasy jelly. "Just relax," the smaller woman continued, removing her finger. "Breathe deep through your mouth."

Germane felt Lila shift on the bed. She knew the smaller woman was strapping on the thick black phallus now, stroking her own clitoris in anticipation. It never took Lila long to come, a fact for which Germane constantly damned the woman.

"Ask me for it," Lila whispered after another minute of silent fumbling.

Her sweet breath tickled Germane's naked back. The hard rubber poked Germane's inner thigh as Lila knelt down close to her.

"No," Germane said. *Just fucking do it already!*

"You have to beg," Lila coaxed, just a hint of disappointment in her low voice.

Germane almost laughed. "No," she said and the fake dick was thrust even closer to her quivering cheeks.

The dildo was on the edge of entering. Germane could feel her anus involuntarily spreading in anticipation. Her body wanted it, but she wondered if she could really take this tonight, if she really wanted it tonight. But as usual, the doubt was working wonders for her libido as the wetness in her sex increased and her breath quickened. She began pressing her pelvis in tight circles against the bed.

"Beg me, or I ram it in," Lila said, the delight back in her voice.

Germane could smell Lila's sex, knew the little woman was undulating her hips in her characteristic little counter-clockwise circles around the hard leather of the strap-on.

"Do it!" Germane cried, and Lila fell down into her.

The dildo spread her wide, filled her. Germane felt her sex flooding, felt the rough bedspread under her coarse patch of brown hair, bunching up her rock hard clitoris, ticking, teasing...

"Do it. Fuck me hard, you bitch!" Germane growled, burying her face into Lila's fruity smelling pillow.

Lila pushed up, forward, and in as deep as she could.

Germane began to cry as she rode a deep orgasm into Lila's bed. And as she shook through her undulation, as the skinny woman lay atop her and pushed the dildo in, up and as deep as she could muster, Germane realized that this had to be the last time she would be with Lila Little.

[Six]

The Guys of the Fourth Floor.

Germane could see it like a title of a movie, on the marquee in lights: National Account Executive Inc., with cooperation from The Girls on the Fourth Floor presents: The Guys of the Fourth Floor.

It was ritual with Germane, her assistant Sally, Ruth, her assistant Kim, Geena, and Bobby Sue. Yes, even here in this Northeast suburb they had a Bobby Sue. When all six women met for their three o'clock break on Monday, they would begin by discussing their past weekends and invariably fall into ribald gossip and spicy speculation about their fellow male workers, or "The Guys of the Fourth Floor."

Germane could be as vocal as the other ladies. She was just as curious about girths, tongue-lashing potential, and the other bandied-about attributes of her fellow male workers. Being a lesbian did not rob one of healthy curiosity, and Germane would be damned if there wasn't a gay woman or man alive who hadn't wondered about their opposite sex. In her years, Germane had done a lot more then wonder, that's for sure. Hell, she knew straight men and women frequently fantasized about homosexual encounters. Wasn't that supposed to be a sign of a healthy heterosexual? Why couldn't Germane join in with a little light teasing and heavy-breath speculation?

True, these days her thoughts never ventured further then the blue walls of the lunchroom, still it was fun to sit and jabber with The Girls, sip stale coffee, and relax. Besides, she enjoyed the often-sideways glances she received when she offered a rather salacious piece of inquiry. It was as if her fellow co-workers knew she was gay—since no one had ever asked, she had never told—or at the very least suspected, and Germane's suggestions or queries startled them into reconsidering her sexual preference. It was a bit of a game and on most occasions Germane would enjoy this half hour, but that day she was thinking only of A.J. and their lunch of five days before...

* * * *

The hour and a half had flown by.

Was Bonnie really THAT wild in college. What's it like to work for that big publisher? Poly-sci looks good, but I'd really like to do something outdoors. Was buying the old Anderson house really expensive? How has the neighborhood changed in twenty years? What's it like in Roanoke? Do you like this coast better than the other? I was hoping on Paris around Christmas, depends on when class ends. Mom and Dad are pretty cool, built me a nice studio in the basement. Most of my friends want to just go out dancing, which is okay, but it is the same ole' thing all the time. A few boyfriends, just friends, nothin' serious. Would love to go hiking.

The conversation had been led by A.J. as she stabbed her salad and literally bounced her tight ass in the straight-backed wooden chair. Germane couldn't keep her eyes from the bright oval-faced girl, staring hard once again but with the implied excuse of listing intently. *Christ, the girl was perky*, she mused. *Deliciously cute.*

A.J. had that verve, that energy that Germane knew she herself had held—although never to this degree—when she was in her early twenties. The whole road is open before you when you are that age; you don't see possibilities as much as feel them in your groin. It's the very best time of one's life, when you are spreading your wings to their widest span and realizing that you are somebody.

Of course, the whole physical package of A.J. was enticing, too: long strong legs, firm bosom, wide smile, pretty teeth. But it was her energy, her youthful lust for life that made her ever so enchanting.

To say the least, Germane had been transfixed all throughout lunch. Nothing more had been said about Germane's lesbianism or A.J.'s interest in it. The two women talked nearly nonstop. Germane paid the check after a minute of A.J.'s admonishments and then the brief, but incredibly surprising kiss outside.

What did it mean? Germane wondered as she had walked back to the office, savoring the taste of her lips. Did A.J. want her? Did A.J. just want to feel what it was like to kiss a woman on the lips? Maybe A.J. had never kissed a black woman before and wanted to see what it was like. Maybe A.J. was a tease. Maybe A.J.'s parting to a friend was always a kiss on the lips. What the hell did...

* * * *

"Is this cool? I'll go if it isn't."

Germane looked up from her coffee to the smiling face of A.J. The young girl was standing in the small lunchroom doorway. Germane swallowed her surprise and managed to rise to her feet.

"They told me at the desk to just come in," the young girl offered the small group of women, smiling lastly at Germane.

"Yeah, ah, hi," Germane managed, walking the five steps to the doorway. "Girls, this is my friend A.J. Her cousin and I were in college together."

"Oh, hi," the group practically chorused and went back to their coffees.

"Let's get some air," Germane said and took A.J. lightly by the arm, ushering her out of the office.

[Seven]

"There're always guys," A.J. admitted, taking another sip from her milkshake. "I've got nothin' against guys."

"Me neither," Germane agreed.

"It's just that..." the young girl said and looked up from her shake. "I guess I'm just curious. Always have been, always will be."

"Curiosity is healthy," Germane said, coaxing the last bit of yogurt off her plastic spoon and onto her tongue.

"In college with your cousin, I did a lot to feed my curiosity," Germane continued after swallowing.

"With guys?" A.J. asked, brown eyes wide.

"Yes," Germane chuckled to the younger woman's surprised stare. "Plenty of guys. But I knew when I was in high school that I was a lesbian. I just wanted to explore other options. There are certain things you can get from a man you just can't get from a woman."

"And vice versa?"

"Yes, and vice versa," Germane agreed.

"I always thought... that you, that you would just use a... a dildo," A.J. continued, whispering the last word. "A strap-on."

"Some women do, some don't," Germane suggested and then continued. "I figured that if I wanted *that* particular sensation, a penis inside me, I wanted it to be the real thing."

This was mostly true. The times Germane had been with man, it was for this very reason. To feel a warm, a live penis enter her, spread, and fill her. The dildo Lila used certainly filled her, but never in her vagina and only during the harsh admonishments of her sadistic games.

"Makes sense," A.J. nodded.

"But I prefer the feeling of a woman beside me," Germane said and reached out her index finger to stroke A.J.'s freckled hand.

"That's the part I guess I'm a little nervous about," A.J. said softly, staring down at the older woman's black finger tickling the back of her hand.

"That's normal," Germane said and traced a tight line up A.J.'s pale hand. The younger girl attempted to lift her milkshake again, but stopped as Germane traced her finger down A.J.'s skin and settled it on the back of her hand.

"Like I told you last week, I'm not interested in pushing anything," Germane added, as both women stared down at the their touching. "We go slow, okay?"

"Yeah, thanks," A.J. said looking up then, smiling at Germane.

The women broke contact and Germane scooped another dollop of yogurt into her mouth as A.J. finally sipped.

If this girl only knew how perfect this scene is, Germane thought, not even attempting to hide her staring now.

The stuffy hot afternoon, the loose crowd of shoppers, the spittle of ejaculate milkshake coming from A.J.'s straw, the melting yogurt in Germane's deep cup; all of it perfect against Germane's light touch and A.J.'s naive cool. To have taken A.J. right there and then, on that blood-red bench, would have been the end for Germane; her life could have easily ended that afternoon with the young girl's firm breasts in her hand, A.J.'s cute bottom stuck against the hard wooden bench slats, her thin pale lips pressed to Germane's...

Germane realized right then that she was most strikingly in love with A.J. Janson and was falling deeper every second. At her age, love hardly came at first sight, and Germane's emotions had waited four meetings and a considerable amount of fantasy time to bring her to this conclusion, but it was no less powerful. Germane was entranced by A.J., and she wanted her more then any other woman she had yet encountered.

"What time do you have to get back?" the younger girl asked, finishing the milkshake with a quick slurp.

"Anytime, really," Germane answered. "Extended coffee break."

"Wanna walk me to my car?"

* * * *

This time the kiss was long and precise. No initiating hesitation. No retreating guilt. And best of all, no confusing intent. A.J. simply turned around after opening her car door, smiled at Germane, and then the two women met. A.J.'s body folded between her Datsun's bright blue side as Germane's strong hands gripped her shoulders. Germane hid her nervousness by pursuing A.J. until she could feel the younger girl's soft mouth part and her tongue cautiously invite touch.

"Wow," A.J. said when they broke from one another a minute later.

The young girl kept her eyes on Germane's, no quickly stolen glance or retreat; a black woman and a younger white girl had just lip-locked in the center of a busy outdoor shopping mall!

Amazing, Germane thought, smiling wide and long at A.J.'s ever-cool reactions. "Wow is right."

"You kiss really good."

"You sound surprised," Germane lightly teased.

"Yeah. I mean no. No," the younger woman tried. "I just never kissed a woman like that before."

"Didn't seem like it was a problem," Germane said and once again walked into A.J.

"Wow," A.J. said, bowing her head slightly. "Wow."

"Call me tonight if you can," Germane said, squeezed A.J.'s arm. "I think we could both use a couple hours to think about all this."

"Yeah, I..." A.J. started, then turned to her car, turned back around, smiled at Germane, turned back to her car yet again, opened the driver side door, sat down in the car, closed the door, smiled at Germane one last time and drove off.

[Eight]

"I really don't know what else to say," Germane tried as the smaller woman turned from the metal barbecue and walked back to the chair Germane was sitting in.

"If it's over, it's over," Lila said, forcing a tight smile.

"I just don't want to hur..."

"Too late," Lila interrupted Germane. "Too fucking late for that, girl."

Lila turned to Germane.

"Who is she?" Lila asked.

"You don't know her," Germane answered.

"If she is a gay woman in this town, I know her."

"You don't know her," Germane repeated, then stood and walked over to the smaller woman.

"It just happened, Lila," Germane added.

"Yeah, it just happened," Lila repeated.

"We had a good run of it," Germane started. "I have great memories. And I want us to stay friends."

"Yeah," Lila said and raised her head to Germane. A thin tear lightly stained her chubby cheek.

Germane stared at her ex-lover and tried not to falter. This would be the time when she'd break, if at all. Lila at her most vulnerable. Lila the wounded. Lila the short, muscular, little package of need. It was at times like this that Germane remembered what it was she had found so attractive in this woman in the first place: the quiet, latent hurt underneath the strong frame and staid brown eyes.

"I really do mean it, Lila." Germane kissed her ex-lover on the cheek. "Your friendship means a lot to me."

"I think you better go," Lila said, a second tear running down her other pale cheek.

"Okay." Germane turned from Lila, walked across the patio, and out of Lila's backyard—and life—forever.

* * * *

Germane had decided that no matter how hard the break-up was going to be for Lila, it was best that she not tell her the whole truth; use the very real feelings she had for A.J. as the one and only excuse. It was damn hard for someone to learn they were being cast aside for another, but Germane knew it would be harder still on Lila if she had told her ex-lover the whole story: how she just wasn't turned on by Lila anymore.

Lila wasn't the kind of person who'd take well to the idea of an attraction just fizzling, especially when she was the person the fizzle was dying over. Lila would never accept the fact that Germane didn't want her anymore. Her ego simply could never accept the truth in those terms. The smaller woman's ordered, neat life could never allow so shocking a revelation without dire consequences. Her perception of the world around her included the very cemented view that she was simply too special. It was a view borne out of insecurity as had been Lila's need to always play dominant in their affair.

Germane knew all of this, of course. Let Lila think Germane crazy for choosing another lover over her. Lila didn't need to know the whole truth if that whole truth would only hurt her more, the slice of information would snap the very core of the tenuous hold on the life she had built around herself. At the very least, Germane owed Lila the delusion of her frail ego. And in the long run, the result was the same. Germane and Lila were no more.

* * * *

"Over!" Germane spat, as she walked across the street to her house. "Finally," she sighed to her two porch steps and blood red screens.

Standing on her quiet porch, Germane looked across the tree-lined street at Lila's house. She couldn't possibly detect the spark in her now that could ever cause her to miss Lila's aggressive attentions. However, she knew she would eventually think back on the more steamy episodes of their relationship, and a part of her would yearn for those nights when she was treated like a dog, subjugated, fearful... and ever so turned on by the promise of Lila's giving pain and humiliation. There would be times she would think of those nights and the wetness between her legs would thicken until she'd have to masturbate to a vivid Lila-memory. Germane's libido was simply too strong to allow her a clean break, even though she was in love with A.J. and could now think of nothing else except laying next to the flaxen-haired tomboy and holding her naked, sinewy body.

Germane wondered if there would come as time when she would wish A.J. to growl orders at her. If one day she'd secretly want that bright, open face to bark commands, those soft long-fingered hands to brandish a riding crop, that tight little lap to support her for a spanking. Could Germane's needs simply disappear and be replaced by a normal—*whatever the fuck that means*, Germane laughed to herself—sexual relationship? She'd had them before, but since Lila, there had been so very few encounters that she really wondered if her sex-life could exist without the master/slave dynamic.

"The thrill is in the finding out." Germane opened her front door, walked across her peach and tan living room and up the short flight of stairs to her bathroom and her usual pre-slumber ritual.

[Nine]

Slowly, Germane had demanded of A.J.'s striptease. There was no pose the young girl could offer, no coy embarrassed stance, no hesitant pucker of hips. Germane simply sat in her kitchen chair and watched A.J. watch her, as the young girl crisscrossed her long arms and lifted off her shirt.

The call had come seconds after Germane brushed her teeth. She couldn't think of a better nightcap to the new life she felt would be unfolding from tomorrow morning onward. A.J. had simply called, asked if she could visit, and a half hour later she was standing in Germane's bright kitchen undressing.

A.J. smiled as her bright face disappeared under her lifted sweatshirt and soon emerged—still smiling—in a soft, pink bra. Since Germane had never seen the girl in anything other than loose button-down shirts or sweatshirts, she never really saw A.J.'s real form. She knew A.J. was more on the slight side than heavy, and Germane was quite pleased with the body now facing her.

She had a firm belly, not hardened to cut, squared proportions, but indented and soft. Her breasts lay with a slight swell at the uppermost part of the bra, which was lace, and fit her size and frame, making the young girl not busty by any means, but ample and firm; a perfect fit for Germane's mouth.

"Pants," Germane whispered, and A.J. remained smiling, reached her long fingers to her faded jeans and unsnapped the copper button with one quick twist. The young girl wiggled out of her pants, coaxing a cascade of denim by pulling the shorts all the way down her long legs and finally off her ankles.

"Come 'ere," Germane said, and A.J. walked the four steps from the end of the kitchen table to the refrigerator where Germane had pulled the wicker-backed kitchen chair.

The black woman opened her legs, and A.J. walked into her sweat-pants crotch. Germane leaned forward and kissed A.J.'s tight, powdery belly as the young girl pressed just a bit forward into the kiss. The older woman put her hands around A.J. and softly grabbed the silk of her pink panty bottom then sat back and brought her hands to the girl's hips.

"How we doin'?" Germane asked, looking up. A.J. had her eyes closed and her tight mouth open in an expression of muted need.

"We are doin' fine," A.J. managed, quickly exhaling.

"Stop me when you want," Germane said and once again leaned into kiss the young girl's belly. "I don't want to do anything you don't want."

Sitting back, Germane traced her hands up the young girl's sides and to her puckered breasts. A.J. gulped deeply at the touch, her hands to her sides. She managed to pucker her sweet lips as the black woman below her cupped one of her breasts in each of her hands, slowly kneading the silk covering them.

"You are making me very crazy!"

"I'm making you crazy?" A.J. giggled, opened her eyes, and looked down. "Wow!"

"Wow is right," Germane said, releasing her hands.

A.J. took a step back as the taller, black woman stood. The women locked smiles, and then A.J. stepped forward and kissed Germane hard on the mouth. Her tongue darted into Germane's open lips as the older woman embraced her.

"I want you to do everything to me," A.J. said after their lips parted. "I want to feel everything."

"I'll see what I can do," she said, smiling.

Germane took A.J.'s hand, kissed her on the cheek and led her from the kitchen, through the living room, up the short flight of stairs, down the hallway, and to her bedroom.

* * * *

Sometimes, it is hard to tell where fantasy ends and reality begins. The meeting of an ideal, the fulfillment of a dream, the actual realization of hope, is not often a possibility one is ready for.

Germane wasn't ready for it.

She stood at her bedroom window, overlooking her quiet backyard, the satiated young girl asleep in her bed. Strawberry blonde hair splayed over her pillow, the pug nose and tight lips quiet in the moonlight. Germane knew this was the moment where fantasy met her reality. She and A.J. had made love like only two women can ever make love, all the best softness and the deepest hunger, wrapped up in long-legged intertwining and deep, wet kisses; A.J.'s quiet shaking in perfect concert with Germane's constant expertise. This was where it would last, this perfect night with the moonlight, the high trees in the backyard and this painfully beautiful girl in her bed.

Can dreams come true at thirty-three?

Just then A.J. stirred, and the soft blue bed sheet fell a whisper off the young girl's naked bottom. There in the blush of one o'clock moonlight, Germane stared at her new lover's excellent easy skin—the firm roundness of A.J.'s downy backside—and a fleeting thought of controlled mayhem flashed through her mind. The older woman thought hard over the devilish scenario, this slice of information, then released it to the moonlight and her 'maybe later' file.

♥

whatralphwrought.com

Around Midnight
© Tex Randall

The call was unexpected and the caller even more so. Penny was a young lady of my acquaintance and quite beautiful in a long-legged, full-bodied, wholesome kind of way. Quiet and shy for the most part. She would be the last person I'd ever expect to call me. I didn't even know she had my number. I do know that I had never given it to her, but then I realized that I was listed in the phonebook.

"Mr. Mark, this is Penny. You know, from the diner." Her deep husky, exotic voice dripped from the phone.

My mind overlaid it on my mental image of her, and I suddenly realized just how erotic she and her voice were. I cleared my throat for a second and asked, "Yes Penny, what can I do for you?"

"It's more like what we can do for each other. Can you meet me somewhere? I need to ask a favor of you."

My mind gave a jump at the first part of what she said. Visions of all the sexy things we could do together crowded my mind as a smile came to my lips. Meeting her somewhere wasn't a problem on my part, but it might be on hers. It was, after all, a small backwoods Texas town, and my being white and her being black could cause problems even in this day and age. My mind gave another jump at the word favor. More visions floated to the surface.

"Okay, where would you like to meet?" I replied in as calm a voice as I could muster. My mind wanted to dwell on naughty things as only the mind of a dirty old man can.

"I have a room at the Parkside Inn. Room 112. Can you meet me here in about an hour?"

"Sure, but can you tell me a little of what this is about?"

"You'll find out when you get here. I promise you won't be disappointed."

Then she hung up.

I stood there with the phone to my ear for nearly a minute more, fantasies buzzing here and there. Finally, the buzzing of a dead line made me put it down. I remained where I was, my mind lost in a haze of what ifs.

* * * *

I drove through the parking lot to the very back and parked. I sat and watched the lot for a while. What I was looking for, I didn't know, and probably wouldn't recognize it if I did see it. I was nervous, very nervous. I had taken a quick shower before I left, even though I had only had one an hour before.

Why was I so nervous? Questions swam around in my head like so many fish. I didn't have many answers. Why had Penny really called me? I had no answer to that question, but it did answer the original one of why I was so nervous. How much did I trust her, and how well did I know her? Yeah, more questions. Could this be one of those set ups that you read about in the paper or see on TV? *Not very likely*, my mind supplied, as I'm neither rich nor famous.

Another answer that was highlighted by my mind was that I had never been alone with a black woman in my life, much less had anything sexual to do with one. That alone scared the hell out of me. Would I or could I measure up and to whom for that matter? Could I go through with it, if it happened?

I'm old and pretty set in my ways. Despite my upbringing in the old south, I don't consider myself to be bigoted. But am I? Color was just that to me: color. Black, brown, red, pink, yellow. Color, like beauty, was only skin-deep. The person wearing it made all the difference, and Penny was one of the nicest, kindest people I had ever met.

I took a deep breath and opened the car door. Now was the time to find out just what was up and how bad my mind was trying to scare me. I was probably making a mountain out of a molehill. She probably wanted me to lend her a little money or something just as innocent.

* * * *

I knocked on the door of her room. No one answered the door. I stood there confused for a second. Did I remember the number wrong?

I started to turn away when the door opened a crack, and Penny's voice said, "I had to make sure it was you."

"Well, I was when I left home," I said to cover my nervousness.

"Come on in, I won't bite you. Well, not unless you want me to," she replied with a deep chuckle.

I felt funny as I slipped into the room through the partially opened door. It was as though I was doing something illicit, something naughty. I hadn't felt this way since before my wife and I had been married. The few times we had slipped away to a motel to fuck our brains out in wild abandon had been exciting, and it felt much the same now.

Penny closed the door and turned to me, a big smile on her face. "I wasn't sure if you'd come or not."

"I nearly didn't," I admitted as my eyes wandered over the wispy white negligee that accentuated, more than hid, her lush body. I could feel my manhood swell in the confines of my left pants leg. I had never seen her in anything but her waitress uniform, and this all felt so unreal for some reason.

"I nearly didn't answer the door," she confessed.

There was a long, nervous silence, and then we both tried to talk at the same time. I couldn't keep my eyes off the dark mystery under that thin, white nightgown, and Penny seemed both nervous and excited by my stares.

"You go first," I told her.

"Okay." She took a deep breath. "I know that your wife died several years ago, but you might not know that my husband died early last year."

"No, I didn't know that. I'm sorry to hear it," I said softly. "Losing a mate is a lot harder than most people realize. How long were the two of you married?"

"Almost twenty-two years. I was sixteen and he was twenty-one, when we ran away together. It was hard at first—no money, lousy jobs—but as the years went by, it got better and better. We were to the point of having it made. Then about two years ago, he got sick. He spent more time in hospitals than he spent at home, and in the end, he died in one."

"I'm sorry. That must have been a very rough time for you. I was lucky in a way, my wife died in her sleep. We never knew anything was wrong with her before that. At least you had a chance to say goodbye."

Her gaze kept to the floor, and she nodded slowly. "Yeah. I guess that was a good thing, but to watch him waste away... wasn't."

The tone of her voice sounded small and very hurt. I stepped forward, put my arms around her, and gave her a gentle hug. Her arms went around me as her head nestled on my shoulder. I could feel more than hear her gentle sobs.

I wasn't sure what to say, so I just held her and rocked her gently.

* * * *

After a while, she calmed and took a deep breath. With a soft sigh, she snuggled closer to me. "It feels good to be held again," she whispered. "It's been such a long time."

I caressed her back slowly. "I understand. I've been there and done that."

"Then maybe you'll understand why I asked you here tonight. I'm not ready for another man full time in my life right now, but I need someone. Someone that can... well... understand my needs and the reasons for them without taking it the wrong way. Someone who's been there and done that, as you said. Someone who won't pressure me."

I nodded. "I will take that as a compliment. But why me, other than I'm a widower? There's a hundred other men around here that meet that requirement and some of them are much more your age. I won't say I'm too old, but I will admit to being a little past my prime."

She moved her head back so she could see my face. "I've watched you as you've come in every morning for breakfast, and I liked what I saw. You are kind, gentle, and funny. You like to have fun, but you are serious at the same time. You remind me a lot of my husband in many ways."

"Was he white?" I asked and then regretted it.

She chuckled deep in her chest and shook her head. "Nope, he sure wasn't. You're the first white man to ever lay a hand on me, other than a handshake. In fact, you're the first man not my husband to ever..." She let the sentence trail off as she laid her head back on my shoulder.

I caressed her back and then hugged her tightly. She hugged me back.

* * * *

We held each other for a long time. I wasn't sure how or what to do next, and I think she felt the same way. She felt warm and comfortable in my arms. I sighed deeply and ran my hand up and down her back, asking, "What now?"

She hugged me and chuckled again. "I'm not sure. I was going to seduce you, but I got cold feet. I've never done this before, remember?"

"It's been a very long time since I have, so I'm way out of practice. Not to mention the fact of being very nervous around you."

"Why do I make you nervous? I'm just a woman. You were married to one and have a couple of grown kids, so I know you know your way around one."

"Yeah, I do, but...."

She laughed suddenly and leaned back to look at me. "Oh, I see. It's the old black and white thing."

"No, not the way you might think," I said hastily. "I've just never been with a black lady before. I'm not sure." I ran down, not sure of exactly what I wanted to say or how to say it.

"Not sure of what? Black or white, a woman is a woman. The size and shape may be different but the equipment is all the same, so I assume that making love to one would be the same as making love to the other."

"I'm not sure I could handle it or measure up." I admitted.

She laughed again and then grinned. "There's only one way to find out. Don't let myths and fantasies mess you up. Do what you would normally do. We'll let culture sort itself out later. I'm old enough to know what I like and don't like, and I won't be shy about telling you, either."

Before I could lose my nerve, I slipped my hand up to the back of her head and pulled her to me for a kiss. One way or the other, I would soon find out the answers to all my questions.

Our lips met softly at first, almost tentatively. We explored the differences. My lips aren't exactly thin but probably thinner than her husband's had been. Hers were so soft and full. I kissed her, licking and nibbling on their fullness. After a moment, she made a soft moaning sound as a shiver ran through her body. I took that as a good sign and added my tongue to the mix.

I felt her hand on the back of my head and the other wandered haltingly over my back. I could feel her nervousness as I used both hands to explore her back and sides. The kiss grew more passionate. The thin gauzy material of the negligee slid smoothly over her warm dark skin. Her back was firm; I could feel the solidness of muscle moving under the skin as she squirmed slowly against me.

My leg slipped between hers, and my hands wandered lower to caress her high, round ass. I tried to squeeze it but was surprised at its firmness. My hands moved lower to cup each cheek. I pulled upward gently, pressing her tighter to my leg. She flexed her hips, rubbing herself against me, a deep groan coming into the kiss. I could feel her heat on my thigh.

She turned slightly and rubbed her upper thigh against my stiff manhood that was trapped in the leg of my pants. Painfully so, in fact. I hadn't even realized that I was hard until that moment; I had been so wrapped up in exploring her lips and body.

The hand that had been exploring my back now came around to run lightly up and down over the outline of my shaft. When she gave me a gentle squeeze, it was my turn to moan.

The next few minutes were a comedy of errors as we both tried to undress me without breaking the kiss. She was fumbling with my belt buckle while I was trying to slip my boots off and unbutton my shirt at the same time. I had one boot off and half the buttons undone by the time she got the belt buckle figured out and attacked the button and zipper of my jeans. I got the shirt unbuttoned and started to pull it off about the time my foot came out of the boot, and she yanked down my jeans. I lost my balance, and she grabbed me by the dick. We ended up in a pile on the bed.

We were both laughing as I finished getting my pants and socks off. When I lay back on the bed beside her, she whispered, "See, that wasn't so bad. Except for maybe the train wreck of getting you undressed. At least we ended up someplace soft."

"It kind of broke the mood, though," I whispered back.

She laughed and said, "Lust ain't a mood. It's a condition, and that ain't changed one bit."

She rolled over on her side and propped her head up on her hand. Her other hand reached for my manhood. She ran her fingertips up and down my length for a moment and then whispered, "You're as hard as I am wet, so we're doing something right."

We both watched her fingers caress me for a moment and then she whispered, "Well, you've got nothing to be worried about in this department. You're every bit as big as my husband—maybe a little more so."

She wrapped her fingers around my shaft and gave me a squeeze. "It's rock hard, too."

Quickly she stood up and peeled the negligee off over her head. For the first time, I saw her nude. Her breasts were large and round, but didn't look out of place with her wide shoulders and narrow waist. They stood out with very little sag. Her skin was a dark, dusky brown, the shadows under her nipples darker yet. Her nipples were a lighter color than her breasts and as big as the end of my little finger.

My eyes wandered down across her belly. It was flat but not muscular. The deep indent of her belly button was a point of mystery. My eyes moved on to the tangle of tight curls on her mound. They were as jet black as her hair. Her sex was hidden beneath them.

She moved forward and placed one knee on each side of me as she got back on the bed. She hadn't been wrong about her wetness, I could see it glisten and shine on her inner thighs, along the bright pink of her slit and smoothly shaven outer lips. Her mound was high and made plump

88

looking by the tangle of curls on it. Her lower lips were small and narrow, and I couldn't see any inner lips at all, except up near her clit. Two folds fanned out below it, setting it up like a bright pink pearl. I licked my lips as she knee-walked up my thighs.

She paused above my hips and looked down, her hands going to my shaft. She grabbed it with both hands and caressed it for a second before she lifted it upright. She held it there for a second and then looked at me. "I'm not sure whether I want to tease myself and you for a while or just drive it home."

"Do what you'd normally do. That was your advice to me," I replied with a grin.

"What I'd normally do is being overruled by the length of time since." She laughed softly. "Good old lust is working overtime, and I'm in a hurry."

With that said, she lifted my shaft and rubbed the spongy head back and forth along the length of her slit, pausing each time at her clit and again at her wet opening. She would shiver as the head brushed over her clit and her hips would flex as it touched her opening. The slippery wetness of her sex against the sensitive head made me groan.

After a minute of doing this, she gave out with a hiss as she jerked in time with her hips flexing. She was trying to get the head lined up with her opening but wasn't having much luck. I think she was having small orgasms each time the head brushed against her. I do know that she was getting even wetter than she had been before.

The next time I felt her sex nibble at the head of my dick, I lifted my hips sharply and entered her. She gave a loud yell and sat down, driving me halfway into her hot, velvety depths. Her mouth was now open—but no sound came out—and her eyes were tightly shut. Her hips and belly moved in a rolling rhythm as she slowly sank down on me.

When her ass met my hips, she groaned loudly and leaned forward, placing her hands on my chest. She started to make little rocking, lunging movements, each accompanied by a gasp. Her vagina would grip and then release me with each intake of breath. I laid still and let her do as she wanted.

After a minute or so, she lifted one hand, made a fist, and slowly but firmly hit it on my chest several times. "Oh, shit!" she said softly and then banged my chest a couple more times.

I grinned as I brought my hands up and caressed her thighs and hips. She was either having one hell of a long, drawn out orgasm or a series of short hard ones. Either way, she was coming. I could feel her warm juices running along my shaft and dribbling down over my balls. The inner walls of her sex were doing marvelous things around my shaft. It was a rippling effect that started at the head and ran down to the base. If I had moved at all, I would have probably exploded myself.

* * * *

Over time, the rippling effect slowed and then stopped. Penny sat still as a statue except for her heavy breathing. When she had caught her breath, she lifted her head and looked at me. A shy grin slowly spread across her face.

"Sorry about that." She paused and took a shuddery breath. "I ain't felt nothing like that since my honeymoon, if you could call it that, twenty-two years ago. I was a virgin then and didn't have any idea of what to expect. My husband was gentle and patient and had me so hot that by the time he entered me, I did about the same thing as I did just now."

She smiled and leaned down to kiss me softly on the lips. When she straightened up she said, "You have that same gentle, knowing patience that he had. I think I made a good choice."

She rocked her hips slowly from side to side and whispered, "Damn, that feels so good in there. I had almost forgotten what it felt like."

I grinned and whispered, "It sure ain't bad from this side, either. You fit like a warm, velvet glove."

She sighed and rocked her hips again. "I've always been tight and very sensitive. I figured it was because I never had any kids. That's the one thing I regret the most."

"Why is that?" I asked softly.

She shrugged and replied, still rocking her hips. "It just never happened. We never used any kind of protection, but I never got pregnant."

All of a sudden, she stopped moving and got a big-eyed look on her face. "Oh my God, we're not using any protection. I don't want to get pregnant now. I couldn't handle it."

"There's no chance of that." I told her. "When my youngest son was born my wife got fixed and a few days later, so did I. It was our insurance policy, so to speak."

"You're sure?" she asked with a suspicious look on her face.

"I can go home and get you the paperwork and the doctor's report, if you really want me to," I said. "I wouldn't lie to you."

She grinned as she lifted her hips a couple of inches and then lowered them back. She made a soft sound and shook her head. "I'll take your word for it. I ain't giving this ride up for nobody and no reason. It's been way too long and way too nerve-wracking to get to this point and time."

She worked her hips up and down slowly. I could feel her moving all along my shaft as she did. I groaned softly and whispered, "I'm sure glad of that but I have a feeling that it ain't going to be a very long ride. You feel so damned good."

She grinned, lifted her hips higher, and then dropped down sharply. "Then I better get all I can, while I can."

I groaned loudly and nodded my head.

True to her word, she rode me hard, with me trying to give as good as I got. We ended up finishing in a dead heat—lots of heat and me nearly dead. I tried to hold back for as long as I could, but that wasn't very long.

As the first jet of hot semen ripped my shaft, she slammed herself down on me and ground her hips back and forth, rubbing her swollen clit on my pelvic bone. The second jet seemed to ignite her orgasm. Her inner muscles clamped down on me as a hot gush washed over my balls.

I had never felt anything like the squeezing, pulling, rolling massage her vagina was giving my dick. I thought she was going to chew it up and spit it out. I'm not sure who was yelling the loudest, her or me.

The next thing I knew, she had a hand on each side of my head and was kissing the hell out of me in a wild passionate kiss that went on and on until we finally had to come up for air.

I lay there gasping for breath, and she lay on top of me doing the same. My gaze connected to hers and we both smiled. She held my head again and lowered her lips to mine in a soft gentle quick kiss.

When she raised her head, she whispered breathily, "Oh, my Lord." And she grinned.

I nodded my head, not trusting that I could talk and breathe at the same time.

"Are you alright?" she asked with concern in her voice.

I nodded again and grinned up at her.

"Don't you go and die on me. I'd never forgive myself," she said, grinning down at me.

"I don't plan on it," I told her, my breathing becoming easier.

She leaned down and kissed me softly, then lifted her head slightly, breaking the kiss. "What do you have planned for the rest of the weekend?" she asked softly.

"Before, nothing. But now..." I let the sentence trail off as I pulled her head down for a long gentle kiss.

She gave a drawn out sigh and sat up. My dick was soft but still inside her. She wiggled gently from side to side and grinned. "I don't think my little pussy wants to give up its dinner."

I laughed. "When it does, there going to be one hell of a mess, believe me. One even bigger than the one we already have."

She wiggled again, and we both could hear the squishing noise from where we were joined. "I think you're right on both counts. So what do we do now?"

"The only idea I can think of, is for you to jump up and run for a towel while I try and dam up the flow. I'll try and keep it between my legs instead of on the bed. Otherwise, we'll have the wet spot from hell."

"We could always move to the other bed." She was grinning like the Cheshire cat.

"I was hoping to save that one for tomorrow. You know, a new day, a new bed. I figure if we keep it up like we've been going, we'll need it. This one will either be broken or a swamp."

She laughed and nodded. "Or it won't matter as we'll both be dead."

"Oh, you'll live, but I probably won't. I won't have one complaint in the world, either. The smile on my face will drive the mortician crazy trying to get it back to normal. Every time he does, this silly grin will return."

"You are one crazy old white man."

"And your point is?" I asked with a big grin.

"No point, just an observation." She said as she laid back down on me for another kiss.

* * * *

As she moved, the cork came out of the bottle and the mad scramble was on. I jammed my thighs together and she ran for the bathroom. She returned with two small towels, one went under my raised thighs and the other on top.

We mopped at the mess, laughing at ourselves, as we did. Finally, I said, "Okay, enough of this. I think it's time we took it to the shower."

I wiggled to the edge of the bed and held out my hands. "Give me a hand. Maybe I can get up without making it worse."

She grabbed my hands and pulled me to my feet. We looked down at the bed. There was a small wet spot near the edge. I picked the towel up. There was another spot about the size of a silver dollar. "Not bad."

"Not bad at all," she said with a smile.

I turned toward the bathroom and took a step. I stuffed the towel I had in my hand between my legs. Penny looked at me funny. "Flee for your life. The dam has broken. Women and small children first." I laughed as I headed for the bathroom and the shower.

I got in the shower and took the towel with me. I dropped it and turned on the water. As I was adjusting the temperature, Penny stepped in behind me. "You're not the only one that needs a lifeboat. I'm sticky in places I didn't know could stick."

I pulled the little knob up for the showerhead and got hit in the face with the spray. I tried to back up but Penny was right behind me, so I turned around. She reached over my shoulder and angled the spray down onto my back. "Now you won't drown from that," she said as she slipped

COMING TOGETHER: AT LAST

her arms around me. "I won't guarantee anything for later, though."

I kissed her and ran my hands over her ass and back. She was warm and slippery in my arms. Her breasts were mashed to my chest, and I could feel her rock hard nipples move as she breathed.

When my fingers dipped between her ass cheeks, she wiggled and broke the kiss. "I'd be careful doing that. You might get a finger or two broke."

"You don't like that?" I asked softly.

She grinned and replied, "I didn't say that. I just said be careful. I do like it but it tends to drive me crazy and makes me go wild."

"If you get any wilder than a few minutes ago, I'm in a world of trouble."

"Baby, you ain't seen nothing yet. That was just a warm up."

"Oh, shit, I need to check on my medical insurance when we get out of here."

"Who said I was letting you out of here?"

Before I could reply, she kissed me and ran her hands over my back and ass. When one of her fingers tickled my asshole, my hips moved forward, pressing my limp manhood against her mound. She moved her hips tighter to me and rubbed the tight curls on her mound against me. It felt odd at first and then very sensuous. Her finger continued to tease me.

My hands had been on her back, but now I dropped one to run my fingers up and down the deep cleft of her ass. She clenched her ass cheeks and stopped my fingers from moving. I tried the same thing but it didn't work as well.

"You need to work on that," she whispered as she broke our kiss. "I can damn near crack walnuts with mine."

"Somehow, I almost believe that."

"Be very careful what you wish for, you just might find out."

"Promises, promises."

Her grin widened and then she kissed me—long, hard, and deeply. Her finger also slipped into my ass an inch or so. I heard myself groan softly as her hips started to move from side to side again. My manhood wasn't nearly as soft as it had been before.

Between her finger, her soft fuzzy mound, and the passionate kiss, it wasn't long before my dick was standing up tall and proud. I tied to tease her asshole like she was doing to me, but I was having no luck. Every time I would touch it, she would tighten up her ass muscles and my fingers would be pushed away.

She slowly broke our kiss and smiled at me. "Time to get cleaned up." She slipped her finger out of my ass and asked, "Where's the soap?"

"Uh, out there somewhere." I replied, indicating the area outside the shower curtain. I pulled the curtain back and picked up the small bar of soap lying on top of the toilet bowl.

As I turned back, something hot enveloped my dick to the very base. I dropped the soap as I looked down and saw Penny with her nose against my pelvic bone and my dick completely in her mouth. She made a soft moaning noise as she sucked in her cheeks and lifted her head. Her tongue was fluttering along the bottom of my shaft as it came out of her mouth. She paused with just the head between her lips and then slowly swallowed me again. Now it was my turn to moan.

She continued to suck on my dick in long, lazy movements from the tip to the base and back again until my hips gave a little quiver. She removed me completely from her mouth and then gave the head a last kiss. Looking up at me, she smiled and licked her lips. "We taste good together."

She picked up the soap and stood up. She took her time unwrapping it, watching me through her lashes as she did. When she had it unwrapped, she handed it to me. "Do me, and don't miss an inch of my body." She turned around and put her hands on the far wall, leaning forward and spreading her feet as wide as the tub would allow.

My hands shook as I lathered them up. I stepped up close behind her and reached up to the tops of her shoulders. I lathered her dark skin from her shoulders to her tailbone, taking my time and savoring the silky smoothness of her skin.

I lathered up my hands again and stepped closer, pressing my hard-on into the deep cleft of her ass as I reached around and lathered up her breasts. I cupped one in each hand and lifted, feeling their weight and firmness. I gave them a gentle squeeze, which got me a gentle squeeze from her ass cheeks.

I lowered my hands and used my forefingers and thumbs to roll her large nipples back and forth. This got an even tighter squeeze to my dick. I gave her nipples a gentle pull as I rolled them around. The pressure on my dick went up, and she moaned softly, her ass moving up and down slowly. My dick moved with her ass, so I did, too. When I released her nipples, her ass relaxed but still moved slowly up and down, my dick now sliding easily between her ass cheeks.

My hands soaped up her belly and ended up rubbing along the insides of her thighs. She would moan softly each time my hand bumped into her sex. I moved my hands to the front of her thighs and ran them up and down, gently brushing her outer lips at the top of each stroke. She shivered and pressed her ass back tighter against me, still slowly moving up and down.

I cupped her sex and mound in one hand and rubbed them in rhythm with the movement of her ass. She moaned loudly. I soaped up her curls and then down between her legs as far as I could reach. As I moved my hand back up, my middle finger dipped into her silky slit. I rubbed up and down. I could feel her hips tremble as the base of my finger rubbed lightly over her exposed clit. Her ass cheeks clamped down on my dick again, very tightly this time. I had to move with her or lose something I valued greatly.

Her hand came off the wall and down to grab my wrist. I stopped moving the hand and slowly her ass cheeks relaxed. "I was about to cum," Penny sighed. "I want to wait, if that's alright with you."

"Fine with me."

She moved her hand back to the wall, and I stepped away from her. I lathered up the cheeks of her ass and marveled at the smooth texture of her skin. I ran my fingers down between her cheeks, and she came up on her toes, sticking her ass out even farther. Damn, what a gorgeous sight! I've always been an ass man and this was one for the record book, in my opinion.

I used one hand to rub between those luscious globes and the other to slide between her legs and cup her sex from the rear. Staying away from her sensitive clit, I explored her opening. When I slipped a soapy finger into it, she gasped and came up higher on her toes. When I pressed a finger on my other hand to the puckered opening of her ass, she pushed back and moaned softly.

I moved the finger in her pussy slowly in and out, as I held a steady pressure against her asshole. Slowly the slippery finger entered her ass. She let out a soft moan the whole time. When my finger was in to the second knuckle, I eased it back a little and then moved it back forward. She gave out with a loud gasp, and I felt her inner muscles clamp down on both fingers.

Her hips began to shiver, so I removed both fingers. I went on by soaping up the backs of her thighs and then down to her calves. Slowly she came down off her toes, sighing deeply. I was kneeling behind her now, and the view was outstanding. The dark shiny skin of her thighs was parted enough for me to see the bright pink of her slit and the lighter brown starfish of her anus. Her ass was stuck out proudly.

I stood up, angled the showerhead so that it rinsed the soap off her ass, and squatted back down. I kissed and licked each slick cheek. When I moved to the center and took a slow lick up it, she came back up on her toes and moaned loudly. I used my hands to pry her cheeks wider apart as I took another lick. She moaned loudly again and pushed her ass back tighter to my face.

I could taste a little soap left from my hasty rinsing, but I didn't care. The tip of my tongue brushed over the tight pucker of her asshole, and I liked to have gotten my nose broken as she jammed her rock hard ass back. I grabbed her hips and jammed my tongue against the opening. She bent farther forward and gave out with a yell. My tongue slowly entered her. Her ass and hips were shaking now.

I felt her hand slapping lightly at my head. With a grin, I let her hips go and stood up. I used my hand to run the head of my dick up and down between those satiny globes for a second, and then I touched the head to her anus. She gasped loudly and tried to move away. I let her.

She straightened up and turned around to lean backward against the wall of the shower, her breathing slightly ragged and fast. Her face had a strange look on it. "I thought you were going to try and fuck me there."

"The thought crossed my mind," I told her.

She looked at me for a few seconds and then dropped her eyes. "I've never... My husband never... You know what I mean."

Her eyes darted to my face with a searching look. "I've had fantasies about it."

I nodded and held my hands out to her. "We'll file that away under things to explore," I told her with a smile. "Along with a bag of walnuts come Christmas time."

She laughed and came into my arms for a kiss.

Later, as we were rinsing the soap off our bodies, she said, "If you promise to be gentle, I might just let you try to fuck me there."

"Woman, do I look that crazy to you? I don't want my walnuts cracked or my dick crushed." I told her bluntly.

Her eyes got big, and she got this incredulous look on her face for a second. I grinned and winked. "I'll be as gentle as you want me to be. I've had a little practice at it. My wife loved it every so often. Not a regular thing, something special, you might say."

She hit me lightly on the chest. "Damn you, you scared me. Here I was offering you my only cherry, and I thought you were turning it down."

"Hey, you're the one that bragged you could crack walnuts with that thing."

"Okay, maybe it was pecans and not walnuts, and I promise not to crack anything of yours. How's that?"

I laughed and gathered her into my arms for a kiss.

* * * *

We were out of the shower, and I was taking my time drying her off. I started at her shoulders and worked my way down the front, pausing to kiss and lick the interesting hollows and high spots. I sucked on one hard nipple and then the other, feeling them grow even larger as I did. She murmured softly in pleasure.

I licked along the bottom of her ribs and flicked my tongue in her belly button. She squirmed and pushed my head away. I grinned up at her as I moved the towel. She spread her feet farther apart and shivered.

I drew the towel down across her thighs. As I did, I leaned in and ran my tongue up one side of her slit and down the other. Her hands were back at my head but not pushing me away. I pressed my tongue to her large exposed clit and held it there. Her hips did a little fluttery quiver as she groaned loudly. I lifted my head and dried her other leg.

"Turn around so I can do the other side."

She smiled as she did. "You're supposed to be drying me, but part of me keeps getting wetter and wetter."

"Don't worry, I have a special way of drying that, but I'll wait until you're lying down." I kissed my way across her shoulder and up the back of her neck.

She shivered. "I'm more likely to drown you, if you're going to do what I think you are."

"I'll take my chances."

Before she could say anything else, I ran the towel down her back to the top of her ass. I followed it with little licks down her spine. I planted a kiss on her tailbone and squatted to kiss my way down one ass cheek and up the other.

Penny took little half steps to the side and bent at the waist to place both hands on the floor. I must say, I didn't expect her to be so limber. In this position, her low-slung sex was staring me right in the face. There was no doubt about her wetness, either.

I licked up and down the tight muscles at the back of her thighs and then took a lick from her clit to her asshole in one long, slow swipe. She made a gasping sound and wiggled her ass from side to side.

"Damn! You sure like to use that tongue of yours, don't you?"

I gave her another lick, pausing to explore the depths of her sex. Her taste was musky, almost spicy. I dipped my tongue in as far as it would go and wiggled it around. She made another gasping sound and pressed back against my face.

"Oh, fuck yes!" she said loudly as I continued to tongue her. Her hips quivered and started to shake.

I moved my head back, dropped down, and sucked in the hard nub of her clit. It was hot and slick as I ran my tongue around and around it. Her knees flexed, and then she pressed back hard against me. I flicked her clit. She gave a soft yell and hunched back against my mouth. My nose was pushing her opening.

"Oh, God!" she yelled as she came all over my face. She was right. She damn near did drown me.

I moved my mouth up and stabbed my tongue back in her sex. This just seemed to heighten her orgasm. She shook and humped my face through a long, drawn out series of orgasms. I had to stop tonguing her pussy a couple of times so I could swallow. She was like a water fountain gone wild.

Slowly her knees buckled, and she went down onto them. I followed her down as far as I could, then I caught her hips as she sprawled flat on the floor. I sat back on my heels and smiled down at her. I could feel her juices running down my cheeks and chin.

* * * *

After a time, she made a soft whimpering sound and rolled onto her side. I mopped my face with a small towel.

Penny continued her roll onto her back and looked up at me. Her face had a blank look for a moment, and then she focused on my face, smiling. "You're going to kill me yet."

I grinned and moved down between her knees. I laid a washcloth over her sex and gently pressed it there. She gave a small gasp and her hips jerked sharply. "I'll let you do the rest. You know where you're the most sensitive."

She moved her feet in and her knees up. She spread them wide and reached for the washcloth. Sighing, she closed her eyes as she cleaned herself up. Every so often, her hips would give a little jerk. After a moment, she opened her eyes, licked her lips, and handed me the cloth. "Rinse, please."

I rinsed it and handed it back to her. She ran it over her inner thighs and down the crack of her ass. "Damn!" she whispered, "Just how many times did I come, or did I have some help?"

"Nope, you did that all by yourself... well, except for the tongue part." I grinned.

"Yeah, the tongue part," she said softly with a slow shake of her head. "That was the special treat in our marriage. Hubby did it to me on special occasions. It wasn't something he was particularly fond of, but he did it for me. I did it for him, and he returned the favor."

"I guess it's one of those cultural things," I said in a similar tone. "I enjoy the hell out of doing it."

She groaned softly. "I was afraid you were going to say that. I enjoyed the hell out of it myself, and it could be the death of me, if you keep doing it."

"I've never heard of anyone dying from being eaten, but then again, it probably wouldn't be listed as the actual cause of death... something to do with the censors on the five o'clock news."

She laughed and groaned again as her hips jerked and the muscles of her stomach rippled.

"Are you alright?"

"Oh, I'm just fine, but laughing moves things that shouldn't be moved right now. Damn, I'm so sensitive I can't believe it. Then again, I can't believe how much different it was. My husband would give me a few licks here and there and then, as I got close, he'd move away and jam his dick in. I'd come hard, but never like I just did with your tongue in me."

"You told me to do it my way, and I was just following instructions." I shrugged and grinned.

She opened one eye and peeked at me. "Yeah, but you're not supposed to enjoy it as much as I do."

"Hey, I always make sure the lady comes first. Well, most of the time. I try to, anyway. Sometimes, it just doesn't work out that way."

"It sure as hell worked out this time." She handed me the towel. "I should feel like I've been run over by a truck, but I don't. I've got those lazy, well-satisfied, damn-that-was-good feels. I just want to lay here and let the glow flow."

"You sleep there, and your back is going to hate you in the morning—not to mention a few dozen of the muscles you've abused in the last couple hours. Anyway, cuddling is going to be a bitch with that door in the way."

She chuckled and shook her head. "Okay, I get the idea. I should make you carry my big ass to the bed, but I wouldn't want you to hurt yourself." She turned onto her side and added, "I'm going to roll over on my stomach so I can get up. You stay in front of me, where I can keep an eye on you. I ain't letting you behind me for a while. You're way too dangerous when you're back there."

"Oh, come on, let me help you up."

"Nope, no way. I'd probably end up doing a headstand in the closet. I got down here on my own, and I can damn well get myself back up."

She got as far as her knees. Her eyes were level with my semi hard manhood. She eyed me for a second and licked her lips. "I know a way to even the score. I'll lay a lip lock on that so good that the white will come off."

I backed up and shook my head. "Oh, no you don't! You're getting up there on that bed and relaxing for a while. We both need it. Anyway, it's around midnight and I, for one, have had a long day."

"Yeah, and you're going to have a longer tomorrow." Penny replied with a big grin. "A brand new day and a brand new bed. What could be wrong with that?"

♥

Tex Randall

Island of Fantasies
© Jude Mason

When the boat bumped the dock, Syne's heart lurched. The invitation she held was a forgery. Her best friend Diane, daughter of European nobility, had left hers out while she'd been visiting, and it just seemed too good to be true—too big an opportunity to let pass. The Isle of Arcadia, and the man who owned it, were renowned for secrecy. Once a year the baron held a ball, but only a few of the world's rich and infamous were ever invited.

She was neither. A freelance writer, she'd seen Diane's invitation and asked if she'd planned to attend. Diane had turned her nose up and replied that of course she hadn't. A masquerade ball wasn't exactly her cup of tea. She was much more likely to go to Aspen and party with the beautiful people on the slopes than to some secretive bash in the tropics.

The willowy blonde had taken her invitation and tossed it at Syne. "I mean, just look at it. A weekend in disguise, no itinerary, no celebrity list—nothing. All it says is: _Live out your wildest fantasy._ I couldn't possibly attend. Daddy would be outraged if he ever found out." And that had been it.

Syne had slipped the invitation into the pocket of her designer jeans and said no more. But, her heart had raced. She'd learned about the annual bash by accident the year before when a news story had been squashed at the paper she'd been writing for. All she'd heard were rumors. Something about the man who she thought owned the island, his incredibly beautiful consort, and a death—

nothing else. She'd tried to find out more, but it was useless.

Once she'd returned home, she'd taken the invitation to a friend—David Caslow, computer geek extraordinaire—and had him work his magic. Two days later, he'd called her, and she'd gone to pick up the perfectly duplicated card. Gold with a darker gold text and outline, the card read:

Make Your Wildest Dreams Come True!

*This document entitles you exclusive entrance
into the Arcadia Island Masquerade Ball.*

*Join us at Plantation House on Arcadia Island
and explore your wildest fantasies.*

*Your All-inclusive, all-expenses paid trip
begins the first weekend of the coming month.*

*Madame Dione de Celeste, Proprietress
Plantation House, Arcadia Island*

She'd made up her mind to attend as soon as she had the fake card in her hand.

And that's how she managed to be there, dressed in her finest white silk gown, waiting her turn to walk the gangplank off the boat. Around her, a dozen or so equally resplendent men and woman milled around. There had been very little conversation on the way over, it seemed even the wealthy liked to keep their quirks and kinks to themselves. Only when they'd drawn into the bay had conversation erupted.

A beautifully pale woman said in a breathy voice, "It's lovely, isn't it? Twice here, and I'll never get over how incredible the island is."

A deeply tanned young man, dressed in a black silk suit that must have cost a month's wage for Syne, replied, "Yeah, it's pretty amazing. When you think that everything had to be shipped in, you realize just how rich this guy is."

The island was breathtaking. The long, white sandy beach rose from the crystal blue waters of the bay. Lush tropical ferns carpeted the area a few dozen yards from the shoreline, and tall trees she could not name loomed high overhead further inland. Some looked like willows and others were some kind of palm, but she couldn't tell what kind and really didn't care. A well-swept wooden walkway led up the beach and into the trees.

"Good evening, ladies and gentlemen. My name is Ares, and I'll be your guide," came the voice of an incredibly tall, incredibly well-built black man dressed in a flaming red sarong slung low on his hips and nothing else. He stood at the end of the gangplank, off to one side in the white sand. "Please, come ashore. It's a short walk to the plantation house, where rooms and refreshments await you all. Please present your invitations as you pass me."

Syne stood back, allowing the other partygoers to push past her. When she was left standing alone, she took a deep breath and walked across the gangplank, praying David's work would pass muster. Standing in front of the black man, she was astounded at just how big he was. He towered over her five-feet, seven inches by at least a foot. His midnight-black skin shone. He looked as if he'd oiled himself. Hairless, his chest and arms rippled with muscles, and his six-pack would be the envy of any man she'd ever known.

"Thank you, milady." His voice was as soft as melted butter—and as smooth. Taking her invitation, he glanced at it and smiled, then slipped it into a fold of his sarong. Nodding, he checked the gangplank before asking, "Is there anyone else?"

"No, I'm the last." Her voice was steady, which surprised her. Her hand hadn't been when she'd held out the small gold card.

"Good, thank you, milady," he replied and let his eyes meet hers. Thickly lashed, almond shaped, and the most brilliant blue she'd ever seen. His eyes were like the sea, full of mystery and depth. His nose was straight and narrow, the nostrils flaring with each breath, as if he was taking her scent. He smiled at her, showing off whiter than white teeth, then winked.

Shocked, she felt herself grow warm and realized she was blushing. Before she could think of some snappy retort, the man stepped onto the walkway and stood looking down at her. From that angle, he looked even bigger.

He smelled of the sea and man, and she very nearly reached for him. The only thing that stopped her was him taking her arm and guiding her towards the trees. She'd worn high-heeled sandals—not the best thing for tramping through the jungle, but the walkway was sturdy and, with his hand on her arm, she walked easily ahead.

On the beach, the heat had been stifling, but when the canopy of the trees shielded her from the sunlight, the temperature dropped to a much more comfortable level. The sweat that had trickled down her sides cooled and dried. She peered into the trees and wondered what animal life there might be, but so far she had seen only a handful of birds.

The guide released her when he was sure she'd follow along after the others, and she felt his eyes on her as he followed. The flush she'd felt before returned, but this time it was excitement. Syne had always loved being watched by an attractive man, and he certainly fit the bill.

The further along she went, the less she worried she was about the counterfeit invitation and the sneaky way she'd gained access to the island. She watched the others sauntering along the path ahead. Each of them looked about as uncomfortable as a person could. The outdoors obviously wasn't their normal environment. Every time a bird or insect flew by, the group of partygoers ahead of her cringed or cried out, or both. Syne began to feel as if she and the huge black man were the only ones who got any pleasure from the walk.

After hiking about a mile, the grumblings of her companions suddenly stopped. They'd gone around a corner, and there was the plantation house.

It rose majestically out of the forest, flower-laden vines and bushes surrounded the enormous building. The air was thick with their scent—spicy, sweet, exotic. Syne inhaled and loved the rich smell as it filled her lungs.

A touch on her arm got her attention, and she moved to one side, allowing Ares to pass. His chest brushed her shoulder, and she thought for a moment about slipping her hand into the sarong to see if it was true what they said about black men. Only his speed saved him. "Almost there," he said to the group as he took the lead position. It was then she realized he'd trailed them, making sure no one lagged behind or got lost.

The plantation house loomed over them as they approached, ominous, daunting. To Syne, it looked like a castle with its tall, slender windows high up the wall. Ornate stone dragons guarded the bottom of the stairs which led to an intricately carved wooden door. More dragons perched along a wide handrail and still more peered from beneath fragrant red rose bushes and luscious rhododendrons in every color imaginable.

"Bloody hell, this place is amazing," said a lanky fellow who stood red-faced and winded before the door. "Why he couldn't have put it someplace a little closer to civilization is beyond me, though."

"Jeffery, you're just out of shape," the woman on his arm chimed in. Her hair, which had been beautifully coiffed at the beginning of the trek, hung in stringy tendrils half way down her back. Her dress—black silk by the look of it—was wrinkled and sweat-stained from the unexpected excursion. "Like we all are." She looked around the small group and chuckled at her lame witticism. When her eyes locked on Syne's calm demeanor, she scowled as if she'd just noticed a spot on a favorite rug. "All of us that matter." The last words came out more like a whine than she'd perhaps intended, but everyone turned to look at who she meant.

Syne smile sweetly, or she hoped it looked sweet. Inside she was livid. How dare the overdressed, underdeveloped excuse for a woman try to demean her? She took a deep breath and let loose. "Some of us prefer to keep in shape rather than look like limp rags after a short stroll."

If looks could have killed, she'd have been tits up in the doorway. But, the aristocrat didn't say anything, just glared at her.

"Ladies," Ares said, a little louder than he needed to, she thought, "and gentlemen, if you'll just follow me inside, I'll show you each to your quarters. Refreshments have been laid out for you." He opened the door and while he held it wide, the group filed in, Syne in the rear.

The entry hall stopped them cold. Even the girl who'd been twice before stopped and gazed around, dumbstruck by the splendor. Where the outside was rustic and appeared ancient, the inside was immaculate and extravagant. Gold met rich, vibrant wood and deep blue velvet. On each wall, gilt-framed pictures of the old Greek gods and goddesses at their leisure looked down upon them. Chandeliers glistened, dark slate floor shone, and in the background soft music played. *It's a castle for the gods*, she thought as she slowly turned, admiring it all.

"Follow me, please," Ares urged.

Syne turned and saw him on the bottom step of a curved staircase that led to the second floor. "My God, this is amazing," she whispered. The tapping of her heels echoed. The others followed her when she followed the beautiful black man up the stairs. She couldn't take her eyes off his ass. High and firm, she had to remind herself that he was just the hired help; she was in for bigger game.

At the top of the stairs, he stopped and waited for them all to join him on the landing. "You'll each have a room," he said in his deep, soft voice. "In your room, you'll find a closet full of costumes. Choose whatever you like, and if you don't find something to your liking, don't hesitate to call for a tailor to assist you." He turned and walked away, slowly down the long hallway. "You'll have time to bathe and take a nap, if you wish. You'll also find refreshments. Please, make sure you drink well before you join your host for dinner."

He stopped in front of the first door and waited while the group joined him. Opening the double doors, he said, "Jacob McEwen, this will be your room while you stay with us."

The room was massive. Dark wood prevailed, but the deep greens and golds complemented it magnificently. The fireplace across from the bed was waiting for a match.

"Come," Ares said, and closed the doors behind the man named Jacob. Each guest was delivered into a room, some larger than other, all resplendent with luxurious décor.

Finally, there was just her and Ares. He turned and smiled, then opened the double doors on the last room. "And here you are, milady," he said as he pushed open the tall oak doors.

For a moment, Syne was speechless. Gold, glass, and white fur surrounded her. The canopy over the bed gleamed gold, the coverlet and rug were sparkling white and so soft-looking that she wanted to go and lie down immediately. The walls, broken by tall windows, were covered in what looked like white fur. The only break in the color scheme was the floor, and it was white marble with gold streaks spreading like tiny rivers across the room.

"Will this be all right for you, milady?" Ares' soft voice interrupted her silent appraisal.

When she turned to face him, he'd moved closer. His naked chest was inches from her nose, his nipples standing erect, hard, for her lips to suck and nibble on. Those thoughts and more raced through her mind, his question forgotten.

"Milady," he repeated in that soft as silk voice, "are you all right?"

Shaking herself, embarrassed at having been caught drooling over a complete stranger, Syne cleared her throat before replying. "Yes, fine. The room is fine. I'm fine, thank you." Her voice wasn't as firm as she'd have liked.

"Very good, milady," Ares smiled down at her. He knew she lusted after him; he had to. "You'll find refreshments over here." He brushed against her as he headed to the far side of the room.

She watched his muscular back and the bounce of his ass for a few moments before following him. With each step, her pussy moistened and her heartbeat increased. The bed, to her right, was like a magnet she fought to ignore, but her eyes couldn't resist just a quick glance. King-sized and luxurious, she wanted to drag Ares to it and try out the springs.

"Here you are, milady." He'd stepped behind a long glass bar and opened a small fridge. "May I get you something while I'm here?" He reached for a small bottle.

"Yes, please. Just something cold, anything." She wasn't interested in alcohol for the moment and the bottle he had looked innocent enough. She was much more interested in him.

He reached overhead for a tall crystal glass. Pouring the amber liquid into it, he then handed it to her. When she took it, their fingers touched. It was as if a tiny electrical charge touched her, making her gasp. Her pussy clenched.

Ares cocked his head and looked at her. "Are you sure you're okay? You look a little flushed."

"I'm fine, just warm," she parried, wondering if he realized the effect he was having on her. She raised the glass to her lips. Taking a tentative sip of the cool liquid, she was pleasantly surprised at the sweet, yet tangy, taste. "This is nice," she purred and took another large gulp. Before she realized it, the glass was empty, and she was mildly disappointed that it was gone.

Ares smiled, and for a moment, she wondered why.

The room spun. Her lips felt numb. Panic rose. She opened her mouth to scream. Blackness closed around her. She felt herself being carried and then... nothing.

* * * *

The spicy scent of flowers woke her. Without opening her eyes, she rolled onto her back feeling the delicious drag of softness caress her breasts and belly. She arched her back and stretched.

Her eyes popped open, and she sat up. The room was quiet. "What the fu..." she mouthed and then realized she was naked beneath the furs. "Shit!" She peered around the room and saw no one, nothing but the curtains billowing in the breeze. Through the window, she saw that it was dark.

She climbed out of bed, grabbing the fur and wrapping it around her nakedness, and made her way to the double doors. Trying one and finding it locked, she reached for the other. Locked. She pulled harder, alarm bells going off in her head.

"Damn!" she roared and pounded a fist against the right hand door. The fur shimmied down her body, landing in a pool of softness around her ankles. She pounded again, anger rising. She'd raised her fist for a third strike, but the door suddenly swung open, nearly slamming into her.

"Milady," came Ares' soft voice, "please, you're all right." He stepped into the room and wrapped his hand around her fist, holding it firmly. "I locked you in to keep you safe. I didn't want to take the chance of any of you wandering about, perhaps getting lost."

She pulled, trying to free herself from his grasp. "Let go, you big ox." Anger flared. "What did you do to me? Where are my clothes?"

Ares released her, quickly stepping past her, a little deeper into the room. "Milady, I'm so sorry. The drink was drugged to make you sleep. All of our guests begin their weekend in that way." He smiled down at her, eyeing her nakedness. "Your clothing is in the closet, along with the assortment of costumes I mentioned earlier."

Syne looked down at herself. Shocked, she reached down and grabbed up the fur. Wrapping it around herself, she stomped over to the closet. Holding the fur snuggly, she flung open the door he'd indicated. Sure enough, there were her clothes, neatly hung at the far end.

Spinning to face him again, she glared and asked, "Who undressed me?"

He looked down, and at that moment, she realized that she'd never see him blush. Dark skin doesn't show its blush as noticeably, but he did sweat.

"I did, milady." His voice was almost too soft for her to hear, but she'd known already. "It's a rule. All guests are to begin the weekend in the same manner—naked, drugged, in their rooms." He raised his face and looked at her. The embarrassment he might have felt wasn't there. Instead, she saw nothing but desire.

"Everyone the same." She reached for the first costume, and pulled it out. A dance hall girl flashed though her mind. The gaudy red dress with its low cut bodice screamed 'Come and get me, cowboy' to her, and she quickly thrust it back. The next was a gossamer thing held together by ropes of coins slung around the wearers' hips and bosom. *Veils*, she thought, and *Arabian Nights*, but again, she quickly pushed it back.

"I'll leave you to your choice." Ares' voice intruded, but pleasantly so. Her anger was gone, her reason for coming to the island resurfacing. A story, perhaps more—more of what, she wasn't sure, but she was there to find out.

She turned and faced him, still in his red sarong; still as masculine, as beautiful as she'd thought when she'd first seen him. And, now he'd seen her naked, and been tactful enough not to say anything. "Ares, when does this masquerade begin, and when do we get to meet our host?"

"At dinner. When all the guests have dressed in their chosen costumes, a bell will ring." The man slowly crossed the room to the door and stood waiting for her to join him there. "Each of you will come down the stairs and when you're at the bottom, you'll be escorted to the dining room." He looked into her eyes, and smiled then. "When you leave your room, that's when the festivities begin. You can do anything you wish, live whatever life you choose, let your imagination run free."

She opened her mouth to ask how anyone could possibly know her fantasies, but he stopped her question with a single finger pressed to her lips. Heart pounding, she wanted to kiss that finger, or gently suck it into her mouth.

"No more questions," he whispered, and ran his finger across her lips, side to side. Then, with a final tap against them, he turned away and opened the door. Over his shoulder, he added, "When you're ready, push the button there." He pointed to an ornate gold button beside the door. And then, he was gone. The door closed softly behind him, and she was left alone with her thoughts.

Sighing, wondering if she'd made a mistake brazening her way in, she returned to the closet. The costumes were well done, exquisite in their detail and she liked many of them, but none caught her attention. None called to her. That is, until she got to the end. Tight against the wall, a simple gown of white cotton hung from a hanger. She drew it out and knew she'd found exactly what she was looking for, only hoping it would fit her curves.

Before she slipped it on, she dropped the fur to the floor and kicked it away. Her hair needed to be done, nothing extravagant she thought as she headed for the luxurious bathroom. White marble and gold fixtures in a room that was bigger than her apartment met her when she pushed through the doors. Pulling open drawers, she found a brush she liked and several elaborate combs and barrettes from which to choose. Sweeping up her long, dark hair, she twisted it in a knot and pushed a beautifully curved gold comb through it to hold it in place. A tendril escaped the comb, curling from behind her left ear and draping over her shoulder.

"Yes, perfect," she muttered and slid another comb in. She posed, turned to the left and then right, and thrust her naked breasts out. Chuckling, she tweaked her nipples, and gasped at how sensitive they were. Imagining how it would feel if her black guide had pinched them, her pussy responded with a pounding heat.

Dragging her hands from her breasts, she groaned. "Enough, or you'll never get out of the damn room." She checked the drawers for make-up and wasn't surprised to find an assortment. Digging through the vials and tubes of this and that, she chose kohl eyeliner. Deftly, she outlined her eyes, then worked the liner until she had the desired effect. Next came blush and lipstick, both a deeper red than she was accustomed, but what she thought would fit the outfit she'd chosen. Absentmindedly, she wondered how the others were fairing, if the women were going to be as beautiful as she thought, the men as handsome.

Done, she went back into the main room and picked up the gown. It was cotton, but a softer, finer cotton than she'd ever worn. She wrapped it around herself, tying the shoulder so that it draped over her breasts and left her back bare to the top of her butt as well as one leg to the hip. The long, gold, braided rope, she wound around her waist then pulled up and crossed between her breasts before tossing the ends over her shoulders. They came around her again, at her waist, and she tied them loosely at her hip.

She walked over to the closet and peered inside for some kind of footwear. High-heeled sandals would be best, something that laced up her legs. She spotted boots and several pairs of stilettos but couldn't see any sandals. Her disappointment lasted only a moment. Pulling back a particularly heavy cape, she saw exactly what she wanted. Gold, delicate sandals with a heel that would make her close to six feet tall and laces up to her knees. Perfect—and best of all, they fit beautifully when she slipped her foot into them and wound the soft strips of leather up her calf.

She checked herself in the mirror and gasped. The white cotton gown was the perfect thing for her; at least she thought so. Her curves were a little more abundant than most women liked, but she'd always been well rounded and had grown used to the remarks and looks she got. Tonight, she'd decided to show it all off.

Satisfied with how she looked, she went to the entrance door and pushed the button. She waited, but not for long. She'd just settled in a chair facing one of the huge windows when she heard a bell chime. Not even enough time for her nerves to kick in—or her lust to completely die.

She got to her feet and went to the door. Taking a deep breath, she opened it and stepped out.

Her will faded. She felt it go, trickling like sand from an hourglass.

A tiny woman dressed in a beautiful blue patterned kimono waited at the bottom, bowing when they had all stepped off the bottom step. "Would you be so kind as to follow me, please?"

She just followed the others, like cattle to the slaughter, into the dining hall. It was a huge room with high ceilings and beautifully-carved marble figures perched on tables and stands around the perimeter. Flowers of all descriptions brightened and scented the hall. The table was set, a lace cloth, fine china and crystal, silver cutlery and more flowers, roses, baby's breath, and something obscenely phallic looking.

At the far head of the table, a throne sat on its raised platform. Beside it, Syne saw a huge red velvet cushion, upon which reclined a gorgeous black man. Not just any man, he was very familiar.

Yes, it was Ares, naked and kneeling. His body was turned slightly toward the throne, but still perfectly visible to anyone who chose to look at him. And look she did. His hands were behind his neck, clasped there or held, she couldn't yet tell. His back was straight and the wide leather collar around his neck kept his chin up, but he still managed to keep his eyes downcast. With his knees spread wide and his ass firmly planted on his heels, his crotch was visible and accessible, if only she was able to move his way.

For the moment, she wasn't. And, for some reason, it didn't concern her. She eyed his genitals, smiling at the bright gold ring at the base of his cock, another one around his balls. He wasn't erect, but he was extremely well endowed.

"Ladies, gentlemen." The voice was smooth and softly feminine, but carried across the length of the room easily. "Please take a seat and we'll begin."

As if in a dream, Syne made her way, along with the others, to the table and found a place. When she was seated she looked around, the first voluntary movement she'd been allowed to make since leaving her room. The others were as 'controlled' as she was. Sitting straight, they peered around, but that seemed to be all that was permitted.

A sudden noise from the doorway got her full attention. But, try as she might, she couldn't turn her head. She strained against the invisible bonds, but it didn't do a bit of good. She was held. All she could move was her head, and even that movement was restricted.

When the woman came into view, Syne could have fainted, if given the option. Tall, slender, incredibly blonde and fair, Diane, her friend and confidant, stood at the head of the table, smiling.

"I am Dione, Goddess here and your hostess." She shifted her gaze from one to the next of her 'guests' and smiled when her eyes came to rest on Syne. The gown she wore left next to nothing to the imagination. Held at the neck by a band of what looked like diamonds, the white gossamer gown covered her to her toes, but revealed everything. Luscious full breasts, their nipples rouged and standing proud, formed tiny pyramids. Another band of diamonds held her waist and was tied on her left hip, the ends left to dangle.

She turned away before Syne noticed if her pussy was visible, but seeing her from the rear, she had no doubt it was. She sidled up the two steps to her throne, her buttocks like two puppies snuggling together. Turning, she stood for a long moment, as if awaiting applause, then settled into the soft cushions of the elaborately carved chair. Her hand, draped over the side, came to rest on Ares' chest.

"Tonight, you'll each live out a fantasy, or so you've been told. That's why you came. But, in reality, it is I who will create and enjoy a fantasy." The smile she shot toward Syne sent a chill through her.

"One of you is going to have a special treat, though; something she's always wanted but never had the guts to do." Diane—Dione—stared straight at her as she spoke, a wicked smile pulling at the corners of her mouth. "She's always wanted a plaything, a man who'll do anything she asks."

Dear God, Syne thought and cringed, wishing the floor would open up and swallow her. How could her friend so blatantly tell these strangers her deepest, most secret fantasy? How did she even know about it? Shaking her head, she willed it all to stop—to be over. But, when she opened her eyes again, Dione was still there, and the rest of the guests were watching her.

"Ah, dinner is here," Dione said in a softer tone.

A feminine hand and arm, covered by a kimono sleeve, placed a plate in front of her. Pastries and succulent vegetables in a sauce that smelled of garlic and butter were piled high. More plates arrived, carried by other kimono-clad girls and scattered along the table. Carafes filled with different colored liqueurs arrived next, their glasses were filled and the rest left for later.

"Eat, drink, and enjoy. The masquerade has begun." No sooner had the words left her mouth, than Syne saw the woman across from her change. Her hair, which had been mousey brown, suddenly became vibrant honey gold and appeared to be growing longer. Her breasts, which had been on the small side, plumped and were suddenly much larger, the nipples more red against the suddenly tight bodice of her slave girl outfit.

The blond-haired man beside her, who had been very nice looking to begin with, was instantly heart-stoppingly gorgeous. He'd been less than powerfully built, but that changed, his body amassing muscles enough to split the cloth covering him. He simply sat there, bewildered and naked, as his body reformed and grew.

Syne watched each of her counterparts changing, becoming more vivacious, more lusciously beautiful. None of them seemed to suffer from the alterations; no one moaned or cried out. The process was either painless or some kind of block was being used.

"Eat," Dione repeated more sternly. "You'll all need your strength, I'm sure."

The cruel laughter that followed made Syne shudder. But her hand, as if it had a life of its own, moved to the plate in front of her. She noted that everyone else did the same. Forks rose, morsels of food pressed to mouths that opened obediently, and teeth chewed. While they ate, the changes finished, and Syne wondered what they'd done to her. She felt nothing. Her field of vision allowed her to see her arms and hands, but nothing more.

Soon enough, the meal ended, much to her relief, and her fork lay across her plate. The others quickly followed, and the same silent servers removed their plates.

Dione watched, not partaking of the meal, not that Syne could see. Ares continued to kneel beside her, his body held erect and his eyes lowered. But, that was about to end.

Tension in the air grew. Syne heard one or two of her companions fidgeting. One of them moaned very softly. Unable to see what those further down the table were experiencing, she returned her attention to those across from her, and gasped. Flushed, eyes glazed with lust, they squirmed and twisted in their chairs as if they'd suddenly grown hot.

"Syne," the sultry voice of Dione called. "Come to me, girl. There's something special here waiting for you."

Syne's heart leaped into her throat. Rising from her chair, she turned and faced the woman whom she thought was her friend. More regal, more impressively beautiful, Dione smiled down at her and nodded. Slightly reassured, Syne squared her shoulders and moved toward the head of the table. With each step, a strange, terrifying thing happened. Her memories shifted. What she remembered of her life as a freelancer, faded.

After only a few forced paces, her mind was almost blank and her terror gone. It was hard to be afraid when there were no memories to be afraid of. Noises from the others distracted her, but she walked on, determined to reach the source of all that was happening to her. Language remained, was enhanced. She realized a new language, or an old one, crept into her mind.

When she finally stood at the bottom of the stairs, Syne was no more. The woman before her was familiar, loved, and admired.

"Dione," she whispered, shocked as her memories flooded back—the masquerade of a year ago, her flight from the island when Ares had confessed his infidelity, again. Confused, angry, she breathed, "How...?"

Dione rose from her throne and stepped down. Holding her arms out, she pulled the shocked woman into them and held her tenderly. "Shh! It's all right. Give yourself a few minutes. It'll all come back."

The name, Mnemosyne, crept in, and with it a million memories. Words, the meaning of things and emotions, of animals and plants, she knew them all, had created them, explained them, loved them all, and now she remembered. The arms around her tightened, as if Dione could read her mind, fathom the shock and anger raging through her.

Syne, the freelancer, the woman struggling to make a living off reporting the tragedy of others, faded into a corner of her mind. She was the Goddess, the creator of words and the namer of everything known. Her year of being simply, and only, human was gone. Her life as the Goddess Mnemosyne, daughter of the sky and earth, she remembered it all—Ares' goading, his infidelity, his tormenting, and how she'd fled the safety of the island.

Her own hands had found their way to Dione's hips, her fingers digging into the soft flesh. Taking a deep breath, she struggled to calm herself. A year was gone, wasted because of anger, and she vowed not to repeat it.

"Thank you," she whispered into Dione's ear and kissed her on the neck. "Thank you." If it hadn't been for the lovely woman in her arms, she might never have found her way back. She'd made sure she found the card, knew she'd find her way here. A debt owed, and she'd remember.

"Ares, I want him." She straightened up and turned her gaze on the kneeling man.

He seemed to know she was watching him, and straightened himself even more. He was smart, though, and never raised his eyes. His dark skin shone, a light sheen of sweat gleaming in the brightly lit room.

"He's yours," Dione said, and stepped back, giving her room to pass.

Mnemosyne took her time walking toward the kneeling god, enjoying the return of her memories and the power she knew was hers. Standing over him, she glared down at the god who had stolen a year of her life.

"Ares," she snarled and smiled when his shoulders hunched. "Ares, you dog, look at me."

His head shifted, raising his eyes to look at her. The blue of the sea gazed calmly into her eyes. There was no sorrow, no plea for mercy or forgiveness there. She saw only determination and—and something else she couldn't name. Shocked, she slid her hand through his tightly crinkled hair, twisting her fingers into it, squeezing, dragging a grunt of pain from him.

"Why?" Roughly, she dragged his head back, forcing him to arch his back.

"Mnemosyne—Syne, it's my nature to wander. You knew that when we joined together. I didn't change."

Her heart sank. What he said was true, and she herself had enjoyed the attention of other men. "Yes, it's in your nature, and you haven't changed. But, you took a year from me and caused me much sorrow. You must pay."

"Willingly, if it will bring you back to me."

For a moment, she was too surprised to speak. Back? How could she possibly take him back after what he'd done? He'd bragged of his conquests, rubbed her nose into them one too many times. How could she forgive him or forget the pain he'd caused her? It was his careless disregard for her that had driven her away, forced her to flee the island.

"You must be punished," she snarled, anger flaring. "For the evening, this night of fantasies and dreams, you'll be my dog, my beast, and be treated as one." Her blood roared in her ears. The punishment she was devising would be harsh, painful for such a man as Ares, but if he loved her as he claimed, he'd agree.

He looked at her with a mixture of lust and confusion. "It seems you've remembered it all, my love." He lowered his head and shuddered. "The dog. Yes, that's what I'm called by some." Glancing back up at her, the determination was back. "I'll be your beast. A well deserved title perhaps, but one I'll gladly endure for your love."

"Not quite my dog, although that may be what I call you. My abject slave." She stroked his head lightly, feeling him tremble at her words. A warrior, he'd balk at her proposal, but she'd give him no choice. "You'll do exactly what I ask of you, or I'll banish you from my presence."

He took a moment to reply. His muscles tensed, she watched them, then slid her hand down over his shoulders and across the top of his broad, black chest. "Damn you,

Syne," he said in a strangled voice. "You know I have to say yes. I love you more than life. I've nearly gone crazy without you."

Triumphant, Mnemosyne smiled and reached a little lower for a tightly puckered nipple. "Damn you, Ares." She tightened her grip slowly, rolling the tiny black nubbin between fingers and thumb, until he squirmed. "Not the nicest thing for a slave to call his mistress, is it?" She twisted her hand.

He grunted, but that was the only sign of his acknowledging the pain. "No, it's not."

"Apologize." She wrenched her hand the opposite way, dragging another grunt from him.

"Mnemosyne, I'm sorry. I'll try very hard to show proper respect for you in future."

Releasing her hold, Mnemosyne turned and faced Dione. "Thank you, my friend. You've given me my life back. I'll never forget the debt I owe you." She bowed low and smiled when she stood tall again; Dione was in front of her.

"You're welcome, Mnemosyne. I'm glad you're with us again." She nodded down at Ares, and added, "I'm not so sure he will be by the time you're finished with him, though." Her laughter was contagious and soon both were holding onto the other, howling with glee.

"You may be right, my friend; but he'll remember, that's for sure," Mnemosyne managed. "We'll be leaving you now. Enjoy your masquerade; I'm sure the others will."

Unwinding a strand of gold belting from her waist, she bent and looped it around Ares' genitals. *He'll heel me well,* she thought, and turned toward the door. Naked men and women, who thought they were there to party and play out their own fantasies, awaited the pleasure of Dione. They knelt, beautifully, exposed and eager for the revels to begin.

COMING TOGETHER: AT LAST

Reaching the door, Mnemosyne heard the lovely goddess' first command of the evening, "Reach to your right and excite the person next to you. I want to see what you have to offer."

Ares heeled her, on his hands and knees. Closing the door behind her, she whirled and thought of her favorite rooms in her palace.

And they were there.

Pale marble with tendrils of gold running through it surrounded them both. Tall pillars of the same stone rose skyward at the entryway, framing the chamber and the pool in its center. Cushions were piled around the pool, all colors and sizes, and that's where she went. A tug on the leash brought Ares scrambling after her.

"Damn!" he cursed as he hurried to keep up with her.

She gave his leash a jerk, forcing a howl of pain from him. "You have a dirty mouth, Ares. I don't want to hear it again."

"Right," he shot back, and realized—a moment too late—that he was in no position to get mouthy.

She jerked on the leash again. No outcry followed, but she saw his muscles tense. "You will also keep a civil tongue in your head, or I'll remove it."

He shot her a look of panic, but kept any comments to himself.

"I'm going to bathe. You're going to wash me. But, before you enter the pool, I'd like a glass of wine." She released the end of the leash and, ignoring him for the moment, went to the side of the pool. *It's so good to be home*, she thought, and stretched languidly. His eyes were on her, she felt them burning a path over her flesh.

Revenge was going to be sweet, she mused as she unwound the strands of gold from around her body. The semi-sheer gown was next. With a shrug of her shoulders, it slid, as softly as a summer breeze, down her arm and off. It pooled around her ankles, hobbling her until she stepped free of it. When she bent forward to unfasten the knotted laces at her knees, presenting him with an unobstructed view of her nicely rounded bottom, she heard him gasp.

Normally, she would have just straightened up and entered the pool. Instead, she stepped out of her sandals, and ran her hands up the backs of both legs. Peering back, she saw him, fixed and staring at her. "Wine," she said, loud enough to get his attention.

He jerked his head up, caught. Mouth agape, he nodded and rose to his feet, or almost did. He stopped when he lifted one foot and placed it on the floor, then looked at her, "May I rise?"

Laughing, she said, "Yes, but don't touch yourself." Nodding at his middle, she added, "That belongs to me for the remainder of the night."

"Yes, it does." He rose to his feet, than asked, "What would you like me to call you, my love?"

"My love will be fine, unless I suggest something else."

"Thank you, my love." He bowed. "I'll get your wine now."

She watched him walk out of the room, his buttocks flexing, the muscles playing against each other. A beautiful man, and hers to play with.

When he returned, Syne was up to her neck in the pool. Sitting on the lower step in the shallow end, she lay her head back, allowing the water to sooth her. Her breasts rose to the surface, the nipples peaking out at him. Each breath moved the water around her and felt like a massage.

She watched him approach her, his cock erect and swaying before him. She loved the sight of him nude, his skin so dark it seemed to suck in the light around him. Walking around the pool, he finally knelt beside her and held out a crystal glass filled with amber liquid.

"Your wine, my love. I hope it's to your liking." The brute knew how to impress her. He also knew her love of water.

When she'd taken the glass and placed it on the edge of the pool, he slipped into the pool beside her. A large basket of soaps and oils waited for him. He chose a lilac scented soap and, with a dollop in his palm, he worked it into a rich lather. He moved in front of her, then carefully nudged her feet apart with his own and stepped between them.

Mnemosyne's blood felt hot as it raced through her. Her knees trembled when she spread them, and she gasped when his thigh brushed hers. His cock, hard and black, seemed aimed at her sex. His hands, slick with lather, slid across her shoulders and over her breasts.

Beneath the water, she took hold of him. He gasped when she eased her hand up and down the shaft. He'd obviously been excited for some time, as he pulsed and groaned, his hips thrusting into her hand. His hands stopped moving. His head was thrown back, and his mouth hung slack as she teased him. Sliding her thumb over the mushroom head, she felt the slickness of pre-come oozing out of him. He shuddered, his hips twitched.

"You're not bathing me." Her voice was thick with passion. She loved to torment him.

He blinked at her and swallowed. "I've missed you, my love," he murmured and slid his hands down her sides. His mouth went to her nipple, his lips puckering for their first taste in a year. His body touched her, his chest slid across her belly, his cock rubbed along her inner thighs. She groaned and dragged him forward, her pussy aching to be filled.

"Fuck me," she growled, all thought of his punishment forgotten for the moment. When he pushed forward, the head of his cock wedged itself against her opening. Easing forward, his mouth tore free of her nipple. The cool air sent a shiver of pleasure through her. His ragged sigh was music to her ears.

"Fuck me," she repeated and to her joy, he plunged in deep. "Yes, but don't come. Don't you dare come."

"My love," he croaked. Breathing like a freight train, he eased himself out of her, and held still with the tip just barely in contact with her nether lips. He moved his hands to the side of the pool, one on each side of her shoulders. His body, slick and wet, covered in the lather with which he'd caressed her breasts, shone.

She leaned forward, kissing his chest, and felt the drumming of his heart against her lips. With her hands on his hips, she pulled him back inside her, groaning as his cock touched deep within her. She held him there, reveling in the wild pulsing of his cock and the way he trembled under her hands. Again, she pushed him away, but just enough. Her pussy clenched, the lips fluttering against his glans.

"Please, my love. Ah!" His hips lurched ahead.

She lost her grip on his hips as he lunged deep. Her clit rubbed against the base of his cock, and she cried out as her orgasm blossomed. Flashes of light blinded her, took her breath and held her captive as pleasure raced through her. Tensed, unable to move or breathe, she basked in sensation. He pounded into her, again and again, slamming his body into hers, extending the blissful explosions.

When her thoughts returned, he'd collapsed against her, cock still buried deep, still hard and throbbing. The ring snug around the base of his cock ensured his erection, although he continued to twitch.

"Ares, dog that you are, get off me." She placed her hands on his shoulders and shoved.

Obviously reluctant, he backed away from her. His cock slid across her inner thigh once again, but this time she let it go untouched.

"Now, I've been alone for an entire year. Had to take care of myself, you see, in all things." She warmed to her little speech and could see from the look of annoyance on his face that he knew where she was going with it. "I don't imagine you kept yourself celibate, did you?"

Shamefaced, he lowered his eyes and muttered, "Uh, well... No, my love."

Laughing, she replied, "No, I didn't think you had." She squirmed, truly enjoying herself. "I want a little entertainment. You, my love, are going to be it. Climb out of the pool and kneel beside me—nice and close. I don't want to miss a thing."

Ares did as he was told, clambering out of the pool, and kneeling very close to her. She glared at him when he presented himself with his knees firmly pressed together. Quickly, he eased them apart and showed himself as he'd been beside Dione's throne, the leash still wrapped around his genitals.

She made him wait, posed, cock trembling with lust. His eyes were lowered so he looked at it, watching it throb and swell as his excitement rose even more.

Mnemosyne reached for her glass of wine and relaxed against the side of the pool drinking. "How many women have you had this past year, my sweet Ares?"

For a moment, he didn't answer. Whether he was unwilling or unable to remember them all, she didn't know. Finally, he replied, "Not as many as I would have liked, my love. There are always women to enjoy."

Temper flaring, she said, "Entertain me. Masturbate, but don't come until I tell you to." She sipped her wine and watched him.

Taking a firm grip on his shaft, he squeezed it first. The head bulged, its eye opening as if winking at her. A pearl of pre-come oozed out, perching atop the bulbous dome. His strokes were slow, uneven for the first few. He got into the rhythm quickly enough, his own private pace that would carry him at length to the heights of bliss. She watched his inner thighs tense, his belly muscles tighten, even watched his tightly held testicles squirm within the confines of the ring holding them. Her wine slowly disappeared, and she waited even longer.

Sweat beaded on his brow and upper lip. The muscular chest heaved with his determination to obey, to show her he loved her through his obedience. She knew him, knew how stubborn he was—how proud and vain—and used it against him.

"Lean back, one hand on the floor behind you."

He leaned back and rested his weight on the hand he placed behind himself. His hips thrust upward, his balls pushed more forward. Covered in pre-cum, his erection glistened darkly, magnificently.

Mnemosyne pushed herself toward him between his wide spread legs. The scent of him was intoxicating. "Do you love me, Ares?"

Gasping, scarcely able to speak, he managed to gasp, "Yes, more than anything."

Smiling, she said, "More than anything. Are you sure?"

Without a moment's hesitation, he said, "Yes, more than anything."

"Good." She leaned forward and kissed his cock head. It pulsed, and he groaned, obviously near to losing control. "You may stop entertaining me now."

A look of disbelief crossed his face. "Stop? Now?"

"Yes, if you love me. You can still come, but it will be me that gives you that gift."

She saw the struggle. His painful realization of what she'd done. She controlled him, owned him, and would decide when—or if—he climaxed.

He forced his hand to release his cock. Curled into a fist, he put it behind his back, resting his weight on both hands.

Mnemosyne eased into a more comfortable position between his thighs and blew on his cock. It twitched in reply. "You may come, but remember this. You come at my command. This," she tapped his glans with a fingertip, "belongs to me."

"Yes, my love," Ares croaked. His eyes were on her, unblinking, desperate.

Her lips touched the tip of his cock, and she allowed the sticky crown to ease them open. She grazed the glans with her teeth, and it pulsed. She carefully followed the vein along its length to the base, then back to the rim. She sucked the tip into her mouth, flicked her tongue back and forth, then around until his gasping became soft, begging her to take him, suck him. Ignoring his pleas, she released his cock and worked on his balls, sucking and nipping at them with her lips.

"Please, my love, please," became a litany of need and one she refused to heed.

When he stopped begging her, simply allowed the pleasure she gave to be what he would have, she stepped up her suction—eased more of his cock into her mouth and urged the come out of him. The first spew was massive and she swallowed it quickly, knowing another would come on the next pulse. Warm, thick, rich with his salty maleness, he pumped another stream of come into her waiting mouth. His groaning returned, and she loved it. She knew he was beyond caring about anything then except the rapture she provided.

He gasped and jerked, and thrust into her mouth until nothing was left but dry pulsing. She lathed him with her tongue then let his softened cock go.

Climbing out of the pool, she got a towel big enough to cover them both and went to him. He'd just managed to pull himself away from the edge of the pool and settle back onto the cushion, but was still gasping. Sitting astride him, she wrapped the towel around them both. "My love, my dog, you'll never learn, I know, but I love you anyway."

Eyes shining with love, he smiled at her and said, "Yes, I'm your dog, your slave even, and if anyone can train me it's you." He laughed for a moment, but then stopped and gazed into her eyes. "I love you, my Mnemosyne, my sweet Syne."

♥

my-haven2001.com

Seafood Cocktail
© Sacchi Green

He emerged from the sea like the incarnation of some primal god: wet, powerful, gleaming like dark, polished rosewood. When he spoke, his voice was deep as thunder, smooth as rain.

"Hey, Lexie, where do you think they've hidden the cameras?"

I rolled out from under the boat's inverted hull. "Come on, Max, you think they could fake a storm like that? Even if the technology existed, they wouldn't pay for it. The beauty of reality shows is the low overhead."

"You're probably right," he admitted, turning away to block a full frontal view, oddly shy for someone who'd signed away all rights to privacy for a chance at fame and fortune.

I still got the benefit of his muscular butt. Droplets of seawater trickled over its curves, forming jaunty question marks. Several intriguing answers occurred to me.

"You'd think they'd still cover all the bases," he said over his shoulder. "Including any island we might get ourselves shipwrecked on. Otherwise, why let us have a boat, even a chicken-shit one like that?"

He might have a point there—in addition to the one he was keeping out of view. "I just hope they know this sand spit exists," I said, peeling off my sodden T-shirt and shorts and spreading them next to his on the hull to dry. "You can search for cameras all you like—I'll even help after I wash this sand off—but our first priority should be figuring out how to survive until they come to get us."

I walked into the whispering wavelets of the lagoon, feeling his eyes on me and feeling my body move in ways subtly different from the strides I would have taken under the gaze of another woman. A tingle spread across my ass and around to my belly, upward to my breasts; it had been a long time since a masculine presence had had that effect.

I swam out until the water was smooth enough for me to float on my back. Images of last night's chaotic storm coiled into and out of each other, like oil on the surface of a whirlpool. The one clear memory was a sexual current intensified by fear. Max and I had huddled through the night under our meager shelter, bodies pressed so tightly together that our clothes, saturated with rain and sweat and seawater, were no barrier to the pounding of each other's hearts. But Max, in spite of the arousal his wet jeans did little to conceal, had done nothing to take it any farther.

I had a pretty good idea why. He had witnessed my girlfriend Tonya's explicitly steamy farewell at the plane and drawn the obvious conclusion. But Tonya had known perfectly well that potential sex was written between the lines of the show's contract, and she'd still pressured me to sign it. I'd only agreed to do the "Marooned" show for my indie-producer girlfriend's sake. If I could get a bit of notoriety, she figured, she'd have a better chance of getting backers for our films.

But last night, while the pounding rain made our shelter into an impenetrable cave, Max's arms around me and mine around him had seemed absolutely right. The lightning flashes outside had built an electric tension deep inside me until I'd been at the point of jumping him myself—when he'd started snoring.

Men! But he'd saved my life more than once in the last few hours, maybe even a time or two more than I'd saved his. Instead of interrupting his exhausted sleep, I'd amused myself with working my hand gently, gently between jeans and skin and teasing his heavy balls and straining cock just lightly enough to make him writhe and groan in his dreams, until, ultimately, his pants were soaked with something thicker and sweeter than seawater. And all without waking up.

I drifted onward in the lagoon, savoring a gentler tension. Unless Max had more reason for resistance than figuring me for a hardcore dyke, being marooned was going to get very interesting, very soon. I swung upright, my toes just touching the sandy bottom. I looked around and saw I'd drifted close to a tiny islet near the center of the lagoon.

A maze of underwater rocks suggested mysterious lurking creatures, maybe octopi. I could see, too close to pass up, clusters of what I was pretty sure were oysters. I wished I had pockets; my built-in ones winced at the thought of rough oyster shells. I dived and grasped a large one in each hand.

Back on the beach, I loped up the slope to where Max knelt. He was piling palm fronds under a lean-to built with the boat and some pieces of driftwood.

"Hey, Max," I called as I ran; he turned and got the maximum effect of my jiggling breasts. It wasn't wasted on him.

"What's up?" he said, and turned quickly back. I resisted commenting on the obvious.

"I found an oyster bed out there. Might be a little hard to get them down raw without lemon or Tabasco, but better than starving. And better than the rats they're eating back at the main base." I tossed my prizes on the sand.

"I guess," he said, clearly not really focused on eating of that kind.

I pressed my thigh against his shoulder. "I don't suppose we'll be here long enough to starve, anyway. But there are things I'd really, really like to fit in while we're still here. Alone."

He'd pulled his shorts back on, but not his shirt. I leaned on his broad back and nuzzled his neck. He knelt, unmoving, supporting my weight, until I began chewing lightly on his muscular shoulders. "Did you know that oysters can switch their sex?" I murmured against his rigid jaw.

"Lexie," he said, his deep voice getting even deeper, "What do you think you're doing?"

"If you can't tell, I must not be doing it right." I brushed my hardening nipples across his back.

"But I thought..."

"I know what you thought. And I know what you're thinking now. Drives you crazy, doesn't it, envisioning what women do with each other?" I reached around his chest to flick his nipples; they sprang to attention. An interesting effect on hard muscle instead of soft curves.

"If it didn't before, it does now," he muttered. I worked one hand down inside his jeans, over the bunched muscles of his buttocks and then in between; suddenly he twisted under me and ended up on his back with me astride. "Damn it, Lexie, you'd better be going somewhere with this!"

There's something about a deep, deep masculine voice. A woman's voice can stroke like a warm, wet tongue, but Max's voice set up reverberations that seemed to liquefy my bones.

"Trust me," I said. "I never met an erogenous zone I couldn't appreciate." I rode the huge bulge in his pants, appreciating the hell out of it. "Check me out, if you need proof." I lifted myself just enough for his hand to test my natural lube. His digital enthusiasm was touching, if a bit clumsy, but I pursued other interests, sliding backward until I had his zipper far enough open to insert two fingers. Then slowly, slowly, the gap widened until my whole hand curved around his hot, hard cock, still trapped by the pressure of his belt.

His hips rose, his hands scrabbled at the belt buckle, and I caught the tip of his cock in my mouth as it jerked free.

I savored it with just enough in-out action to keep him breathing hard without rushing things. Then I hitched my body along his until my knees clutched his hips. My own hips moved as my cunt lips slid back and forth over his swollen, eager cock. Too bad, I thought, that our sense of taste is limited to the mouths we eat with. And a taste was all I was going to get.

"Max, you wouldn't happen to know what the Swiss Family Robinson used for condoms, would you?"

"No, damn it. They must have cut that part from the movie to get a G rating."

"Don't worry." I played him with my hand, stroking from the root of his balls all the way up his shaft. "Just lie back and let me run this fuck."

"You're the boss," he said, his voice rising into a gasp. I had pressed my knuckle firmly below his scrotum and was working my thumb back toward his asshole.

"I'll bet you'd like something really kinky," I teased, "to tell your grandchildren."

"I'll bet you have inside information," he said, not too steadily, "about what Robinson Crusoe used for sex toys!"

"Is that a challenge?" I watched a gleaming pearl of pre-cum form at the slit in his cock. "If so, I accept."

I yanked the belt from his shorts; he lifted his head in alarm. His expression went from apprehension to horrified awe as I leaned over to grab an oyster.

The belt buckle was just the tool for prying open the tough shell. "No pearl in this one," I said, bringing the opened bivalve close to his erection. "Maybe you could share." I tapped his cock; it jerked. I just managed to catch his dewdrop on the oyster, while some of the liquid cupped in the shell dripped onto his balls. I bent to lick it off, then touched my tongue to the glistening shellfish.

"Hmm, needs more sauce." I slid the oyster into my mouth and held it there, excitement balancing revulsion, while I worked Max hard, inexorably, with both hands. At the penultimate moment, when his deep moans rose in pitch and nearly flowed together, I worked my full mouth down over his cock. I barely managed to keep the slippery oyster from being rammed down my throat until Max's storm of cries rattled my bones and the hot flood of his come burst over my tongue.

Swallowing had never been quite like that before.

Finally, Max regained enough breath to speak. "Lexie," he said, "it's your turn." He was trying not to look at the remaining oyster. It was a very large, very juicy oyster. I plucked it from its shell. Liquid dripped between my fingers into my lap and seeped downward to mingle with my own juices.

I leaned back and spread my legs. The oyster was cold against my tender heat, but I kept pushing. Between its slippery coating and my own wetness, it slid in easily. My cunt tried to grip the slick, yielding pressure, and the teasing subtlety of the stimulation began to drive me crazy. "No, it's your turn," I said, gasping. "Eat!"

"Well, considering the gourmet dipping sauce..." And he ate, his willingness to learn exceeded only by the length of his truly phenomenal tongue. It was a long time before I realized that the throbbing sounds filling the air weren't all coming from me.

"A search helicopter," Max said, wiping his mouth.

"Damn!" I groped for the belt buckle and rolled over until I could reach inside the prow of the boat. I started gouging the splintered wood around what seemed to be a bolt; then Max's large, dark hand took the buckle and finished the job.

"How long have you known it was there?" he asked, when the tiny camera lay at last cupped in my hand.

"I noticed it when I woke up," I said. "Want me to send you a copy on disc?"

"You'd better," he said. "Not that I'm likely to forget any of it."

"Not as long as there are oyster bars in the world," I agreed.

"I don't think I'll be eating any more oysters," Max shouted over the increasing noise, "unless that special sauce comes with them."

"Sauce for the goose as well as the gander," I called, but my voice was swallowed by the roar of the rotors. The chopper was so close now we could feel the wind. I scrabbled for my clothes.

* * * *

From high above, the little crescent of sand and rock seemed to smile in the liquid embrace of the ocean. I shifted in my seat in the helicopter, new waves of tingling overlapping the residual glow between my legs.

The camera was in my pocket. I knew where I could hide the chip later, if I had to, to get it home; I might even manage the whole miniature camera, if only briefly. I grinned to myself. Max probably thought I was thinking of him, but I was really filled with images of how Tonya would get the most out of a cuntcam.

It was a damned shame, though, that she was allergic to seafood.

♥

Alessia Brio, ed.

sacchig.livejournal.com

Instinct
© Chloe Waits

Samantha looked out her small office window at the traffic below, tucking her light brown hair behind one ear. She gave a rueful smile as she thought of everyone else in the office clock-watching this Friday, desperate for the weekend to begin. And yet Samantha knew their plans would be very different from hers.

She slipped into the tight bathroom stall, quickly removing her navy business suit and pulling on jeans and a T-shirt. Outside by the sink, she ran her hands through her hair to tease its volume and applied fresh gloss. She smiled at the effect in the mirror. She was ready for her 'date.'

Samantha walked out of the building into the sunlight and traveled the few blocks to her destination. She'd started passing this way a couple weeks ago—something she hadn't done in years. In that time, it was quickly becoming a weekly routine to visit on her way home. Every Friday she came, paying her admission and making her way in until she had reached her final destination. And every Friday she came to stand in front of his cage as he stalked it. Eyes locked and hissing. Flashes of yellow, of foamy spittle. Sleek muscles rippling.

She leaned on the metal railing fascinated with the panther's raw energy. It seemed to draw her in. Felt the shame of it closed in a cage; a hundred square feet to prowl in, never again to be the hunter it was meant to be. Samantha thought of human nature in the same terms: how we scale our hungers down to adequate size—afraid to eat, drink, even fuck too much. Afraid to want things. To be too much and take too much. A veneer of civility over all things.

The panther had none of these concerns. It was its appetite. She admired its struggle to be free, the way it tore into the flesh of its food with sharp, shiny claws.

The animal seemed to study her sometimes, as though in kinship. Other times it growled low, chilling Samantha to her core. Licks of fear up her back excited her. Her legs trembled. Sometimes, she wanted to bare her teeth right back at it.

What had drawn her back to the zoo after so many years since her last visit? Some dim childhood memory? It seemed sheer impulse that had made her go inside one day after work, abruptly turning off the street on her way home. Perhaps a factor, too, that she had not wanted to go home that night. She had, after all, broken up with Tim that week. And yet if Samantha was honest, she felt more disappointment then regret. She had to admit to herself that she was bored with the men in her life. More interested in their jobs and cars than her, it seemed. More interested in stocks and their bank accounts.

And the sex? Sterile and boring. Samantha tried to block out images that thought drew. Awkward fumblings. Missionary thrusting. Oral sex performed on her badly—and then only if she was lucky. Watching the panther was exhilarating. This animal had more life, more instinct than all her previous lovers put together.

In fact, everything seemed a bit grey to her lately. Her job as an analyst was bland as well. Numbers after numbers to tabulate. She longed to escape the office building that looked like a beehive and breathe the summer air. Her clothes felt restricting and stiff on her body.

Her conservative office did not have a casual dress Friday. So, when another Friday arrived, Samantha again brought a change of clothes to signal the start of her weekend. She squeezed into the bathroom, changed out of her work clothes and slipped into a black miniskirt, applying more kohl to her green eyes and shaking her long brown hair loose from its smooth pony tail.

This is me, not some suit, she thought.

As she left her workplace her walk changed, became freer. Samantha allowed the natural sway of her hips to dominate. Her heels clicked as she walked, slipping through the turnstiles. She stopped briefly at the exotic birds, listening to their calls, admiring the bright saturated colors of their feathers, their movements in the cages. Then she continued until she came to front of the panther cage.

He was lying down, tail tapping against the ground, lazily taking in his surrounding through half-hooded eyes. The panther seemed oblivious to the crowd of people, mothers with children passing through. It was as though his wildness had been bleached out.

She fought back disappointment, gazing and willing the beast to come to her. Her eyes locked with the panther's. *Show me who you are,* she thought. She slipped under the railing, closer to the black barred cage as the panther eyed her approach warily. She stood in front of it, mentally inviting it to smell her scent, to welcome her as one of its own. The animal made a low keen in its throat, but did not move. She placed her hands on the bars, legs apart. Samantha felt so alive. Her skin tingled with energy as her heartbeat increased.

The panther leapt toward her suddenly, mouth stretched, teeth bared. Growling ferociously. Samantha sprung back from the cage as it pounced at the bars. Strong hands gripped her shoulders, righting her.

"Miss, are you okay?" asked a deep voice.

She nodded wordlessly, looking up into the face of a tall, dark man with a zoo logo-emblazoned hat.

Embarrassed, her eyes darted away, but not before she saw how black and intense his eyes were. It was like being watched by the panther. She pushed the thought away.

"You shouldn't get so close. Raven can seem tame at times, but he is wild."

She swallowed, nodding, and turned to leave on unsteady legs. "Thank you."

"Miss, are you sure you're okay?" he asked.

"Yes, I am fine." she assured him.

Was she fine? She was trying to communicate with a wild animal. What was she doing? She left quickly, trying to ignore how the man's gaze had held hers.

At home, Samantha winced as she replayed the event at the zoo. She tried to block out the image of his large build, his probing eyes. Did he think she had some kind of death wish? She had heard of people climbing the cages to get close to the zoo animals—even parents who would put honey on their children in order to get a wild bear to lick it off. Just for the photo op. Did he equate her with those people? Was she like them? Was she an adrenalin junkie? How could she explain her admiration of the panther's feline grace? Its strength? Its danger?

She flushed as she thought of the feelings of excitement, almost sexual as she faced the panther down. Maybe that's what was missing from her life. Her life was too safe—and so were her men. Maybe that was at the heart of her feelings of restlessness, of boredom.

That night she dreamt of being in front of Raven again. This time she was inside the cage. The eyes of the panther and the man blended together. Strong hands were pulling her out.

* * * *

It was two weeks before she went back. She felt subdued as she walked in, wandering restlessly through, stopping at animal exhibits without really seeing them, wondering if she should leave. Yet her feet seemed to go—of their own volition—slowly to the feline section. She went to the railing, a safe distance away. She leaned against it, watching Raven. The panther was pacing his cage. Yellow eyes sharp and feral. Samantha became aware of a presence next to her. Out of the corner of her eye she saw dark hands folded on the railing.

"So, you're back. I'm glad Raven didn't give you a permanent scare."

She glanced sideways, seeing a flash of white teeth. "I don't scare quite that easy."

"I guess not, not someone who would go up to the cage and have a staring match with a panther."

"It wasn't a staring match, it was..." Samantha felt helpless to explain.

"I understand," he said slowly. "I am fascinated by these animals, too."

"I like how they are real. Really themselves. With no preconceived notions, no worries..."

"Yeah," he laughed, "other than getting their next meal."

She tried to smile at his joke but continued, "They're free. They know real freedom." She stopped awkwardly, realizing the contradiction of describing the freedom of a caged animal.

He stopped grinning, grew thoughtful. "They are true to themselves."

She turned to look at him. His eyes were so dark she could barely see the rings around his irises.

"Yes," she replied softly.

"So, are you true to yourself as well?"

It sounded like a subtle challenge. His deep eyes hypnotic.

"Is anyone?" she challenged back, "Don't we have different constraints on us than animals? We have our

nature shaped and molded since we were born. We're...
institutionalized."

"Perhaps. But some of us have an easier time living by
our passions. Some... block them out."

It was hard for Samantha not to flush at his words.
Every time he spoke it seemed to take on different layers of
meaning, as though he was talking about something else
entirely.

"Anyway, don't they scare you at all? Part of being free
is being wild..." He growled suddenly, deep in his throat.

Her hands tightened on the railing, pupils wide feeling
the vibration. Like a call inside her. He stopped short
seeing her reaction, his eyes not missing a thing.

"I should go," Samantha said abruptly, starting to turn
away, heat rising in her cheeks.

"I look forward to seeing you again. My name is David,"
he called to her back.

"How do you know I will be back?" she called over her
shoulder as she kept walking.

He caught up to her quickly. "Because, I think you like
it here. I think you like Raven, and I think," his voice
dropped to a soft silky whisper, "I think you like to be a
little afraid sometimes."

Samantha hurried away, feeling her secrets on her face
for him to see. She walked quickly without stopping until
she reached her door, slamming it shut as she entered her
apartment. *You like to be a little afraid* echoed in her mind.
His face seemed to follow her around as she paced her
room. How did he seem to know what she was barely able
to admit to herself?

* * * *

Samantha was at war with herself about returning the
following week but her intrigue with Raven—and David—
drew her back. She slowed her walk as she got closer to
where the panther was housed. She tried for an air of cool

COMING TOGETHER: AT LAST

nonchalance in spite of the tightening in her stomach. Her wavy hair was piled on her head, lips painted a wine color in sharp contrast with her light green eyes. She thought of passing Raven's cage quickly.

"Hey," David came sprinting up. "I am glad you kept our Friday date."

"It's not a date," stated Samantha coolly.

"Well, your date with Raven, then," David conceded, laughing.

Samantha looked at him carefully. About six-four, he was powerfully built. His face was sculpted with high cheekbones, and a wide generous mouth.

"Do you see anything you like?" he asked, noticing her appraisal.

She turned quickly towards Raven's cage. "How long have you worked with Raven?" she asked.

He removed his hat, scratching his head. "About two, three years," His head was neatly shaved, and his fingers rubbed it briefly. His hand spanned over his head, large fingers extending out of his palm. He glanced over at her. "Now I have a question for you. What is your name?"

"Samantha."

"Samantha," he repeated to himself softly. He said her name like he savored it. "Samantha, I was wondering if you would like to go to dinner with me this evening. I am off at eight-thirty. We could grab a bite, or a drink... I know a great place for ribs a couple blocks from here. I promise I will change before we go," David stated, indicating his khaki shorts and T-shirt with a grin.

Samantha tried not to focus on his muscular calves, how wide his wrists were.

"That is, when you're finished with my friend here."

* * * *

David appeared at the gate dressed in tan pants and a white T-shirt. Her pulse quickened at the sight of him.

"I'm parked right up here." He opened the door to a jeep, helping her step up inside. "So, do you want to check out that barbeque place?"

Samantha just nodded.

"Good, we're in for a treat. I found this place by accident. It has a live blues band every Friday night, too."

David placed his hand on the small of Samantha's back, as he led her into the restaurant. His hand warmed her skin through her clothes. The place was dimly lit with blues music playing in the background.

He leaned down and spoke into Samantha's ear, "The show starts around nine. I've seen this band before," he said gesturing to the name, Mitch Trio, printed on a chalkboard.

They sat down, David trying to push his chair back to fold his long legs under the checker cloth table. "What would you like to try?"

"A plate of ribs—hot—and a rum and Coke," she stated, looking at the menu.

David motioned the waiter over and placed their drink and food orders.

It was disconcerting the way he looked at her. She wondered when a man before had ever stared so intently at her. She cleared her throat.

"So how did you get this job, David?"

David looked down, and gently peeled the label off the beer. His face grew pensive. "I have loved animals all my life. I volunteered at the zoo out in Detroit as a kid. My mom would take me a lot. I also loved biology, so I jumped at the chance to study zoology. Then I moved to Toronto about two years ago to work here. I basically never left the zoo, I guess.

"Here's our ribs." He picked one up, sucking the flesh with his teeth, watching Samantha.

Following suit, she did the same, licking the spicy sauce off her fingers as he watched.

He smiled, "You know, Samantha, I love to see a woman with an appetite. I like watching a woman eat."

"Well, enjoy the show," she said, smirking.

David paused. "I have seen you before," he said softly.

Samantha looked at him. "I have seen you coming, watching Raven. Before the day we met, I mean. You have the same look you have eating now."

Samantha looked at him levelly.

"That same look of hunger."

"Hungry for what?" It was hard for Samantha to keep the edge out of her voice at what sounded like a cheap line.

"I don't know. I guess you know better than I do. But I am thinking there is part of yourself you see in Raven. Something is drawing you in." As he spoke, Samantha felt David drawing her in as well. "There is nothing to be embarrassed about. We're all fascinated by them. There wouldn't be zoos otherwise. Animals have no self consciousness, no inhibitions. Not like us."

David took Samantha's wrist, rubbing the inside slowly as he spoke. "Do you know why Raven reacted that way to you? It's mating season for them. Panthers secrete pheromones, just like we do, only way more powerful. The female has to invite the male to her. That is the way it is with them. When I saw you with Raven, it was like you were inviting him to you." *Like you were inviting me in...* hung in the air unspoken.

Samantha said nothing but held his gaze as he spoke. As he stroked the delicate pale skin of her wrist with his large fingers, she admired how his skin looked like polished dark wood, how his forearm flexed with the simple movements. Desire started in her stomach, a warmth that emanated there.

David looked down at her wrist, "Raven is going to have a female introduced to him soon...from another zoo. What most people don't realize is the mating process takes days. The female panther will secrete her hormones—even calling out to the male—without being ready yet for mating," David looked directly in her eyes. "The male has to approach her slowly and wait."

Samantha took a sip of her drink, trying to clear her thoughts, but the potent libation stirred them even more.

"Oh, here's the band," stated David, as the musicians approached the small stage to their right. Music filled the room for a few songs with Samantha lost in the beat. The blues guitar slowed, and couples started to fill the floor.

"Will you do me the honor, Samantha?" He pushed back his chair offering his hand.

She placed hers in his, allowing him to lead her to the open dance floor. Samantha was aware of his height against her petite frame as her head rested against his chest. A faint smell of musky cologne teased her nostrils, and something indefinable blended in.

His heart thudded against her ear, his massive leg muscles rippled as they danced. She felt his hard erection against her stomach. She remembered the width of his wrist and shivered.

She pictured his cock, imagined it brushing against her panties, rubbing against her clit insistently. And, after tiring of the game, his hand twisting them aside to gain entrance. Nudging her wet lips open. Swollen. Widening, widening.

David lifted her chin, bending down to brush a kiss on her lips, tasting liquor and her desire. The kiss deepened and his tongue explored her mouth. They broke off, at last aware of their surroundings.

The way to his car and back to her place was punctuated by hungry kisses. Her mouth felt bruised as she stumbled out of his Jeep. Samantha felt her back hard against the wall of the apartment building as their kissing resumed with urgency. The texture of the concrete was imprinted on her skin. His hands cupped her face. David pushed his erection against her stomach. His fingers laced through her hair. She felt his hand mold to her breasts, sliding down her stomach.

Too fast, she thought. Her lips came away from him shakily, and he opened his eyes to focus on her. He brushed a strand of hair off her face gazing at her, his hands encompassing her face.

"When can I see you again?" she asked.

David let his arms slip from her neck reluctantly, fighting for control. A muscle flexed is his jaw. "Um, soon, hopefully." He laughed and straightened up. "I know it's not your regular time, but do you want to stop by the zoo on Wednesday?"

She cocked her eyebrow at him. "I thought you might want to view your competition. Lily—the female—is being introduced that day to Raven."

"Oh, I don't think she will be much competition for me," stated Samantha softly. "Um, come to think of it, yeah, you're right."

David smiled at her, "But it would be a good night to come. I am off at eight. You could come by after work...if you want."

Samantha held his gaze.

"Sure. I guess I better check things out." They started walking up to the lobby door of her apartment.

"Samantha? Sam," he said. Her face flushed as he used the intimate form of her name. "I had a good time tonight. A really good time." He kissed her forehead and started walking a short distance before turning, his voice lowered with promise. "Sam? Raven and I... we have that in common. I can wait."

Samantha opened her door, dizzy. What was she doing? She didn't sleep with men on the first date! She practically threw herself at him tonight. Closing her eyes, she could hear his growl in her thoughts. The smoky smell of his skin clung to her. She brushed her teeth furiously, shaking her head.

What would it be like to have a near stranger in her bed? She shivered, maybe they would not use the bed at all.

Turning on the shower, she peeled off her clothes. The spray felt like warm, hard needles on her skin but did nothing to shift her mood. A layer of steam rose, and Samantha felt her frustration throbbing painfully between her thighs.

She took the soap, creating a lather over her arms and moving down her chest. Her nipples were tight and pink. She felt a flicker as her hands moved over them. Passing them again, moving down her stomach, her thighs. Moving her soapy hand against her full cleft, feeling the swollen bud of her frustrated desire. The wet folds thick and full. She trembled as her hand explored it, picturing his face, imagining his naked body. Stalking her. Like a panther waiting. For the right moment. Fingers up inside her wet opening. Three fingers rubbing circles on her clit. Grabbing the soap rack for support. Tightening...building... shuddering.

Samantha leaned against the stall, gasping, her fingers against her throbbing clit. Shaken at the strength of her orgasm. Was David the hunter, waiting for his moment? It was his game. And she was his prey. Samantha yanked on a light nightgown and pulled up the covers. Only half satisfied.

The feeling stayed with her all week. Licks of desire, even fear of being so out of control. So out of her element. It made her feel alive, half-drunk on something... forbidden. Her demeanor was slow and sensual as she entered the bathroom stall to change for her Wednesday date. Samantha smirked in the mirror at her reflection as she took in her outfit: a micro black mini, white cotton pleasant blouse.

David's eyes widened for a second as Samantha approached. "Um, I see you're ready to give Lily some competition."

Samantha just smiled, standing on tip toe to graze his lips with a kiss. She put her hands on the railing looking in. There were two panthers in Raven's cage. Raven seemed to be stalking a short distance away from a smaller black panther that was lying down.

Samantha felt David's body heat as he stood at her back. His powerful arms gripped either side of the railing around her, enclosing her, leaning over her shoulder.

"They're almost getting along now. We introduced them slowly. She has been on the periphery of his cage all day. Lots of hissing and territory issues. But, of course, it's mating season, so I think they'll get over it soon."

Samantha looked at the female, half-lidded eyes calmly observing as Raven paced, hissing occasionally. Raven circled closer. Lily rose quickly in a growl, causing Raven to back off.

"So, what are they doing? This is the mating dance?"

David's fingers grazed up and down her arms as he spoke. "You could call it that. She's not ready. She is kind of sending mixed signals. She has hormones being secreted right now, and she may sound like she is calling to him, but she is likely not ready and will rebuff him when he approaches."

"Mixed signals, hmm?"

"Well, I am sure we all do it. For us, sometimes the body is ready before the mind... or vice versa."

"So we wait for it to catch up..."

His hands played on her forearms, causing her to shiver. Was that what David was doing, getting her ready for him?

"When they're finally together the mating may last up to four days in a heat."

His lips were at the nape of her neck. Her eyes glittered looking at Lily, admiring her nonchalance as Raven prowled angrily around. The original tease, she mused.

"I guess we should give them some privacy, eh?"

Samantha turned to face him, looking up at his face, taking in his smooth skin and full lips. She tiptoed and captured the swelling of his lower lip, tugging it lightly with her teeth.

As David pressed against her, she broke off contact, looking at him through her lashes.

"I should let you get back to work. We do have the constraints of society, now, don't we?"

David laughed low. "And I do have to go, it's a weeknight."

She turned away winking then turned back. "I have that in common with Lily, I guess. I like to send out all those different signals."

David strode toward her, quickly clasping her wrist. She felt the power in his as he gently caressed it, looking in her eyes.

"Okay." He smiled intently. "I guess I will have to wait 'til Friday." He leaned in to her ear. "You're lucky I'm at work. I wouldn't let you leave otherwise." He nipped at her ear. "I do hope you will be rested up for Friday. I think the night will end much differently."

She shivered, weakening, but straightened up, smiling sweetly. Looking up at him, she whispered, "We'll see."

* * * *

Friday at work seemed endless. Samantha watched the clock, unable to concentrate on anything except seeing

David again. Her heart thudded in anticipation as she entered the washroom cubicle, pulling on the light denim skirt and blue tank top. She looked in the mirror as she freshened up her gloss. She kept her makeup light and natural, hair loose around her shoulders.

Samantha looked around expectantly in front of Raven's cage, but David was nowhere in sight. She fought back disappointment as a couple minutes passed, scanning the crowds for him. She turned her attention to cage. Raven was lying a short distance away from Lily. She swatted her tail at him occasionally but otherwise seemed to tolerate his presence. Samantha watched the courtship, fascinated.

A man wearing a zoo uniform approached, smiling. "Are you Samantha?"

She nodded.

"David is in the observatory, would you allow me to take you to him?"

She followed him, intrigued as he led her to the small building toward the back of Raven's cage. He escorted her to the door, and she entered alone.

"David?"

She walked a small distance in, her eyes adjusting to the gloominess from the bright sun outside. A strange noise reverberated in the building, a low guttural growl. Samantha froze unable to source the sound. Were there cages in here? The growling seemed to move directly behind her. It was circling. Samantha could not move, too terrified to turn around.

"I thought you liked to be afraid."

She whipped around to see David standing there, looking dangerous. Samantha felt off balance. Adrenalin surged through her along with a delicious fear. It rippled through her, making her nipples taut with desire.

David did a slow appraisal up her body, noting her hard nipples and the slight tremor in her legs. Reaching her face, his dark gaze seemed to pin her to the spot.

"I thought you might like a closer view of our friends..." He pointed out the window.

Samantha turned. She felt David approach as she looked out. Her back tingled and legs trembled. Raven was still close to Lily and there was tension in the air. The animal seemed to circle now slowly.

David whispered, "He has been getting closer for the last couple days." He circled her as he spoke. "Maybe she does not know what it is that she wants, but all her instinct is crying out for him. And he hears her—and answers." Samantha backed up to the small railing a couple feet in front of the window inside. David followed. "Look."

Samantha looked outside, seeing Raven creep closer to Lily, then stop. David's breath was warm on her ear. "Panther males take their mates from behind. They stimulate their partner with a bone... inside their member." He pressed his erect cock against her. Samantha felt faint. "The female panther signals she is ready by laying on her haunches... her tail aside to allow him entrance. Are you ready for me, Samantha?"

She leaned back against him, wordlessly. David kissed her neck. Fingers stroked up her sensitive forearms, teasing her flesh. Her breath caught as his hands molded to her breasts, dipping under her shirt to feel her skin. Samantha groaned as his hand contacted her tight nipples.

David pulled the back of her skirt up, hooking his fingers on the top of her white lace panties and tugging them down to her thighs. His hand snaked around to the front to cup the heat of her mound. His fingers searched her slick wetness, rubbing her clit and biting her neck.

She dug her nails in his hand as it moved, moaning. David's fingers moved away, pushing suddenly into her tight flesh, moving his finger in and out as Samantha gasped to his rhythm. Feeling one finger, then two, three.

He knelt down at her feet, kissing the backs of her legs. His hands spread out, feeling her, sucking and licking at her flesh. Samantha gripped the rail to stay upright during his sensual assault. She felt his big hands turn her around. David quickly removed her panties entirely, positioning his head between her thighs.

Her legs rested on his shoulders with her back half over the railing. Samantha felt him explore her wetness with his tongue as she closed her eyes. She could feel the ridge of his nose against her sensitive flesh. Her clit was starting to throb. Blood was rushing in her ears.

David stopped abruptly, only to turn her toward the window, presenting her back to him. Samantha felt naked and exposed as he bent her body. She heard a rumble in his throat, the sound of his zipper. Felt the heat of his cock searching her wet folds, nudging against them, then surging in.

Samantha gasped at his full length. His hands gripped her hips as she pushed back against him. She was losing control. Samantha closed her eyes to the image outside the window of Raven approaching Lily, the sound of their calls as David bit her shoulder gently, moving strongly inside.

She closed out everything except his heat and smell, the sweet, sore stretching of her flesh to accommodate him. She dug her nails in his hands on the railing, pushing back to his movements. Samantha did not recognize the moans as her own. They sounded deeper and strange to her ears. She thought the sounds were from the panthers—mating at last.

♥

www.chloewaits.com

My Secret Beauty
© Jolie du Pré

[One]

My Razr's been blaring Madonna at least three times in the last hour. I can tell it's Christy by the Caller ID, and I know she won't leave me alone until I answer.

The girls are going to Sea Breeze tonight, and of course, I'm expected to join them. It's is one of the most popular bars in town, even though some people never get in. You have to stand in line, behind a rope, as if you were at some New York night club. You have to be attractive, and your clothes have to be the latest fashion.

"I've been trying to reach you, like, forever."

"I know."

"You know? Well then, why didn't you answer, dork?"

"I was cleaning my apartment."

"Whatever! Like you really clean."

Christy's right. I never clean. There's so much dust on some of my tables that I could write my name in it. "I don't think I can do the Breeze tonight."

"What? Are you serious? It's ladies' night! Free drinks!"

"I know, but..."

"No buts, and wear that green dress you bought. You look hot in that. We'll get you around ten."

She hangs up before I can say anything more.

When it's January in Chicago the air is so cold it rips through every inch of my body. Tonight, like most winter nights in the Windy City, all I want to do is relax inside my warm apartment. The only way going out is worth my time at all is because of Erika. She's so incredibly hot.

I've known Christy and Peggy for about ten years and Erika for three. From the moment I first laid eyes on Erika, she's been in my thoughts.

The day I met her, I was playing poker at Peggy's. I remember it because when Erika walked in, I looked at her and promptly lost my concentration.

"Well, what are you gonna do? Bet or what?" Christy had screamed.

"I fold." My heart was beating hard against my chest, and my brain seemed to go blank.

"Hey, girl! You're late," Peggy pulled a chair up to the table, right next to mine. "Ladies, this is Erika."

The first thing I noticed about Erika was her creamy brown skin. It doesn't matter how much I smooth my skin with oil and budget my sessions in the summer sun, I can never get it that shade of brown.

Erika is a mixture of many things, mostly African-American, but with some Irish, German, and Native American, too. I wonder what that's like, since I'm not such a kaleidoscope, just Irish and Polish.

"You smell good," Erika had said to me. I remember trying hard not to blush. It was bad enough that she was sitting right next to me. I could barely look her in the eyes.

"Yeah, I splashed some of my perfume on her," Peggy blurted. "She needed it."

Peggy is brash. Christy is all about Christy. But Erika is special. It's not just that I find her beautiful. She has a sweet, sensitive personality that always puts me at ease.

She's not as thin as me, Christy, or Peggy. She's always asking for diet advice, which Christy, who is as skinny as a flag pole, is happy to provide. I long to tell Erika that I'd love to drown in her womanly curves. But, of course, I can't say that. So, I keep my thoughts to myself and instead try to get her to appreciate her body.

None of the women I've been with measure up to what I want. Erika is what I want. But it's a secret, and it's got to stay that way.

* * * *

"Get your ass out here!" Peggy screams.

It's around ten at night. I'm wearing an old brown coat over my dress, but it's too short for this weather. I'm freezing. The cold wind hits my face and my legs as soon as I step outside.

Peggy has pulled up in her brand new, bright red Exhibition that she can't afford. Christy opens the door. She's in the front with Peggy. Erika sits in the back. I hurry back there with her. Like me, she's wearing a short coat that doesn't cover all of her legs. Our thighs touch.

"Hi everyone," I say to the group while looking at Erika.

Peg breaks my trance with her overly loud voice. "Hey, slut! Rocco's working tonight. He'll spill all over himself when he sees you in that dress!"

"It's a sexy dress, Monica," Erika says.

I smile. God, how I wish it were just her and me tonight.

Sea Breeze is lit up for a Friday. The line of people has already formed and winds around the building. Some people are jumping up and down, trying to stay warm. Others are huddling close. It doesn't matter how cold it is outside, people are willing to stand in line in hopes of getting in. Fortunately, the girls and I never wait.

We get out of the car, and Peggy hands the valet the keys. "Come on!" She saunters across the street like she's Paris Hilton. We follow close behind like a herd of sheep. She's always been the one to take the lead in the group. Maybe it's the fact that she's got fiery red hair and an attitude to match.

Sure enough, it's Rocco's shift. Peggy doesn't bother getting in line. Instead, she walks right up to Rocco.

"Dude! Let us in?"

"I was hoping you lovely ladies would be out tonight. Sure, come on inside."

We enter. It's dark. Everybody is dressed liked they're ready for the catwalk. We check our coats and walk up to the bar to get our drinks.

"I'll catch you guys in a minute. I need to visit the ladies room," Erika says.

"I'll come with you," I say, even though I don't need to go.

"Great. Come on. I've had to pee ever since I got in the truck."

Erika is wearing a short, tight blue dress that hugs her bottom. I'm staring at her ass as she walks in front of me. Nobody should have an ass like that. It's a crime for anything so round and luscious to be presented to the world.

The ladies room is empty, just me and Erika. "You like this bar?" I ask her while she's in the stall.

"Yeah, don't you?"

I lie. "Yeah, sure."

She comes out and leans over the sink to wash her hands. Her full breasts spill a little out of her low cut top.

"It's just that this place is such a meat market. I mean, is this really the right place to meet guys?"

"That's not really why I come here, Monica. It's just fun to go out with you girls, that's all."

She's smiling at me, and I smile back. I really want to spend some alone time with Erika, and it's come to the point where I need to do something to make it happen. I've never felt this kind of urgency before. Tonight, in this bathroom, I take the first step.

"You and I should go out sometime."

163

"Okay sure. Weekdays are bad with classes and stuff, but let's hook up some weekend. Cool?"

"Cool." I'll try to finalize a date later. I knew she'd say yes, but that's because she doesn't know what I'm up to. How do I expect to tell her that I'm attracted to her, and what makes me think that I can?

[Two]

It's a Saturday. The girls and I didn't meet last night because Peggy is sick. She informed all of us that we can't go out together again until she's better. I could care less, but it's interesting the control she has over us.

Today's the day I've decided to give Erika a call.

"Hi, Monica. How are you?"

"I'm good. Was wondering if you'd like to go to dinner tonight?"

"Sure, but I thought Peggy was sick?"

My heart sinks, but I'm determined to get what I want. "I thought you and I could just go."

There's a little bit of a pause, and my butterflies start to act up. I wonder what she's thinking.

"Okay, that sounds nice," she says, finally. "It'll just be you and me. Peggy would die if we all got together without her, anyway. Where do you want to meet?"

I feel like doing cartwheels. At the same time, I'm creaming at the thought that I'll be able to stare into her big, brown eyes and not have to compete for her attention. I try to think of some place cozy. "How about that Italian restaurant we pass on the way to the club?"

"Oh yeah, that place sounds perfect. I'll meet you there. Say around seven?"

"Great!"

* * * *

I sit in the back of the restaurant staring at the door, waiting for her to arrive. What do I expect out of this? She's straight. She doesn't have the slightest inclination that I'm a lesbian. Why should she? I've never given her any reason to think that. I've never told her that I've been on dates with women, kissed women, slept with women.

She opens the door and notices me right away. I rise and try to quash my enthusiasm.

"Hi!"

"Hey!" I give her a hug. Instead of sitting across from her, I wish I could squeeze in next to her. She pulls off her coat and sits down.

"I found a parking place right in front. Sure helps with it being so cold out!"

"Lucky you! I took a cab. Didn't feel like driving today."

"After our meal, I'll give you a lift home!"

"That would be nice, but you don't have to."

"It's no problem, hon. So, have you ever been here?"

"Been here once or twice. The food is really good."

"You and I have never met like this before. It's nice."

"Yes, very nice." I look down at the menu. I know that if I stare into her eyes for too long, I'm finished.

"I wish Peggy would get better so we can all go out again."

I try not to curl my lip, which is what I do when I'm sick of something. I look up from my menu. "Why do we listen to Peggy? If she blinks, we all jump. Don't you get tired of that?"

"Um... well... maybe."

I've never discussed Peggy in any sort of negative way, so of course Erika is confused. I don't want to talk about Peggy or Christy. I just want to be here with Erika.

"May I bring you ladies something to drink?" the waitress asks.

"A glass of white wine sounds really nice," Erika says.

"Yeah, make that two. Chardonnay?"

"Chardonnay sounds good."

The waitress looks at Erika. "May I see your ID please?"

She doesn't ask me. Erika has the fresh face of a teenager.

When the waitress leaves, I look at Erika. "Why don't we talk about you? How's school?"

"Oh, nursing school is horrible, but it's all starting to kick in. My grades have been good, and I'm certain I can get a job when I graduate. You? How's your job?"

"Same old shit. I live for the weekends." The light from the candle on the table gives her face a pleasant glow.

"Erika, I just have to tell you that I think you're really beautiful."

She smiles.

"I mean it. I really think you should have been a model."

"I'm too fat to be a model. You know that, Monica."

"I hate skinny women. On the other hand, I love a woman with curves."

She looks down at her menu. Suddenly, I feel awkward for having said what I said. But at the same time, I've wanted to say it for so long that I'm willing to take the risk.

"You know, I've been thinking that we all should try that new club on Clark. We always go to the same place; it might be nice to go somewhere new."

I take a deep breath. "My club hopping days may be coming to a close."

"Why? We have so much fun."

The waitress brings the wine. I take mine and drink half of it. Erika watches me with a look of amazement in her eyes, but doesn't say anything.

"Would you ladies like to order now?"

"No, we haven't decided yet, but in about ten minutes, you can bring me another glass of wine. Erika?"

She laughs. "No, let me finish this one first."

The waitress walks away. I down the rest of my wine. My courage is bolted.

"Erika, the reason I don't want to go to those clubs anymore is because I'm gay."

Erika spits the wine that she has in her mouth back into her glass. "What?"

"I'm a lesbian."

"There's no way in hell you're a lesbian. What about all those boyfriends you've had?"

I hate to think about those men or the fact that I slept with them in some hope that feeling a man on my body would change me in some way.

"If you notice, I haven't had a boyfriend in months, and when I go to the clubs now, I barely talk to guys."

Erika laughs. "You're not gay, Monica. I know you."

"No, Erika. You don't know me."

She takes another sip of her drink. Her eyes stare down at the menu again, but I can tell she's not really focusing on it.

"You're a lesbian?"

"Yes."

"How long have you been a lesbian?"

"All my life, I guess."

Erika looks at me. "Do you like me?"

I pause. "You mean, am I attracted to you?"

"Yes. That's what I mean."

"I am."

She shakes her head. "That's not good, Monica. That's not good at all."

She pulls ten dollars out of her purse, slaps it on the table, grabs her coat, and rushes out.

The waitress brings the other glass of wine. I drink it down and ask for another. It doesn't take long for me to start to feel like I'm losing control.

I motion for the waitress to bring me the bill, and then I call a cab. When it arrives, I stumble out of the restaurant. I'm so drunk that when I get to my place the cab driver has to help me take the money out of my wallet so that I can pay him. I manage to get inside, and then I run for the toilet and vomit the wine.

* * * *

The next morning, I'm lying in bed, topless. The bottoms that I wore last night are still on. My head feels like someone pounded it with a hammer. I stagger over to my purse and see if any money is left and if I have all of my credit cards and identification. Amazingly, I have about twenty bucks left and all my other stuff is still there. Then, I stagger back to bed and stare at the ceiling, thinking of Erika.

What was going to happen now? I'm sure she told Peggy and Christy about me.

I grab the covers and pull myself into a ball. There's no doubt in my mind that telling Erika was a huge mistake.

[Three]

Around mid-afternoon, I've managed to take a shower, but I feel so sick to my stomach that all I can do is sit on the couch and stare at the television. I'm supposed to feel good after doing this. That's what Robin told me. Robin is the woman I met at the health club. The first time I saw her she was wearing a gay pride t-shirt. That's how I knew she was a lesbian. Eventually we started chatting, just as friends.

She told me that when she came out, she felt like a huge weight was lifted off of her. But I don't feel that way at all. I don't even want to leave my apartment.

The doorbell rings. I don't want to see anybody, so I don't get up. Now there's a pounding.

"Monica! Open the fucking door. We know you're in there."

"We got food, and it's getting cold."

I've got a hangover. The last thing I want in my stomach is food. I can't even think about food. But I let them in.

"You look like shit!" Peggy says. She and Christy whisk past me and put the stuff on the table.

Christy plops down beside me and lights a cigarette. "So you're a dyke, huh?"

"Yeah, you freaked her the fuck out," Peggy laughs.

"You know how she is." Christy blows some smoke out of her mouth. "She takes everything seriously."

I feel myself sliding back into the closet. I just want to shake Christy and tell her just how serious I am. But having them here, stinking up my apartment with cheap food and cigarettes is something I don't want to lose.

"Erika's so easy," Christy continues. "She gets on the phone—'Oh, my God, you won't believe what happen to me. Monica says she's gay.' Blah, blah, blah. She believes everything."

I stare at the television, watching the movement on the screen. I want to cry, but I don't want the tears to come.

Peggy is looking at me now, and she's not laughing anymore. "You need to call her. Let her know it was just a joke."

Christy loves to lighten things up whenever Peggy starts to get serious about something. "You're a ho, not a dyke, Monica!"

I jump off the couch and almost knock over a lamp.

"Look, you guys! I'm gay. I'm very gay. All those men I slept with? They didn't mean shit to me. I didn't want any of them. And... I *like* Erika." There it is. My secret is out.

The two of them just look at me.

"Well she doesn't fucking like you, dyke!" Peggy screams.

For the first time I feel scared.

"Okay Peg! Calm down! Wait... are you a freakin' lesbian, for real, Monica?"

I look at Christy, but I don't say anything.

"She's serious." Peggy walks to the door. "Let's go Christy."

Before they leave, Peggy turns and gives me a look I've never seen before, no matter how worked up she's gotten about something in the past. "Leave Erika alone, do you understand?"

The door slams in my face.

[Four]

At work the next day, my cell phone doesn't ring. I usually get a call from at least one of them. Christy calls to gossip. Peggy calls to complain about her job. But today, silence. They've all gotten together and decided not to speak to me. It's obvious. For how long? I don't know. Maybe I've lost them forever.

I've been trying hard not to cry at work. Robin says I shouldn't be friends with people who can't tolerate gays. I know that. I know I shouldn't. But it still hurts to be ignored.

I look around at my co-workers. I've wanted to come out to them, too, but after the reaction I got from my friends, I don't dare risk it. I can't afford to create an unpleasant work environment for myself. I need this job.

After work I go home. My cell hasn't rung all day, except once, and that was from my mom. I still remember the look that Peggy gave me when she left my apartment.

I'll leave Erika alone. I'll leave everyone alone. The tears are welling up, and this time I can't stop them. Right now, all I want to do is leave Chicago and never come back, but I can't just pick up and go. If it were only that easy.

[Five]

About two weeks have passed. I haven't heard from any of the girls, and I haven't the courage to call any of them. It's gotten a little easier. But just a little. Tonight, there's a huge party downtown that we had all planned on attending, so I'm sure they're headed for that.

I've been watching a lot of television. More than I usually do. I guess that's all I can handle right now—mind numbing stuff to make me not think about them.

Sometimes I sit around and wish I were straight, and when I do that, I usually cry. I cry a lot.

As I'm watching television, my doorbell rings. It's got to be the girls. Despite everything that's happened, I rush to answer it.

I look through the peephole and my heart awakens in my chest. It's Erika.

"Can I come in?"

"Of course, come in."

Erika takes off her coat and sits on my couch.

"Would you like something to drink?"

"Water would be nice. Thanks."

I look like shit in sweatpants and a sweatshirt, but at least I've showered. I notice my hand is shaking as I'm filling her glass with water.

I take a seat next to her. She sips her water as we stare in silence at the TV.

Then she puts her glass down. "Monica, I'm really sorry about what Christy and Peggy are doing. I don't care that you're gay, and I feel horrible for letting them know what happened. I don't think it's right for them to shut you out. I've been very torn up about this."

"I'm sorry I did what I did."

"Don't be sorry. I'm sorry for the way I reacted."

"I don't want to lose your friendship, Erika. Let's just forget everything I said in the restaurant."

Erika grinned. "How do you suggest we do that?"

"Well..."

"Because I know you like me. I've known that for awhile."

I could feel myself go flush. "You know? How did you know?"

"I just had a feeling. I should have told you that in the restaurant instead of acting out the way I did."

"It's okay, Monica. Really, it is."

"No, let me finish. You see, back there in that restaurant, I wasn't prepared to face the fact that I could feel the same way about you."

My eyes grew wide. "You feel the same way about me?"

"I think so. What does that mean for you?"

It would be an understatement to say that I was at a complete loss for words.

"Does it mean you want to go to bed with me?" she continues.

Erika is not the kind of woman who says what's on her mind. She's often very shy, and I've always thought capable of being manipulated, especially when Peggy and Christy work on her. I never expected Erika to say what she was saying. It didn't seem real. But it *is* real. Of course, I want to sleep with her, but I didn't want her to think that's all I wanted.

"Erika, I'm not like that. We should get to know each other first."

She laughs. "Monica, I met you years ago. We already know each other. If you're going to take me to bed, then do it. I passed on that party to be here with you, so let's make a party of our own."

She jumps up and heads for my bedroom. There was nothing left for me to do but follow her. She plops on my bed face up. I stand over her, still amazed that this was happening.

"Are you going to kiss me now?"

I don't hesitate. "Yes."

I climb on top of her, and for the first time, my lips meet hers. She has the softest lips I have ever felt. I put my hands in her hair and slowly move them down to her shoulders. I feel her hands on my waist.

She smells like strawberries, the scent I had grown accustomed to ever since she bought that new perfume. The scent I want to inhale up close as I put my lips on her neck and kiss her skin. I hear her moan when I do that. I feel her hands grab my waist tighter.

She kisses me hard and slow. She wants it. There's no doubt in my mind about that.

I put my hand on her breast. I'm not afraid to do it.

She whispers in my ear, "You've always liked my breasts, haven't you?"

I'm sure my face is beet red as I gush in my panties. Here I am, with this beautiful woman who wants me as much as I want her.

She unzips her blouse and removes her shirt. I stare at her bra and the mounds of her creamy flesh. She brings her hands to the center of her bra and unclasps it, removing it completely, allowing her breasts to fall out.

My cunt can't be any wetter at this point. I drop my lips on her nipple, moving from one to the other, like I'm sex starved.

She pulls my face away from her breasts and kisses me again. She's breathless and topless. I want her naked.

I unzip her pants, pull them off, and throw them down by the side of the bed. Her panties are pink, outlined in maroon lace.

I stand up so that I can take off my sweatshirt and pants. I'm wearing nothing underneath. I never wear underwear when I'm hanging around the house.

Erika stares at my naked body and smiles a little, blushing at the same time.

I climb back on top of her and kiss long trails down her neck, on her chest, and down to her full breasts, and then further to her perfect navel.

"I'm ticklish," she laughs.

"Good! I like making you laugh."

"No... don't!"

"Okay, I'll stop."

I'm staring at her panties. I want to take them off, but I feel like I should ask her first. No need. She does it for me. She knows what I want to do.

She has this perfect little patch of black hair between her thighs.

"Open your legs for me," I whisper.

She does, closing her eyes and blushing again. Erika gets this look on her face when she's shy about something. She has it now. It turns me on.

I lean up to her and adjust the pillow under her head.

"Are you comfortable?"

"Yes." She closes her eyes.

I lower myself down and nuzzle my nose into her cunt. Her scent is enough to put me over the edge right there. My mind is willowing, because I can't believe I have my face in the woman I've been lusting after for three years, not to mention the fact that she tastes better than any woman I've ever had.

I look up at her. Her head is back, deep into the pillow. Her eyes are still closed. She has a lustful look on her face. It feels good for her, and I'm confident of that.

I lick her more, sucking her clit into my mouth as she grows increasingly wet.

"Oh...God, God."

"I'm not God. I'm Monica."

We both laugh as I dive into her more. She puts her hands in my hair.

"Mmm...keep doing that!"

I'm licking her clit as fast I can, loving every inch of her. She's wet. Really wet. Her juices leave a spot on the sheet.

The more vocal she gets, the faster I lick. She grabs a fistful of my hair, pushes my face into her, and opens her legs even wider.

After Erika comes, she lies very still. I move up to her, lay down by her side, and put my arms around her. She moves in to me, and I feel better than I have in my entire life.

"I love you, Monica."

She loves me. And I love her. Of course, I do. We've known each other for years.

"I love you, too, Erika."

Later we make love some more. She kisses my lips, caresses my nipples, but she's a little hesitant to do more than that, at least not yet. I'm not offended. I've had the best night of my life, and we've got plenty of time.

[Six]

Around midnight, we're starving. I don't have much in my apartment, so we decide to make a run to the store. Junk food, pop, all sorts of stuff that we don't really need, but want.

I'm strutting down the street like a rooster, because I've got the girl of my dreams by my side. She grabs my arm sometimes, but doesn't hold my hand. Once again, I'm not offended. Erika's never been with a woman, and even I am not at the point where I'm brave enough to walk down the street holding a woman's hand, anyway.

"So what do you want?" she asks, as we enter the store.

"Barbecue chips."

"Yuck! I want plain."

"We'll get both and some soda, too."

"Diet?"

"Yeah, cool, sweetie. Diet. This stuff is my treat, okay?"

"No, Monica. I'll help pay."

"No woman of mine is paying tonight."

"Oh... I'm your woman?"

"Tonight you are."

"I can live with that."

The biggest smile *ever* appears on my face.

Then, after we pay, just as we're about to leave, the door opens and in walk Christy and Peggy. I can't believe it. We all visit this store a lot, but why did they have to come in tonight?

Erika had been holding my arm, but she let go as soon as she saw them. Christy and Peggy walk up to Erika, acting like I'm not in the room.

"What are you doing here?" Christy asks. "I thought you had to study? That's why you didn't come out with us."

"I thought I'd visit Monica tonight." Erika's voice is low.

"Believe it or not, the party was lame. So a bunch of people are coming over to my place. Kevin will be there. Remember that guy you met? He asked about you.

"Thanks, but not tonight."

"What? Didn't you hear me? Kevin will be there."

"Maybe she doesn't want Kevin. Maybe she wants Monica." The glare on Peggy's face is as sharp as it was the last time I saw her.

"Peggy, please. Monica, let's go." Erika rushes out, and I follow her.

"Don't ever call us again, you dykes!" Peggy screams.

"We won't," Erika yells back.

In the dark, we walk a few blocks in silence.

"That was a nice thing you did back there. Are you okay?"

"I'm fine, actually," she says. She takes a deep breath and seems to stand taller. "I've been getting tired of them for a while now."

We don't say anything, just walk to my apartment. I put the key in the lock, but before I open it, she gives me a kiss on my cheek.

"With all this junk food your woman would like to get a real breakfast tomorrow, okay?"

I laugh. "Of course!"

♥

joliedupre.com

Unchained Heart
© Jae Knight

New Orleans, Louisiana, March of 2001

In what other city besides New Orleans could you expect to see a Goth band fronted by a vampire? None came to Marty's mind.

She stared at the newspaper spread out before her on her kitchen table. She drummed her crimson-painted fingernails on the glass surface and bit her lip, wondering. Marty had attended two of Symphonic Dream's concerts. Their music was lovely, as was their guitar player—Cameron Mayhem—who was six feet and six inches of solidly-muscled, dark-skinned, alpha-male deliciousness.

There she sat, staring at an ad in the paper for a new bassist and back-up female vocalist. Marty could sing. She could play the bass guitar. And she was female. Check, check, and check.

The other vampire, their previous bassist, was apparently no longer with the band. If the lead singer—Vallon Paige—was a vampire, and the ex-bassist—Korinna—was a vampire, why *wouldn't* they let her join their band? Provided, of course, they liked her skill enough.

Still, a part of her balked at the idea of making herself so visible to a crowd, to the human fans that flocked to see Symphonic Dream at every gig around town. Hadn't she suffered enough rejection in her life to satisfy her masochistic side? Apparently not, for Marty could already feel steely resolve straightening her spine. That position was going to be hers.

The man named Cameron would be, too... or so she hoped.

* * * *

"How many band members are we going to go through before the year is out?" Adam Zanders huffed in frustration as yet another hopeful left the room. The auditions for the next female backing vocalist and bassist for Symphonic Dream drug on.

"I've got a good feeling about this, Adam. I think once we find the right woman, we'll have a band member for life," Cameron answered. He ran a large hand over his smooth, shaved head. He, too, was feeling the strain. The auditions had been going for two hours already.

Adam raised a brow at his friend. Usually Adam himself was accredited the description of positive and always smiling. But after Azure had been murdered and Korinna had left the band inexplicably a couple months prior, Adam's upbeat attitude had taken a beating.

For Cameron Mayhem to be the voice of optimism was downright stunning. For as long as he'd known the man, Cameron had possessed a serious and quiet demeanor, almost to the point of being funereal. It was touching that Cameron tried to boost his band mate's confidence, especially as it was so rare.

Not that Adam would ever admit it.

Adam watched as his friend's dark and handsome face lit in surprise, and perhaps even lust, as the next tryout walked in. At first Adam only heard her heels tapping the concrete floor of the back room of the tattoo parlor that the band's lead singer owned, but as his head turned to greet the newcomer, his breath left his lungs, too.

She was fair skinned and quite tall, although not as tall as Korinna had been, and dressed in low-rise jeans with a black tank top. She carried a black leather guitar case slung over one shoulder. Her dark brown hair reached just past her shoulders, sleek and shiny in the overhead fluorescent lighting. The eyes that glittered at them as she smiled were the most striking sky blue either man had ever seen.

Cameron cleared his throat and cleverly disguised his face into an expression of relaxed concentration and polite interest.

"What is your name?" Adam asked, as he was the primary 'interrogator' at this audition.

"Martina Cassidy, but I prefer to go by Marty, if you don't mind," she answered and gave them a winning smile, made all the more lovely by the adorable Monroe piercing she had. Adam saw Cameron shifting uncomfortably in his seat beside him.

"It's a pleasure to meet you, Marty. Whenever you are ready..." Cameron prompted, and Adam's jaw fell open in shock. Marty was the first girl Cameron had spoken to all day.

Marty murmured her thanks and set her guitar case on the floor. She pulled out a hot pink bass guitar and set its pink leopard-print strap gingerly around her long, slender neck. She bent over to hook it up into the amp and a smile crept across Cameron's face.

Her eyes focused on Cameron as she strummed a few experimental chords and then parted her lips to let loose a voice that raised chills on Cameron's strong, tattooed arms. He didn't know what song she sang but he knew it was the most beautiful he'd heard. Was it because the song reached his soul or merely the fact that it came from her? Cameron couldn't say.

"Love will set you free and lift you up out of the darkness once you let it inside. These chains around my heart have at last been broken. Never say that love is impossible for it has even found its way to me," she sang, her gaze never leaving Cameron's own chocolate brown eyes.

When she finished, no one spoke. It was as if she had woven a spell. A spell with which she had Cameron fully ensnared.

"Wow. That was great. We'll call you if..." Adam started but Cameron cut him off with a gruff response, "The position is yours."

Marty laughed and flashed that engaging smile of hers.

"What was that song you sang?" Adam asked, hiding the frown that pulled at his mouth from Cameron's hasty decision.

"It is called 'Unchained Heart.' I wrote it when I was fifteen and decided to perform it here for you guys on a whim. Now I am glad I did," she answered with a laugh.

"Adam, why don't you go let the others know that try-outs are over?" Cameron asked him, and Adam decided not to argue. It was plain his friend wanted to be alone with the new bassist.

* * * *

Marty put her guitar back in its case as Adam left them. She bit her lower lip as she thought of how she could make an excuse to hang back with the man with the deep, velvet voice that had sent shivers all over her body and turned her insides to jelly.

Marty snapped the case shut and rose slowly to her full height as she heard him rise from his seat and step softly toward her. When she turned she could see his gaze whip dutifully back to a clipboard he held in his hands.

"If you could leave us your information so we can contact you about practices..." he began awkwardly, and took a deep breath. She almost laughed at the expression in his dark eyes that said he wanted to kick himself.

"Oh, of course," she replied, taking the clipboard from his hands. He had strong, long-fingered hands that she suddenly envisioned on her skin, running over her breasts and down her hips to grasp her buttocks. Marty bit back a moan. Her mouth went dry.

"So, uh... I didn't catch your names," she stammered as she handed the clipboard back to him.

"The redhead is Adam Zanders, drums. I play the lead guitar. The name is Cameron 'Mayhem' Lucas," he answered with a bone-melting smile and extended his hand, his delectable hand, in greeting. She grasped it in her much smaller one and almost sighed as his warm fingers closed over her own.

He was so tall. His shoulders were wide and bared to her by his black tank top, so like the one she wore but filled out with rock hard muscle instead of her smallish breasts. He wore black jeans covering long legs and big, black combat boots. God, he was amazing. Intimidating, perhaps, to some, but irresistible to Marty.

The mocha-toned skin of his arms was covered in tattoos to the wrists with tribal designs, and she could imagine those arms holding her. She flicked her eyes away from his in hopes he would not be able to read the thoughts swimming in her head.

"About that song," Cameron began, and Marty smiled.

"I wrote that after I was adopted when I was fifteen. I spent many years of my childhood being moved from one foster house to another. But my parents adopted me and showed me what it was to be loved, and this song was a result of that new feeling. Did you like it?"

"Yes, I did. Perhaps sometime you'll play the song for our lead singer, Vallon. We might like to perform it, if that's okay with you," he told her while he awkwardly held the clipboard as if he knew nothing else he should be doing with his hands.

"Really? That'd be great. I've never performed it for anyone but my parents before. I'm flattered that you think it is good enough for a live audience," she told him, then cleared her throat.

What else is there to say? she wondered. She was used to getting a little flustered around attractive men but never like this. Cameron turned from her, striding with his long-legged gait back to the table where he and Adam had sat. He set the clipboard down and leaned his hip against the table.

"Perhaps you would let me take you to dinner or out for drinks sometime?" he asked, and Marty almost dropped her guitar case. Marty thought he must have misread her surprise, and he hastily added, "Now that we are band mates, we should all get to know one another."

Now or never, Marty. Go for it.

"Or we could go alone. Just the two of us," she said, surprised at her own audacity.

Cameron smiled widely at her, and his warm, chocolate-hued eyes caused her breath to catch in her throat. She returned his smile, hoping to let him know with that one look that she was interested. The ball was in his court now, so to speak.

"Alright. I'd like that. I know a good place to eat. My uncle owns a restaurant. They serve barbeque, seafood, and good old-fashioned Southern soul and comfort food as well," he suggested.

"Sounds perfect, Cameron. Give me a call sometime this week. I'll be looking forward to hearing from you," she told him as she walked up to him. She shook his hand and felt a little ridiculous doing so, but she couldn't do what she really wanted to do and kiss the man.

Not yet, at least.

* * * *

Two days later, Marty ran naked from her bathroom, dripping wet, into the living room of her small apartment to answer the phone.

"Hello?" she asked somewhat breathlessly.

"Hey, it's Cameron. I was wondering if you'd like to meet me at the tattoo parlor on Friday around seven o'clock, and we'll go to dinner."

His deep velvet voice sent shivers all over her damp body. Belatedly, she realized she was soaking her carpet but couldn't summon concern about it. "Yeah, sure. Sounds great," Marty answered and wondered why she couldn't manage to sound cooler.

"Great. I'll see you then?" he asked.

"Yeah, for sure," she said, slapping her forehead in frustration as she said goodbye, hoping he hadn't heard that loud, wet slap.

* * * *

Friday came, and Cameron waited outside the tattoo parlor, Under the Gun Tattoo. He looked at his watch for the fiftieth time and wished he hadn't headed out so early. He'd already been there a half an hour and there was still a good ten minutes until she was due.

"Still waiting?" Lily asked, and he about jumped out of his skin. Lily was Vallon's wife and Symphonic Dream's new manager, and he hadn't heard her come out of the parlor.

"Yes. I arrived too early," he answered and felt his cheeks heat.

Lily smiled, her golden eyes alight. "She must be quite a girl to have you blushing like that, Cameron Mayhem. Don't be embarrassed. Vallon's blushed a time or two, as well," Lily confided, and he laughed a little.

It seemed to Cameron that he and his friend had more in common than he had originally thought. Vallon had never made a fool of himself over a woman, either. Not until Lily. What could that mean for Cameron? Was he drawn to Marty because she was beautiful, or for something deeper?

He found a part of himself desperately wishing that there was more to his attraction to her. He wasn't immune to the love he saw between Vallon and Lily and between Vallon's employees, Loki and Marlena Hartwick.

Cameron wanted that, too... someday.

"I'm going to head back inside. She'll probably be on her way any minute now," Lily told him with an indescribable look upon her face.

He hoped she was right. He watched her walk back into the parlor and pull Vallon aside, and he wondered what she whispered to him as he watched his friend's dark brows draw together in a concerned frown.

A minute later, Marty came into view. Her dark brown hair was twisted up in a messy knot, and she wore a simple, black halter dress and black stilettos. She wore no jewelry, and he doubted she would ever need any, for her beauty shone through without the added glitter of cut stones or precious metals.

"You look beautiful," he whispered.

Marty shyly smiled and gave a little pirouette, the skirt of her dress billowing out and giving him a teasing glimpse of shapely thighs. "So where are we going to eat? Your uncle's restaurant?" Marty asked him and linked her arm with his.

"Yes. My Uncle Jimmy's restaurant is down on North St. Peter's Street near the French Market. It's called Jimmy's Southern Soul and Seafood, and they have great food there. Wait until you try it," Cameron answered in a flustered rush and led her to where he had parked his car. It was an old black Caddy that had belonged to his mother before she went into rehab. Again.

* * * *

Marty smiled as he opened the door for her. She scrambled in as gracefully as she could, but she strongly suspected she may have flashed a little too much thigh by first date standards. Not that she cared overly much. This man could look as much as he wanted.

Marty asked him about the menu even though she knew she could read it when they arrived at his uncle's restaurant. Mainly, she just wanted to listen to that voice.

"...lobster, shrimp, crab, and prawn. Any kind of fish you can think of, really Uncle Jimmy barbeques steaks, ribs, hamburgers, bratwursts. There's fried chicken, fried catfish, and fried green tomatoes. You can get just about anything fried there. My uncle believes any food can be improved just by deep frying it, and he proudly states that he has the gut to prove it." He listed a few more of the items on the menu.

Her stomach growled loudly.

"Am I making you hungry?" Cameron asked, and he looked over at her with an amused grin.

"Very much so," she answered, and she didn't mean just for food. Marty stared at thick thighs filling out the soft-looking black leather of his pants. She bit her lip to stifle a moan as she noticed the outlines of a rock-hard six-pack under his snug-fitting T-shirt.

"Well, here it is. Don't let the humble appearance fool you. I'd lay money on the line you'll never taste ribs like they have here," he told her as they both got out of the car. It was a rather simple looking building, painted white with bright blue shutters. It looked more like a cozy cottage than a restaurant.

"Hey, Cameron, my boy! What brings you out here tonight? You smell the barbeque on the wind?" his uncle asked him from the front porch of the restaurant where he sat in a weathered rocking chair with a glass of iced tea in one hand and a cigarette in the other. He resembled Cameron but older and with graying hair. He had a thick mustache and wore wire-framed glasses.

"I followed it home. This is Marty Cassidy, Uncle Jim.

COMING TOGETHER: AT LAST

Marty, this is my uncle, James Lucas," Cameron introduced as they climbed up the creaking porch steps and stood before his uncle.

James 'Jimmy' Lucas stubbed out his cigarette and stood to his full height, only being slightly shorter than Cameron. He clasped Marty's hand warmly and gave her a wide smile.

"Nice to meet you, young lady. Cameron been telling you about my food? I know he can't stop once he gets going. Grew up on this food, he did."

"He has indeed been telling me about the food, but in all fairness I did ask."

Her stomach growled again, and Jimmy Lucas laughed, gesturing to the front door. "Y'all head on inside and order. I'm due in the back. Ribs should be about done by now."

The interior instantly gave her a feeling of home. The atmosphere was very casual, very down to earth, and filled with the smells of home cooking. There were wooden tables all around with red and white checkered tablecloths. The pictures on the walls, she assumed, were photos of family and friends. There were a few notable jazz and blues musicians, as well. A small stage was tucked into the corner where there sat five wooden stools and an upright piano.

"They have live bands every once in a while. A lot of jazz and zydeco. My uncle likes to sing the blues on some nights," Cameron explained.

"Maybe we could come back up here some night to hear?" Marty asked and swung her gaze around from the stage to his face. She could see the pleasant surprise on his face.

"I'd like that, Marty."

"Cameron, come on and sit over here. I'll take care of you tonight."

"Hey, Leda, how are you tonight?" Cameron asked as

she waved him over to an empty table near the kitchen doors. It seemed a dangerous place to sit as they were sure to be tormented by the smells wafting out of the kitchen every time someone opened the door.

"I'm doing well. Working my butt off. Like always. You see Dad yet?" she asked. Marty took a moment while Cameron and Leda talked to observe the woman. She was gorgeous with her smooth, caramel-toned skin and golden brown eyes. Her hair fell in long, tiny braids to her waist, and she wore slender gold hoop earrings.

Leda balanced a tray of appetizers on her curvaceous hip and gestured wildly with her free hand while she talked.

"Well, I have to get these wings over to table three. I'll be back in a minute to take your order when you are ready," she told him and was off with her tray of hot wings.

"That was my uncle's daughter, Leda. She's working her way through college right now. She wants to be a nurse," Cameron explained and pulled out a seat for Marty.

"She's very lovely," Marty answered as Cameron took the seat across from her.

"Okay, I'm back. Well, excuse my manners. You have a guest. Hi, honey. I'm Leda, Cameron's cousin. Would you like a menu?" Leda said, and as she talked with her hands, the gold bangles on her wrists tinkled prettily, accenting the jazz that spilled from the jukebox.

"Nice to meet you, Leda. My name's Marty, and yes, I would like to see a menu—although I have a pretty good idea already of what I want." She couldn't get over what a nice family Cameron had. Of course, she had good family now, too, but it had taken fifteen years.

"I'll give you a minute to go over the menu." Leda went over to another table where a group of old men flirted good-naturedly with her.

"Do your parents work here as well?" Marty asked as

she idly scanned the menu.

"Um, no, they don't actually. My mother used to but..." he trailed off, and she looked up into his eyes and immediately knew that somehow she had just managed to ask the worst possible question.

"I'm sorry, Cameron. You don't have to answer..." she started to tell him, but then he smiled at her.

"It's okay, really. My mother is in rehab, and my father was never a part of my life. My uncle and his wife pretty much raised me. My mother would go off for days or even weeks at a time. We never really knew where. I was a parent figure to her more than she ever was to me. At least I was whenever she was actually around. Don't be sorry you asked, Marty," Cameron reassured her, and she smiled weakly back at him.

Maybe I can go out back and put myself on the barbeque pit, or maybe go hang out for a while in the freezer? How could I have asked him that? But at the same time, it was reassuring to know that his childhood hadn't been perfect, either. Marty felt closer to Cameron having learned all that.

"I can relate in a way, you know. My mother died when I was little, and my father—Ben—is in and out of jail for stealing and breaking into people's homes. Even once or twice for armed assault. Foster families really are nice people, but sometimes something just doesn't work out or they already have kids that ended up hating me. But all that is behind me now. My adoptive parents are the best. My dad's name is Bryce Cassidy, and my mom's is Hope.

"They never had any children. They were unable. So they adopted me," she told him, surprised at how easy the words came. It was not a story she trusted many people with. If you tell someone your dad is in jail, they look at you like you might pull a gun on them or try to steal their purse or wallet. Not to mention that her adoptive parents were actually changeling vampires, and they adopted Marty when she was seven-and-a-half and already as grown as a human fifteen-year-old. Not that he'd be hearing *that* from her at the moment.

Cameron just looked at her for a full minute and she felt as if her lungs were being compressed.

"I've never had anyone to 'relate' to, Marty. Thank you for being so honest with me. My mother—her name is Caroline—is in rehab for perhaps the twentieth time. She keeps saying she wants to get better, but then she relapses and picks up another bottle. Caroline couldn't pay for her apartment or her car. The car belongs to me now, and the apartment belongs to a new family.

"I don't know where she'll go when she gets out again, but I can't keep bringing her back into my life. I've lived this life for so long already. I'm tired of it. I want to live *my* life on *my* terms," he told her, and she reached across the table for his hand.

She heard his intake of breath, and then his other hand came to rest over hers. Cameron smiled and leaned over the table toward her. Marty leaned in to meet him, and as his soft lips brushed across her own, it felt as if sparks shot from the nerve ending in her lips straight down to her toes. Her free hand cupped his face, and she deeply inhaled the scent of his cologne.

Her tongue met his as she parted her lips for him. Marty sighed and deepened the kiss. She couldn't help herself. This was the most beautiful kiss she had ever experienced.

"Oh, excuse me. I'll just come back in five." They heard Leda's low murmur, and they laughed while they gazed into each others' eyes.

* * * *

"Those was the best ribs I have ever had! I was a bit worried about ordering them, to be honest. I didn't want to be covered in barbeque sauce on our first date, but that meat comes right off the bone," Marty exclaimed as she sat back in her seat and took a long sip of her cold beer.

"I was hoping I'd hear those words," Jimmy laughed from the kitchen.

"Best ever! If I had a blue ribbon, it'd be yours," Marty joked, and he came out of the kitchen laughing and wiping his hands on a towel.

"Cameron, you be sure to bring her back. There's more on that menu than ribs, and my wife makes the best cakes you will ever taste for dessert. Room for it?" he asked, and she shook her head.

He laughed again and clapped Cameron on the back, nodding to him. Cameron knew his uncle liked Marty at that moment, and he was glad for it. He liked her, too. If 'like' was an appropriate word for what he felt for Marty. She followed him back out of the restaurant and to his waiting car with a happy smile on her lovely face.

How could it be that she was a musician, loved good food, had gotten on well with his family, and could even understand the childhood he had had? Marty seemed too good to be true.

Is it just my imagination or did her smile just slip a little? Cameron wondered. He opened the door for her and watched her climb inside. Once Cameron was in the car as well, he asked her, "Is there any place else you would like to go? I can take you home if you want."

Marty felt tears prick her eyes but fiercely blinked them back. She couldn't let him see her like this. But how could she explain to him who she really was? *What* she really was? When she had walked into that audition, Marty hadn't expected to fall so hard for Cameron. She had not expected to find the one man that would make her heart beat faster and make her future look brighter.

"I'd like to come by your place, if that's okay," she told

him.

Cameron's couldn't believe his ears. Then he blinked and covered his surprise with a his most beguiling smile.

"As you wish."

* * * *

While Cameron was in his kitchen making her a drink, Marty took the time alone to look around his living room. There were no pictures she could see of the woman named Caroline, his mother. But there were plenty of Jimmy and a woman who must've been his wife and, of course, Leda.

There were a few of his band, as well. Now also her band. The band she had heard was fronted by a vampire. She jumped a little when she heard Cameron's phone ring.

As she waited for his conversation to end, Marty continued to look around the living room. It was definitely a bachelor pad. The furniture was black leather. There was a huge, flat screen television and an entertainment center filled to bursting with all kinds of electronics any guy would lust after.

A few minutes later, Cameron joined her with two glasses in his hands.

"That was Vallon. He figured we could all get together tomorrow evening to get acquainted. Are you game?" he asked her handing her one of the drinks.

She took an experimental sip and licked her lips. "Not bad. I think I like Southern Comfort and Coke. Yes, I would definitely be up for it. I'm eager to meet Vallon," she answered and took another sip from her glass.

"He can't wait to meet you either. Symphonic Dream has had it pretty rough lately," Cameron told her and took a seat upon the black leather couch. She sat beside him.

"First out, bassist and backing vocalist, Azure, is killed. God rest her soul. We finally find another to replace her but she inexplicably leaves New Orleans, and we were left without a bassist again. We were growing quite popular around here, and Azure's death was a hard blow to us," he continued, and Marty could guess that he was hoping she would not abandon the band as the woman before her had done.

"I've lived in New Orleans all of my life. I have no plans to leave. I love music and always have. I'd like to think I'm in it for the long haul," she told him, and Cameron nodded approvingly to her. He set his glass on the glass-topped coffee table, and Marty followed suit.

She sighed as his lips pressed softly against hers. Her mouth parted on a gentle moan as his tongue traced her lips, begging her to let him inside. Marty followed Cameron's lead. His mouth tasted sweet from the SoCo and Coke.

Marty's hands came up to grip his wide, hard shoulders and guided his body closer to hers. He leaned over her, pressing her back into the soft, leathery cushions. As he settled his hips between her legs, Marty's breath caught and her heart skipped a beat. Marty let go of Cameron long enough to untie the knot behind her neck and to peel the top from her breasts.

As the cool air struck her bared flesh, her nipples hardened, and Cameron's eyes devoured her.

"You are so beautiful," he whispered, and she felt beautiful—for the very first time—reflected in his dark and sensual eyes. His impressive arousal bulged at the front of his leather pants, and Marty's fingers raced to free it from confinement. When his cock sprang forth, Marty's eyes widened.

Cameron laughed and then dipped his head down to her breasts. Marty's eyes rolled back as the pleasure slammed into her. His tongue stroked her like velvet, and the heat of his breath raised chills all over her skin. He gave her a devilish smile and plucked an ice cube from his glass.

"Oh," was all she could say before he idly traced the melting cube over and around her nipples then replaced it with his burning lips and tongue. The torture was exquisite, teasing until the cube was nothing more but chilly rivulets trickling down her ribcage and onto the sofa.

Cameron peeled his shirt off and flung it onto the floor. The shirt was followed by the leather pants, his large black boots, Marty's stiletto heels, and her slinky dress. All that remained between them was a tiny scrap of cloth, her turquoise silk thong.

That piece of material seemed to fascinate Cameron, as he stared with a hungry expression and licked his lips in anticipation. His hands found the thin straps and slid them slowly over her hips and down her legs. He gently raised one of her legs and planted a kiss on her calf before dropping the thong on the floor with the rest of their shed clothing.

Cameron's lips teased a white hot trail of kisses and nibbles up her leg to her thigh. She held her breath as he hesitated, then she let loose a small scream of ecstasy when his tongue swirled over the sensitive folds of her sex. She bit her lip as one, and then two, long fingers entered her and started a devastating rhythm with his expert tongue.

Tendrils of white hot pleasure coiled in her belly, making Marty nearly mindless in her passion. He laughed huskily as her breath slammed out of her in harsh pants.

Her breasts bounced and her body quaked from the building pressure inside her, finally bursting as she came with a series of loud moans. Marty's hips jerked as Cameron planted one last kiss upon her throbbing clit.

Once Marty had gained enough of her senses back, she took control and gently pushed Cameron back into the soft leather of the couch. She had him sitting up so she could straddle him. Cameron let out a groan as Marty lowered herself onto him.

Marty bit her lip, feeling herself stretched to take him. She paused once she had him buried to the hilt within her.

* * * *

Cameron closed his eyes and took a few steadying breaths as the slick muscles surrounding his hard flesh throbbed rhythmically. He chanced a look at her face and sighed. Her head was tilted back, mouth parting on a soft moan. Marty's eyes flickered open and gazed deep into his own. It was as if Marty was looking deep inside him, and he prayed she liked what she saw.

Cameron's large hands settled on her rounded hips, and he lifted her—slowly—up and down. His cock burrowed in and out of her moist heat, and her thighs quivered against his. He watched through lowered lids as she leaned back, bracing her hands on his knees, pushing her breasts outward. Marty was beautiful.

Her hips undulated in a hypnotic dance, and he could feel his orgasm building. Cameron's heart was pounding, his blood rushing. How could one woman hold so much power over him?

Marty's lips parted as she cried out her release a second time. Cameron joined her with a low moan, and she collapsed against him. She lay there against his heaving chest, satiated and relaxed. His arms came around her, holding her against him like something precious. A small smile curled her lips.

Cameron lifted Marty as he stood and carried her into his bedroom. She smiled sleepily at him as he eased her onto the large, comfy bed. She turned into his embrace as he settled in next to her.

* * * *

Marty came wide awake an hour before dawn broke. She bit back a curse as she realized her large wings were cradling them both in a warm cocoon. How could she have allowed herself to sleep? The power it took to maintain a perfect human glamour while awake was hard enough, and near impossible in sleep.

She gently extricated herself from Cameron's arms and tip-toed into the living room to get dressed. Her clothes were still in a heap on the floor where they had been left. Her wings were once more hidden from human eyes as she pulled on her dress.

Should I leave a note? He might wonder why I left so early. Marty looked around for paper but couldn't see any, and she wasn't about to rummage through his things.

With a shrug, she was out the door and on her way home. She could feel that people were beginning to stir and awaken from their sleep. Some were already up and ready for a day's work. One was even out on the street with her. She could hear footsteps behind her.

A chill crawled up her spine, and she burst into a run, faster than any mortal would be able to follow, much less see. She heard the gun shot not a moment later and knew her instinct to run had been correct. Who wanted her dead and why?

Marty Cassidy had always been careful about masking her appearance. None of her foster families had even known that they were housing a Halfling demon, although they had often realized that Marty was somehow different. Who could know? Her parents knew that she was Halfling but they themselves were Changeling vampires and would never tell anyone that couldn't be trusted with the information.

Had she slipped somewhere along the line? That thought taunted her as she reached her apartment and let herself in. Perhaps she was getting careless. For so long she'd had nothing to worry about. Her family knew what she was and accepted it. She was free to be herself with them. Had she become too comfortable in that knowledge?

Marty sat on her couch and put her head into her

COMING TOGETHER: AT LAST

hands. What if they knew where she lived? Knew that she was now in a band? She was exposed and did not have a single idea who could be behind this.

What about Cameron? The shooter must have been waiting for her! It was too late to go back now and warn him, look after him. The sun's first rays were already reaching across the sky. She reached for her phone but hesitated.

There was no reason to suspect Cameron was in any immediate danger. The shooter had come after her, not him... or them. If Cameron was a target, the shooter would have stayed behind. Even if she did call Cameron, what would he say in answer to her dire predictions? He wasn't familiar with her world or the beings in it.

Despite the fact she had met him mere days ago, she cared deeply for the human male. Perhaps she even loved him.

Love Cameron? It's too soon but... yes, I do. I love Cameron Lucas.

Cameron was all the things she looked for in a mate: strong, understanding, sincere, and thoughtful. The list of his wonderful qualities could go on forever, and the last thing she wanted to do was jeopardize their budding relationship. She could easily lose him forever.

Marty then thought about calling her parents, but what good would it do to worry them? It could have been a random criminal, hoping to gun her down and take her money. Sure, the shooter was now aware there was something unnatural about her—what with the way she, to all appearances, disappeared into thin air—but they would likely never cross paths again. New Orleans was a large city after all.

In the end, she decided to go ahead and call Cameron. Marty left a nonchalant message saying that she had to leave early in order to get ready for work. A small but necessary lie. She told Cameron that he should call her after he got her message. Then she would know for sure he was alright.

* * * *

Marty nervously checked her appearance in the mirror. It was now evening. The shooter was far from her mind, as she'd convinced herself the man hadn't known her nature, couldn't *possibly* know it, and hadn't been trying to assassinate her because she was a Halfling.

Now, her only concern was making a good impression on the band's lead singer and the band's manager, whom she was meeting with tonight. Cameron was dropping by her apartment to pick her up. His knock sounded as she finished that thought.

She greeted him with a kiss.

"Hello, gorgeous. Are you ready to go?" he asked her and she nodded, smoothing her skirt with her shaky hands. She had worn a black halter top and a peacock blue peasant skirt. She wanted to look nice and make a good impression. Especially since she not only needed Vallon's approval as a band member but also as a Halfling demon dating his best friend.

Now that she had Cameron, she was wondering if it was a good idea to meet Vallon Paige. Vallon would know what she was, she was certain of that. There was no way she could hide it; not when she had already made up her mind to be honest about it. He could very well remove her from the band and see her as a threat to Cameron.

She kept her smile firmly in place for Cameron even though her heart pounded with fear.

Would he say something to Cameron? Did Cameron even know Vallon was a vampire? she wondered as she and Cameron rode in silence to Under the Gun Tattoo. His eyes kept flicking her way, and she realized he knew something was up.

"I'm just nervous," she told him with a laugh, and he smiled, relieved. Marty crept into his mind, feeling like a thief indeed. Cameron had thought she was having second thoughts or regrets about him, about what they had done last night. She turned to look out the window to hide the big grin that crept across her face as she could plainly see he cared for her, too.

Falling hard for her, to be exact. Cameron was stunned and confused by the realization. He had never been one to buy into the whole love-at-first-sight deal, but it was quickly becoming apparent that it was possible after all, and he was victim to it.

Cameron parked not far from the tattoo parlor and turned to Marty.

"Ready?" he asked, and Marty nodded, taking a deep breath. More than just her fate with the band depended upon this meeting. They could easily take Cameron away from her.

The tattoo parlor came into view too soon, and she was stepping through its door once more, this time for a different kind of audition. This one would be for her right to pursue Cameron, and she wouldn't give him up that easily. If mascara and eyeliner were war paint, then she was ready for battle.

Vallon and the band's manager, Lily, another Changeling vampire much to Marty's surprise, stood side by side and extended their hands to her. She shook their hands, smiled and exchanged greetings. Their eyes were knowing but their talk remained mundane with Cameron present.

"Cameron, I believe Adam wanted to speak with you. He's upstairs. We'd like to talk more with Marty though," Vallon said, and Marty took a deep breath.

This was it.

Cameron kissed Marty on the cheek, much to the

surprise of his friends, and left the shop to go around back and upstairs to the apartment above.

"Let's just cut to the chase. You know what we are, and we know what you are. My only question for you is what are your intentions with my best friend?" Vallon asked her, and she appreciated his upfront honesty. There was no malice in his words or expression, only concern.

"I care for him. I know it's soon, but nevertheless I feel for Cameron in a way I've never felt for another person. I would never cause him harm, you must know that," Marty answered, and Lily smiled kindly at her.

"I know all too well what that's like, Marty. Your mind rails against the idea of loving someone so quickly, but it doesn't change the fact that you do. Perhaps since we are vampires it is easier for us to recognize that feeling, that connection, than it is for humans," Lily told her and laced her fingers with Vallon's. He smiled and nodded at the truth in her words.

"Does Cameron know about you two?" Marty asked.

"No. Neither does Adam. I do not know how I could make them understand. I keep thinking of ways to tell them, but then I think about how they might react. Either they'd think I'm insane, or they'd be lost to me forever," he answered her and leaned back against a glass counter that held body jewelry of all kinds.

"But if you are serious about Cameron, you will have to tell him sooner or later. Normally, Cameron is very serious, quiet. He's different around you. He smiles more. That alone tells me what he feels for you."

She felt pleasure at Vallon's words.

"I must ask, do you live in Tenebrae?" Lily asked. Marty knew they would be concerned that she held an alliance with the demon realm.

"I've never been to Tenebrae. My mother, a demon, died when I was not even four years old. Everything I know about demons and vampires was taught to me by my adoptive parents who are Changeling vampires like the two of you. They serve the Gods, if that is what you truly wish to know," she told them and Lily nodded with a smile.

"Then we are glad to welcome you," Vallon told her, and she almost skipped with joy.

"Adam isn't upstairs, Vallon," Cameron said as he came back into the tattoo parlor.

"Oh, well, he must have left then. Guess whatever he had to say wasn't that important," Vallon answered and smiled sheepishly at Marty as she lifted a brow at him.

"Okay, then. Well, if you are both done with Marty, I'd like to take the lady out for drinks," Cameron told them and put an arm around Marty's waist.

"By all means, you two go out and have some fun. I think the wife and I are going to head out, as well. It was a pleasure to meet you, Marty. We'll have a practice soon," Vallon said to her, and they parted ways.

Marty couldn't stop smiling as Cameron walked her back to the car. "I like them. They are good people."

She could feel the pleasure those words made him feel. He wanted her to get on well with his friends, and it pleased him that their meeting had gone smoothly.

"They are. Vallon and I have been friends since we were in school. He's my best friend. I know if I ever needed him for anything, he wouldn't let me down. His wife has done so much for our band. It is because of her that Symphonic Dream is starting to get booked for gigs outside of New Orleans. She's even going to get us into a studio to record a CD.

"She wants to send our demo CD in to radio stations and try to get us airtime. Now that we have a bassist that wants to stick with us for good, we can start to get serious." She could feel his excitement. It bubbled up in her, as well.

Marty would *belong* with her band. They accepted her,

even knowing what she was. Her smile faltered as her thoughts came back to the matter at hand. Cameron was human, and she was not. She had to tell him but how? When?

He opened the door of his Cadillac for her, and she climbed inside. She kept her happy face on all throughout drinks and dinner. They were headed back to his place, and she wondered if it were too soon to breach the subject.

Cameron talked about Symphonic Dream and what it felt like to be on stage in front of an audience, keeping her somewhat distracted. Marty listened eagerly, desperate to escape the thoughts running through her head.

I could lose him still. What if he were to hate what I am? What if he thinks me to be evil?

Marty mentally shook herself. No. Cameron would not be like the others. Not like the numerous foster families she had stayed with. They had always found something odd about Marty and the fear would enter them. She had grown too fast, healed too quickly, and could do things no human should be able to do. Marty had been a child, a foolishly trusting child. She should have hidden it better.

It had brought her heartbreak again and again until that fateful day that Bryce and Hope found her. They had looked at her and grinned. Bryce winked, and she could hear his voice in her head, telling her it would all be alright. She had to hope it would turn out alright this time, too.

Cameron was silent as they came to his door. It was open.

"Stay here, Marty. I'm going to go check it out," he whispered, and she could see the fear for her in his eyes. She let him go in first and followed quietly behind. There was *no way* she'd let him walk into danger without her. Besides... she couldn't shake this odd feeling, like a forgotten memory, struggling to resurface.

The living room was empty. Nothing was disturbed. The same with the bathroom and bedrooms. But in the kitchen, an older human man with gray hair and wild blue eyes sat at the kitchen table with a beer in one hand and a revolver in the other. And it was pointed right at them.

"Who are you and what are you doing in my apartment?" Cameron asked the man, eyeing the gun warily as he realized Marty had followed him into the apartment. He cursed.

"My, my, what filthy language you possess, young man. Let me ask you something. Do you have any idea what you have there standing at your back?" said the man as he took a long swig of beer.

Cameron didn't answer but he heard Marty gasp in shock.

"So, you remember your Pop, then, girl?" he asked, and Cameron knew this man had to be the father she had spoken of, the one that was in and out of prison.

"Why are you here?" Marty asked and came to stand beside Cameron, as if she were clueless to the gun pointed at them.

* * * *

"I've been waiting for a chance to get rid of you, girl. Young man, this woman is no woman at all. She is the spawn of a demon, and she must be killed for the greater good," the man said, and Cameron thought he had a nutcase on his hands. Spawn of a demon, indeed.

Not *his* Marty. Cameron's Marty was sweet, gentle and loving. This man was the monster, not his daughter.

"Wait. You killed her didn't you, Ben?" Marty asked, shocked to her very core. Her sky blues eyes were wide as she struggled to accept the fact that her father had murdered her demon mother.

"Of course, I did. I was sick and tired of being under her thumb. The sadistic bitch had to go, and I smiled when the life left her eyes because I was finally free of her. I shot her in the head with a gun that I had loaded with earth-packed bullets. But there was a witness, and even though there was no body, the police still found enough stolen property in my house to send me away for a few years. They took you away before I could do the same to you," Ben answered, glaring hatefully at Marty.

Cameron stepped forward and positioned his own body a little in front of Marty's. He had to protect her from this madman at all costs.

"That's why you're here? To kill me?" she asked him, and he laughed, downing the rest of his beer with noisy gulping sounds.

"Yes, Martina, that is why I am here. To save other people, like that young man there, from the likes of you. I'm here to send you back to Hell," he said and pulled back on the hammer. The ominous click echoed in the small kitchen and when the loud blast came, Cameron pushed Marty out of the line of fire.

Cameron's body slammed back into the wall behind him as the bullet tore through his chest and out of his back. Warm blood poured down the front and back of his shirt, and Marty's scream pierced his ears. He fell to his knees on the floor and slumped forward.

* * * *

Marty watched in horror as the man she loved took a bullet for her. She centered all that pain and rage in her chest like a weapon and flew over the table. Her father's eyes widened in fear, and he lifted the gun again but never got the chance to fire. Marty crushed his heart in her fist the moment her fingers tore through his chest and shattered his ribcage.

Her eyes bore her hatred into his as he died. The gun fell to the floor with a loud clatter. She rushed to Cameron's side, shaking her head as his pulse slowed. He was dying.

No. Not like this.

Marty slit her wrist with her sharp fangs, and when the blood began to seep, she lifted Cameron from his position on the floor, laying his head gingerly in her lap. Her blood coated his lips, and she let out the breath she had been holding when Cameron's mouth opened wide to cover the wound and suck the blood from her.

Her hands stroked and soothed him as the change came over him. His muscles tightened from the pain, and his body curled around itself. She could sense his organs failing, his thoughts fading and then—just as suddenly—coming into sharp focus.

Cameron's fangs grew and pricked his lower lip. His eyes searched and found her. She heard the questions buzzing in his brain.

"My father spoke true. My mother was a demon. Not a demon like you think. Not like in the Bible, Cameron. They are a race of beings spawned from the shadows, and they live in a dark realm known as Tenebrae. I am only a Halfling demon," she told him and dropped her glamour. Her black wings spread out, filling the kitchen with their impressive span. She smiled, showing him the fangs she had kept so well hidden.

"I am not like them. I do not kill when I feed. I follow the will of the Gods and protect the human race, not harm them. You are now a Changeling vampire. You will need blood to survive and will not be able to abide the sunlight. I am sorry for changing you without your consent, but I love you, Cameron. I couldn't leave you to die. You wanted only to protect me," she told him; and she knew he could hear the awe in her voice that he had taken the bullet for her.

"I'm not asking that you love me now. You owe me nothing for giving you this new life. I'm not even asking you to accept me for what I am. All I want is that you understand, that you live on, even if it must be without me," Marty whispered and held back the tears that threatened to spill. Her wings folded behind her and truly, she felt, he wasn't disgusted. Cameron wasn't afraid.

* * * *

He couldn't explain why. All he knew was that in that moment when he had thought this woman might die, he had needed to save her life. Even at the cost of his own life. The mere thought of Marty's death had made his blood run cold.

"You are beautiful," Cameron told her, and her eyes widened in surprise. A smile toyed at the edges of her mouth. "I love you, Marty. I thought he was going to kill you. I had to keep you safe no matter the cost and that is how I know I *do* love you. Very much."

She bent down to kiss him where he lay on the hard floor of his kitchen. "I love you too, Cameron. More than anything in this world, I love you."

Cameron stood shakily to his feet, trying to accustom himself to everything he was sensing, to everything he was feeling. He saw the corpse still sitting at his kitchen table and felt only satisfaction that the man was dead.

Marty stood and faced him, "I'll take care of him. You might want to take a warm shower. You've been through a lot tonight." She reached up to caress his cheek, and he smiled.

"I could use a shower. Should it bother me that I can't mourn his death?" he asked her.

"No, this man was once what we Guardians term a zombie, a human that is enslaved by a demon or vampire to do their bidding. He has taken lives and brought misery to many. He will not be missed," she answered and took the man into her arms. Cameron watched as she disappeared and shook his head.

There were many things he wanted to ask her, but for now, he craved a shower and clean clothes. Besides, they had plenty of time now, didn't they?

* * * *

Four months later

Cameron and Marty left the recording studio and walked back to their new house hand in hand. The CD was finished, and Lily was ready to send them out. Adam was still unaware that all his band mates and his manager were vampires. They all thought it was for the best that Adam remained in the dark for the time being.

Cameron had become a Guardian, taking an Oath to protect mankind from demons and other beings that sought to harm. The knowledge that he served the God and Goddess still stunned him, As had learning there was a race of Guardians, the Fae and the Familiar, that were created by the Gods to protect mankind from the demons. Not to mention that the Isle of Atlantis was no myth. It was home to the Fae folk and the shape-shifting Familiars.

Once inside their home, Cameron spun Marty into his arms and lowered his mouth to hers. She sighed as his tongue teased her lips.

"Alone at last," Cameron murmured against her lips as he unzipped her jeans.

Clothes flew this way and that as Marty and Cameron raced to the bedroom. Marty was lifted into Cameron's strong, tattooed arms, and she wrapped her legs around his waist. She laughed as he fell with her onto the bed and rolled her underneath his large body.

Marty's laughter faded into wordless, breathy exclamations as his hands and lips trailed over her sensitive flesh. She shivered violently as his warm breath raised gooseflesh on her skin. The hard ridge of Cameron's erection fit snugly between her legs, and Marty moved against him, chuckling playfully as she heard his rough intake of breath.

Cameron slipped into her damp heat, and his tongue sparred with her own. Marty's hips surged to meet his powerful thrusts, and she cried out as his teeth broke the skin on her neck. Cameron lovingly suckled her throat as he rode her, bringing her closer and closer to a climax.

Marty screamed as the force of her orgasm slammed into her, and Cameron came in short, hot bursts. Her tight muscles clenched around him, taking every last drop. Cameron rolled onto his back, pulling her with him until Marty lay sprawled on top. She dropped her glamour and when her dark, leathery wings enfolded them, she knew Cameron didn't think her any less beautiful.

Finally, after all these years, both Cameron and Marty were free from the chains that had bound their hearts, and they had an eternity to love.

♥

myspace.com/jaeknight

Synchronized
© Allison Wonderland

Lips latched onto cinnamon skin, my nails scrape the teeth
of the zipper, eliciting a faint grating sound.
    I locate the silver tab, seizing, easing.
Peppermint lip gloss fuses with tangerine. Moans expelled,
consumed by concave caverns, dark and slippery.
Mouths detach.
Distended pupils seek one another.
Piercing, probing, penetrating.

I burrow my face in your neck, imbibing the aroma of
apricots and chamomile. My hand sweeps the ebony ripples
aside. Mouth cleaves to your bare shoulder. Tulip petals
traipsing along honey-brown skin. Lush, plush,
    the texture of velvet.
Goose bumps sprout in the wake of each kiss.
    Miniscule, raised, like Braille.

In between kisses, we discard the remaining articles of
clothing, fold back the violet coverlet,
    reunite in the center of the bed.

Eyes embark on a visual expedition.
Hands conduct a corporeal navigation, traversing unveiled
skin, caressing curves and contours, crests and canyons.
Minds compose identical thoughts: At last.

In tandem, two vertical bodies incline toward one another.
Arms encircle torsos, legs engird waists.
Te amo, you whisper,
    the words infused with tenderness and sincerity.

209

My mouth seeks yours: *I love you, too.*

The relentless whump-thump of heartbeats fuse into one.
A complete and total immersion,
    nothing separating us but flesh and bone.
It is a symbiotic moment, like when the tide merges with
the shore, and the boundaries between the two
    are no longer discernible.

I feel you tighten your hold, constricting the flow of oxygen
from lungs to brain.
We can't get any closer, I murmur.
I know. Frustration. *I just want to try.* Determination.
Desperation.

Entangled limbs.
Synchronized movements.
Stifled screams.
Fractured utterances.
Fingers threaded through tousled tresses.
Our bodies generate a heat that is at once
    sweltering and hypnotic,
    inducing a kaleidoscopic trance
    behind clench-closed eyes.
Beads of perspiration trickle from our foreheads,
    like raindrops on a windowpane.
A throbbing, inebriating feeling of rapture.

Te amo, you whisper,
    the words infused with tenderness and sincerity.
My mouth seeks yours: *I love you, too.*

♥

aisforallison.blogspot.com

Shorn
© Selena Kitt

Several pictures of her were tucked into the sides of the mirror over his dresser. Most were school pictures, and one was of the two of them together, their arms wrapped around each other, both of them smiling at the camera. My hand, holding the brush that I had picked up from amidst the clutter on his dresser, stopped in mid-air as I peered at those pictures.

I glanced from her to my own reflection in the mirror, unable to prevent the mental comparisons. She looked so young, her skin lighter than his, like a sweet latte to his dark, black—no cream, only sugar. She was beautiful in a fresh, natural way that made me blink with envy. For me, that time in my life was gone—it had passed away somewhere between college frat parties and establishing my first IRA.

A heavy, sodden dullness settled somewhere in the pit of my stomach as I glanced from her picture to my naked reflection in the mirror and then to Del, who was behind me, hauling up his jeans and cramming in the tails of his shirt.

"I've gotta shave." He moved to look over my shoulder. The mirror revealed him rubbing the top of his head. There was a fine stubble there he inspected, his eyes like smoky gray glass. He had a durably boyish face, but he was only twenty-one. His features would change by the time he was my age—but his eyes, those incredible eyes—they wouldn't change. His eyes were the thing that attracted me the most; there was some sort of reserve there I still couldn't place.

"What do you think?" He pushed his bottom lip forward in thought and studied his face in the mirror. "Should I grow a beard?"

"If you want." I found my voice—I thought I couldn't speak through whatever seemed congealed in my throat.

"I could leave the stubble." He wrapped his arms around my waist from behind and rubbed his cheek against my neck. I shrank away a little from the feeling, smiling indulgently. I loved the feel of his clothed body against my bare skin.

"Yuck." I wrinkled my nose, turning in his arms, away from the mirror and the pictures of his girlfriend.

"Okay." He smiled. "Want to come watch me shave?"

"Do we have time?" I put my arms around his neck and massaged the back of his head. He was right, he did need to shave.

"My mom won't be home 'til after three." He glanced at the clock over the bed we'd just vacated.

"Okay." I pulled out of his arms and reached for my T-shirt. "Let me put something on."

"Nuh uh." He grabbed my hand and pulled me in to him, kissing my shoulder, my neck, nibbling on my earlobe. "Stay like this."

I raised my eyebrows at him but just smiled when I followed his lead out of his room and down the long hallway to the bathroom. He moved with a slim, languid, muscled grace that still made me turn to watch him as he walked away.

I loved his bathroom and the bathtub most of all, a marble sunken thing that I'd been dying to soak in since I'd seen it three months ago—when Del and I had first started coming to his house on Saturdays when no one was home. I still hadn't had the chance, and I didn't know if I would.

COMING TOGETHER: AT LAST

Maybe there would be time this summer, if his parents went out of town for some reason before I went back to teaching in Japan in the fall.

I slid up on the counter and watched him take out his razor, the shaving cream, and a towel. I loved to watch him shave, to see him leaning over the sink to look into the wall-to-wall mirror, long-legged and slender, razor poised in mid-air. It was such a masculine thing, shaving, something that made me feel more a part of him.

I watched him lather the top of his head and thought of the picture in his bedroom of him and Tracy. I remembered her arm around him in such a casual air of ownership. That bothered me. The picture itself bothered me, and what bothered me more was the absence of my own picture in that mirror. It was crazy, I knew—impossible.

It wasn't the first time that I'd been back to his room, or the first time I'd seen those pictures, but I think it was the first time I realized what they meant. They held the sweet promise of a future, something he and I didn't have. He said he loved me, and I believed him, but it was a foregone conclusion that the relationship would be over when I went back to Japan and he started college.

So, what did I expect? I knew, when we'd started seeing each other, I was going to be the "other woman." I knew it all along. He didn't lie to me. There was no future for us. There was only right now. I realized that he was looking at me, half-shaved, razor poised, giving my face a long and interested search.

"Should I ask?" He raised one eyebrow in my direction. I loved that.

"Ask what?"

"What you're so lost in thought about." He raked the razor over his scalp, looking back in the mirror. "You're usually chatting a mile a minute when you watch me shave."

I just shrugged, planting an elbow on my knee and resting my chin on my cupped hand, my eyes following the razor's path, my mind wandering. I hadn't planned on getting involved. I was home to take care of some things with my parents' estate, just a few months, and hadn't planned on meeting Del—or falling in love. It just wasn't the right time or place. Still, things had happened as naturally as breathing, his seeping into my life, filling the cracks, dulling the cutting edge of my loneliness. I hadn't planned on any of it, but how could you plan to fill a void that you didn't even know existed?

"Are you going to see her tomorrow?" I slanted him the question.

He hesitated, and I wondered if he was going to play dumb. He didn't, but—as usual—he didn't give me a straight answer either. "You have a beautiful cunt, you know that?" His eyes fell to the triangle between my legs.

"Thank you." I smiled, knowing he was trying to distract me, and I let him. I put my feet up on the counter, opening my thighs, giving him a better view. "So, are you going to see her?"

"Samantha." He said my name with a sigh. I didn't reply but just watched him instead.

"I might." He used the razor over the few spots he'd missed. I waited. "Probably." I just gave him more silence as he wiped his face clean with a towel. "Yeah, I guess."

"I figured."

He put some shaving cream on the tip of his finger and touched my nose with it.

I rolled my eyes. "Jerk!" I wiped it off with my hand, dabbing it onto the tuft of my pubic hair with a grin.

His eyes lit up, and he reached over and opened the top drawer under where I was sitting, pulling out a pair of manicure scissors.

"I was kidding!" I grabbed his towel and wiped off the shaving cream.

"I'm not." He snapped the scissors open and closed, his dark eyes flashing, his grin devious.

"I thought you liked it!" I cried. He had often said how much he liked that I was a natural redhead, the hair between my legs just a shade darker than the strawberry-blonde hair on my head. Our physical differences, the natural contrast, the strawberry cream and black coffee of our skin together, only served to drive our passion to further heights.

"Mmm, I do." He knelt on the floor so he was eye-level between my legs, leaning in and kissing all around my pubic hair. "But I'd love to lick your pussy when it was shaved."

I touched the curly, wiry mass of hair. I had never trimmed or shaved there. "I wonder what it would feel like..."

"Want to find out?" He showed me the scissors again. Seeing him eyeing my bits with a sharp implement in his hands was quite a shock.

"I don't know." I bit my lip. "Do we have time?"

"Plenty." His lips brushed my thigh as he breathed my scent. The sight of his dark, smooth, newly shaved head between my legs elicited an immediate response, and I felt myself opening to him. "Don't you trust me?"

I sighed. "Should I?"

"Yes." His fingers probed my slit, spreading it open. He kissed my clit, his lips soft against my flesh.

"Okay," I breathed, leaning back against the mirror as his tongue moved through my wetness.

"I want to kiss her goodbye." He eased his way through, making his tongue into a sharp little point to probe inside of me. I moaned when his fingers replaced his tongue, sliding deep into my flesh as his mouth moved over my clit.

I was still surprised at how skilled he was at this, how attentive, how eager to please.

I moaned as he gently sucked and nibbled my clit, his fingers moving in a slow, steady rhythm. I cupped my breasts in my hands, tweaking my nipples as I watched him lick me, his eyes on mine, watching my response. I lifted my breast, reaching my tongue out for my nipple, a fat, pink bud. He watched me lick at it, making it wet with my saliva, and he groaned, the vibration sending a quick jolt through my pussy.

I closed my eyes, my head going back, shifting my hips forward toward his mouth, letting the sensation build, like the spark of a flame starting a wildfire between my legs. I loved the wet noises he made as he urged me on with his tongue, the squelch of his fingers pistoning in and out of me. I grabbed the back of his head, calling his name, rocking my hips with him now.

He murmured something, but I couldn't hear the words as I pressed him harder against me, using his mouth now, moving my hips in easy circles. I was close, my thighs trembling with the effort. Del pulled his head back, shaking off the hand at the nape of his neck, his face glistening with my juices. I looked down at him, surprised, bewildered, and he grinned at me.

He lifted the scissors again, and I gasped, my pussy swollen and throbbing and aching for release.

"Now?" I panted, reaching for him, longing to press his face between my legs again.

"Yes. Now." He started to trim the hair between my legs. "I want to taste you when you're all smooth."

I groaned, watching him pull the hair taut with his fingers and snip it, bit by bit, working his way up one side of my labia and down the other. The pulse between my legs was an incessant reminder, and feeling him pushing and pulling at my lips, watching his tongue sneak out of his mouth as he concentrated, was making it worse. I rubbed my fingers over my nipples, feeling it immediately in my clit, and shivered.

"Hurry," I whispered, looking at him through half-closed eyes, and he smiled, watching me pull and twist my nipples, his eyes darkening with lust.

"God, you make me so hard." He reached down to adjust himself in his jeans.

I studied what he'd done so far. There were light red pubic hairs all over the counter, and my mound looked like it had undergone a military buzz cut. "What if your mom finds red pubic hair in the bathroom?" I brushed it off my thighs. "Wouldn't that kind of be a tell-tale sign that a white girl had been in her bathroom?"

He chuckled. "I'll clean it all up." He was changing the blade on the razor and running it under water. Then he put some shaving cream on his hands and started lathering me up between my legs. I wondered for a moment if it would sting or burn and was relieved to find it didn't.

My lips still felt so swollen, my clit throbbing. He was being much more careful with me than I'd ever seen him be with himself. He shaved downward at first, rinsing the razor under warm running water after each pass, and then he shaved upward, clearing every last hair away with the sharp, double-edged blade.

The air on the wet skin of my vulva was cool, and I shivered. It was a strange sensation. He rinsed the razor again, and then got the towel wet, wringing it out before beginning to wipe me down with it. I whimpered as he rubbed it over my pussy, again and again, making a few passes over my thighs and down my ass. Then he used the towel to wipe down the counter and the floor beneath my feet before tossing it into the sink.

He stood back, his dark, muscular arms crossed, admiring his handiwork. I could see the bulge in his jeans and knew he was just as excited as I was.

"How does it feel?" he asked me with a smile.

"Cold." I laughed, reaching down to touch myself. *So smooth!* The air had dried my skin, and it was as soft as rose petals under my fingers. I stared at him, amazed. "Can I see?"

"Turn around." He came to stand in front of me, helping me swing my legs around on the counter, leaning back against him for support as I did.

The mirror filled the whole wall behind the double sinks. My eyes were drawn between my legs, and I gasped. Completely shorn, my pussy looked so tiny, almost like a little girl, no more hair spreading upward in a triangular thatch to give the illusion of larger proportions. My lips were pink and swollen, parted enough to show my clit peeking out at the top. I touched it and moaned softly, the sensation intense.

"She's beautiful." Del held me against him, cupping my breasts and then moving one big hand down my belly, seeking the wetness between my thighs. "You're beautiful."

His hand stroked my hairless and exposed labia, and we both watched in the mirror as his dark fingers parted my pale, creamy lips, sliding a finger into me. He lifted his finger to his mouth, tasting me, and I moaned.

"Let me kiss her." He held my shoulders and turned me back toward him.

I wrapped my legs around his waist, my tongue seeking his and finding it, tasting my juices in his mouth. He pressed his crotch against me, his cock hard—*big*—straining at the fabric. The roughness of the denim over my exposed skin was a powerful sensation, incredibly arousing in a way I'd never experienced before. I rubbed myself against him, sucking his tongue into my mouth.

He groaned, breaking the kiss and adjusting himself again as he knelt between my thighs. His breath over my now-bare skin was a panting heat, and I wiggled and moved my hips closer to his mouth. He feathered kisses over my pussy lips, moaning at the smoothness, and I marveled at it, too. My wetness had nowhere to go, nothing to contain it, and I felt my juices beginning to flow, a steady trickle between my legs.

"Oh, God!" I felt him spreading my wetness over the sensitive, unprotected skin of my lips, his tongue lapping it off. He nuzzled my clit with his nose, delving in with his tongue to find more of my juices, drawing me out. He made his tongue flat, moving it over my whole pussy in long, easy strokes, bottom to top, stopping just short of my clit every time.

I grabbed for something to hold onto, to pull him in, my fingers finding only the smooth skin of his scalp. I moaned in frustration, "Lick it! Please!" directing him there with my hands, my hips, and sighing as his tongue finally swept over my clit, still flat and soft and open, teasing me with slow, gentle strokes. I watched him, my now-bald pussy lips disappearing when he opened his mouth to suck on them. It may have appeared smaller and more dainty, but my cunt felt three times more swollen and sensitive in this unveiled state. I moaned and rolled my hips, spreading my legs wider and pressing up against his mouth.

He slipped two fingers into me, pumping them through the dripping, soppy mess I was making all over him and the counter, but it felt so good I didn't even hesitate when I started fucking him back, thrusting my hips against his hand. He groaned an encouragement, his tongue moving fast and furious against my clit now, his fingers matching my fierceness.

"Close," I whispered, but he knew it and didn't stop, giving me more and more, until I bucked and twisted and shuddered, coming in a flood all over his face. I shivered, the cool air over the bare moisture between my legs giving me goosebumps, and let my body start to relax, my feet slipping off the counter and resting over Del's shoulders. I gasped and panted, still feeling a quiver deep in my lower belly.

Del stood then, grabbing my ankles in one hand and putting them over his shoulder. His mouth and face were glossy and slick, his eyes burning as he unbuttoned his jeans to reveal his hard cock. It was beautiful, thick and uncut, and he pulled the dark foreskin back, revealing the pinkish head.

I gasped when he shoved it up against my pussy, my legs still pressed together, straight up, my ankles crossed against his left shoulder. He rubbed the fat head of it all through the wet heat of my now-smooth skin, my slit squeezed together, tight, a moist resistance against the force of his hard cock slipping through, up and down, again and again.

"Fuck me," I begged.

The wet, smooth entrance of my pussy now gave him no fuzzy obstruction as he slid the head of his cock down and pierced my flesh. He groaned, stopping when he was fully in, the saddle of his hips rocking me back toward the mirror. I moved to open my legs, but he held them tight against his shoulder, beginning to fuck me that way, my pussy a snug, smooth, shaven crease, all wet heat and tight friction. He cupped my breast with his other hand, pulling and twisting my nipple. He felt enormous inside of me this way, and I trembled as he drove into me, his breathing harsh.

The sensation of my now hairless pussy being squeezed and pummeled at once, the delicious, damp grinding of his hips against mine, feeling him shove into me faster and harder as he worked his cock through my flesh, was almost too much. I had never been the kind of girl who had multiple orgasms, but the stimulation between my legs now was fast driving me toward the contrary.

"I love your shaved pussy," he growled, moving his hips in small circles, working his cock against the pressure and tension of my legs squeezed together, my pussy lips closed firmly around him. I arched my back and moved my hips with his, straining to grind my clit toward ecstasy.

Closing my eyes, I felt him start to thrust deeper and make the low, grunting noise he always made just before he came. I strained against him, twisting in exquisite torture with my clit trapped between my swollen pussy lips, my compressed thighs, and then I felt a dam burst, a violent shudder racking my body as I came again.

Del groaned and pulled quickly out of me, opening my legs and aiming his cock directly at my clit, finishing himself off quickly with a few strokes of his hand. The heat of his cum over my pussy was a burning shock, and I gasped, writhing as wave after wave seared the bare skin of my vulva.

"Incredible." He smiled as his fingers spread his seed over my lips. "So, how do you like it?"

"I love it." I sat up and put my arms around him. "I can't believe how sensitive my pussy is now."

He groaned. "Don't start tempting me again! My mom will be home in an hour!"

Well, let's get cleaned up before Mommy comes home." I slid off the counter, wiping up with Kleenex and looking longingly at the marble bathtub. Then I followed him into the other bathroom where there was a shower stall, and we spent entirely too short a time lathering each other up and rinsing each other off.

Then, déjà vu, I found myself back in his room, brushing my wet hair and contemplating the pictures of his girlfriend tucked into the mirror while Del pulled on his jeans.

"I want to meet her some day." I fingered the edges of one of the photos. He stared at me for a moment.

"That would be interesting." His voice said otherwise.

"She doesn't even know I exist." I frowned. "No one knows I exist."

He came up behind me, wrapping his arms around my waist. "I know you exist."

He kissed my neck, and I got an even stronger wave of déjà vu, looking at my body in the mirror, the triangle between my legs a now conspicuous absence, a point of reference.

"You're both very different." He ran his hand over my hip.

"I figured." I stared at the smooth skin between my legs, the tiny cleft. Why had I let him shave me? Why had I let him? "Aside from the age difference, I mean."

"Your pussy looks so sweet like this." Del's eyes and fingers caressed me there.

I smiled, twisting out of his arms and grabbing my panties and jeans off the end of the bed. "So, tell me the truth, did you get involved with me just because of the sex?"

"No, Sam." Del finished tucking in his shirt. "You know how I feel about you."

"She's your girlfriend." I glanced back at the mirror as I did up my bra. "But I'm your lover."

"Do you mind?" He smoothed his hands over his bald head, as if there was hair there to smooth down. I understood the feeling, shifting as the seam of my jeans rubbed my now-exposed pussy.

"Do I mind being your lover? No," I assured him, reaching for my T-shirt and pulling it on. "Do I mind that she's your girlfriend? Yeah. A little. I guess I do."

"Not enough to leave though." He came to stand in front of me, putting his arms around me. His tone soft, knowing—too knowing. It was true, and in many ways, I resented that he knew it. I rested my forehead against his neck, feeling him long and lean against me.

"I love you, Sam." He hugged me, and I squeezed him back, wondering if he realized I knew how much he manipulated me. How much I let him.

"I know." I made my voice light, easy. "We'd better get out of here before Mommy returns to find her little boy in his bedroom with some older white woman."

Del laughed and pulled back. "Okay."

I looked into his eyes for a moment, wondering if I really knew him—or if I even really wanted to. My pussy ached, blazing like a fireplace with no screen, exposed, vulnerable, the heat seeping out around the edges, uncontrollable. What had I done?

Del smiled as he took my hand and led me out of the bedroom.

And I let him.

♥

selenakitt.com

She's No Shrinking Violet
© J.M. Jeffries

"Violet Carsdale, I cannot believe you carry this sort of filth in your mother's bookstore."

Violet turned her head away from her computer screen to see the mayor's wife, Tibby Maxwell, waving a copy of Anaïs Nin's *Delta of Venus* in the air.

"It's my bookstore, Miss Tibby." Well, at least it was for the next six months until her mother's estate was settled. After that, she would sell the store to Bree and blow this Popsicle stand of town, head back to New Orleans and concentrate on her writing career. She was counting the seconds.

"Then why are you allowing this in your store? In this town? Your mother, God rest her soul, would never allow pornography in her store." She slapped the book on the counter with a large thud.

Who died and left her the thought police? Did she wake up in Iran this morning? "Because this is America."

"This is pornography."

Violet put her elbow on the counter top and rested her chin on her fist. Her dark spiral braids curled around her mocha skinned arm like black snakes. Actually, *Delta of Venus* was pretty tasty read that got her motor running when she needed a little inspiration. In her mind, it was necessary like... oh, air. But she wasn't going to say that to Ms. Starchy britches. "No, it's classic literature."

Tibby huffed. "I'm complaining to my husband, and I'm never going to frequent your tawdry little shop again."

Violet shrugged. "Okay." Wasn't any sweat of her nose.

"Well, I never." The short woman squared her pudgy shoulders.

It was on the tip of her tongue to say: *Well maybe you should*. But, she didn't. "I'm assuming you don't want to buy this book."

Tibby pale, thin lips puckered. "I'm going to put a stop to this immediately."

She lifted her hand and waved at the new mayor's wife. "Have a nice day, Miss Tibby."

"That's a powder keg ready to explode." Violet turned to her employee and best friend, Bree Hanigan.

"The only reason, she came in to this shop was to gloat."

Bree's blonde head nodded. "I know. It's all my dad's fault."

Had Bree's father not had a heart attack and been forced to retire as Kenyon's mayor, Miss Tibby's husband, Floyd, would have never run unopposed and she wouldn't be lording it over everybody. "I'm going to your parents' house and slap him in the face after I close the store."

Her blue eyes twinkled. "I'll meet you there to help."

Violet went back to putting in a new book order and, just to get a little back for herself, she ordered several erotic titles. If old Tibby was going to start a ruckus, she was going to give her something to really get riled up about. Step on her right to do business? Oh, hell no! Erotica was one of her hottest sellers and plus, unknown to the town of Kenyon, it was paying her bills in a style she'd become accustomed to. Nobody told her what to read or sell. Write? Yes, but then she loved her editor, who gave her a sweet three-book, six-figure contract deal.

* * * *

As she walked on the sidewalk the next morning, Violet inhaled the tempting aroma of caramel, coffee, and fresh whipped cream, courtesy of Wallace Vance's dairy cow

Lulubelle. For eight months, Wallis had been making her the Red Star Diner's version of the caramel Macchiato on the sly. God forbid anyone in Kenyon knew he was making fancy coffee, but the five spot she slipped him—three fifty of which he pocketed—went a long way to convincing him to do her a little favor.

She turned the corner of Jackson Street and looked up, stopping dead in her tracks. Tibby and her gang, the Poly Esthers, were picketing her store. Catching the words on one sign, her mouth dropped open. *Smut Peddler* in big block letters. Oh no, she didn't!

Violet fished her cell phone out of her pocket and dialed the store's number, knowing Bree opened early for children's story hour. After one ring, Bree answered. "Good morning. Carsdale's Books."

"How long has that bitch and her posse been in front of my store?"

"They got here five minutes after I opened."

Violet forced her voice to remain calm. "How is business?"

Bree sighed. "Half of the story regulars didn't show up. Most of the kids came for story hour. We're getting a lot of calls for delivery. The book club crossed the line and—get this—they decided to an erotic book this mouth. I sold eight copies of *Bound Heat.*"

That was one of her books. "Bitch."

"I called my brother."

Violet took a sip of coffee letting the sweet taste of caramel roll over her tongue. She could handle this herself. "What do I need a lawyer for?"

"Not Sean. Flynn."

Violet groaned. Not him. Flynn Hanigan still had the power to make her panties wet, then melt right off of her. Six and half feet of blond-haired, blue-eyed god. He was the last man she needed getting tangled up with again. Five minutes alone with him, and she be begging him to do all the things she wrote about, but didn't have the time to do. All the things they used to do in the bed of his daddy's Chevy truck. She gulped. She'd made a point of avoiding him since she returned home to care for her dying mother. She didn't need the temptation.

"Do I need a cop?" Yeah, that question sounded good. She didn't want Bree to be suspicious or anything. Back in the day, they kept their little fling on the Q.T., not thinking that Kenyon was ready for their version of a meeting of the races.

"Miss Tibby and the Poly Esthers are as mean as snakes. You never know what they are going to do. Better safe than sorry."

Violet felt her eyes roll so far back in her head they were sliding down the back of her calves. "Shit."

"Go home. Flynn will meet you in a couple of hours. I can take care of the store. And, worse thing you can do is confront them. If we ignore them it will irritate the more."

"I want to jump her." Knowing Bree was right didn't make it any easier not to march up to those old biddies and give them a piece of her mind. She growled.

"Let it go, Vi."

Violet hated being out maneuvered. She wanted her pound of flesh or... to kill them with kindness. That would get their polyester panties in a twist. She was raised right. "Do me a favor. Call Wallace and have him send over some drinks and snacks for them. Have him put it on my tab."

There was dead air for about five seconds. "What the hell for? They are cutting into our business."

She could be civilized. "Make sure he adds his lemon cookies. You know Raylene Lavell can't resist them."

Bree snickered. "You are so sneaky."

"But not in a bad way." She could fight dirty. "I was raised right." Just to prove a point, she'd get all up in the mud. No problem.

* * * *

Flynn Hannigan got out of his squad car and walked up the steps to Violet's house. There was a fresh coat of yellow paint on the old Victorian and a For Sale sign in the front yard. So she wasn't sticking around this time either.

He was later than he said he'd be, but earlier than he expected. This was last place he wanted to be. She was the last person he wanted to see. After a seven-car pileup on the interstate, he was in no mood. For the last six months she'd been in town, he'd been able to avoid her. No use bringing up the past. And he wanted to keep her there. He had to. Thirteen years later, and he still wasn't quite over her. But do you ever get over your first love?

The scent of the roses permeated the air. The porch swing squeaked in the slight evening breeze. One hot summer night, he'd made love to her on that swing. Was his dick getting hard? Jesus Christ, was he still sixteen when a stiff breeze could get it up for him?

He walked up the steps and knocked on the door. No answer. Now that was strange. Her black Honda was in the driveway. He leaned into the door and heard the faint strains of music. Bob Marley, he assumed. She was still a big reggae fan. That was comforting.

Why wasn't she coming to the door? Had the situation gotten out of hand already? On instinct, he reached down and unsnapped the flap on his service weapon. He tested the doorknob, finding it locked. Almost forgetting that she'd been living in New Orleans, she still kept her doors locked. Kind of like her heart.

He moved off the veranda and headed around the house. The wooden door of the fence didn't squeak as he opened it. The music became louder as he turned the corner

of the house, and he found himself tangled in lacy purple
lingerie. Backing up a step, he discovered he'd walked right
into the clothes line. And what a sight to see! Bras and
thongs of every color a man could want to see were hanging
from the lines. He got even harder. Slowly, he reached up
touched the silky material. He let his fingers run down the
narrow crotch string, just imagining what parts of Violet's
chocolate skinned body this tiny bit of material caressed
day after day. Her hot little pussy. Her hard sensitive clit.
Her tight, high ass cheeks.

He remembered when they were all his, and she'd let
him do everything he ever wanted to her body. He'd hoped
that had been enough to keep her here, but it wasn't. No
matter how many times he could make her come, she still
left him.

"Are your enjoying your time alone with my panties?"

He dropped his hand to his side and looked in the
direction of the sultry voice. "Always have."

Her hands were on her curvy hips. The red tank top
looked stark against her creamy chocolate skin.

"Do you want to take them home with you?"

A slow smile formed on his lips. The red tank top was
molded to her lush breasts. God, he loved women with a
little meat on their bones. And her bones were covered just
fine. "I already have a pair of yours."

Her head tilted to the side and her long braids danced
over her shoulder. "Which ones?"

He'd even taken them to Iraq with him when his guard
unit was called up. Those panties kept him alive. She
wasn't even supposed to be his date, but at the end of the
night he'd ended up with her in his arms and in the back of
his mother's Caddy. "White cotton, senior prom."

"That was a lot of years ago."

How could he forget that night? That was the first night he got into those pristine panties. "Those underwear are holding up well. Considering."

Violet grimaced and held up her delicate hands. "Don't share. Please." Violet's gaze narrowed in on his crotch. "Jesus, Flynn, do you still get a boner at the drop of a hat?"

"Not for everyone."

Brushing past him, she headed for the panties. "I'm flattered, but you're late." She started picking her underwear off the line and throwing them into a wicker basket. "What are you going to do about Tibby picketing my store?"

Pushing his Stetson back on his head, he took a deep breath. "I'm going to try and handle this the easy way."

She tossed a lacy black bra in the basket, her black eyes glittering with annoyance. "I think you should arrest her."

Frankly, he was a bit surprised she didn't want him to shoot her. And, for a second, if he thought it would get her back in his bed, he might consider it. He was a cop. He could probably get away with it. "Why?"

"Because then she blows a gasket and calls her brother Billy Mac in the state assembly, and he'll alert the media, and we could have a huge censorship protest, and the it will be funny when the rest of the world finds out what every citizen in Kenyon already knows."

Pain hammered at him, and he pinched the bridge of his nose. Did he really want to know? Oh, what the hell. He had to ask. "Which is?"

"Tibby and Floyd are stupid."

A stabbing pain hit again, and he couldn't decide if the ache in his pants was worse than the one in his head. "Did you put a lot of thought into that one?"

"I didn't have to."

"Is it such a big deal to keep the porn under the counter?"

"I don't carry porn. I carry *erotica*." She tossed an emerald green thong at him.

He caught it, and for a second, he contemplated slipping it in his pocket and using it to beat off with tonight when he was alone with his memories. "What's the difference?"

"Erotica is classy." She plucked the panties out of his grip and dropped them, missing the basket completely.

"Is that a legal definition?"

She bent over to pick up the free range panties. "The Supreme Court hasn't figured out what porn is, why do I have to?"

Not so discreetly, he checked out her cleavage and the spotted red lace cupping her breasts. He almost groaned. "You're the one selling it."

She stood. "And according to the First Amendment, I have every right to. And just so you know, I put the ALCU on speed dial."

The flesh of her breast jiggled again, and he thought his eyes might fall out of his head. "And once Tibby gets a permit, she has every right to peacefully protest in front of your store, as I'm sure the ACLU has already told you."

She huffed. "How long will it take for her to get a permit?"

More jiggly flesh happened. Was he starting to sweat? "Normally, a couple of weeks, but since Miss Tibby is connected. I'm going to give her a couple of days. By the way, she already packed up her signs and promised not to come back until she has the proper paperwork."

"Look, I understand she has every right to be out there on the street, but she's a pain in my ass."

Flynn held up his hands. "So, whose freedom do I tramp all over?"

She put her finger on her chin. "Hmm, let me think about it. I'm the victim. Not mine."

"You look good, Vi."

Violet had to stop herself from being all tingly. She hadn't expected to get all worked up by him. But there he was, touching her underwear and stirring up way too many memories. "And you want to avoid this whole issue, don't you?"

His blue eyes trained in on her mouth. "You know what I want?"

No, no, no, she thought. *Don't push.* She knew she wasn't strong enough to resist him. Not after today. "You've never been shy about sharing that with me before."

"I still want you."

His words worked their way into her brain—deep down in a place she didn't like to visit often. "A lot of water has past under that bridge."

Flynn shrugged his broad shoulders. "You asked."

God, why did he have to look so good? No, better. His body filled out, and he'd become a man. His face was leaner, more masculine. His body was tall, muscular, even more so than in his football days. There was a sense of ease about him. He was comfortable about the man he'd become. That was so compelling. Her chin raised more in defense then defiance. "I'm not going to be here much longer."

"Then that makes it perfect."

Violet bit her bottom lip. A heat she was trying to control was surging in her belly and in her pussy. "I am tempted."

He held his big hands out. "Consider me research?"

What did he mean by that? Had Bree told him? She knew her mother wouldn't. As much as her mother supported her career, she'd been embarrassed that her daughter wrote dirty stories for a living.

"For what?" There. That sounded so convincing to her. Not.

"Your book writing."

"You know? How do you know?"

His broad shoulders shrugged. "I read one of your emails to Bree."

Did he just try to look guilty? Nope. That was her imagination. Bree would take her secrets to the grave.

Flynn filled her in. "She had to take Roy, Jr. to the ER and called me to watch Melissa, and she'd been answering email on her laptop. I saw it while I was feeding Melissa. You were telling her about how much you hate your cover."

"Bound and Determined."

He took a step closer to her. "I had no idea that you wanted to take on two guys at once."

For the first time in his presence, she felt like prey. And he was the big, blond wolf. Okay, Bambi, you are toast. "You read the book?" Did her voice just squeak?

"I've read all your books." His full, seductive lips smiled.

Violet covered her face. A flush burned her fingers. Of course, it was nothing compared to the heat in her belly or the wetness seeping into her panties. She was going to have to change her pants after he left. "This is the first time I've ever been embarrassed someone's read my books."

"Why?"

She had a flashback of those beautiful lips and what they had done to her body once upon a time. "Because..." She couldn't finish her sentence.

"You write about taking it up the ass. How can you just say *because?*"

God, the slow sexy voice made sound so naughty, even naughtier than she could write it. She rubbed her forehead, trying to come up with an answer that would get him off her back. "Listen I really have to go." She picked up her laundry basket and turned to head back into the house.

Flynn grabbed her upper her arm stopping her. "No, don't avoid this conversation." He took the basket out of her hands and dropped it on the grass.

The heat of his touch made her dizzy. "You're still in uniform. You still have to work?"

"I'm off the clock and on my way home. I have all the time in the world."

She was tempted. Really tempted. Her body was screaming, *Yes! Yes! Yes!* Frankly, her brain was kind of agreeing. She was in trouble. "What are you going to do about Tibby?" Time to get the conversation back to the original topic before she whipped off her jeans and begged him to fuck her.

He cupped his big bulge. "What are you going to do about this?"

God, he was a healthy boy. Her mouth went dry. This was so not how this was supposed to go. "Speaking of books, I really have one to finish."

Those thick blond brows wiggled. "You need a little inspiration?"

He inspired all of her heroes in one way or another. She just didn't admit it to anyone. "I'm good."

"You sure?"

Just standing there in there in that khaki uniform with a big hard on would fuel a hell of a love scene in the next chapter. She wondered if her editor, Kym, would be mad if she changed the hero to a small town sheriff. "Yes. Please go so I can get some work done."

"Not going to happen that easy. I never thought you left because you didn't want me anymore."

Now the man was getting all cop on her, trying to confuse her. "I wanted to get out of Kenyon. I don't belong here."

His head shook. "You belong where you want to belong."

He was still angry with her. He didn't ask her stay. Why, she didn't know, but maybe if he had she would have. But she was kid. Hell, she barely knew her own mind, certainly not his. "Where do you think you belong?"

"Inside of you."

She yanked her arm away from him and dropped the basket of laundry. He had to power to make her stay and forget her dreams. He could make her be happy just being his woman. No, she had things to do with her life. Places to go and things to accomplish. She couldn't stay in a town that called her a smut peddler. "I can't do this Flynn. Not again."

"I'm only asking for right now."

He made sound so easy. So right. Damn him and his blue eyes. "No."

He pulled her into his arms. "Tell me you don't want me. Tell me you're not wet."

Pressed close to his hard body, Violet couldn't think. Desire flooded her, stopping her brain from intelligent thought. She was seventeen again, and he'd picked her over every girl in the world. His cock throbbed, rubbing into her belly.

"Doesn't mean I have to do anything about it."

"We're grownups." He tilted her chin up until she met his gaze. "You're leaving. Why can't we have some fun?"

Think, girl. Think. "What about Tibby?"

He lowered his mouth until their lips almost touched. "You want her to join us?"

Warm cinnamon breath fanned her cheek. Her hands rested on his lean hips as she tried to find some anger to push him away. "You know what I mean."

"Yeah, but right now I just want to crawl between those long legs and ride you hard."

She let out a long breath. "Damn, you *have* read my books."

He cocked a blond brow, then he leaned down until his lips touched her ear. "Let me see if I give you something to write about."

There she was listening to her pussy again. That's what got her trouble in the first place. She was so weak. "I'm going to regret this."

"Only that you waited so long."

* * * *

By the time she got to her bedroom, she was naked. Flynn stalked behind her like a big jungle cat who knew his prey was cornered. Frankly, she liked it. Now if someone would've told her this morning that he'd have her naked by evening, she'd have laughed her ass off. But he was right. Why not play while she was stuck here? They were grown-ups, and they knew the score.

He caught her around the waist and tossed her on the bed. There was enough light in the room to see him slowly peel off his uniform. The gun belt dropped to the floor followed by the shirt, and she had a wild thought. The house was off the main road, so no one could see the squad car parked in her driveway unless they were coming to the house, and she didn't care.

After taking off his boots, he started to peel off his pants. His big cock sprang free, already hard and throbbing and just for her. "Mother nature has been good to you."

"And I'm going to be good to you."

"God, yes."

He bent over, grabbed his belt, and took off his handcuffs.

"Am I under arrest?"

"Just some inspiration." He climbed on the bed, then lifted her arms over her and cuffed her wrists to the wrought iron head board. His cock was so close to her mouth, she stuck out her tongue and gave him a little lick.

He groaned then moved away.

Violet adjusted herself into a more comfortable spot. Flynn grabbed one of the pillows behind her head and shoved it under the small of her back. Then, he leaned over and took her mouth in a searing kiss. Their tongues seemed to war with each other, and Violet thought she was going to explode. He pressed his big body into hers, and she could feel every inch of his rock hard body. His cock was touching her stomach, and her legs just seemed to wrap themselves around his lean hips. He had just enough hair on his golden body to make things interesting. She ground her clit against him, feeling the hot moisture creaming from her body. She was on fire. The only thing she wished was that she could touch him.

He moved his mouth down her neck.

"Come on, baby. Fuck me."

"Not yet, I'm gonna play."

"Flynn."

His mouth moved down to her breast, and he grasped one hard nipple with his mouth. Gently, he bit the peak, then pulled with his teeth and ground his hard cock on her labia.

Violet screamed and vibration shot through her entire body. She wasn't sure, but she thought she heard him laugh against her skin. Then again, she just about came all over herself. When he moved his mouth over to her other breast and did the same, she was sure she'd died and gone to orgasm heaven. Her hands fisted, and she tried to escape the handcuffs, but she couldn't. She just wanted to touch him one time.

Flynn nibbled his way down her stomach until he reached her drenched pussy. Then he swiped the long talented tongue down her slit to the crack of her ass. Violet's eyes rolled back in her head, and this strange needy sound just rushed out of her mouth.

Then she was sure she heard him laugh.

"You are way too easy."

In a bad way? She didn't think so. Doesn't every man want a woman who could come at the drop of a hat?

Flynn propped her legs on his shoulders and went down again. He sucked on her clit so hard she thought she was going to buck off the bed. But that wasn't all, The long, naughty tongue went to work on her pussy like she had ice cream down there. Almost all coherent thought stopped.

Then, he inserted a long blunt finger and started massaging her G-spot. She could feel her internal muscles clamp onto him and move inside of her. As his tongue worked her clit, another finger joined the first, and Violet bucked when he coaxed her G-spot into action. Her whole body quaked with the force, and she gripped him so tightly as she rode out the orgasm. "Flynn, damn it. Oh God, that..."

He didn't answer because he was busy licking up her juices. Slowly, her body came back to itself, and she thought he would let her go. Well, more hoped because she just wanted to roll over and go to sleep.

"We're not done."

She opened her eyes and watched him reach into her table and pull out a condom.

"How did you..."

"You're a modern woman and from the looks of what's in this drawer, a very horny one."

"Wait until I get out of these handcuffs.

He didn't answer. He just put the condom on and got back in between her legs placing his penis at the entrance of her pussy. He massaged the tip of his cock on her clit slowly back and forth, just smacking it hard enough to drive her insane, but not enough to make her come. *Bastard*, she thought. Violet started wiggling her hips trying to get him inside. Damn, when did he learn to wait like this? "Flynn."

"What, Slick?"

"Fuck me."

"Ask me nice."

"Flynn, fuck me, please."

He pushed the head inside.

Her pussy was dying here! She tried to scoot down and get him inside her, but he pulled out. "Please."

He laughed. "Please what?"

"Please, baby, just fuck me."

There was a long, drawn out breath. "I'm so weak." And he plunged inside her to the hilt.

Violet screamed in sheer pleasure. Her muscle clenched around him, and she felt so full.

"You are so wet."

Violet couldn't say anything as he pounded her. She looked up at his face, and the handsome features were twisted with tension. Skin slapped against skin as he pumped. Her juices flowed, and she felt a finger circle her tight asshole and push slowly inside her. She clenched his finger and his dick, letting him ride her both of her holes. Something inside her tripped, and a hard, fast orgasm ripped through her. Her blood rushed from her head and she thought she blacked out for a second. When she caught her breath, she felt his hard cock slip out. She moaned in distress.

"We ain't done, darling." He adjusted her body, and she felt the tip of his cock pushing into her anus. Her first reaction was to tense up, but then she realized she wanted him to do this to her. After some gentle persuasion, her tight hole opened, and he pushed inside.

Violet gritted her teeth as he filled her in an exquisite moment of absolute pleasure. He worked his way in slowly until his entire dick was inside her. Then he began fucking her ass. He braced himself over her, and her head thrashed back and forth as she took him completely. As Flynn increased his pace, Violet ground herself against him, trying to get him in deeper. This did something to him, because he started pounding inside her and rubbing her clit. Then tension built inside her, and she felt herself crashing to the edging. With one hard thrust of his cock, she screamed and came. A second later, she felt his body shake, and he came hard inside her.

* * * *

Three days later, Violet stepped into the crowded meeting room at city hall. As she moved through the packed room, the sea of people parted, and a hush fell over the room. *Great*, she thought. *This is going to turn into an event.* Spotting Bree near the front, she headed that way.

As she took her seat, she saw Tibby Maxwell sitting with the rest of the Poly Esthers, staring at her smugly. Flynn had been right. They'd gotten their permit in record time, and today they been out in front of her store with their picket signs and megaphones. All and all, it had been a quite day at the store. But book deliveries had been up almost fifty percent. No one wanted to piss off the vindictive Tibby, but they certainly didn't want to go without their books. So, she rented a Vespa and spent most of the day zipping around town dropping off books. It was an end run around the problem, but she was willing to be creative.

Floyd patted his bald head with a snow white hankie then banged his gavel. "Is there any new business?"

Tibby raised her hand. "I would like to speak, Mr. Mayor."

"Of course, you can, Ms. Maxwell."

Tibby rose with flourish and moved to the podium. "I would like to address an insidious plague that has infected our beautiful little town..."

Violet went off into her happy place and pretty much knew that woman was going to take up about a half an hour ranting and raving.

"At least look like your paying attention." Bree leaned over to her.

Violet lifted up an eyelid. "Why?"

Before Bree could answer, her parents walked up to them and sat beside them.

Sweet. Now she had some powerful allies on her side.

Tibby even stuttered a few times, which made her have to bite her tongue so she wouldn't start laughing. Violet leaned back and smirked at Tibby, whose unibrow was creased in what could only be described as an unattractive way. But, she still kept yapping.

Discreetly looking at her watch, she noticed the old girl had been at it for almost fifteen minutes. Violet looked around the room, and she could see the signs of the crowd getting bored. She also saw Flynn heading straight for her. A little tingle started in her pussy as he slowly made his way through the crowd. There was some shuffling beside her as Bree moved over a seat to let Flynn sit beside her. She smiled at him. He winked at her, then mouthed the word *tonight*.

They'd been playing prisoner interrogation for the last three nights, and she was having a grand old time. Of course, she didn't think about the ramification of their little game. But then she hadn't always been the smartest of women when it came to her heart. "Hell, yeah."

"And in conclusion, we, the decent God-fearing citizens, must protect our town from the encroachment of smut. Thank you."

Floyd banged his gavel one more time. "I think we've covered all the business, thank you—"

Violet stood. "Don't I get a chance to speak?"

Floyd almost looked guilty about trying to rush the meeting so she wouldn't have a chance to talk. "It's nearly eight o'clock, and *Reba's* coming on."

Oh, dear God, redneck culture at its finest. "The show's in syndication. You can catch the same episode in three weeks." Violet walked to the podium.

"But—"

"Mr. Mayor, it wouldn't look good to show favoritism, now would it?" Violet glanced over at Tibby and almost laughed as the woman tried to keep a straight face.

"Could you make it quick, Ms. Carsdale?"

Planting an elbow on the podium, she gave Floyd a sweet smile. "I aim to please."

There was a round of muffled laughter throughout the hall.

She wished she'd written something down. She was a seat-of-the-pants writer. She could be a seat-of-the-pants speaker to. "I thought really long and hard about this problem and what I was going to say tonight." *Well, not really.* "First, I want to commend Tibby and the ladies of this town for exercising their right to protest a situation they don't like. America was built on the backs of people who had the power of conviction to change their circumstances. Although I don't agree with your stand, I do salute you ladies for taking action. There are too many times when people remain silent because of fear or laziness or apathy. But, I too must let my voice be heard." Was that the national anthem playing in her head, or had she had too much coffee? "No one should live in fear of reading a book. We are not a group of Iranian women risking torture and death to read *Lolita*. We're Americans—with a written guarantee called the Constitution that says we are allowed to read pretty much anything we purchase. I want Tibby to keep protesting at my store, because I'm going to keep selling books that my customers want to read. But more importantly, it is proof that we live in the world's greatest country, because we can all have a voice no matter if we agree or not. Thank you." The crowd jumped to their feet and applauded her for nearly two minutes. She smiled and realized she'd beaten Tibby at her own game. If her arm were long enough, she pat herself on the back.

She walked over to Flynn grabbed her purse. "See you later." Then she walked out.

* * * *

Two days later, Violet walked around the corner, coffee in hand, and stopped dead in her tracks. No one was picketing the store. What the hell happened? She hurried to the store and rushed through the door. She found Flynn standing near the erotica section of store reading a copy of *Exit to Eden.*

She placed her purse and her coffee on the counter. "You know, that's going to rot your brain."

Flynn closed the book and put it on the self. "What it's doing to my dick will compensate for that."

She looked at the boner straining to get out of his pants and bit her bottom lip. How can a girl look a gift cock in the mouth? Or was that: not put it in her mouth? "Where is your sister?"

"Chicken Pox."

"Why are you here?"

He wiggled his eyebrows.

"I don't have any fantasies about fucking you in the store." Okay she did, but the book club was going to be there at ten thirty, and it would have to be a quickie.

"I didn't come for sex. I wanted to you sign my petition."

Well, damn, she was juicy and ready now. "What petition?"

"To get my candidate on the ballot."

They weren't supposed to have an election for another two years. She'd be long gone by then. "What?"

Flynn started walking over to her, and he reached behind him and pulled some folded papers from his back pocket. "There is an old law on the books that states if only one person runs for office they must have another election in six months and another candidate must run against them. I need signatures to get my candidate on the ballot." He held out the papers to her.

Violet held up her hands. She couldn't sign anything. "That's great, but I'm still registered in New Orleans."

He kept pushing the papers at her. "No problem, I can register you to vote here."

God, he wasn't going to give up. Violet shook her head. "I have to live here to vote here. I'm going home soon."

He sighed and put the papers on the counter. "Then how do you expect to be the mayor if you don't live here?"

Did he just tell her to run for mayor? "Say what?"

"You're my candidate." He flashed her the sexiest grin ever.

He'd just taken a turn for crazy land. "I'm not going to run for mayor."

The glint in his eyes was telling her a different story.

"After your speech, I don't think you have a choice."

"Do most of these people know what I do for a living?" her voice lowered. Why was she whispering? There was no one else in the store. Oh, he could always confuse her.

"I don't think they care if you can get Floyd out of office."

Okay, that was one thing in his favor, but she still wasn't running, because she wasn't staying. Although deep down, she would love to still play with Flynn. Okay, more than play with him, but that wasn't the point—at least not right now.

"Why don't you run?" He was standing so close that he reached out and gave her butt a little squeeze. "I like being the man behind the power, especially if the power has an ass as fine as yours."

Now she was really distracted and tempted to put the CLOSED sign on the door and show him the fold out sofa in the reading area. He had to stop touching her, or she'd be in house wearing an apron cooking him waffles in the morning. "Why isn't Tibby outside?"

He started laughing. "Tibby has to marshal the forces to keep Floyd in office."

Violet put her head on his broad chest. "You did this on purpose."

He was now rubbing her ass. "For the town."

"Yeah, right."

"Okay, I'll be honest. I'm not letting you go this time."

Violet stepped back and put her hands on her hips. "You can't keep me here."

"I can transfer to NOPD."

She let those words play over in her head. He loved this town. He was made for Kenyon, not the big bad city. Yet, he'd leave it for her. That was a lot to take in. "You'd leave here for me?"

He shrugged. "You got me by the dick."

Those weren't the words she wanted to hear, but she knew they were true. The chemistry between them was undeniable. She wanted—needed—more from him, though. "That's just wrong."

"Try telling me that about five seconds before I come."

She took a big breath. She wanted to be with him as much as she could, but she just wasn't ready to throw all her cards on the table. "I'm thinking about keeping the house and coming back on weekends."

He shook his head. "Marriage or nothing."

Her body went rigid. "What are you saying?"

"I thought I was pretty clear."

Only men got to be that blasé about their feelings. That was just plain annoying. "You didn't even ask if I love you."

"Well?"

Okay, now they were just playing power games. And to be honest, it was fun. She was going to say *yes*. She should of yes years ago, but she'd had some growing up to do. Now she was ready—even if she didn't know it until just then. "Well what?"

Flynn leaned on the counter. "Do you love me?"

She wanted him to say it first. He was the guy after all. "Do you love me?"

His head nodded. "Oh, yeah."

Growling she crossed her arms over her chest. "You think you could, like... Oh, I don't know... say it."

There were a few seconds of silence. "I. Love. You." He said each word slowly.

"Good."

His blond eyebrow cocked. "Anything you need to say?"

Violet pursed her lips. "I'm making you work for it."

"I have handcuffs."

Her kind of man. "I love you, Flynn."

♥

jmjeffries.wordpress.com

Just Be

© Andrea Dale

I was convinced Sarita was going to leave me. The signs all pointed to it... The hushed phone calls, hanging up when I came into the room. The fact that we hadn't had sex in over a month, and over a month before that, and probably more, but I'd blocked it out. And even those had been rushed. The suitcase I found in her closet yesterday morning when I was looking for a scarf I thought she'd borrowed, although she hadn't mentioned any trips to me.

But it had all probably started before that. The night I was late to her birthday dinner, rushing into the restaurant from a study session that had run long, and her looking up from the table, her luminous brown eyes glowing disappointment in the candle flame even as everyone at the table fell silent for a moment.

We'd known that my going to law school would be a burden on us both. At the time, we'd made the decision together, discussed the potential problems, worked out solutions. I'd gotten scholarships, so money wouldn't be a big issue. I'd be too busy to spend frivolously, anyway. We'd have to cut back on traveling, but there would be summers. That sort of thing.

Going back to school, especially the kind of intense studying necessary, was harder than I expected. I guess when you're thirty, you don't have the kind of resilience you do in your late teens and early twenties. You don't have the momentum of coming out of high school straight into college, or cannon-shot from college into grad school.

Sarita and I barely saw each other, and when we did, my head was spinning with torts and US Code sections, and I was rambling about fellow students whom she'd never met.

Add the screeching halt in our sex lives. Well, nobody would have expected us, with our reputation of being screwing-like-bunny dykes, to be falling asleep with no more than a brush of a kiss and a snuggle.

Every damned night.

I'd abandoned her, and she was probably just being her usual wonderful self by waiting until after my stress-crazy finals to tell me that it was over.

I don't know how I made it through finals. I remember waiting to be handed the Constitutional Law test, on the verge of tears from thinking about my life empty without her. Then, the paper was in front of me, and my world narrowed to articles and amendments.

Hours later, I looked up, and my stomach twisted again. You'd think I'd feel relief that finals were over. Instead, I was sure they spelled the beginning of the end.

I grabbed a Snickers from the vending machine—I didn't remember eating breakfast, and I'd skipped lunch in favor of some last-minute cramming—and headed to my car.

Sarita was standing by it. My steps slowed even as my body tingled. With her dark East Asian complexion, she could pull off fire-engine red like nobody's business. The little stretch lace tank top hugged her high breasts. She'd paired it with khaki shorts and a pair of red thong sandals.

Her toenails were the same shade of red as her shirt. Sexy right down to the details. Did she have to look so good just to dump me?

"Hey," she said when I got close and stepped forward into a kiss.

Out of familiar habit and familiar desire, I responded,

letting myself focus on nothing more than the feel of her soft mouth moving against mine, her teeth gently nipping my bottom lip before she stepped back.

"Will your car be okay here over the weekend?" she asked.

Confused, I nodded. The student lot was open 24/7.

"Good. You're coming with me."

I followed her, too brain-fogged to form a coherent question. She asked about the tests, and I told her how I thought I'd done: Contracts, pretty well; Criminal Law, hard to say. It wasn't until we pulled onto the freeway in the opposite direction from home that I had the presence of mind to ask where we were going.

"Yosemite," Sarita said, flashing me a grin.

That was entirely beyond my current comprehension level.

"You need a break, sweetheart," she said. Her hand on my knee wasn't helping, but I tried really hard to concentrate on her words. "You've been studying your ass off, and now that finals are over, you deserve a vacation. We both do. You get to decompress, and we get to reacquaint ourselves with each other."

I took her hand from my leg and pressed my mouth against her palm. It was the only way I could express my gratitude and relief.

And then I did something I wouldn't've thought possible. I fell asleep. And I stayed asleep until we were pulling up to the ranger station to pay our entrance fee, bleary and blinking and needing to pee.

I apologized to Sarita for not helping with the driving, but she waved my contrition away. "You were exhausted. I'm glad you were able to sleep. It means you're starting to relax and let go."

We stopped to stretch, pick up a few last-minute supplies, and change into hiking gear, then continued on into the park. Apparently, Sarita had thought of everything, including packing all the stuff I'd need. That explained the suitcase in the closet and the mysterious phone calls.

Despite my nap, I still felt groggy and overwhelmed, like I was wandering around in a fog. Strapping on the packs and hiking up to the meadow went a long way to clearing that fog. We didn't speak much, just occasionally pointed out an eagle overhead or commented in awe over the views. All of Yosemite looks like a postcard, a surreal, impossible beauty.

Kind of like Sarita. Dazed and confused as I was, as the hike progressed and the weight and stress of school peeled away, feelings I thought I'd lost resurfaced. Arousal. Desire. Lust.

It wasn't just the brisk air that quickened my breath and hardened my nipples. Oh, no. Watching Sarita's lithe form moving gracefully up the path was doing wonders for my formerly buried libido.

The sun was no more than a blushing glow behind Half Dome by the time we had the tent set up and the fire going. Since it was late, supper was simple: canned stew, fresh sourdough bread, and cherries for dessert.

In the flickering firelight, I watched the cherries stain Sarita's lush lips a deeper red, and I quivered right down to my clit.

She looked up, saw me watching her. Must have seen the look in my eyes, because she smiled, tossed the pit in the fire, and leaned over to kiss me.

Like the kiss at the car, it was slow, gentle, gradually deepening. Dimly, I realized that I understood the cliché of air to a drowning man. I breathed the feel of Sarita against me and felt alive again.

The skin of her bare arms was satiny under my hands. Suddenly, I wanted to be naked, feel my body against hers:

soft belly, hard hipbones, sharp nipples, silken hair above and coarse below. I wanted it so badly my hands shook.

"You taste so good," Sarita whispered, licking the hollow of my breastbone. "I've missed the taste of you."

"I've missed you, too. I'm so sorry—"

She pressed her lips against mine again until she was sure I'd stopped trying to talk. "Don't talk. Just be."

I let tears of wonder drain down the back of my throat and kissed her, cupping her beautiful face in my hands. Her tongue darted in and out of my mouth, teasing and playful, and my pussy contracted as I thought about how that teasing touch would feel on my clit.

We tumbled back onto the sleeping bag. Sarita kneeled over me, unbuttoning my shirt and leaving trailing kisses along the exposed skin, then deftly undoing the front hook of my bra. Cool air slid over me before she took my breasts in her hands and warmed first one, then the other nipple with her wet mouth.

It had been so long since we'd touched that my cunt ached from the sudden rush and swell of desire. I think we might both have had it in our heads to take this slowly, to savor and celebrate. Our bodies, however, had other plans.

I reached up to brush my palms across her breasts. She was braless beneath the tank top, and her nipples distended the fabric. She hissed as I pinched, first gently, then harder. Her hips twitched, pressing her crotch harder against mine.

"Sarita!"

It wasn't quite an orgasm, or maybe you could call it a mini-orgasm. I know I shuddered with pleasure, cried out her name. Whatever it was, it was enough for her to expertly strip me of my shorts and part my thighs with her long-fingered hands.

Then her mouth was on me. She licked and sucked my swollen clit, and that was enough to send me off on a real orgasm, an incredibly long one or maybe a string of them.

She kissed me, her face covered in my juices. Moments later, I was between her legs and returning the favor, two fingers stroking her deep inside as I licked her until she screamed.

After that, we slowed down, stroking and whispering and luxuriating in having all the time in the world to make love. Sometime after *that*, with a waxing moon high in the sky and stars like you've never seen, we threw half the sleeping bag over us and finally talked.

I admitted I'd thought she was leaving me. She was shocked, protesting until I kissed her quiet just as she had done to me earlier.

"The look you gave me when I was late to your birthday dinner..."

"I was worried about you," she said. "You'd been working so hard and not eating, and you walked in and you looked so pale and gaunt... I wanted everyone else to go away so I could feed you and take you home and put you to bed."

"I'm sorry things got so crazy," I said.

"I'm sorry I couldn't do anything to make it easier," she said.

Then we both laughed, because we knew we were being silly apologizing for things we couldn't control. We'd find a way to work it out, to communicate better, to take the occasional weekend or even just a day or an evening to reconnect during the most stressful times.

As the embers pulsed orange and hot in the fire ring, I looked up and watched a bat swoop overhead.

And just let myself be.

♥

cyvarwydd.com

Send More Japs!
© Robert Buckley

The scrawny captain looked like he'd been pushing papers all his life. Tommy and I held out our hands, but he kept our discharges just out of reach.

"Don't you men understand? They're only going to haul you back in. No one's staying out of this one. Hell, why would you want to?"

"Captain," I said. "Tommy and I are going home. The Army can come get us after we see our families."

He shook his head and handed us our papers. I glanced at the date: December 8, 1941.

Tommy Gennaro grew up in East Boston; I grew up in Southie. For all we know, we may have traded punches after one of the Thanksgiving games when the micks and wops mixed it up. We ended up in the Army pretty much the same way. A judge said we could either serve our country or serve some time.

Tommy and I met up in some dusty armpit of an Army camp in Texas. He bumped into me in the chow line and said, "Hey, Donovan, you know what sound a toilet makes when you flush it? Irissssssshhhhh!"

I knew it was the start of a beautiful friendship, forged by ever more outrageous insults upon each other's national heritage.

I liked the Army. Tommy did too, but he hid it behind all his belly-aching. The day we were discharged, I left with three stripes. Tommy had two.

We started our odyssey with our uniforms on and our thumbs out. We didn't pay for anything all the way from Texas to Boston. Servicemen used to die along the sides of roads waiting for a ride. Folks would just as soon give a lift to an entire chain gang. That sure changed after Pearl Harbor. People nearly had accidents trying to pick us up.

We made great time. One guy went nearly a hundred miles out of his way to bring us to New Orleans. He even let Tommy sit in back with his teenaged daughter.

In the Big Easy, we drank and ate for free for nearly three days. Folks were falling all over themselves to show us a good time. One old gent brought us to Madame Louret's, where we had our pick of the most beautiful girls I'd ever seen in my life.

Tommy didn't waste any time. He went upstairs with a girl who was a dead ringer for Carole Lombard. I picked a colored girl—the first one I ever had. But she wasn't like any colored girl I'd ever seen before. For one thing, she had green eyes, and long soft, flowing hair, not like a lot of the Negro girls you saw in the South, with tight, kinky curls and funny clothes that reminded you of the kids in the Our Gang shorts.

This girl was long-legged, with a big old behind that swayed and bounced just so sweetly. She was the color of light caramel, and she did things to me I didn't think were possible.

In the morning, we caught a ride with a truck driver who was on his way to Birmingham, Alabama. When I told Tommy I'd fucked the colored girl he looked at me kind of funny.

A while later he said, "Aw, she wasn't colored. She was what they call Creole. It's a New Orleans thing. Yeah, a Creole. She was just a dark-skinned white girl, is what she was."

I shrugged. "If you say so, all I know is she could really 23-skidoo. But, okay, she was really a white girl."

"Creole."

"Yeah, right, Creole."

We made our way through the South, got invited to bars and church dinners, brought into folks' homes where we were fed like kings by families who laughed at the way "the Yankee boys talk."

We traveled up through Georgia and the Carolinas. In Virginia, we even got picked up by the cops, who brought us over the bridge into Washington. Lots of people were wearing uniforms in that town, but we still made out all right.

We practically got kidnapped by a woman in a big white Studebaker who brought us to a suite in the Willard Hotel. A big party was going on; classy looking guys and dames with backless dresses that you could see right down their ass cracks. It turned out the woman who brought us was married to some senator. He bent our ears about how Roosevelt had plotted to get us into the war all along. Then he invited Tommy and me to bang his wife. He said it was the patriotic thing to do.

And we were just loaded enough to take him up on it. She looked a little like Barbara Stanwyck, and she liked being done from behind while she sucked another guy's cock. So Tommy and I loaded her up and fired her off like a howitzer. Tommy had passed out when she asked me to hit her.

"Huh? Guys from my neighborhood don't hit women— unless they're married."

"C'mon, big brave soldier like you? Afraid to hit a girl?"

I gave her a little light chuck under the chin, but she wanted more.

"C'mon, pansy boy, paste me."

I did to her pretty much what Jimmy Cagney did to that dish with the grapefruit in "Public Enemy." Then I grabbed Tommy and we staggered out of there. To hell with her, maybe she could get one of the bellhops to smack her.

Tommy and I were so loaded we didn't even notice we had parked our asses in front of the White House. We must have been pretty loud though, because all of a sudden we were surrounded by a bunch of guys in suits yelling at us to get up and show them our papers. I was getting ready to swing at one, when a big black Packard cruised by and pulled into the driveway. The rear window rolled down and a hand beckoned to us.

"C'mere, boys."

Those guys in suits shut up quick, and we tottered over to the Packard. About all we could make out was that jutting jaw and a big grin clenching a cigarette holder.

"Where you headed, boys?"

"Boston, sir."

"Know it well. Ever eat at Jacob Wirth's?"

"Yes, sir, but I like Amhrein's."

He chuckled. "Well, boys, let me buy you your tickets home." He handed each of us a twenty dollar bill, waved and gave us a big, "So long."

The Packard continued on and stopped under the portico.

One of the guys in a suit said, "All right, soldiers, time to amscray." He gave us a ride to Union Station.

We bought coach tickets, but a conductor let us flop in a sleeper that wasn't being used. We didn't wake up until a couple of twin sisters stumbled in at New Haven and announced we were occupying their sleeper. But they were great girls. Tommy and I swapped and compared all the way to Boston.

We were pretty ragged when we stumbled out of South Station. I hopped on the D Street bus while Tommy took the MTA over to Eastie.

My mom almost had a heart attack when I walked in the door of the old triple-decker, but she recovered pretty quick, and she and my little sister set about making a big meal. But I had plenty of cash left over, so I took them to Amrhein's for dinner, and then the owner tore up the check. Life was good, but it wouldn't last.

I got to sleep late, but in the morning, Ma said a couple of MPs were waiting in the parlor for me with my reactivation orders. It was time to go back.

* * * *

I met up with Tommy again at the South Boston Army base. Before we knew it, we were back on a train with about twenty other guys. More guys got on in Connecticut, New York, and Philadelphia, then the train started heading southwest. We figured we were headed for the Pacific, but that was applying logic to an Army situation. I bet they would get us as close to the West Coast as they could before they shipped us to Europe.

A loud-mouthed private by the name of Kelso was driving everyone nuts about how many Japs he was going to kill. "I'll roast their little brains inside their ugly skulls," he said.

I had to wonder how a guy came up with an image like that. He didn't say if he was going to eat them too, but I wouldn't put it past him. But it was Kelso who picked up the jackswop that we were on our way to Arkansas.

"God damn it!" he fumed. He was always bitching about something, but our ears perked up when he said, "They're sending us to be some kind of fucking jail guards. Damn, I want to fight."

"What the hell are you talking about?" Tommy growled. "Guards?"

257

"Yeah, for Japs. Can you fuckin' believe that?"

"Malarkey!" A guy from the rear shouted. "We ain't even captured any Japs yet."

"I got it from a corporal who read it off a copy of orders when he was looking over the colonel's shoulder. We're gonna be babysitting Japs."

The whole car went quiet. I said, "Aw, that's for the birds. He probably misread it. Besides, we're getting our asses kicked pretty good. How many Jap prisoners could we have?"

Kelso exploded. "Hey! The only reason the Japs are doing so good is that they got help."

"Huh?"

"Yeah, someone tipped the sneaky little rats when to hit us. Anyway, look what happened at Wake Island. They nearly got their asses wiped by those Marines. How'd you like the CO saying 'Send more Japs!' like he couldn't kill enough of them. Oh, baby, that's what I want, a crack at those little yellow monkeys."

Send more Japs? Wake Island got overrun because we couldn't even organize a half-assed relief expedition. That shit was good for public morale, but any vet knew the last thing those poor bastards needed was more Japs. I looked at Kelso and shook my head.

But then we arrived in southern Arkansas and got marched to a camp. We thought it was an up-overnight Army camp, but then we saw the buses—whole convoys of them—and civilians getting off with luggage. Families, it looked like. Goddamn! They were all Japs.

We formed up and our captains read our orders. FDR had decided to round up anyone of Japanese ancestry on the West Coast and lock them up in camps like this all over the West. It was being done for their safety, but we knew the real reason. People just didn't trust them.

Contractors were still working on the barracks where these people were supposed to be kept, and they looked damned flimsy. It was winter, and I thought the wind could blow right through them. The area was scrubby pine and dusty. A small stream ran just outside the perimeter.

We were marched right past the civilians. Jesus, they were a sad lot. The men's shoulders were hunched, and most of the women were crying. Maybe they thought we were going to shoot them. The little kids clung to their mamas, and I swear you could see a collective tremble go through the entire line.

We got settled into our barracks and got read the riot act. No fraternizing with the "detainees." Yeah, they didn't call them prisoners.

The next day, I was ordered to the intake and interrogation office. I just couldn't see these people giving us trouble. Most of them bowed when they approached an officer or private soldier. But while they all seemed meek, a few glared like they knew one day they'd even the score.

A little old guy showed the captain a Bronze Star he got in World War I. I guess he thought it would buy his ticket out of that rat trap. The tears poured down his cheeks when he was assigned a berth in the bachelor barracks.

It went on like that for hours. Names were checked and barracks assignments made. Then there was a slight commotion. It looked like one of the dads was having an argument with his daughter. You didn't have to understand the language to know it was your typical family argument.

The girl was tall. Well, tall as compared to most of the girls. She was maybe five six and curvy. I mean this girl had more curves than Lefty Grove. She wore a baseball—Dodgers—cap, but her long black hair poured around her shoulders like a shiny shawl. It looked like she was doing the talking for her family.

"Name?" the captain ordered.

"Mickey."

He went down the list. "M-I-K-I?"

The girl rolled her eyes and tilted her hip. "C'mon, don't you know how to spell Mickey? Like Mickey Mouse, for Pete's sake."

The captain was steamed. "What's your Japanese name?"

"I don't know what you're talking about. I'm an American."

"Now, see here …"

"Don't you wag your finger at me, you maroon!"

The captain started to get up, but the colonel put his hand on his shoulder. Meanwhile, I was trying real hard not to grin.

Col. Grayson asked, "Please, Miss—your family name?"

"Yamura."

The colonel traced the list with his finger. "Ah—would you be Michiko Yamura?"

"Yeah."

The colonel nodded his head. "Mickey, huh?"

He turned to me. "Sergeant, escort this young woman to interrogation room B."

"Huh?" the girl protested.

I stepped beside her and pointed the way to the room. Her family called after her, and she turned briefly to try to calm them.

"You like the Dodgers?" I asked, but she said nothing.

"Too bad there aren't any West Coast teams," I continued. "You're from California, right?"

She turned on a dime to face me. "Hey, buddy, you writing a book or something?"

"I dunno, maybe."

"Well, leave my chapter out."

The colonel followed us into the room. A couple of types I recognized as Army intelligence and a suit—probably FBI—were already there.

They told her to sit, and then the AI guy said, "Michiko Yamura, your pilot's license has been revoked."

"What? Damn, what for?"

"You flew for Yoshi Crop Dusters?"

"Yeah, for my uncle. Why did they yank my license?"

"Because, Miss Yamura, your aircraft on numerous occasions violated government airspace. You were observed dropping papers over military facilities in San Francisco. Do you deny that?"

"Big deal, so I buzzed the Army base a few times."

"Maybe you were trying to record the prevailing wind currents with those papers."

"Why would I want to do that?"

"It would come in very handy for a bombardier."

"Oh, for crying out loud, what a lot of baloney. Besides, I wasn't throwing papers, I..." She stopped short, her features frozen in an expression of guilt.

"Yes, Miss Yamura? If they weren't papers, what were they?"

"Ah, nothing."

"You'd better come clean, young lady."

"I... I... Okay, gee... They were my undies."

You could have heard a pin drop in that room. The AI guy's jaw fell open like a trap door. The girl blushed fiercely.

"Excuse me, Miss?" the colonel said in a gentle, fatherly inquiry.

"You know—panties. Gee, you guys have heard of girls' panties, haven't you? And, it wasn't as if they were new. I'd pretty much worn them out. Gee."

The colonel swallowed hard. "Miss, why would you toss your... underthings... out of a plane over an Army facility?"

The girl stared at her feet. "I used to like to fly over when the guys were formed up at attention then watch them break ranks and try to snatch them. It was funny, that's all."

The AI guy spoke up. "Weren't you pursued by a pair of fighters after one of your... panty runs?"

"Aw, those guys and I were just playing," she said. Then she grinned. "They didn't think I could dogfight in that old biplane, but I gave those P-40s a run for their money. It was fun. Hey, they knew I was a girl. They were having fun, too."

Everybody huddled for a bit. I stood in the corner like a good soldier, but I allowed myself a grin while everyone's back was turned. The girl turned and caught me. At first, she looked sore, but then her lips curled into a grin, too.

Finally, the colonel said, "Okay, Miss Yamura, you may return to your family."

"But, what about my pilot's license? Hey, this isn't fair! I was born in this country. I want to do my bit, too."

The AI guy sneered, "The Army Air Corps isn't taking on female pilots, especially..."

"Especially what?" If looks could kill that AI guy would have exploded into smithereens. He just waved her toward the door.

I walked her back to her family. She was proud, and trying real hard not to cry.

* * * *

Any time something was popping up at camp, I could expect to find Mickey Yamura in the middle of it, and somehow she got the idea that I was the go-to guy in the camp. I guess it started the day she collared me about getting some wood for the stove in the camp classroom.

"The kids are freezing, for crying out loud," she complained.

"Yes, ma'am."

I put the guys to work chopping wood as a regular detail after that. Then she came around sniffing for more text books. I had to go to the colonel for that. He made arrangements with some of the towns around the camp to send in some old ones. He really had to plead for that, because people who lived around the camp didn't start out being sympathetic to *the enemy*.

One thing we never had enough of was medical help or supplies. Five babies were born in the camp that winter. Three died. So did a lot of the elderly people with influenza and pneumonia. Colonel Grayson begged for more medics and supplies. Finally, he sent out a request to town doctors to volunteer at the camps. A couple showed up and did a great job. Then the docs took word of the suffering in the camp back to townsfolk.

It used to be kids would ride by and mock the "dirty Japs." But then groups of women came by with blankets and any sort of supplies they could spare. Maybe it was the sight of those three baby graves in the makeshift camp cemetery that tugged at their hearts. Maybe it was because, like most of the soldiers there, they could see that a lot of regular folks like them were having a hard go of it.

We had some suicides. The worst was a guy who got under the wire and made it to some railroad tracks. He just put his head on the rail and waited for the freight to come by.

"How do you like that stupid Nip?" Kelso roared. "Fell asleep on the track. Hey, now he's a good Jap."

A large group was transferred to a maximum security camp in Nevada. They had expressed an enthusiasm for Japan to win the war. Some renounced their U.S. citizenship. It rankled everyone, including most of the detainees, but I had to figure, I couldn't blame them.

But at the same time, the draft board arrived and took about twenty-seven young guys. They went enthusiastically, and bunch of others enlisted when given the chance.

Spring was wet but welcome, and as the weather improved, the camp kids came out looking for pick-up baseball games.

Mickey came to me. "Hey, Donovan, some jackass took the kids' bats and balls away. He said they were dangerous weapons or something."

"I'll check into it."

We got the colonel to step in, and the bats and balls were returned. Then one of the guys said we should build a diamond. By that time, the no fraternizing rule had pretty much gone by the boards. We all pitched in, except for a few hardasses like Kelso.

Mickey supervised, then later she coached one of the kids' teams. One day, I watched her showing a kid how to hit. She whacked one that must have landed in New Mexico. Then she whacked another. My eyes didn't follow the ball; they were glued to her breasts as they jostled under her T-shirt. Then they drank up the long, smooth line of her thighs beneath her khaki shorts.

The guys and I had just cleared up the area around the diamond when I felt a gentle tap on my shoulder.

It was Mickey. "Hey, Donovan, thanks."

It was her eyes—the way they fixed me in her gaze, promising all sorts of dark, mysterious wonder, but glinting with a mischievous sparkle. I just nodded my head. I couldn't speak.

Spring lasted a few days—just a brief respite between winter's cold and summer's oppressive heat. The camp was hot and dusty. We bitched in our barracks, but the detainees' barracks were worse. A few little kids with diarrhea made living inside a nightmare.

At night, I walked the perimeter hoping to get a little relief. One night, a sentry stopped me.

"Sarge, I think I saw some Nips sneak under the wire."

"Where?"

"Halfway between the towers where the scrub pine backs up to the fence."

"Okay, keep your eye out for any more. I'll go after them."

"Alone?"

"Hell, it's probably a couple of kids hoping to take a dip in the stream."

I went out a utility gate and followed the stream. About a half mile down, it pooled into a good sized swimming hole. We'd already yanked a few kids out of it. As I got closer, I heard the unmistakable sounds of splashing. I crouched behind a withered tree just as a cloud cleared the moon to reveal the shimmering body of a naked water goddess. Her head was thrown back with her arms held out from her sides. She stood out of the water, just below her deep-shadowed belly button. She held that pose for a moment, then slid back into the water.

I winced from the suddenly tight confines around my dick. The girl emerged again from the water, backstroking to one end of the pool, then turning and breast stroking the other way. The globes of her ass shown like beacons in the moonlight.

I sat and watched her for about twenty minutes, and caught myself trying to reach for my cock more than once. But finally, I had to put an end to her idyll.

"Miss, you're in violation of curfew and outside the camp perimeter without authorization. Get out, get dressed, and let's go."

"Donovan?"

"Jesus! Mickey, is that you?"

"How long have you been there?"

"Ah, just got here."

"Malarkey!"

"Damn it! Where are your clothes? You're damned lucky I found you instead of someone like that knucklehead Kelso."

No sooner had I said that than Kelso's voice came booming through the woods. "Who goes there? Come out, you little fuck-stick Nips."

"Aw, shit!" I whispered and plunged into the water after Mickey.

"Wait, my clothes!"

"No time!" I lifted her out of the water, and we climbed out the other side of the pond. I tugged her by her left arm, and her right couldn't make up its mind whether to cover her tits or her snatch.

We crouched behind some scrub brush. Then Kelso came bumbling through the trees. He held an M1 fixed with a bayonet. "I'll fuckin' shoot yas and ask questions later!"

Mickey trembled next to me, but I couldn't tell if she was scared or just chilled. We waited Kelso out, then he turned and stomped back toward the camp, but not before he stumbled over Mickey's clothes.

He picked them up and yelled, "Ha! Try getting back bare-assed you dirty Jap whore."

He hesitated a moment, then he left. We stood, and I turned my back and wrestled my shirt off. I held it for her, and she took it hesitantly. I waited a bit before I asked, "Are you decent?"

She had put on the shirt, but it hung open, barely covering her breasts. I must have stood there like a jamoke with my mouth hanging open.

All she said was, "I..."

I didn't think about it at all. My hands slid over her hips and around the small of her back. I pulled her close and kissed her.

My God, the way she felt in my arms! Her skin was softer than I could imagine, and her body hummed with some kind of electricity that found its way right to my cock. I kissed her again, and our tongues twirled and danced. Then she shrugged, and my shirt fell off her shoulders.

I stood back and looked at her in the moonlight. For a brief moment, I wondered why they called Japanese yellow. She was white as snow, paler than any girl I'd ever known, and that included the red-haired colleens from the old neighborhood.

She stepped back. "God, Donovan—are you? I mean... aren't you..."

"Oh, Christ! I don't have a rubber. Mickey, I... want to..."

We just stood a moment and said nothing. Then she picked up my shirt and put it on. It just barely covered her. She led me to a place the kids used to get in and out of the camp. None of us guys ever knew it was there.

She slipped through the wire and turned. "I'm going swimming tomorrow night, too."

* * * *

The guys were excited the next day because movie night was coming up. Then the word went around camp that the colonel had canceled it. Everyone was looking at everyone else wondering who screwed the pooch and being generally surly.

I asked permission to see Colonel Grayson to ask him why. It was hard enough keeping up the morale of guys who were itching to fight but were stuck stateside minding a bunch of *mama-sans*.

"It's not a punishment," the colonel said.

"Yes, sir, but a lot of the guys look at it that way. Was there a problem with the film?"

"Not with the film—the film *is* the problem. It's 'Wake Island.' I told the damned fools not to send us war movies. I had reservations about letting the men see 'Sergeant York,' but at least that was about fighting Germans in another war. But you're right about morale. Okay, I'll permit it in small groups just to keep a lid on things."

That night after the movie, Kelso was regaling the guys about the "dirty Japs" again.

"'Send more Japs.' Did you hear that guy? We should send them all these Japs we got here, right back to Nip-land. Load 'em all up into a B-17 and drop them on Hirohito's ugly monkey head."

One of my younger guys piped up. "Hey, you hear about the guy in C Barracks who got the stockade for making time with one of the Japanese girls?"

"What?" Kelso roared. "I'd just as soon kiss a nigger. They ought to shoot the son-of-a-bitch for treason. At least he couldn't have pumped her."

"How come?"

"Cause white guys don't have flat dicks—and you need a flat dick to fuck a Jap, on account of their twats go side-to-side instead of up-and-down, see."

The room was silent for a second then everyone burst out laughing. The scary thing was, Kelso wasn't in on the joke. He really believed that shit.

I told Tommy to keep a lid on things, then I went out around eleven o'clock. By then, my nightly walks were routine, and the sentries didn't pay any particular attention to where I was going. I slid though the opening Mickey had led me to the other night and made my way down the stream.

Mickey was splashing in the pond when I got there. When she saw me, she lay back gently pedaling her legs lifting her knees out of the water.

I stripped and jumped in. She made a break to slip away, but I caught her, and we wrestled and splashed until she slipped out of my grasp, giggling and kicking water in my face. She moved like a torpedo, but I managed to lunge and grab her above her hips. We must have made a hell of a racket. Then I caught her in a tight arm lock and she stopped giggling. I kissed her—a kiss as delicious as the one the night before.

She broke our kiss and in between feathery pants, she whispered, "I have a blanket on the bank."

We left the water and made our way to the blanket spread in a clearing. The moonlight was doing wondrous things to Mickey's shimmering body. My cock was standing out—almost painfully. The rubber was already in my hand. I tore the packet and rolled the condom over my pleading, weeping cock.

Mickey took my hand and guided me onto my back, then in a one fluid motion straddled me, easing her pussy over the head of my dick. It seemed to take her forever to slide down its length, and I was seeing stars. Mickey began to swivel her hips and piston her body. Her head was slightly thrown back as she licked her lips, eyes closed.

He breasts swayed with each motion, and she moaned musically. I wished I could fuck her without the rubber.

Then she shuddered, held her breath, and then shuddered again. She bent forward until her breasts touched my chest and her long, wet hair draped around my shoulders. I was still hard and deep inside her. Gently rolling with her until we swapped positions, I resumed my thrusts, building speed and straining to penetrate her as deeply as I could. She was making squeaks and little cries as I drilled my cock into her tight channel. Her inner muscles grasped and kneaded me until I launched my fluids into the rubber. I wished I had filled her with them instead.

I had never been so thoroughly fucked out in my life. I practically collapsed on top of her, then I snuggled her in my arms.

We dozed, alternately waking and kissing. I made love to her nipples with my lips and stroked the coarse dark patch that adorned her pussy. We lay there until the sky turned pink, then hurried back to camp. I'd committed a court-martial offense, and that was just jake with me.

* * * *

Mickey and I met every chance we could at the pond. Tommy knew something was up, but he kept it to himself. None of the other guys suspected anything.

Another batch of kids from the camp reached enlistment age, and everyone signed up. A lot of the guys in the outfit were becoming resentful, fueled by the ever louder ravings of Kelso.

"Shit, you got real Americans right here who want to get into this fight, and what do they do? Take these damned Nips and leave us here to mind their bug-eating mamas. They'll probably shoot our guys in the back the first chance they get."

Most everyone thought Kelso was a little crazy, if not a whole lot crazy, but what worried me was they were beginning to listen to him, and giving in to their own frustrations. Tommy kept telling me I had to knock some heads to keep them in line, but my mind was on a swimming hole and a girl who was taking me all kinds of magical places.

It was almost midnight when I headed for the barracks door. The other guys were asleep, but Tommy came after me.

"It ain't none of my business, Sean, but you gotta start taking care of business. These guys are ready to pop and—damn, if word gets out that you've been—you know, with Mickey..."

"Jesus, Tommy, she's not the goddamned enemy. None of these people are."

"Hey, I know that. If things were different... If we weren't at fucking war, I'd say good luck to both of you, but damn it... you're juggling gasoline with a cigarette lighter."

He was right. I patted his arm and nodded, as if that was reassurance I could avoid a mess.

I went out and made my way to the pond. Mickey was waiting on the bank. She hadn't even been swimming. I waded across, and before she could speak, I began to strip her. She was tight and hesitant. In frustration, I tugged her T-shirt off and kissed her tits. But she pushed me away.

"What? What's the matter?"

Tears poured from her eyes. "Damn it, Donovan. You're my jailer. My family and I are someplace we don't deserve to be, and you're helping to keep us here. And what am I doing? Screwing you like some... some whore."

I felt like I was kicked in the heart. "How can you say that? Who's been telling you such nonsense?"

"It's just... I guess I've been thinking, that's all. I applied to an outfit of women pilots. They'll be used to ferry aircraft from factories to debarkation ports, maybe even all the way to Europe. But they turned me down right off the bat, because I'm a Jap, and because I'm on some damned watch list."

"I'm sorry, Mickey, but you can't blame me..."

"It's not you, Sean. It's this whole damned thing. I'm as good an American as you or anyone, and so are my folks and my brothers. So, what did I do to get put in jail, huh? Because my eyes look different?"

"But, Mickey..."

"I like you Sean, I may even love you, but I can't do this anymore, not while you're my... keeper."

I couldn't help but admire her pride. It shone in her eyes, even in the way her little breasts perked up. I pulled her close and she cried into my shoulder.

"Goddamned fucking traitor!"

I turned and stood between Mickey and the voice I hated so well. Kelso had found us. Worse than that, he was holding an M1 and swaying on his feet. He was three-goddamned-sheets-to-the-wind.

"Lousy Jap lover! I'm marching you and your little Nip slut to the stockade, Donovan, you lousy prick, you fucking Jap cunt-licker."

"Kelso, you're drunk. Drop the weapon."

Instead, he aimed. "Better idea, I shoot the little yellow cunt, then I shoot you for helping her escape. Maybe they'll give me a medal."

His thoughts of homicidal glory ended with a loud metallic *thunk*. Tommy Gennaro hit him over the head with his steel pot. Kelso was out like a light.

I snatched up Mickey's T-shirt and like a gentleman, Tommy turned his back while she put it on.

"Sean, Kelso's going to tell Grayson no matter what. Better you and I tell him first, huh?"

Tommy was right. We humped it back to camp with the unconscious Kelso. Then I woke up the colonel and told him what happened and what had been happening with me and Mickey. He sent me back to the barracks and ordered me to stay put.

It was late afternoon when I was finally summoned to the colonel's office. I was shown into his private office, and the door closed behind me. I was looking for another officer to witness the formal charges, but it was just me and the Old Man.

"Sergeant, you're a good soldier, you know how to handle men, you're intelligent. How the hell did you let yourself do something so damned stupid?"

"No excuse, Sir. But, she's not like any girl I ever..."

"Yes, yes, Miss Yamura is a force of nature, but damn, you've put me in a difficult situation."

"I understand, sir. Kelso..."

"Forget Kelso."

"Beg your pardon, Sir?"

"Kelso's getting his wish. He's going to fight. I just signed his transfer papers."

"Oh..."

"You and Gennaro are, too."

"What?"

"That's right. They need you. I'm releasing about twenty men to combat units. Kelso won't say a thing, and you and Miss Yamura will go your separate ways."

"But, Sir, Mickey... I mean, Miss Yamura deserves a chance, too. She's a loyal American, Sir, so are all of these folks."

"Don't you think I know that?" The old man pushed a buzzer and a second later, his aide peeked through the door.

"Send in Miss Yamura."

Mickey entered the office and gave me a sidelong glance.

"Colonel Grayson, I'm so sorry to cause this trouble, but..."

The colonel raised his hand and cut her short. "Miss Yamura, I don't have a lot of juice in this man's Army, otherwise I wouldn't be at this camp. But I pulled what few strings are available to me. I've approved you for the Women's Auxiliary Air Unit."

I thought she would jump out of her skin. "What?"

"Congratulations, Michiko. You'll get a chance to fly them all: Lightnings, Wildcats, even B-17s."

Mickey nearly bowled him over when she rushed to kiss him. The colonel acted like a flustered dad.

The colonel dismissed us with orders to keep our distance until we left camp, but we arranged to meet one night behind some supply shacks.

Mickey didn't say much. We just held each other and kissed. Then Mickey looked into my eyes for a moment before she kneeled and worked loose my belt buckle, then drew down my fly. She reached into my pants, and her silky soft hands closed around my cock. She licked the tip and then took it into her mouth.

It wasn't something that nice girls did in those days, so I understood what a special gift it was. Her tongue swirled, setting off charges of electricity that meandered the length of me. I lost all sense of the outside world and gave myself up to the sensations. Then a steady flow of fluid roared out of me.

Mickey stood, licking at the corners of her mouth where my cum still drooled down to her chin. I kissed her, tasting her and myself.

"I wanted to do something... special for you," she said.

We kissed again, and I held her a long time. Finally, she slipped through my arms.

"Goodbye, Donovan."

I never saw her again.

* * * *

A few days later, we were in Fort Dix, New Jersey, and from there it was on to North Africa, Sicily and Italy, where Tommy met up with a few of his relatives. I got myself a field commission to lieutenant. Otherwise, Italy was a nut-busting, ass-breaking slog up one mountain, and then up another, fighting every goddamned inch.

I remember when we blundered right into an SS Panzer division and got chewed up pretty good. That's the fight in which Tommy bought himself a little piece of Italy. He's lying there still.

I might have been lying next to him, but just in the nick of time, we got saved by some hard-chargers from the 100/442nd—a Nisei regiment, Japanese Americans. Those guys kicked some Nazi ass that day and saved ours in the bargain.

When it was all over except for the mop-up, the CO rang me up from headquarters.

"Need anything, Lieutenant?" the Old Man asked.
I knew just what to tell him. "Yeah, send more Japs!"

♥

Enough Said
© Bridget Midway

[One]

No one should be forced to live an entire life in a week. Autumn stared out of her upstairs bedroom window searching for Sean's truck, although there was no way could she miss its thunderous rumbling. It provoked complaints from their elderly neighbors who called him a nuisance.

As she thought about his unintended ruckus, she smiled. A laugh managed to cough its way through her lips, a first in several weeks.

Autumn chewed the soft, fleshy inside of her cheek. Standing in her bare feet, she rested one foot on top of the other, then swept her upper toes over her planted ones. She crossed her arms over her chest. When a hand rose to her mouth to begin the habitual fingernail feasting, she slammed it back down. For Sean, she would keep her manicured fingernails intact.

Occupying her thoughts became harder and harder. If Autumn kept her gaze directed outside of the home she shared with Sean, she would be able to get through these last hours. As time passed, she stopped counting down from month to month, then week to week, and day to day. She now had to mark the remaining time by hours. Soon, it would be minutes. One-hundred sixty-two minutes to be exact.

A booming grumble growled down the street. Autumn braced her hands on the windowpane and scanned the road for her man. Her heart sank to see her neighbor riding up his driveway in his new Harley-Davidson.

Damn.

Tired of waiting and being disappointed, Autumn swung her head around and looked into bedroom. In the expansive room with the canopy bed she shared with Sean, the dresser and chest-of-drawers she purchased with him over a year ago, and the forty-two inch plasma screen TV she couldn't talk him out of buying, her gaze connected with the picture that sat on top of the nightstand. With so much to look at in the room, why couldn't something else capture her attention?

Unable to disconnect herself from the sight, Autumn padded over to it. She sat on the bed before picking it up, remembering the exact moment the picture had been taken: Fourth of July in her parents' backyard, a month or so after they moved in together.

Her father had had anything and everything that once breathed cooking on his grill. Her mother led off all of the dances, from "The Electric Slide" to "The Boot-Scoot Boogie." And, the entire day, Sean wouldn't let go of her. Autumn remembered how he held her around her waist the moment they had gotten to the cookout.

"No one's going to bite you," she remembered telling him. "You don't have to hold me all the time."

Sean had said with that deep voice of his, "Maybe I'm just using you to cover up my hard-on."

Thinking about it now, she laughed through her tightening throat.

Don't do this, girl. Don't let him see you break down. Not now.

Autumn took a deep breath and stared at the picture again. The muted colors in the background faded as she studied the two of them. The sun had given Sean a great tan that summer. Autumn recalled how good he looked, even with his head shaved. His darker skin made his gray eyes even more pronounced.

That summer, she had opted for braids, and he had called her his African princess. She called him her white knight in shining armor. Their friends had other names for them. Thomas Jefferson and Sally. The Swirl. Zebra Duo. All names said in fun. Sean had made sure the teasing remained in good fun, always making sure Autumn was protected. Now, Sean would be defending other people—strangers—whether they liked it or not.

She shook her head, not wanting to think about that now. Her mind had been filled with those thoughts for the last several months. She wondered if Sean knew at the time the picture was taken that duty had called. Was that the reason he held onto her like a prized possession, like a security blanket, like another wounded soldier? If he knew, why hadn't he said anything?

She slammed the frame down, attempting to block out all thoughts about his departure—even with it being days away. Autumn jumped to her feet and strolled around the bedroom to take in other sights or find something else to occupy her mind, her senses.

Music. She scurried to the sound system in the corner of the room. Unlike some men, Sean never flinched when Autumn touched his precious and expensive electronics. Once, she managed to erase all of his settings by accident. He didn't get angry. Instead, he had kissed her on her temple, sat down with her, and showed her step-by-step just how to work the pricey equipment.

Sean's patience was what drew her to him. For such a big man, he never lost his cool around her. The arguments they had—which weren't many—never had him raising his voice.

Now Autumn, she would rant and rave and jump around like a mad woman. It used to piss her off to no end when Sean would watch and smile at her antics.

"Babe, you don't have to shout in order for me to understand that your argument means a lot to you," he had told her. "If it comes out of your mouth, it's important."

Responses like that got him sex every time. As soon as sex entered her mind, Autumn's hand hovered over her romance CDs. Robin Thicke, Barry White, Boyz II Men, Jill Scott. She stopped at The Isley Brothers. Classic slow jams got to her more than the modern stuff.

Autumn popped in the CD and put it on the song that she and Sean first made love to shortly after they started dating. *Shortly after*, she snorted. Who was she kidding? She had met him that morning in the grocery store in the produce aisle and asked him out. That night they had sex in her apartment. Since then, they'd been inseparable.

Her eyes itched again with the realization that they would soon be separated. Separated. Departing. Departed.

Stop it, Autumn! Stop it!

She wiped her eyes to arrest any wayward tears. As soon as the first note from "In Between The Sheets" sounded, Autumn strolled around their bedroom. With time winding down, she wanted to fill her senses with everything related to Sean.

At his tall dresser, she pulled open the top drawer packed with white T-shirts and Jockeys, also white. Just like a good military man, he had everything folded in small, neat bundles and organized in rows. Her drawer looked nothing like it.

She closed it and opened the next drawer. Colored T-shirts arranged by hues filled the second drawer. Autumn removed a dark blue shirt. Holding it around the collar, she snapped it open. Damn if it wasn't the same shirt Sean had worn to the cookout in the framed picture.

Wanting to feel close to Sean, she sat the shirt on top of the dresser and pulled off her own T-shirt. She tossed hers to the floor, then stripped off her bra. His oversized shirt draped her body like a dress, coming down far enough to cover the cotton shorts she wore.

To feel it tighter, she tied a knot on one side and had it resting high on her hip. When she brought her arms down, a faint aroma of his cologne wafted up to her nostrils. No, she needed more.

With two long strides, she ran to the bathroom and scanned the counter for his regular cologne. Buried behind her bottles of scented oils and sprays hid a squared bottle of the scent that drove her crazy every time he wore it. Autumn removed the cap and took a whiff.

Her mind traveled back to that day in the grocery store when she first walked by him. She'd noticed other women watching him. Who wouldn't have? A six-foot-six sexy brick of a man carrying a small green basket and palming honeydew melons like they were as small as golf balls. Only Autumn had been brave enough to approach him. His aroma enraptured her, a strong, musky smell that fit him to a tee.

Autumn sprayed the cologne on the shirt, set the bottle down, grabbed the front of the garment, and took in a strong inhalation. She closed her eyes, and Sean's image populated. Her Sean. Not Major Sean Littleton of the United States Marines. He was her Sean, the man who shooed away spiders and who held her during scary movies and cooked blueberry pancakes in the nude. That was her Sean.

She smoothed her hands over her breasts, aware of how hard her nipples had become. Her small hands with their slender fingers could not compare to Sean's mitts. Much like the melons, her breast disappeared in his grasp. She felt captured by him, and the feeling suited her.

As the music continued, Autumn swayed her body. She danced in front of the mirror, and it reminded her of the first time she gave Sean a lap dance. She'd bound him to a chair in her bedroom, then swayed her body around like a snake.

"Baby, are you trying to torture me?" he'd asked her.

She had continued dancing, stripping off her clothes ever so slowly until she stood in front of him in the nude. Before she untied him, she got down on her knees in between his legs. She undid his pants and pulled them down to his feet. The sound of the handcuffs she'd used to bind his wrists sliding up and down the chair railings echoed in her head.

His cock was long, thick, and hard. She'd wrapped her hand around the base of it and slid her mouth down as far as she could go. His body twitched, and he growled like a grizzly.

Thinking about his primal reaction now released Autumn's juices. She leaned against the bathroom doorjamb and slid her hand into her shorts. Through her panties, she rubbed her thumb over her clit. Her other hand occupied itself by snaking its way up her shirt and cupping her breast.

As her heart pounded, she continued with her fond memory of sucking Sean's cock. She could almost taste his tangy saltiness now.

When she'd felt him shaking out of control, Autumn let him go long enough to strip out of her panties, straddle him and ride him hard. He devoured her mouth until she tilted her head back. Then he sucked and licked her neck.

When they both came, their bodies covered in sweat and the room smelling of hot sex, he'd said, "Marry me."

Not missing a beat, Autumn had said, "Ask me when you don't have your dick inside of me."

The question and response had become their running joke. Marrying Sean wouldn't be a joke. Aside from how she'd met Sean, Autumn planned everything about her life, even down to her wedding. She would be damned if she allowed the United States government to dictate how she ran her life. It was bad enough that they had to celebrate holidays and special occasions in a week.

Not satisfied with fondling herself through her thong, she slipped her hand inside. Her expert middle finger found its way inside of her pussy as the heel of her hand brushed her clit.

"Oh God!" Autumn scrubbed her back against the doorframe as she pleasured herself.

She squeezed her eyes shut and only imagined Sean, his body, his eyes, his large, calloused hands, his mouth, his tongue, and that deep voice that would whisper "I love you" in her ear.

The song ended and the next song started, but Autumn wasn't done with the first song. She wanted more. On shaky legs, she stumbled to the sound system and figured out how to put the song on repeat.

As the song started over again, she plopped down on the bed and continued exploring her body. This time she brought the T-shirt over her bare breasts. She relieved her shorts and thong of their duties and piled them on the floor at her feet.

With her legs spread open, she moved her finger in and out of her in a fast and steady rhythm. But it wasn't enough. No matter that she inserted a second finger; they couldn't match the girth or heat that she would get from Sean's perfect penis.

Autumn opened her eyes and rolled onto her side. She crawled over the bed to the nightstand and dove into the drawer where she found a friend she hadn't used in long, long time. The bright pink plastic phallus hummed and vibrated as soon as Autumn turned the switch at the bottom.

This unique vibrator worked in water. Remembering its capabilities, Autumn ran to the bathroom and turned on the shower in the cramped stall. Without taking off the T-shirt, she got inside, letting the cool water attempt to lower the temperature of her overheated flesh.

She put one foot on the wall next to the spigot and braced her free hand on the built-in soap dish. She slipped the vibrator inside of her, slowly at first. Once she got it all the way inside, she let out a long, low cry. The feeling couldn't match Sean's dick, but it was very close.

Autumn moved the vibrator in and out of her at a faster pace. The music echoed in the bathroom. The sound, the smell, the feeling, they were all like Sean, almost. Things like this would have to pacify her in his absence.

The leg supporting her body trembled, and she leaned her head back. Autumn's stomach compressed into a ball as she squeezed her nipple. The build up to the orgasm churned at a slow pace, but at least she knew she could get there. With Sean, he could just look at her, and she wanted to claw her clothes off and spontaneously combust right on the spot.

As the climax started to build, her strength began to wane. Autumn slipped down the wall, continuing to piston the vibrator in and out of her greedy cunt.

"Sean! Sean! Sean!" Even with her eyes closed, she noticed an immediate shift in the lighting in the stall, as though someone had flashed a light on her.

Autumn opened her eyes and turned to the glow. Sean stood next to the shower stall with the curtain pulled back and carrying a self-satisfied grin. Without a word, he covered her hand holding the vibrator, and he removed it from inside of her. Not bothering to turn it off, he tossed it to the floor.

Autumn hooked her hand behind his head and pulled him, clothed and all, into the small stall. Sean craned his head down to kiss her while both of their hands worked on his shorts, trying to undo them and get them down.

Once his cock was free, Sean took no time in looping his arm under her leg as he guided his head to her pussy. He stared into her eyes as he pushed his way inside of her.

Autumn clawed his wet shirt as it clung to his back and wrapped her other leg around his body. Just like she liked, just what she wanted, he pounded inside her fast and hard. Cramped space or not, he knew how to please her.

Sean massaged her breast as he kissed her, darting his tongue in and out of her mouth. Autumn's hand moved up the back of his neck to his head where she immediately noticed his new shorter haircut.

At that point, he let her breast go, brought her hand down, carried her outside of the stall to the counter, and left the shower running. The old Autumn would have yelled at Sean for getting the bathroom floor so wet. Now it seemed so trivial.

Sean cupped her ass cheeks as he slid himself in and out. Even with his tan, his cheeks flushed red. Autumn framed his face with her hands. His strong jaw line now had a fine sandpaper grit covering it. Trying to capture a new sensory detail, she smoothed her hands over his face, letting the prickly hairs tickle her palms.

As soon as Autumn felt Sean's legs shaking, her pussy twitched, tightening around his shaft. The feeling provoked a moan from Sean. He squeezed her ass cheeks, then nibbled her earlobe.

She coiled her legs around his body and released a scream that would have been worthy enough to alert the police. It didn't take Sean long to follow suit, letting out his own guttural growl to complement her shriek. His muscles tensed in an instant as she felt his hot cum bathing her insides. That feeling she wouldn't be able to duplicate.

After a tense moment, Sean exhaled. His shoulders and back relaxed as he kissed the side of her face and moved to her mouth. When he broke from the kiss, he said, smiling, "Marry me."

"Ask me when your dick isn't inside of me." Autumn laughed.

The smile dripped from Sean's face. He pulled out but kept his hold on her. "Marry me."

Autumn regarded him for a moment. She laughed at first, thinking the joke was still rolling until she noticed how stoic his face had become.

"Marry me," he said again with the beat of their sex song playing in the background.

Autumn wriggled away from him. "No."

[Two]

One thing Sean loved about Autumn was her fiery spirit. That same bullish attitude grabbed his attention the day they met in the store. She had approached him like she knew she could get him. And she did.

Sean remembered staring into her dark brown, almost black, eyes. In her tiny short shorts and the halter top, she showed off her dark brown skin—skin that he got to lick the very night he met her—she possessed a swagger that couldn't be ignored. She made him dinner, then rocked his world.

He hadn't planned on getting into a serious relationship. With Autumn, pairing with her couldn't be avoided. She was a force of nature that he could either fight or allow to blow him over. He went with the latter.

Seeing her masturbating in the shower stall when he had gotten home drove him crazy. It was bad enough he had driven from his parents' house to the home he shared with Autumn with an erection the whole time. She had sent him off to see his family by telling him, "I'm going to fuck your brains out all this week." It was all he could do not to think about her tantalizing body while his mother went through photo albums and showed home movies of the family.

Autumn sobered him when she turned down his impromptu marriage proposal, a serious one this time. He shut off the shower and stripped out of his wet clothes and shoes. Autumn took off his T-shirt and dumped it in a plastic laundry basket. Then she picked up the still vibrating toy from the floor and ceased its intended duty.

Without a word, she summoned him to deposit his wet items into the basket as well. Sean dried off his body, keeping his bandage side from her view. Then mopped the puddles off of the floor. He added the wet towel to the basket.

"Don't worry about the clothes right now." He held her upper arm.

"Let me do this, and I'll be back." She moved away from him and walked downstairs naked with a hamper on her hip.

Sean removed the CD from the player and inserted a mellow jazz CD, something to help them wind down. He wanted a beer right now, but he'd done so well to wean himself for the last month, he didn't want to ruin it now.

With his head on the pillow, he glanced to the side at the picture of the two of them. He remembered the day that picture was taken, not because of the kick-ass food Autumn's father had made, or the way her plump mother had shimmied and shook when she danced. It was the day he'd told Autumn he loved her for the first time. Too bad it was also the day he had been told about his future assignment. The year had flown by fast. He needed more time with Autumn.

He'd never told Autumn that he had been given his oversees assignment on that day. She didn't need to know. It was bad enough she cried in her sleep, calling his name out on most nights. Holding her helped, but it tore him up to think that she would be home alone to deal with the nightmares. All he could do was to assure her.

Autumn waltzed into the bedroom, sashaying her hips with every step.

"Stop." Sean held up his hand.

Autumn halted in her spot.

"Slow." He lowered his hand and watched her swaying even slower as she moved toward him.

Snakes would have been envious of her moves. At the foot of the bed, she climbed on and crawled to him. She slithered over his body and rested her head on his chest.

With his arm around her waist, he said, "I wish I could capture that look before I go."

Autumn wrapped her arms around him and brushed against his bandaged skin, making him wince.

She sat up and peered over to his side. "What's that?"

Sean stared at her, gauging if she had the strength to hear the truth right now. Regardless, he had to tell her.

He sat up higher, leaning against the headboard. "It's my name, rank and serial number tattooed on my side." With slow and careful precision, Sean removed the bandage from his skin, showing off the greenish tattoo.

Autumn trailed her fingertips around the spot without touching it. "Why do you have this on your body?"

Sean affixed the bandage back into its spot. "In case while I'm there, if anything happens to me, if my dog tags get separated from me or out of my boot, they'll know who I am and what to do with my body.

He heard Autumn swallowing hard. She gazed up at him, connecting her gaze to his. In her gape, they shared a silent conversation. In his mind, he heard her asking him if he was afraid, if he was scared that he wouldn't come home from this mission.

Sean smiled to assuage her fears. He ran his hand up and down her arm. "Mom missed you. She thought you were coming with me."

Autumn shook her head. "Right now, I can't be in the same room with her. One look..." She trailed off and turned her head away from him like she wanted to hide her emotions. But now was the time to get all of her emotions out. Everything. Love, hate, confusion, anger, regret, all of it.

"Afterward, when you're... I'll see her then." Autumn wiped her face. "So what did you do today?"

"Family movies and pictures. Dad thought it was all silly. He did 'Nam with less fanfare. Didn't understand what all the fuss was about." Sean kissed Autumn's forehead.

"A year. You'll be gone for a year." She curled her body closer to his.

"Or less. You never know. Peace may break out in the Middle East as soon as I get there." He laughed and, thankfully, it elicited a laugh from her.

"Hoo Rah." Autumn pumped a weak fist in the air.

"Oh no, honey. If you're going to do it, do it right." He covered her fist in his hand. "Hoo rah! Say it, babe. Hoo rah!"

"Hoo." She choked on the word. "Hoo." The second time she said it, the word broke.

Sean had to get her to talk. Aside from her plans for his final week home, Autumn hadn't opened up about how she felt about his deployment.

"My checks will be direct deposited into our joint account. If something happens to me, clean out the account before the government or anyone else tries to seize the money, understand?"

Autumn sat up and glared at him.

"My mother has power-of-attorney. Anything happens with the house, she'll help you work it out so that you keep it."

"What are you doing?" Autumn's voice came out soft.

"Briefing you. I mean, preparing you. Whatever clothes my brother doesn't want, give to Disabled Vets."

"Stop it." She backed from him, but Sean held her hand and pulled her close.

"If you don't want the truck, Mom knows to sign it over and give it to my brother or donate it charity."

Autumn pounded on his chest. "Stop it! Stop it! Stop talking like you're going to fucking die!"

"That's it, honey. I want to hear it. Tell me what you're feeling. Are you mad at me?"

"What?" Autumn furrowed her eyebrows.

"For being a Marine."

"No. I'm— I'm—"

"Say it." He let her hand go to allow her movement.

Autumn could be very physical and passionate when she argued.

"I don't understand this fucking war! Why do you need to go? I just got you in my life, and now I'm losing you. It's not fair. It's not goddamn fair! I could care less about oil or weapons of mass destruction or whatever else may be going on over there. I want you here. I want to be able to yell at you when you leave the toilet seat up. I want you home when thunderstorms roll through and I'm afraid. I want to remind you every Thursday to take the trashcan to the curb." She straddled his body. "And I want to be able to make love to you morning, noon, and night. I want to be able to pick up a phone and call you to talk dirty like I do now when you're at work."

Sean smiled thinking about her previous calls where she got him so horny that he couldn't stand up for over an hour.

"I can't do this alone." Tears streamed down her cheeks. "Fuck! I promised not to cry in front of you before you left." She attempted to get up but he held her down on top of him.

Sean wrapped his arms around her body and stroked her hair. "I'll be fine. My guys are trained to watch my back, and I'll cover theirs."

"But you watch the news and—"

"Don't watch the news, not while I'm gone, okay?"

She nodded. "Sean?"

"Yeah, babe?"

"I'm not giving your brother that blue T-shirt." She looked up at him and smiled.

"You're such a sentimental softie. I thought I hooked up with a tough girl." He kissed her forehead. "So what do you have planned for me this week?"

Autumn stared at him, her eyes full of suspicion. "Did you look in the refrigerator?"

Sean waited a beat before answering. He'd never lied to Autumn. He wouldn't start now. "Yes."

Her shoulders slumped down. "So you saw it?"

"Maybe." Sean wouldn't say outright that he saw the birthday cake in the refrigerator, although the blue-and-white monstrosity couldn't be missed.

"Damn it. I wanted it to be a surprise." She pounded her hand into the mattress.

"Honey, you've already told me that we're packing a year into this one week. I knew what was in store."

"Fine. You wait here." She leapt from the bed and scampered downstairs again.

About five minutes later, he heard her climbing the stairs. At the middle landing, she stopped and asked him to turn off the lights in the bedroom. Without question, Sean doused the lights and climbed back into bed.

"Happy birthday to you." Autumn sauntered into the room with a circular cake in one hand and two bottles of water in the other. "Happy birthday to you." She sat the cake with the numbers *three* and *six* lit on the top on the bed next to Sean. "Happy birthday, dear Sean." She sat down on the other side of the cake. "Happy birthday to you!" After placing the two waters on the nightstand, Autumn applauded. "Make a wish."

Sean peered up and thought for a moment before blowing out the two candles.

"Should I even ask what you wished for?" She tickled her fingertips over his outstretched legs.

"I've already got half of it. You're here naked, and I have cake."

"So what's the other half of the wish?"

"I eat the cake out of your sweet pussy, then fuck you senseless."

In the darkened room, he heard Autumn's breathing turn into a pant. "You might get your wish. But before anything happens, you have to open your presents." She jumped from the bed and ran into their spare bedroom.

When she returned, Sean asked, "Are all of my presents in there?" He started to sit up.

"Don't you dare! I'll make sure you don't make it to your assignment."

Sean laughed.

Autumn handed him three big boxes. "Open them."

In one, she had gotten him the complete DVD collection of the "Shaft" movies. Sean laughed so hard, his side hurt.

"I remembered you said you liked the movies." Autumn took the balled gift wrap from his hands.

"I also said I had a crush on Pam Grier."

As she chewed on her lower lip, Autumn glanced at another gift on the bed.

Sean opened it and found all of Pam Grier's old 70's blaxploitation movies. "Your dad is going to be so jealous."

"I know. White or black, he always saw you as another son." She looked away and coughed a little before returning her attention to him and plastering a smile on her face. "Last one."

The last gift contained items for things he'd always wanted to do—like scuba and skydiving.

"We can do them now." She peeked at him under heavy eyelids. "Or when you get back."

"We? What happened to, 'You can't get a sista under water'?" Sean punctuated the question with Autumn's trademark head roll, which made her laugh.

"I decided that life is short. If I'm going to do things with you, I have to start now. Plus, this will give you hope to come home in one piece."

He nodded. "I do my damndest." Then Sean set the items on the floor. "Is that all?"

"Those are all of the presents. Why?"

Sean crawled over the bed to Autumn. "I hope you didn't think I was kidding about the cake."

As he hovered his body over hers, he swiped his finger on the cake, scooping up some icing on his fingertip. Like lipstick, he smeared the white, sugary coating over her lips—not that he needed something to entice him to lick and kiss her, Sean enjoyed nibbling her full lips, removing the fluffy topping.

Autumn let her tongue touch his until he moved down her body to her breasts. There he covered each nipple with frosting. Just like with her lips, he licked her breasts, dragging his wide, flat tongue over her hard peaks. Each time he touched her, Autumn arched her back in response. Sean wanted to tease her until he had her levitating.

With a scooping motion using three of his fingers, Sean picked up a hunk of cake as he made his way down her body and positioned himself in between her legs. Staring at her protruding clit, he couldn't wait to lick it, devour it, make her come so hard that she would forget about his impending departure.

With the ease of a sculptor, Sean placed the dessert on top of her pussy, right over the hardened nub.

Autumn jerked her body. "So cold."

"I'll get you hot."

True to his words, each swipe of Sean's tongue over her wet, shaved pussy coupled with eating the cake he had sitting on top of her, drove Autumn's body temperature higher. Had he not finished off the pastry, he was sure it would have melted. The thought of licking off the melted sweet cream from her already tasty center propelled him to delve his tongue inside of her even more.

Autumn screamed. She held his head in its spot, right between her legs and at her pussy. Her back arched with each long, loving swipe. When Sean felt her body trembling, he knew she was close. As much as he wanted to have her come with his cock inside of her, he wasn't about to break her moment, her flow.

Sean massaged her thighs and continued his oral assault while Autumn began bucking he hips. He wouldn't tell her, but it was moments like these, going down on her, tasting her salty juices, making her come, *hearing* her come, that would drive him insane while he was thousands and thousands of miles away from her.

This was a path he'd chosen before he met her. He wanted to be just like his father, a fearless Marine. Although bold in his job, one thing did scare him. He didn't want to go away for a year without having Autumn as his wife. It had nothing to do with trust. The reason had deeper roots, one he didn't think he had to explain to Autumn. Sean believed certain things didn't have to be said.

He must have slowed down his tonguing technique. Autumn lowered her hips and peered down at him.

"Babe?"

Without a word, Sean covered her clit with his mouth and sucked on it, making Autumn jerk off the bed. His finger circled her pussy opening before delving deep inside, finding a hearty welcome within her moist, thick walls. His other hand continued massaging her thigh.

Sean's heart pounded as hard as Autumn pounded the mattress with her fists. Her body convulsed. At once, she froze just as she released a howl that turned him on rather than make him question the sound.

Sean eased his finger out of her as he backed away. After sitting up on his haunches, he scanned her body. Sweat made her glow. Her black hair, now in a short hairstyle, was spiked all over head. She was absolutely breathtaking.

"Now that I don't have a dick inside of you, I'll ask you again."

Autumn removed her hand from her face and peered down. "Don't."

"Autumn, will you marry—"

She wriggled away from him and had to fall on the floor and pull herself up on the bed in order to get her feet under her. "I'll start dinner."

"Why don't you want to answer me?"

She didn't respond, which was unlike Autumn. In every argument and every conversation, she had to have the last word. Why change now? He needed that fire back inside of her. And he needed an explanation.

[Three]

For their Veteran's Day, a holiday that Autumn had never truly celebrated in the past, she surprised Sean by dressing as a candy striper, complete with a short uniform that barely covered the tops of her stockings, and a traditional nurse's cap.

"Hiya, soldier." She gave him a salute from their bedroom doorway, then sauntered inside in her five-inch white patent leather stilettos. "I hear you're on the mend."

Sean snickered as he remained in bed, covered by a thin sheet that did a poor job of covering his growing erection.

"Is this what I have to do to get you to wear more costumes in the bedroom? I have to get deployed?" He laughed.

After a tense night, when he'd asked her to marry him again and, again, she refused, it was great to see him smiling. Hopefully, she could get him to forget about asking her to marry him. Her answer would be the same—and it wasn't because she didn't love him. Her heart ached each time she thought about him leaving. For that reason, she knew she couldn't be his wife.

"Costume? Why, I'm not wearing a costume, honey." She touched the white curved hat on her head, which made the hem of her dress rise, evident from the way Sean's gaze dropped down. "This is a regulation hat." Then she smoothed her hands down her body. "And this is a regulation uniform. I found it a bit confining, so I made some alterations." She pulled down the zipper in front. "I can pull this down to give myself some breathing room. And I raised this up so that I can move better." She pulled up on her dress, showing off her thong panties that had a big Red Cross emblem on the front.

The sight forced a hearty laugh from Sean.

"What? You don't like my panties?" She hooked her fingers on the sides and pulled them down. Then she twirled the undergarment around her index finger. "Better?"

Sean shook his head. He motioned for her to come closer to him. Autumn dropped the panties to the floor as she strolled to him.

He kicked off the sheet, peered down at his erect cock, then brought his attention back to her.

In mock surprise, Autumn covered her mouth with her hand. "Oh, my! Major Littleton, why, you're not sick at all."

"You're damn right." He grabbed her hand and pulled her on top of him so that she straddled him.

"If my nursing supervisor catches me, I could get into a lot of trouble," she said as she held the base of his shaft and positioned her pussy over him.

"Tell her this is a part of my treatment." Sean raised his hips, stabbing his dick inside of her.

Damn, he felt so good there. The length and girth of it fit inside of her like he had been made just for her. Autumn held onto his shoulders as she rode him, slowly at first.

"You're awfully wet, Nurse Autumn." He held her hips. "Did you know you were going to come in here and fuck me?"

Unable to speak, Autumn nodded her head. She leaned forward and connected her mouth to his. Her tongue explored familiar territory. Like a good ally, his tongue touched and teased hers.

Autumn picked up speed, undulating her hips. Although she wanted this session to last forever, she already felt her stomach tighten. Sean must have felt her body's responses.

"Come if you want to. I'm not done with you yet." A sly smile curved up.

Autumn gripped Sean's shoulders as wave upon wave or orgasmic intensity hit her. As promised, as soon as her body settled down, Sean pulled her off of his lap and rolled her next to him so that she was positioned on her stomach. Then he got on top of her.

"Time for the patient to take the nurse's temperature." As soon as he brought her dress over her lush ass, and Autumn raised it in the air, the phone rang.

"Don't answer it, please." Autumn craned her head around to look Sean in his eyes. "This is our time."

Sean nodded and held her hip in one hand as he guided the tip of his cock to her puckered asshole. At the fourth ring, the answering machine kicked on. Damn. Why didn't Autumn think to either unplug the phone or turn off the answering machine?

"This is Lieutenant Colonel Musser," the authoritative voice bellowed through the answering machine.

"Are you serious?" Autumn tried not to laugh, but it popped out anyway. "Colonel Mustard like in that board game?"

Sean hopped off of her and scurried to the phone. He picked up the receiver to stop the recording.

"Yes, sir." Sean sat on the edge of the bed with the phone pressed to his ear. "I understand." He paused before speaking again. "I'll see you then. Yes, sir." Then he disconnected the call. He turned to Autumn, but from the look of his deflated erection, it looked like their party was over. "Change of plans."

Autumn got excited. A call from his commanding officer about a change had to be a good thing, right? So why wasn't Sean looking any happier?

"You're not going?" she asked.

All Sean had to do was stare at Autumn for her to know the answer. She shook her head.

"I guess Dad can go on with the barbeque." Autumn climbed out of bed.

The mood had been broken.

Sean jerked to his feet. "Come on. Get dressed."

"Why? Where are we going?"

He didn't answer. As a matter of fact, that was the last statement he'd made before Autumn and Sean both showered, dressed and got into his noisy truck.

Autumn didn't care if Sean drove them down to Mexico from Virginia to start a new life and hide out from the Marine's kung-fu grip. When it came to Sean, she trusted him completely. That was until he drove until the city clerk's parking lot and parked his truck up front.

"What are we doing here?" A sinking feeling weighed down Autumn's stomach. Her hands became cold and clammy, and she tried wringing them to bring back the feeling.

Sean turned to Autumn. "Applying for a marriage license."

That was what she feared the most.

He opened his door, then, as usual, trotted around to her side to open her door. That gentlemanly gesture would never get old, but it would be missed while he was away.

He took her hand and led her inside the building.

"Sean, I told you I didn't want to get married. Not now." If the ceramic floors weren't so slick, Autumn could have dug in her heels more convincingly. As it was, she looked like a scared poodle at a veterinarian hospital going in for a checkup. All she would need would be a leash.

"I know." Sean opened a door that read "marriage license" right above "fishing license."

Maybe Autumn could convince him to get the fishing license instead. She'd much rather wake up at an ungodly hour, put swishy, squirming bait on a hook and catch a slimy fish than marry Sean right now.

"If you know that this is not what I want, then why are we here?"

Before Sean answered her, he requested the applications and sat down with her away from the clerks.

He stared at her after he wrote in his name. "I'm hoping to convince you to change your mind before the week is up." Then he completed his application.

Autumn fixed her gaze on her application. It all seemed so standard. Her name. Her parents' names. Place of her birth. She started to fill it out until she got to the section that asked for their intended wedding date. She glanced at Sean.

He must have known where she stopped. He pointed to the filled in area on his application. He noted the last day he would be home.

The date should have been encouraging. But he was looking for something that, if Autumn had caved, would have torn out her heart.

Although she signed the document, she couldn't fill in the date. Sean took her application and walked up to the counter. Autumn followed him, although she wasn't sure how she managed it. Everything around her felt like it was all melting away. The floor seemed soft and unstable, and every step she took felt like she was sinking into the ground.

The clerk looked over both completed documents carefully. "The date's not completed on this one." She held up Autumn's form.

Autumn's paralyzed vocal chords prevented her from screaming that she didn't want to be here at all. Filling out that paper felt like she was completing Sean's death certificate. There was no joy in the action. It all came off rushed and manic.

"It's the same day." Sean commandeered her form on the clipboard when Autumn didn't make a move to correct her intended oversight. He filled in the date and handed it back to the clerk.

The elderly clerk took Sean's money, and made a couple of official stamps on both forms. "If you're unable to marry on your scheduled date, you two have sixty days from your application date to do so. After that—"

"There is no after that." Autumn shook her head as she backed away. "I won't even have *him* for another sixty days." She ran out of the office and back to Sean's truck.

Autumn tried the passenger side door, but it was locked. When she saw Sean walking out of the office, she jumped on him. "Why the hell would you lock this piece of shit? Who's going to steal it?"

Sean said nothing as he unlocked the door and opened it for her. Once she was secured inside, he went around to his side. In his hand, he held a piece of paper.

Before he started the truck, he said in a calm voice, "If we do get married, we just need whoever is officiating to sign this." He handed her the official-looking document.

Sean must have had a lot of trust in her. Autumn fought to keep from ripping it up to shreds. Instead, she sat it on the seat in between them. When they arrived at home, Sean didn't park his truck. He pulled up to the driveway and kept it running.

"I don't understand you." He shook his head. "Do you understand what's going on here?"

Autumn rutted her eyebrows. "More than you could possibly know."

"I'm leaving. I'll be gone for a year. I love you." He held her hand. "Why do you keep denying me the one thing that's going to help me get through this?"

When Sean said it that way, Autumn couldn't talk. Her throat squeezed shut preventing her from even breathing. She wanted to tell him that her decision wasn't meant to hurt him. Didn't he understand that she wanted more from him, from the situation? Not everything about their lives needed to be dictated by this one event.

Sean pounded his fist on the steering wheel. That expression was the first time Autumn had ever seen him lose it, show his anger. She blinked, then stared at him.

Before speaking to her again, he composed himself. "I have some errands to run. I'll be home later." He kept his stare straight ahead.

The last thing Autumn wanted this week was a fight, and one about something as big as this. How could she tell him that the reason she didn't want to marry him right now was because she was so afraid of losing him? Here she was trying to keep him happy before he had to go to war. Autumn cupped the side of his face and kissed him with so much passion that she wept.

"I'll be back." Sean kissed the side of Autumn's face and nodded his head.

He loved her, but he didn't understand her pain, her anguish. Autumn got out of the truck and watched the love of her life drive away.

She slumped into the house, determined to fall asleep and awake to find that all of this, with the exception of meeting and falling in love with Sean, was a dream. She plopped down on their bed and kicked off her shoes. The ache inside of her would not dissipate.

When the phone rang again, she'd hoped it would have been that damn Colonel Mustard. She wanted to tell him what pulling Sean from their home was doing to her, to them. She wanted someone to scream at for this fucked up situation. She wanted her Sean.

"Yeah!" Autumn screamed into the phone.

"Oh, is this a bad time?" Sean's mom's voice sounded so fragile.

Autumn relaxed her shoulders and leaned back against the headboard. "Sorry, Ursula. I thought you were someone else."

"Everything okay over there?"

Autumn tried holding it together, but once Ursula asked the crucial question, she crumbled. "Can I come over and talk to you, please?"

"Yes, you know you can. Is Sean okay? Is he there?"

She wiped her nose with the back of her hand. "No. He had to run errands."

"You want me to come pick you up? Are you able to drive?"

Autumn nodded like his mother could see her. "I'll be fine. Let me clean up, and I'll be over there in a few."

"Be careful, dear. I love you."

Again, Autumn nodded but she couldn't squeak out the same sentiment to the mother of the man she loved, not because she didn't feel the same. She loved Sean's family as much as her own. Images of Autumn standing by Ursula and Bob, Sean's father, as they buried Sean flooded Autumn's thoughts.

If she didn't talk to someone, though, about her fears, she would crack. What better person to talk to than his mother?

[Four]

As soon as Autumn emerged from her car, Ursula was waiting at the front door. It always amazed Autumn that his barely five-foot tall mother could produce a giant like Sean. As always, she welcomed Autumn with opened arms.

"I've made iced tea." Ursula wrapped her arm around Autumn as she ushered her into the house. "Or would you prefer something a little stronger?"

Autumn chuckled and wiped away an impending tear. "Stronger would be way better."

Sean's mother walked her into the cozy family room, then she ducked behind a bar to make their drinks. "So how are you holding up?"

"Probably as well as you are." Autumn crossed her legs.

Ursula shrugged. "I think I might be holding up better than you. You have to remember. I've been through this a few times with Bob. And you weren't with him then, but I've gone through this with Sean when he went off to Desert Storm."

Autumn blinked at Ursula's admissions. How could the woman be so calm? And why would she welcome this type of upheaval in her life?

Ursula walked over to Autumn and handed her a peach-colored drink. Then she sat down next to her holding a similar drink. "So what's going on?"

Autumn downed some of the liquid courage, then sat the glass on the coffee table in front of them. "Sean asked me to marry him... a few times."

"Was it during sex?"

Thank God Autumn had already swallowed her drink, otherwise it would have been all over Sean's mother.

Ursula continued. "Sex was like a truth serum to his father. I could get him to confess what he got me for my birthday and anniversary every time."

Autumn hoped the confession was intended to make her laugh because she did, and couldn't stop.

"I knew it! Like father, like son."

Autumn wiped happy tears away. "Yeah, we just got back from applying for a marriage license."

The smile dropped from Ursula's face. "You two are getting married?" Then she pint-sized woman squealed and wrapped her arms around Autumn's neck. "That's the best news I've heard in a long, long time." Then she backed away. "Well, unless you have other news to tell me." She put her hand on Autumn's stomach.

"No." Autumn pulled Ursula's hand away. "I'm not pregnant. And I don't want to get married."

If Autumn wasn't mistaken, she could have sworn she heard Ursula's jaw crashing through the floor.

"I thought you love Sean."

"I do. God, of course I do." Autumn gripped Ursula's hand.

"Then I don't understand, dear. What's the problem?"

"In a week he'll be gone. He may be gone for a year. Or he may not come back at all."

"So shouldn't that be a good reason to marry him?"

Autumn shook her head. "No, I don't want to feel obligated to marry him because he's being shipped out. Ever since I was a little girl, I've dreamt about my perfect wedding day. I know exactly what my dress would look like. I know where I want to have it, who I want to marry us. I even know what our first dance would look like." She still had the scrapbook with pictures of just what she wanted tucked away in a shoebox in the back of her closet. "I never wanted to feel pushed into getting married because of time."

Ursula patted Autumn's hand, but said nothing.

"I know I must sound selfish. I just never imagined getting married to the man of my dreams only to have him leave me so that we have no chance to start a life together. Is that wrong? Am I wrong for feeling this way?" Autumn ran her fingers through her hair. "Sean looked so angry. I've never seen like that before. He's always been composed, even through our arguments."

"His father is the same way."

"He must think that either I don't love him or that I'm the most unsupportive person in his life right now. I want him. But I want him in the right way. Should I feel bad for that?"

Ursula shook her head. "No. This is your life as much as it is Sean's. I can't fault you for standing up for what you want. I did the complete opposite from you when I met Bob. We met at a dance. We knew instantly that we would be together forever. Sean talks about you the same way."

Autumn smiled at that admission.

Ursula finished her story. "The following week, he was due to be sent to Vietnam. Before he left, we eloped. I didn't tell my parents or my friends or anyone, and he did the same. When he came back home, we told everyone. Some were angry, but we didn't care. This was our lives, and we did it how we wanted. As much as I would love to have you as a daughter-in-law, I'm not going to pressure you to marry my wonderfully handsome, extremely polite, smart-as-a-whip son."

"No guilt, huh?" Autumn smiled.

"I didn't say I wouldn't brag on him." Ursula laughed, then became somber. "Life is short, dear. Just keep that in mind."

"Don't you ever get angry at all over these wars and what it's done to your family?"

Ursula stroked Autumn's face. "You'll learn how to deal with it when you're a military wife." Then she winked at her.

"No guilt."

Ursula shrugged. "No guilt."

"Will you and Bob be able to make it to the barbeque at my parents' at the end of the week?"

"Of course. Wouldn't miss it for the world."

"Good." At this time, Autumn would need her family around her just as much as Sean.

* * * *

"Merry Christmas!"

Sean glanced outside of the window at the searing summer sun, then back at Autumn who bounded into the bedroom carrying brightly-wrapped presents and in the cutest little elf costume he'd ever seen.

"Again, had I known you were going to do the costume thing, I would have deployed a long time ago." Sean sat up in bed as Autumn set the presents in front of him.

"Let's see. We've done my birthday, Valentine's Day, Thanksgiving."

Autumn rubbed her ass. "Yeah, my butt is still a little sore from that celebration."

"Sorry." Sean smiled.

"No, you're not." She sat next to him. "But it was good."

"Just good?" He hitched up an eyebrow.

"Great." She kissed him. "Wonderful." And again. "Magnificent." And a third time, this time, making it linger.

"So now we're up to Christmas. Next will be New Year's."

"New Year's will be tonight at midnight. Tomorrow—"

"My last day."

Autumn glossed over his statement. "Will be the Fourth of July celebration at my parents'."

"Just like last year."

"Except your family will be there this time."

"Don't let my little mother fool you. She knows how to party."

"I hope so." Autumn smiled at him.

Sean pushed the gifts to the side, then pulled Autumn close to him. "I don't know why you don't want to marry me." Autumn started to open her mouth but Sean stopped her. "And you don't have to tell me. I know you love me. And you know that I love you. But I know how you are. I'm sure it took you the entire time after I told you my assignment for you to plan this entire week, didn't you?"

Autumn dropped her gaze. "You know me so well."

"That's why I think I know why you've been turning me down." He pulled Autumn onto his lap. "I know getting married now is not the most ideal situations. I didn't see myself getting married like this either. I saw us getting married on the beach."

Autumn wrinkled her nose. "Really? I was thinking something more homey and intimate."

Sean put his hand on Autumn's belly. "And I want us to have children."

"Lots of them." She beamed.

Sean smiled with her. "Yeah, a house full of them. But I would be crushed if you got pregnant now, and I missed seeing your belly grow and missd the baby being born and everything. Just like I get that when you get married, you want everything that goes with it. The honeymoon, setting up house."

"Again."

"Yeah, again. Planning our family." He pressed his lips to her forehead. When he broke from the warm gesture, he stared into her eyes. "Just know if it doesn't happen before I leave, I won't be angry. I have a feeling like you're going to beat yourself up if you see me off, and we're not Mr. And Mrs. Littleton. Don't. If we don't get married, it'll give me hope to come home and ask you to marry me in the right way and do it up right."

What could Autumn say? She wrapped her arms around Sean's neck so hard that he nearly gasped for air. He held her just as tight. It was this feeling that he didn't want to forget.

She pulled back from him. "So can I ask you one thing?"

"Of course."

She interlaced her fingers with his. Her soft hands felt heavenly on his.

"Did you already get the ring?"

Sean cocked his head.

Autumn nodded, apparently getting her answer from just looking at him. "Can I see it?"

He shook his head. "You know better than that."

"Oh, come on. Just give me a peek. Is it in the spare bedroom?" She started to run out of the room when Sean grabbed her arm and pulled her back. "No, you don't, Nancy Drew. We're going to celebrate Christmas. Then I'm going to ring in the New Year having sex with you in the backyard."

"Oh, great. You go away, and I'll be here for the neighbors to think I'm a freak."

"Honey, I think they already know that." Then Sean simulated a high-pitched squealing noise that sounded a lot like Autumn when she hit her peak.

She playfully slapped his arm. "Not funny. It's better than you." Autumn growled like a bear, then said, "Holy shit, fuck, damn!"

Sean laughed so hard that his side hurt. "Do I really do that?"

"Among other things. I like your sex face." She squeezed her eyes shut as tight as she could and gritted her teeth.

"Baby, you look constipated."

"No, *you* look constipated. Good thing you're cute."

"I could say the same about you. Your eyes roll to the back of your head, and you hang your mouth open like a big-mouth bass." Sean mimicked that look, opening and closing his mouth like a fish. "I just want to put a hook in there and reel you in."

"You've already got me. You must have had amazing bait."

"I guess not good enough bait. It wasn't enough to get you."

Autumn opened her mouth to refute his claim when Sean held up his hand to stop her.

"Let's not argue. Let's just enjoy Christmas and New Year's in June."

"I do love you, Sean."

Sean stared at Autumn, who looked close to tears, the same expression she'd been carrying for weeks now. "I know. I love you, too."

"Will you do me a favor?"

"Anything."

"Will you at least let my family see the ring tomorrow night? I want them to see it."

"So your brothers can take pictures of it with their camera phones and show you later on what it looks like? Oh, no."

"Please?"

How could he say no to the most beautiful woman in the world? "Fine. No pictures. They can describe it to you, but you can't see it until we're married, got it?"

Autumn made a crossing motion over her heart. "Cross my heart. I promise."

"Good. Now, I've been a good boy this year." He pushed the wrapped presents to the floor. "I want to open up this present first." He reached under her skirt and found she wasn't wearing any panties.

"Ho, ho, ho."

[Five]

Autumn glanced over at Sean as he drove his truck onto her parents' street. She held his hand and stared at him. The thought that this would be the last time she would see him, hold his hand, touch him, hit her immediately. She had to stop thinking about that or she would cry before she got to the party.

"My face isn't going to change before we get to the party." Sean split his attention between her and the road.

"You never know. You might get slightly more handsome if I look at you long enough." She caressed his cheek.

"Is that even possible?" he joked.

"Oh, one last zinger. The man still has it."

Sean parked in the circular driveway behind other cars. "Babe, I never lost it."

"There he goes again, folks. He's playing here all week."

Sean laughed as he got out the truck, then he helped Autumn from her side. From the front of the house, she heard music blaring from the backyard. The closer she got to the house, the more she smelled the spicy barbeque sauce. Her father really must be going all out for Sean. Autumn didn't expect anything less.

Autumn smoothed her hands down her white sundress. She held Sean's hand as they walked to the backyard. It was then she noticed that Sean walked slower than normal.

"Are you okay?" Autumn stopped at the back corner of the house.

"Someone wore me out yesterday." Sean winked.

"Yeah, I am a weapon of mass destruction." She flexed her arms to show off her less-than-impressive biceps. Autumn started toward the backyard when Sean pulled her back.

He embraced her in his massive arms and pressed his lips on hers so lovingly, Autumn thought it was a dream. Her heart opened up fully. The music that overpowered the area disappeared. The only things that existed were her and Sean.

"I'm glad we're not getting married now," Sean said in a whisper.

Autumn felt a prickle on the back of her neck. "You are?"

"Yeah. Gives me something to look forward to when I get back." He framed her face in his hands. "And I *will* be back."

She nodded. "I know. I know you will." Autumn took his hand and brought him into the festivities. "We're here!"

The throngs of people turned to them and cheered. It was a hero's welcome, and Sean hadn't gone anywhere yet. Both her parents and Sean's raced to them. Ursula and Bob captured Autumn in an embrace, while Autumn's parents surrounded Sean.

"It's about time our girl let you out," Autumn's father patted Sean on his back.

"Don't worry about me, Terance. It's been the best week of my life." Sean put his arm around Autumn.

"Come on, you two. Get something to drink, and let's party!" Autumn's mother swayed her ample hips back and forth to the groovy seventies tunes blaring from the speakers set up in the four corners of the yard.

"Don't tire yourself out, Bonita. Save a dance for me." Sean kissed the side of Autumn's mother's head.

"You got it, sweetie."

The party beat any house party Autumn attended in her teenage and college years, or any wedding reception she'd ever attended. This time, it was her turn to cling to Sean. She wrapped her arms around him whenever he wasn't dancing with her mother or shaking hands with her brothers.

"Honey, you don't have to hang onto me so much. They won't bite." Sean winked at her again, proud that he could use her words against her.

"You're cute." She glanced at the gate leading into her parents' backyard to watch the new guests filtering into the yard. "You're right, Sean." She pulled away from him. "I need to make a special announcement anyway." She ran to the patio and asked her brother to turn off the music. Then she grabbed his microphone. "Hey, everyone. I have a quick announcement."

The crowd of people turned to her.

"I don't want to talk for Sean, but I just want to thank everyone for coming out and wishing him luck when he's deployed tomorrow."

The people surrounding him patted Sean on his shoulders and back. Her man looked so good wearing the white shorts and crisp white shirt she'd bought for him for this special occasion.

"For those who don't know, Sean and I have been dating for a little over a year now. He's my best friend, and the best man I've ever known." Autumn's throat tightened.

Come on, girl. Don't cry. Not yet.

"Hey, I thought you said I was your best friend and the best man you've ever known!" her father screamed.

Leave it to Autumn's dad to lighten any mood.

"Hush up, Terance. Let the girl finish." Autumn's mother smacked her husband on his backside.

"You keep that up, we'll both miss her speech." Her father tickled her mother, then pinched her ass.

The crowd erupted in laughter. When the laughing died down, Autumn finished what she had to say.

"Like I was saying, Sean and I have been together for a year. I've never loved someone as much as I love him. I would give my life for him, although I'm not sure Sean believes that."

"I know you would, honey. I'd give my life for you, too." Sean scanned the group. "I'd do it for you all."

"We know, Sean." Bob put his arm around his boy.

"It might surprise you to know that all this week Sean has repeatedly asked me to marry him."

A gasp sounded through the group. A couple of the women started to cheer until they all glanced at Autumn's hand and noticed it was devoid of a ring.

"I turned him down. You see, I've always had a fantasy of my dream wedding. I knew where I wanted it, the guests I would invite, the food we would eat. I had it all planned."

"That's Autumn for you," her older brother began. "Always over-thinking things."

"You're right, Cole." Autumn nodded. "I was looking for perfection when I had it right in front of me." She stared at Sean. "I got so caught up in what I wanted, I wasn't looking at the big picture. In the big picture, I would hate for Sean to leave thinking that I didn't love him enough to take that leap. I want him to look forward to something when he comes back home." She sauntered to him. "Sean, I hope you have that ring on you." She turned to the side where she and Sean had entered.

Sean glanced that way and saw Reverend Wilmore from Autumn's church.

"I called a family friend to see if he would do me a favor." Autumn held Sean's hand. "Sean, will you marry me?"

"No." Sean shook his head.

Another gasp rippled through the crowd. Autumn's heart sank when he made his abrupt response.

"*I'm* going to ask *you* again. I suggest you answer right this time." Sean dropped down to one knee in front of her and pulled out a black velvet ring box from his pocket. "Autumn, I know I won't be here long enough for you to get on me about taking out the trash or turning down the thermostat so that you're freezing. But I want you to save up all of that for when I come home. Will you—"

"Yes!"

"No, wait. Wait until I ask you. Will you—"

She smothered him in kisses. "Enough said. You have me. You'll have a wife before you go."

Sean lifted Autumn in his arms as everyone cheered. When he let her go, he stared at her. "You planned this the whole time, didn't you?"

Autumn shook her head. "I was determined not to marry you until you came back home. Then I talked to a really wise person." She looked over at Ursula. "She didn't tell me that I should marry you. But she did make me realize that if I didn't, I might regret it. I don't want to regret anything when I'm with you."

Sean winked at his mother.

"So I bought your outfit and mine. I made a few phone calls. Except for the reverend, no one here knew what I had planned."

"I knew you would do it." Autumn's mother put her hand on her hip. "You came here in white. Hello!"

"I thought she wanted to match him." Autumn's father pointed to Sean.

"I was hoping." Ursula hopped from one foot to the other as she gazed at Autumn and Sean.

"I'm tired of talking about it. Can we get these two married now?" Bob said.

"Oh, wait. You're going to need this." Autumn handed Reverend Wilmore their marriage license. Then she looked at Sean. "I didn't want to make a liar out of you." She winked at him.

"Stay exactly as you are when I come home. Don't change." Sean held her hand as they stood in front of the reverend.

"I'll make a deal. You come home to me, and I promise I won't change." Autumn chewed her bottom lip. "I did make one change." She turned her back on him. "At the small of my back, I had them tattoo your name, rank and serial number." She glanced over her shoulder. "In case something happens to me, people will know I belong to you forever."

"God, I love you." He kissed Autumn. "Now I really have something to look forward to when I'm over there."

"Yeah. You had better be thinking about coming home and making grandbabies."

"Mom!"

"Oh, wouldn't twins be great?" Ursula held Autumn's mother's hands as the two women clucked on about babies.

"Before we go any further, let's get the marriage part out of the way, shall we?" Reverend Wilmore said in a calm voice.

Autumn felt good about taking this step in her life. It wasn't the end. This was the start of a great new beginning. While Sean was away and fighting, Autumn would be praying for his safe return home. Enough said.

♥

bridgetmidway.com

Black and White
© Chloe Waits

Smooth
polished ebony
lying in his arms
wonder at the translucence of my skin
with blue tracings
under surface
his fingers strong dark sure
on my pale flesh
knowing
coaxing
oily essence
and
slippery need
mouth prying open
tender flesh
succulent meat of oysters
greedily
searching for his pearl

♥

www.website.com

About Coming Together

Coming Together is about giving and about sex—a tantalizing combination in any context. Conceived online in the Literotica®com Authors Hangout, a forum for erotica writers, Coming Together is the passionate product of many talented individuals. It's grown way beyond its original borders.

We were all amateurs when the first erotic cocktail was served. In the years since the inaugural volume hit the cyber shelves of Café Press, many of the original contributors have become successful professionals: authors, poets, editors, and artists. Traditional, small press publishers have picked up many of the self-published titles, and Phaze has continued to pour our philanthropic elixir into its catalog. Both Charles River Press and eXcessica have e-published Coming Together titles, and in the spring of 2009, All Romance eBooks will be added to that list.

To date, Coming Together has compiled ten collections, with several more in the works. I am thrilled with and humbled by both the quantity and quality of the submissions received. Support from publishers and booksellers has been exemplary, as well. The critical acclaim is the cherry on top.

In each volume, we strive for an inclusive mix, embracing the diversity of desire. The causes we champion cross all demographic groups, and so does Coming Together. While each individual intoxicant may not suit the tastes of every reader, the savory cocktail is sure to stir every imagination.

Note, however, that these pages may contain stories in which the characters do not practice safe sex. Everyone involved with the publication of Coming Together encourages its readers to act responsibly and to take appropriate precautions against both unwanted pregnancy and the transmission of disease.

All proceeds from the sale of this volume of Coming Together will be donated to Amnesty International (amnesty.org) which campaigns for internationally recognized human rights for all.

Bottoms up!

peace & passion,

Alessia Brio

www.eroticanthology.com

Sex-Kitten.net

Sex-Kitten.Net is pleased to support this edition of Coming Together ~ and the project in general.

We admire the work of editor Alessia Brio and all the talented authors who have made this book truly something amazing. They along with you, the buyer of this book, are proof that fans of erotica are more than just some dirty-minded selfish folks ~ you are all proof that sex & arousal, even the solo acts, are indeed acts of love.

We sex kittens would like to officially salute you all ~ but with copies of this book so near, our hands are working their way towards our panties...

~ Gracie Passette

Alessia Brio, ed.

With Special Thanks

As I once commented in an interview: *Giving is just plain sexy!* There are some damned sexy people involved in the publication and promotion of Coming Together.

I'd like to extend my heartfelt thanks to all our wonderful authors. Please visit their sites and support their work. There are website addresses immediately following each story or poem.

In addition, each of the following has gone above and beyond to help ensure the success of Coming Together. Please find a way to show your appreciation for their generosity:

Phaze Books
www.phaze.com

All Romance eBooks
www.allromanceebooks.com

Lucrezia Magazine
www.lucreziamagazine.com

Romantic Times
www.romantictimes.com

EPIC
www.epicauthors.com

ScrapFairy Designs
www.scrapfairydesigns.com

Erotica Readers & Writers Association
www.erotica-readers.com

Alison Kent
www.alisonkent.com

Barry Eisler
www.barryeisler.com

Charles River Press
www.charlesriverpress.com

Printed in the United States
152345LV00003B/56/P